The Apocalypse Crusade 5

War of the Undead Day 5

A Zombie Tale by Peter Meredith

Fictional works by Peter Meredith:

A Perfect America
Infinite Reality: Daggerland Online Novel 1
Infinite Assassins: Daggerland Online Novel 2
Generation Z
Generation Z: The Queen of the Dead
Generation Z: The Queen of War
Generation Z: The Queen Unthroned
Generation Z: The Queen Enslaved
The Sacrificial Daughter
The Apocalypse Crusade War of the Undead: Day One
The Apocalypse Crusade War of the Undead: Day Two
The Apocalypse Crusade War of the Undead Day Three
The Apocalypse Crusade War of the Undead Day Four
The Apocalypse Crusade War of the Undead Day Five
The Horror of the Shade: Trilogy of the Void 1
An Illusion of Hell: Trilogy of the Void 2
Hell Blade: Trilogy of the Void 3
The Punished
Sprite
The Blood Lure The Hidden Land Novel 1
The King's Trap The Hidden Land Novel 2
To Ensnare a Queen The Hidden Land Novel 3
The Apocalypse: The Undead World Novel 1
The Apocalypse Survivors: The Undead World Novel 2
The Apocalypse Outcasts: The Undead World Novel 3
The Apocalypse Fugitives: The Undead World Novel 4
The Apocalypse Renegades: The Undead World Novel 5
The Apocalypse Exile: The Undead World Novel 6
The Apocalypse War: The Undead World Novel 7
The Apocalypse Executioner: The Undead World Novel 8
The Apocalypse Revenge: The Undead World Novel 9
The Apocalypse Sacrifice: The Undead World 10
The Edge of Hell: Gods of the Undead Book One
The Edge of Temptation: Gods of the Undead Book Two
The Witch: Jillybean in the Undead World
Jillybean's First Adventure: An Undead World
Expansion
Tales from the Butcher's Block

Prologue
Day 5
Oneonta, New York

Fear was the one true constant. It was all-powerful. It permeated everything. The stench of it hung in the air with a sour smell. It rose up out of the dark earth like cold tendrils and ran like an electric current down the chains that strung one man to the next.

The men, thousands and thousands of them in long lines, shivered from the fear and the chill, making their chains clink, clink, clink. On and on, maddeningly. They had the fear of trapped animals, and more than one had torn flesh from their ankles trying to escape their shackles. To make everything worse, the fields were shrouded in a chilling night fog that hid the dead.

As the men waited on the onslaught, most of them prayed to a God they had actively despised throughout their brutal lives. Watching murderers get on their knees to beg and plead and make promises they had no intention of ever keeping was both laughable and annoying to Juan "Cobre" Santiago. He was a man with few morals, and yet he despised hypocrisy.

Even if he had been a hypocrite, he knew better than to waste his breath. What god would ever want him? He was a demon, worse than anything he was about to face. The truth: he was cold-hearted, evil through and through, and ugly inside and out. His face ran with tattoos and scars, as did his gleaming bald head, his muscular torso and his long arms.

Besides, he didn't think he had enough time left to ask forgiveness for all of his crimes. He had killed a lot of people in his time with the Los Zetas cartel, and he had killed them in an astonishing number of ways. It was a thing he prided himself on. He had beaten seven men to death using only his fists. He had stabbed fifteen others—on some occasions, he had pounded the knife home, breaking bones in the process, and on others, he had given his enemies just a little poke in the liver, so he could watch them die slowly. He had used hammers and saws, a homemade guillotine, rope, chains, and gardening implements, including a trowel. Once he had tried to kill a prostitute with a sink disposal, although that had not worked nearly as well as he had hoped, and in order to silence her caterwauling, he had thrown her down and dropped a refrigerator on her head.

Cobre was a horror of a human being, but interestingly enough, no one thought he was insane. He certainly didn't think he was insane. Being part of a Mexican cartel meant that killing people with revolting barbaric cruelty was sometimes just a way of life.

The only reason he was even thinking about his mental state was because he found himself chained within in a few feet of David Berkowitz, the "Son of Sam" killer. Berkowitz was famous, although for the life of him Cobre couldn't understand why. All through the long march, Cobre had stared at him trying to puzzle it out.

"Shiiit, he look like a retired janitor," Cobre muttered to himself in heavily accented English. And he did, too. His heyday as a killer was long in the past. Berkowitz was now in his late sixties, and was portly and bald save for a half-ring of greasy hair that ran from one ear around to the other. His janitorial appearance was cemented by the grey little fag mustache that for some reason made Cobre want to punch him.

Supposedly Berkowitz was a psycho, and everyone looked at him with side eyes. Cobre, who had known his share of crazed, twitchy mother-fuckers didn't see it.

"How many people you kill?" Cobre demanded.

"Six," Berkowitz replied in a soft voice, looking down over his round belly at his feet. "And this is my punishment…my final contrition. I am born again. God loves me, and this will set me free."

Cobre snorted, shaking his head. "You kilt six people and you think God loves you? Shiiit, God must really love me. I kilt a whole mess of people. More'n I can count. What about you, yo?"

There was only one man between them: a short, squat, bulked-up negro who had been busted with thirty pounds of weed in the backseat of his car and a dismembered corpse in the trunk. His birth name was Jamal. "None," Jamal whispered, sticking to his lie right to the end. His lawyer, who had managed to plea bargain the murder charge down to a possession with intent to distribute, had drilled it into his head never to admit anything to anyone.

Jamal licked his full lips with a pale tongue. He had never been so unhappy in his life. "I'm only inside cuz the white man is…" A sudden high scream split the dark and Jamal took a step back, only to be brought up short by the chain around his ankle.

The scream had been inhuman. No person could ever have let out such a hideous shriek. It went on and on, and now the moans were growing louder in response. Jamal was on the verge of pissing himself.

The lip licking started going nonstop, his eyes huge and round. "The, the, the white man did this. He did all of it. He messed this world up. It was a paradise and he messed it up."

Once more Cobre snorted. Jamal turned on him, glad for any excuse not to have to think about the fact that he was chained in a long line with hundreds of psycho killers all passively waiting to be eaten alive. It was crazy. It was all crazy, and the need to piss was so great that he fumbled out his cock and let out a gushing stream as he snarled up at Cobre. "Snort all you want, spic. The white man is holding you down, just like he's holding the black man down."

"Which white men?" Cobre asked. "Is that one holding you down?" He pointed at Berkowitz, who was praying again, his thick, pale lips moving quickly. Cobre laughed easily. "No mother-fuckin' white man ever held me down. Shiiit, don't you know that even saying that gives them power they don't fuckin' deserve? You know who you sound like? *Mi padre*. He was poor as shit, just like his father. And you know who made him poor? Other fuckin' Mexicans. All they ever did was bitch, just like you. That's all they ever did. Bitch, bitch, bitch. Wah, wah, wah. But that wasn't me. I did something. I made myself fuckin' rich. I came here and lived the American dream!"

Jamal began to splutter, half in hysterical laughter, half in hysterical fear. "What? You're in prison, you fucking freak. They got you in chains! They got you just like they got the slaves. Don't you see that? The white…" Just then they caught the squeak of overloaded wheels and the scrape of metal. A cart was being pushed down the line. Quieter now, Jamal hissed, "You know what you are? You're brainwashed."

"Shiiit, I ain't here because of no white man. I'm here cuz I kilt people. I kilt a lot of fuckin' people. The problem was doing the work myself. That was a mistake. I'd still be chillin' in Florida if I done some of that delegating." The cart came even with them. It was stacked high with all sorts of tools and strange weapons. A long-handled shovel was held out to Cobre. "Naw, man. Gimme the pick-axe. A shovel won't do shit." The shovel was tossed at his feet. Jamal got the pick-axe, which he gripped with both hands and hugged to his chest as if Cobre was going to take it from him.

Cobre thought about it, then realized that Jamal with a pick-axe was a better sidekick than Jamal cringing behind a shovel. Besides, he had killed men with a shovel before.

He fingered the metal edge and, like everyone else, glanced down at his shackles. Despite the fact they had been warned, in the very clearest of terms, not to try to escape, thirty-eight men had been shot to death during the endless marches of the last three days. The guards weren't playing games. One of the would-be escapees had been shot in the leg and instead of giving him a bandage and a second chance, a guard had walked up and capped him at point blank range, then just left him there. Another man had sat down and refused to get up; he had been executed on the spot. There had been no questions, no repercussions, and certainly no admonishments.

Even with this ingrained in everyone's memories, somewhere down the line there was a hard *CLINK!* as some fool gave his chains a whack with a metal tool. A few guards surged forward with guns leveled. Fingers were pointed and the offender had his sledge hammer pulled from his hands. He was left without a weapon of any sort, and he mewled petulantly.

His cries meant nothing to the guards.

The world, as far as the prisoners knew it, had been turned on its head. No one cared about them; not even a little. From the worst offender, a title Cobre relished since it had once given him cache, to the man serving two years for tax fraud committed by his now ex-wife, their lives were now utterly forfeit.

Three days earlier, the governor had given the order to "rescue" them from the New York State prison system. That same governor was currently under arrest for a vague federal crime that would find justification just as soon as the President got around with charging him with something. In the meantime, a general was running things in New York and when it got back to him that there were thousands of prisoners sitting around doing nothing but eating, he had set them marching to the very edge of the front lines north of Oneonta where there were just a smattering of farmers and reservists holding down an area a hundred miles long.

The army of prisoners was 51,000 strong, and heralded from forty-three different correctional facilities, including Shawangunk, Sing Sing, Attica, "The Hill" at Elmira, and the infamous S-Block Special Housing Unit from the Fishkill Correctional Facility.

The men from these maximum-security prisons were some of the most hardened, toughest criminals in the world. Now they were little more than cannon fodder.

"Stand and fight," a man in dark body armor said, walking down the line handing out little blue surgical masks. It was hard to tell if he was a guard or a soldier; they were mixed together now. "Anyone who tries to run will be shot down." It was as simple as that.

"What if we win?" Jamal asked.

The man laughed, "Then you get to fight again tomorrow, the same as the rest of us."

Jamal muttered something that sounded like, "Stupid mother-cracker-fucking shit-headed, honky, mother-fucker." It all sort of ran together and was muffled by the surgical mask. Someone hissed him into silence. The shadows not far in front of them were moving. The moans were now louder and closer. And the smell…the smell of the dead was revolting, and more than one man began retching.

With his head canted back toward the oncoming horde of undead, the soldier with the masks shoved the box at David Berkowitz. "Take one and pass them on." He then disappeared, running to the rear. The box made its way down the line in a blur as the first of the undead came close enough to go from shadowy myth to terrifying reality. It walked on stumps, its clothes and flesh hanging like rags. One arm ended not with a hand but with two sharp bones protruding from a mangled wrist. Its face was shredded and looked like it had been dragged behind a car—and somehow it was moving.

It wasn't even a big zombie; still, it sent a portion of the line reeling back. A gunshot stopped the movement. One man challenged the creature. He held a post-hole spade up threateningly. The spade had a long narrow metal head, which the man sent right into the thing's throat, practically decapitating it. The zombie collapsed at the man's feet.

A wild ignorant cheer went up by the men chained to the victor. Looking more astonished than anything, he raised his bloody tool and crowed over his victory.

More zombies stumbled out of the dark, all just as disgusting, though not all so easily destroyed—some were big, strapping humanoids that had to be beaten to the ground by half a dozen men. It was especially frightening when they came in throngs of ten or twelve. The first couple would be killed with a few swings of a mallet or crowbar, but sometimes there would be three or four right there in a man's face. A concerted effort by all the prisoners nearby would be enough to destroy them, but this didn't happen as much as it should have.

The prisoners were selfish and stupid, concerned only with their own survival, and many times wouldn't attack a zombie, even a few feet away if they didn't think it was a danger to themselves. Men began to die and gaps appeared in the line. The zombies didn't pour through these gaps, instead they turned and attacked the men on either side—and the gaps grew.

Like everyone else, Cobre had been foolishly optimistic when he saw how easily the first zombie had been killed. It didn't take long before he saw that the only way to hold the line was if someone assumed a strong leadership role. He saw that the twenty-man chain-gangs could be formed into platoons, dead bodies could be removed to give the platoons more mobility, weapons could be reassigned based on need and effectiveness, and a round-robin system could be used to allow platoons to rest or act as reinforcements.

It was either do that or try to run away. The night was filled with high screams, thousands of moans, angry shouts and gunshots. It was loud enough that no one would hear a single man trying to break his chain.

"Here's the plan," he told Jamal. "I'll hold them off while you use the axe to free me. Then I'll free you. We can both escape."

Jamal held his pickaxe away from Cobre. "No way. I'll do me first."

"Shiiit, you'll run," Cobre answered.

"You'll run if I do you!" Jamal shot right back.

Their argument was going in circles, and all the while more of the dead were coming closer. There were eight lurching, groaning things coming right for them.

"We'll do a fuckin' compromise," Cobre told Jamal. "Cut yourself free of that Son of Sam mother-fucker and then cut me free of this guy." He jerked his thumb at a near-toothless, spidery-thin man from Guatemala, who had been in the joint since the early eighties. The Guat seemed lost in the outside world and was spooked as much by the dark as he was by the zombies.

"Once you do that, you cut this chain and…"

"We'll both be free," Jamal finished as he caught on. He immediately started swinging the axe down: *CHANG! CHANG! CHANG!* There was no disguising the sound and someone behind them took a loose shot at Jamal. The bullet winged off into the dark, and Jamal only paused a second.

Cobre gave him a shove. "Come on, ese! Takin' a motherfuckin' slug is the easy way out, so don't sweat it."

Jamal went back to hacking at the chain and, as he did, Cobre faced the monsters coming at them. With a muttered curse, he hefted the shovel and decided that it wasn't the worst of weapons. It was long enough for him to heave zombies away, pushing them down the line; and it was rangy enough that he could kill without letting them get too close. Using a winding, over-hand swing, Cobre brought the shovel down on the head of one of the zombies—*Thwap!* The top of the thing's head compressed by three inches as black blood squirted from both its ears, and its teeth broke like glass and shot out of its mouth.

"Nice one, ese," the little Guat mother-fucker said, grinning and holding what was essentially a long branch like it was a baseball bat. He took a Babe Ruth swat at one of the zombies and broke its jaw, turning it toward Cobre in the process.

"Stupid Guat mother-fucker," Cobre said, before jabbing his shovel spear-like at the thing's throat. It fell and he was just about to bitch at the Guat when Jamal gave a relieved cry; the chain had broken.

"Look out. Move. Give me some room." Jamal started hacking at the next section of chain: *CHANG! CHANG! CHANG!*

As he did, Cobre was battling five zombies at once. He was strong and fast; they were strong and slow. They were also stupid, attacking with only their teeth. Sure, they tried to grab him with their scraggly claws, but most of their nails were torn down to nothing, and those with nails couldn't rip their way past his heavy Carhartt coat.

He slung the first two left and right, letting Berkowitz and the Guat take care of them. The next took the point of the shovel straight through the eyes. It was still alive, but blind and stumbled into the fourth. The two fell, as behind Cobre the sound of Jamal hacking and hacking rang out even louder: *CHANG! CHANG! CHANG!*

The fifth zombie toppled over the previous two and fell into Cobre's legs. He tried to leap back, but just then the chain sprang taut and pulled his right foot out from beneath him. He fell and before he could get up, there was a sharp pain in his knee. "Mother-fucker!" The thing was biting him. Or at least it was trying to. Human teeth were poor weapons and made worse shears. It couldn't get through his jeans.

Cobre kicked it away with his free foot and brought the shovel up...*CHANG! CHANG! Thud.* At the sound, he looked over and saw the Guatemalan standing over Jamal's unmoving body. The Guat gave Cobre a semi-apologetic grin, showing off two yellowed teeth that looked oddly like fangs in his empty mouth. He grabbed the pickaxe.

"Go on," Cobre told him. "Get us out of here."

The skinny Hispanic was much more at home with the tool, and before Cobre could kill all the zombies in the squirreling mass in front of him, the two men were free. Cobre snatched the axe from the Guat. "Don't even think about messing with me, you little shit. Do what I say and we'll get out of this. Start with putting on your fuckin' mask." The moron was wearing it on the top of his head like he was some sort of Guat-Jew.

Cobre didn't like Jews. His lawyer had been Jewish and for some reason Cobre had expected that one fact to make him a cut above the other lawyers. And maybe it had; Cobre knew nothing of civilized law. The only law he respected was the law of the jungle. The strong survived and fed on the weak. The concept was playing out all around him. The prisoners were fighting in spurts along a three-mile line; it was hard to tell who was winning or if anyone really was.

In a manner of speaking, the humans were fighting with as little strategic forethought as the zombies, and the battle waxed and waned, wholly dependent on the number of zombies that straggled up at any one time.

There were large gaps among the advancing dead that Cobre was sure he'd be able to exploit. "Let's go," he said to the Guat, and took off at a jog, leaving the other prisoners to their fate. Forward seemed like the wrong way to be going and the Guat yanked on his jacket and pointed back. "Go on if you want, you stupid Guat mother-fucker. If you go that way, you'll get fuckin' shot. This is the way to freedom."

Cobre knew what he was about. He had listened. He had paid attention. He knew that their flank was up in the air, which meant that no one was guarding it. If he could run around the end of the line, he'd have a clear shot of running all the way to Canada.

But he couldn't run straight across the line; the mother-fuckin' guards would shoot him. He had to take a chance and go out into the unknown. A hundred yards forward and then a mile or so to the left.

He didn't think that was very far even for a smoker who'd been caged up for the last three years. He hadn't counted on so many zombies, however. The further he jogged forward, the more of them there were. So far, they had been coming in little gangs of eight or nine. Now there were twenty at a time. Cobre dodged these, trying to angle to the north, only more of the dead swerved in at them from every angle, cutting them off.

Soon the pair was going the wrong way, heading to the right instead of the left. They ran on, burning up their lungs and wasting what little energy they had.

Precious minutes passed before the Guat whined, "Ya vienen!" meaning: *They're coming!*

Cobre knew this without looking back. He could feel the creatures pressing in closer and closer; their stench became a nasty cloud and their moans grew in eagerness. He couldn't afford to look back. There were too many in front of them to worry about those coming from behind. They were everywhere and there seemed to be no end to them. The gaps between the groups became smaller and smaller until there was almost no room to slip by.

Then suddenly they were at the end of the field. In front of them was a ditch four-feet deep, and beyond that was a head-height wood fence, and a house set in among a little copse of fir trees. The wiry Guat was faster and was halfway over the fence before Cobre even crossed the ditch. Cobre was winded and flagging badly.

"Is it clear on the other side?"

The Guat squinted into the shadows beneath the trees. "Si nos apuramos…" *If we hurry.*

Hurrying was no longer an option. Cobre's legs were wooden and his breath came out in burning gasps. He needed a way to slow the beasts down and there really was only one option. As the Guat was trying to lift a leg over the fence, Cobre grabbed him by the back of his coat and the seat of his pants, and lifted him bodily into the air. The Guat screamed high and piercing as he tried to twist around like a cat held over a bathtub filled with ice water.

Cobre was too strong. His fingers were like iron and his arms were filled with desperate power. With a grunt, he heaved the Guat down into the ditch, which roiled with grey bodies, fighting and squirming to get to the other side. When the shrieking Guat dropped among them, there was a huge surge as every zombie in sight poured into the ditch to get at him.

"Mierda santa," Cobre swore, as he tossed the pick-axe over the fence and mounted it, scraping his feet on the boards. There was no looking back for him. There was only Canada. From the top of the fence he could see a perfectly good 2002 Honda Accord sitting tucked up next to the house. He had stolen a half dozen of these in his younger years.

Three minutes later it was purring nicely as he ripped north, absolutely covered in zombie blood. It didn't occur to him to wash his hands for another hour and by then he was ten miles from the border and looking for a way to cross.

Chapter 1
1- 12:06 a.m.
Boston, Massachusetts

Christopher Gore hurried up the steps of the Massachusetts State House, his breath panting in and out of him, his belly jelloing up and out of his cinched-in belt. Although he'd only had three cups of the blackest coffee imaginable, his bladder was near to bursting. Normally, he could hold two quarts of urine before he felt like this—like he was about to wet himself.

"Make way," he said to a crowd near the door. He had meant for it to come out as a command from a senior member of the Governor's administration. In reality, it sounded like a blubbering whine and no one so much as glanced his way. The crowd was angry and was demanding answers.

Christopher waved his ID over their heads. "Excuse me! I work here. Soldiers, can you clear a lane. Thank you."

With the help of four armed men, he was through in seconds and climbing more stairs, sweat dripping down from his thin hair. Inside the building, he was more his own man. He knew people and people knew him. Even the vultures in the press were somewhat reassuring. "Christopher! Christopher! Is it true that the President has ordered the arrest of the Governor?"

"Chris, can you tell us, is the front holding? Are we safe?"

"The rumor out of Worcester is that we won't be able to hold the city. What will we do then?"

The real answer: *Run for your lives*, couldn't be said out loud. The panic from such a statement would spell the doom of not just the state, but also of the five million people crammed into the city of Boston.

"No comment. Sorry. No comment," he repeated as he hurried past them, heading for the Governor's crowded suite of offices. Governor Clarren was in the main conference room at the far end of a long cherrywood table. It was so overflowing with charts and notes and maps that not an inch of wood was visible.

He didn't look good. The circles around his now shockingly baggy eyes were so dark that they appeared practically purple. It looked as though he'd been punched—and he was about to be punched again.

Christopher gave his head a little shake when the Governor glanced up. That slight movement of negation caused Clarren to wilt in his chair. He sagged, his back hunched in defeat. After a moment, he took a heavy breath. "I'll be right back," he told the men and women working around him.

He crossed to the door that let into his personal office and Christopher followed him in, whispering, "It's what we thought."

Clarren waited until the door shut before asking what he already knew was true, "The marines?"

"Yes sir. We think about eight hundred of them. For whatever reason, they decided to land down in Plymouth."

A derisive snort escaped Clarren. "Oh, it's obvious why. The President thinks he's being clever. He thinks he'll gain some sort of moral upper hand by landing at Plymouth Rock. All it does is give us time to come up with some sort of delaying strategy. Eight hundred men is not that many."

"They are marines, sir." Christopher started to stutter, "And, and, and they have t-tanks." Clarren's mouth formed the word *tanks* in something of a question; however, no sound came out. Christopher nodded. "Yes, and you know we don't have anything that can stop them."

Clarren knew perfectly well. When it came to bad news, he was very well informed. "And our offers?" he asked in a whisper.

"Rejected out of hand—all of them." Clarren's first offer was to make a public apology. His second was to retain his title but cede all executive power to the federal government. His third and final offer was to be given safe passage to Canada. "You are to be arrested and tried for treason. Along with…" Christopher choked before he could go on. "…Along with your cabinet, the lieutenant governor and others."

"Others?"

Christopher dropped his eyes. "They weren't specified, though I think some of…us your, your staff will be charged. And the military people, too."

Did "others" also mean his wife and kids? What about his brother? What about Christopher's wife? Clarren lost the strength to speak properly and could only summon more whispers: "How do we fight this?"

"There's no way to fight it," Christopher said. "Colonel Randolph was tipped off by one of his old contacts that the Navy is moving in a cruiser to provide support with their missiles. He says they've got hundreds of them on board and they don't ever miss. I think…I think the only thing we can do is try to slip out of the city."

Clarren didn't have the heart to laugh at the idea. He was being watched night and day by journalists, reporting on his ever move. And if that wasn't bad enough, there were drones constantly overhead. The President probably had spies in the building as well; after all, almost everyone in the legislative branch was politically aligned with him and at least half of them were weaselly enough to sell their souls for a presidential pardon. Clarren knew he'd never be able to leave, and if he stayed he would be tried and executed.

A weak, mad laugh bubbled up out of him. He was being screwed for trying to do the right thing, for trying to be a real leader. The laugh ended in something of a growl, which made Christopher even more uncomfortable. He was about to excuse himself to call his wife, so he could tell her that it was time to run, when the Governor slammed a fist down on the table, making him jump.

"Alright," Clarren hissed, his eyes focused on a small potted plant that had been a gift from an elementary school out on the cape. "Our backs are to the wall. We can either fight like men or run like cowards."

"There's no fighting tanks and missiles," Christopher moaned. He could feel the sweat right through his shirt. "It'll be a waste of manpower. Randolph said so."

Clarren stood up straight and cinched his tie down tight. "I'm not talking about fighting the marines. I'm talking about fighting the dead. If I'm going to die, I want to go down swinging. I want to take a few of them with us."

"Us?" Christopher asked. "Sir, I have a wife and kids. And…"

"So do I! So do a lot of people. We'll send them north. I'll call Adams and see if he'll open the border for them. In the mean time, I want you to call a meeting. I want the entire cabinet there, the Lieutenant Governor, as well as everyone who has been backing me. The President is going to come down on us hard and no one is going to be safe. That bastard's going to use us as an example to the rest of the country."

Christopher was starting to go numb. The only thing he could feel was the growing, terribly urgent need to pee. "But fighting the dead? We've seen the p-pictures, sir. We know what they can do." He took a deep gulping breath, ready to take a stand against taking a stand. "Sir, please. I'm old, okay? I'm not a fighter. I'll just be in the way."

"Then stay here and be executed. Those are the only options left to us."

2-12:17 a.m.
South of Pittsburgh

The exquisite, pounding headache had ripened to a point that took Elizabeth Seatter beyond fear. Two hours before, it had made her nervous because it was common knowledge that headaches were the first sign of the zombie disease. But she had told herself it was also a sign of dehydration, of having a hangover, or the flu.

"Hell, it could be cancer," she had whispered and then took another hit from the joint that was being passed around. She had lost count of the number of joints she had sucked on. There seemed to be no end to them and the haze of smoke made seeing from one end of the minivan to the other difficult. They also didn't help the appalling stench clogging up her nostrils. The interior of the minivan stank of armpits, old socks and weed. No one cared, least of all Elizabeth.

As long as she was high, nothing mattered—that had been the mindset which had carried her this far.

There were nine of them in an eight-seat Toyota Sienna, and so far, other than her headache, they had been lucky. Elizabeth had begun her trek almost forty hours before in Trenton, New Jersey. She had escaped that hellhole by the skin of her teeth, driving through fires, smashing through roadblocks, and running down zombies. Except they hadn't been all zombies; she just told herself they were.

Elizabeth had been, and still was, in survival mode. She had started off alone; her husband Milt had never come home from a stupid and pointless trip to check on his sister and her kids. It was a two-hour trip there and back, but he never showed. She paced and packed, and paced and repacked for six long, frightening hours as terror began to grip the city.

Finally, she had made the decision to leave, and not a moment too soon. Although it was only four miles to the border and into Pennsylvania, it took her over five hours, and just as she crossed the Delaware River, the army had closed the border behind her.

That had been her first stroke of luck. Her second came when traffic snarled to a stop a few miles later and she found herself idling next to a tank-sized truck with a flat tire; the tire was huge, half as tall as she was.

The owners did not have a spare and were just about shitting bricks. Elizabeth offered to let them tag along with her if they gave her half of their gas, which turned out to be many, many gallons. Beneath a scrum of suitcases, boxes and bags filled with odd items, the entire bed of their truck was lined with twenty-gallon gas cans.

"I guess it depends on where you're going," the husband replied.

"West," was her vague answer. The plan had been to head to Oklahoma and stay with Milt's mom. One little problem, though: Milt's mom hated her. Elizabeth could easily picture herself showing up at her motherfucker-in-law's door and having it slammed in her face.

West was good enough for the Crenshaws and, after loading up the Sienna with just about everything from the truck, they took off at a snail's pace. It seemed that half the population of the east coast had either become a refugee or a zombie, and the roads were bumper to bumper.

It got so bad that before long, every other car ran out of gas, which, of course only made things that much worse. To save fuel, one group of men simply pushed their car along, jumping in whenever the gridlock inexplicably opened up for a stretch of a mile or two.

Worried that the traffic would remain this bad all the way to the Mississippi, the three of them tried to push the Sienna on flat ground or on downhill slopes. It was dangerous getting out of the minivan. People eyed the gas-cans strapped to the top with undisguised hunger and more than a few demanded that they "share." Things became tense in the slow-moving caravan, but luck was with Elizabeth again.

They crawled past a battered, more rust than not, Jeep Wrangler. Inside was a worn, rawboned, greying old man sporting a dirty VFW hat and worn fatigues. He offered to buy some gas off them.

"Fifty dollars a gallon," he suggested. This was laughed off and although he went as high as a hundred and twenty a gallon, it still didn't seem like enough. "I got guns," he whispered, tipping them a wink.

"Meaning what?" Elizabeth demanded. "You think you can rob us?"

The notion made the old man contemptuous. "No. I figured a trade. Or better yet, I can ride along with you guys. You know, for mutual benefit. There's safety in numbers."

His name was Grizz Johnson and he had two shotguns, three pistols and a black gun that frightened Elizabeth just looking at it. She thought that only the military were allowed to have those sorts of guns. The arrangement was agreed to and after some haggling, the Crenshaws agreed to jettison some of their less essential gear and Grizz moved in, taking up the third row.

A day passed and their pace was so slow that they could hear the battle for Philadelphia raging southeast of them. As the hours ticked by, the battle spread, enveloping the oddly named city of King of Prussia, then Pottstown, and Reading. The crowded Sienna seemed always just an hour or two ahead of the wave of undead.

At some point, they picked up a loose bag of pale flesh with overly large bones named Darren Sproul. He'd been walking along the side of the road, begging for a ride, lugging two suitcases. One suitcase overflowed with marijuana and the other was one-third filled with bricks of twenties, one-third filled with clothes, and the last third filled with beef jerky. Elizabeth allowed him in, taking the cash in exchange for a ride as far as they could go.

After that everything was something of a haze. They picked up a little speed after Harrisburg and somewhere along the way, three other people found their way into the Sienna. Elizabeth had no idea where they had come from, and with the ganja smoke sifting out the windows at a constant rate, she didn't much care, until the headache started thumping in her temples. She wasn't nervous at first. A man on the radio had listed the signs to look out for: a sudden, almost debilitating headache was the initial symptom. Vicious, inexplicable anger was the second—it was an encouraging sign that she was not really angry at all, at least not while she was high, and she made sure to keep a joint in her hand whenever possible.

19

The third symptom was photosensitivity and since it was after midnight and she kept herself slunk down in the back row next to the old geezer, she was fine.

The fourth symptom—eye color change—went unnoticed for a good stretch of road. Because of all the weed she was barely cracking her lids to begin with and it was only when she rubbed her eyes with the palm of her hand that she noticed the black smear. It was then that felt the first rush of fear.

Despite the terrible ache in her head, she sat up quickly and tried to see her reflection in the rearview mirror. No matter how much she squinted, her face seemed small and far away.

Mr. Crenshaw, who was at the wheel, saw her craning her head back and forth. "You okay?"

"Yes," she answered, too quickly. "I-I was just trying to see what time it is." This seemed to satisfy him and she sat back, her paranoia rising. She had the disease, but it wasn't so bad. The headache was nasty and yet she wasn't clamoring for human blood. Making a concerted effort to be cool, she told herself that she only had a minor case and that it would probably clear up in a few days.

Until then she would find out who had done this to her. Yes, one of *them* had done this to her and when she found who it was, she was going to make him pay. She tried to spy on them from the corner of her black eyes to see which one of them had turned.

It should have been obvious except they were all sleeping. "Or pretending to," she hissed, feeling the anger rise in her like a black wave. Quickly, she took another hit from the joint, sucking it down until it burned her fingers; she barely noticed the blisters.

She gave Darren a shove. "I need another."

He was sitting in the seat in front of her and he groused, "Not cool, man. I was trying to sleep."

"Just give me some, damn it," she snapped. The shards of glass in her head were going deeper now.

He fumbled a baggie from his pocket and flipped it to her, accidentally tossing it on Grizz's face. Groggily, the old man batted at it as if it were a large butterfly. It fell on his coat and the next thing he knew claws were ripping at him.

"What the hell?" he demanded, raising his hands to protect his face and getting scratched in the process.

"Nothing!" Elizabeth barked as she yanked the baggie open. "Nothing's the hell. Go back to sleep and shut up!"

Grizz leaned back from her. "Your eyes," he gasped, pointing at her face. "Everyone! Look at her eyes!"

Before Elizabeth knew it, the entire van-load of people was gaping at her. A few were too high to realize the problem and those that did were too far away to stop her as she suddenly attacked Grizz. She went for the pistol at his hip. The weapon was unfamiliar and heavy, and yet her thumb almost magically found the safety and switched it to *fire*.

"No one move," she hissed, waving the gun around. "Except you, Darren. Get me a smoke, damn it." She badly needed something to calm her down, because all of a sudden she had the near overwhelming desire to start shooting.

It wasn't just one of them who had done this to her; it was all of them. She could tell by their wicked eyes. They all had the same wicked, wicked eyes.

No one knew what to do. Mr. Crenshaw kept driving, while next to him, Mrs. Crenshaw slipped her shirt up to cover her mouth and nose. He gave her the smallest of nods as in front of them brake lights flared for the millionth time. She nodded back and when he came to a complete stop, they both leapt out of the van, she with a piercing shriek.

For a reason Elizabeth couldn't name, at the commotion, she shot Darren in the back of the head and then turned her gun on Grizz. He was fast for an older man, but she was fiendishly strong and although he had both hands on the pistol, she slowly forced the gun toward him.

"Don't," he begged.

She pulled the trigger three times, killing him. The gunshots were so loud that she thought she would go insane from the pain. In a fury, she crawled over the bodies and stepped out into the night. The three people she didn't know were foolishly racing down the lane between the lines of cars. She almost didn't need to aim as she emptied her magazine. Two of them were hit and their cries brought a smile to her face.

"That's what they get," she snarled before jumping back into the van. She needed more ammo and more weed. With fumbling hands, she rolled a joint as thick as her thumb, and with it cocked into the corner of her mouth, and the pistol in her lap, she crossed the median and drove down the wrong lane towards the Ohio border. A mere thirty minutes later, she died in a gun battle with a dozen Ohio State Troopers.

But the damage was done. The Crenshaws, both of whom were infected, slipped across the border on foot two hours later, each with a raging headache.

The infection was now heading towards middle America.

Chapter 2
1-1:13 a.m.
New Rochelle, New York

Thuy had been pulled aboard the helicopter, shuffling like a living manikin. She stared out the door as someone, or maybe more than one someone, coated her in bleach. It was only then that she began to cry. The fumes kicked the tears off and they wouldn't stop after that.

Regardless of the tears, and the people around her demanding answers, she didn't stop staring—or hoping—until the research facility had disappeared from sight.

Impossibly, Ryan Deckard had saved her…again. Somehow, he had battled through hundreds of zombies to shoot Eng. But there had only been that one final shot and nothing more. Why hadn't he fought his way out of the building? Why hadn't they seen him running out the front doors, waving his arms?

Almost in answer, Special Agent in Charge, Katherine Pennock reached over and squeezed her hand. They locked eyes for all of a second before the FBI agent dropped her chin and began shaking her head. The simple movement was a code that was easily translated: *No one could have gotten out of there alive.*

Not even Deckard. And yet that last shot had told Thuy that maybe he could have if he had wanted to. Deckard had been trapped in a staircase on the other side of the building. Instead of escaping, he had fought through what had been a kind of hell on earth and had given up his life for hers.

He had loved her to the very end.

Finally, she pulled her eyes from the night blurring beneath her and cried from deep within her soul. Her chest ached and her breath caught in her constricted throat. She grieved for a hero of a man whom she had loved…she grieved for all of ten minutes before a hand shook her on the shoulder.

It was one of the officers; he was pointing toward the floor of the chopper. He mouthed: *We're setting down.*

A glance out the door showed Thuy that they weren't over the R&K research facility in New Rochelle. Instead, they were dropping down on what looked like a golf course. She knew there were two or three golf courses near the facility; "near" being a flexible term in the middle of an apocalypse. Without a car, two miles felt like an impossible distance.

23

She wanted to question the wisdom of this, but without a helmet and microphone, no one would hear a thing she said. They dropped down like a rock and landed with a surprisingly heavy, jarring thump. Before Thuy could even blink, the power to the engines was cut and someone was pushing her back out the door and into the darkest night Thuy could ever remember. It was as if the utter blackness of space was pressing down on the Earth, trying to swallow it whole.

"You're going to have to carry these," the same officer half-whispered into her ear, shoving two heavy briefcases into her arms. "And this" he said, adding a camouflaged backpack to her load.

There was no use complaining, especially as she seemed to be carrying the least amount of equipment. The officers, including Major General Mark Axelrod, were draped with green bags and camouflaged rucks. They also carried rifles. One wasn't offered to her, which made her feel decidedly vulnerable. Her only consolation was that Anna Holloway had been stripped of her weapons and was weighted down with so much gear that she looked like a small blonde pack-mule.

Altogether, there were fourteen of them: seven greying officers, three Blackhawk crew members, Anna, Courtney Shaw, Agent Katherine and Thuy.

Without Deckard, Thuy didn't like their chances. He had been something of a force of nature and she had thought he was virtually un-killable. A sigh escaped her. It didn't seem to matter to her what their chances were; she couldn't summon the energy to care. For the time being, she was past fear. She had one job left to her: find a cure.

It would be an impossible task in the time frame she was being given. At the rate the zombies were spreading, she had only days before a critical mass was reached. At that point a cure would be too late, at least as far as North America was concerned.

Had she known what was happening in China, she might have given up altogether.

"Keep it tight people," General Axelrod said to the little crowd standing around him. "We have a mile and a half to go. Hopefully, we'll only have sporadic resistance. Try to keep the shooting to a minimum, it'll only attract more of them, so if you have to fire a weapon, make it count."

Two of the crew members took point, while the pilot and a major walked at the rear of the formation. Thuy found herself somewhere in the middle. On one side of her strode Katherine Pennock, her M4 held easily. On the other was Anna, looking left and right, and jumping at every sound.

"Why the hell did we land way out here?" Anna demanded. "We're still in the goddamned zone for Christ's sake! I have a pardon and I'm supposed to be…"

"Someone shut her up," a colonel hissed from behind them.

Anna turned and glared. The colonel was a buffalo of a man, his large head thrust haughtily out as he glared right back, not realizing just how dangerous the slip of a woman was.

Since Katherine was equally clueless as to why they had landed in the middle of nowhere, and Thuy refused to even look at Anna, Courtney jogged up and whispered, "We didn't want to lead the President right to us. There's a good chance his men are tracking us."

"So? That's a good thing," Anna said, coming to a halt. "The President is the one that sent us!"

"He might have sent you," Courtney explained, taking her by the arm and marching her forward, "but he didn't send the rest of us. And if we get caught…" She had to stop as the repercussions hit her hard. "He'll kill us all."

Anna stopped again and stared hard at Courtney, finally realizing that they had met before and not under good circumstances—she and Eng had left her and Thuy, as well as dozens of others, to die in a state trooper's station that was surrounded by thousands of zombies. She guessed that it was too late to apologize now.

"The President wouldn't kill *me*," Anna said, arrogantly. "Not only do I have a pardon from him, I was also sent by him personally to find the cure. He might not kill you either, Thuy." She was lucky that Thuy wasn't armed. The petite scientist dropped the heavy briefcases and threw a punch into Anna's face.

Punching was not something she was particularly efficient at; the blow glanced off Anna's cheek. The looping left hook that followed would have landed flush had it not been for Katherine, who caught Thuy's arm.

"Stop it, Dr. Lee. This is not the time or place. There are zombies nearby." Everyone took their eyes from the minor tiff and stared out into the dark, their guns up, waiting for an attack.

25

Having never been in actual contact with the dead, the men were more frightened than the women, and when a moan wafted out of a line of trees that separated the fairway they were on from the next, they all jumped.

The moan ended the fight. Axelrod let out the smallest whistle and made a chopping motion with his hand, his fingers pointing south. As one, the group headed in that direction walking in a strange hunch that made them all look like beggars on a winter day. They crossed out of the golf course and slipped into an upscale neighborhood that appeared so completely normal that it looked as though the apocalypse had skipped right over it.

Other than the block being dark and deserted, there wasn't any sign that the end of the world was imminent.

The ranking crew member, Sergeant Dave Carlton paused behind a hedge before scampering across the empty street as if he was expecting someone to start shooting at him. He looked silly in Thuy's opinion. The dead had terrible eyesight but could still track movement. When they were near, it was better to be low and slow—and at least one of the creatures was near. She could hear a thumping from up the street that suggested one was stuck in a house.

Without waiting for her turn, she followed after the next crewmen. "We'll be at it all night this way," she said over her shoulder. "We're going to run into some of them. We might as well get used to the idea." The rest followed her in a clump, some of them cursing under their breath. Thuy didn't care.

As she expected, they ran into zombies and no amount of sneaking could have prevented it. They were creeping through a neighborhood when Sergeant Carlton practically stepped on a half-eaten creature that had been lying in the dark shadow of a bush. It seemed impossibly alive. Its face was near featureless and looked like raw hamburger that had been left out for a week. One of its legs was straight up missing and the other had its foot chewed off.

Although it barely possessed enough of a throat to shunt blood back and forth to its brain, it still retained an unholy strength. One blackened hand clamped down on Carlton's ankle, sending him face first into the grass.

His reaction was one of hysterics. At first, he tried to kick away from the creature, but the thing's grip was too strong. Next, he tried to use his M4. He brought it around and very well might have shot his own foot off if Katherine hadn't acted. Seeing the poor state of the zombie, she leapt forward and stepped down on the gun before he could shoot.

"No!" she cried in a harsh whisper. "Hold on." Although the zombie, even wrecked as it was, had the strength of three men, the bones of its wrist were still thin and relatively brittle. Katherine stomped her black combat boot down on it, hearing a crunch with each strike.

With his heart racing, Carlton jumped to his feet the moment he was free. "Son of a fucking bitch! It just grabbed me and I..." His face froze, locked on something behind Katherine. Too late he started to warn her, "Zom..."

Something huge crashed into her, throwing her off her feet and crushing the side of her face into the finely manicured lawn of a two-million dollar mansion. It felt as though she had been hit by a car, when in reality it was only two-hundred and fifty pounds of ex-housewife with hellish black eyes, grey flesh, and a terrible thirst for clean blood. The thing's gaping jaws came down on her shoulder with a frightful crunch.

"Shoot...it," Katherine gasped.

Sergeant Carlton was too afraid to. Too much could go wrong; he could miss and hit her or she could get showered in zombie blood or he could bring an entire mob of them down on the little group. Instead of shooting, he lunged forward and slammed his own boot into the side of thing's head. He connected with a sickening thud, and it would have been lights out for any normal person. The beast only turned and snarled at him.

"Jesus!"

He dropped to one knee and shot it through its wide expanse of forehead. There was no exit wound and, for a moment, as the monster knelt on the FBI agent with a stunned expression on its grey face, Carlton worried that the worst of the rumors—that the beasts were ultimately immortal—were true.

Finally, it fell to the side and Katherine lay gasping, staring up at the night sky, where the stars seemed oddly small, mere dots of light that didn't sparkle at all. She didn't have time to wonder why they looked so strange. The sight was replaced by the black bore of a rifle, a little feather of smoke coming from the opening. Katherine couldn't comprehend why it was there. It made no sense.

Carlton stared down the sights and was just a bit out of his mind. He thought he had been ready for this, but he obviously wasn't. "You're going to die," he stated.

"Get that away from her," Axelrod barked, striding through his stunned, huddled officers. He didn't want to push the barrel of the gun away, afraid that touching it would make Carlton jerk. "Look at her. She has armor on. She might be okay; let's see if you're hurt, Agent." Katherine rolled over and everyone leaned in and saw that there were grooves in the fabric of her ballistic vest. Otherwise she hadn't been touched.

"I'm alright. It...it didn't get me." But it had been close. She could still smell the horrible rotting stench that had come from the creature's dank mouth. Her stomach rolled, rebelling. "S-Someone spray me."

The big bull of a colonel doused her with bleach, enough to cause her to gag, and now she was nearly puking for a separate reason. She needed a minute to recover, only they didn't have a minute, or even half of one. The gun shot had woken the sleepy neighborhood and now the sounds of hungry moans and the awful scraping of bone being dragged across cement filled the air around them.

The colonel reached down and picked Katherine up with one hand and hurled her forward as the group ran, again in that unnecessary hunch. They sprinted for only fifty yards before either their age or the heavy loads they were carrying became too much. After that, they staggered on for a few blocks before they had to stop; in front of them was a ragged line of the dead marching across their path.

Like children, they quickly hid behind anything they could. All of them were gasping from their sprint and their fear, but when the dead got close, they covered their mouths or breathed into their shirts, all except for Katherine. She had never stopped gagging on the bleach. She tried to hold back the sound coming from her heaving throat, but the more she did, the more her body fought her.

Anna shoved her shoulder and hissed, "Stop it."

There was no stopping it and out came a rush of stomach juices and chunks of the dinner she had scarfed down hours earlier. The nearest zombie turned right for her. It had been a black man once; now it was a demon the color of midnight, all save for its flashing white teeth.

"Damn it," Axelrod said, straightening. He'd been in a stoop, which hadn't been kind to his aged back. "Everyone up." There was no need to order the creature killed. As if they were part of an execution squad, three of the men shouldered their rifles and fired. All three bullets struck home, staggering the creature, and knocking it on its side. It was still alive, however.

Two of the three went to shoot again. "Don't waste your ammo," Thuy said, remembering the nightmare inside the Walton Facility. "It's harmless to us now and we need to conserve our bullets." The three looked to Axelrod for confirmation.

"She's right. We should get out of here." If there was ever an unnecessary order that was it. With fifty or so zombies racing at them, Anna hadn't waited to be told and was already taking off, running deeper into the neighborhood, with Sergeant Carlton right behind her. The entire group followed as quickly as they could. In no time, they lost what cohesiveness they'd had earlier. The younger and faster among them sped ahead, while the heavier and slower ones slogged after, casting frightened looks back as the zombies formed into a shadowy evil mob, filled with sharp teeth and raging screams.

Katherine and the colonel, whose name was Kyle Taylor, were at the very back. Her lungs felt like they had shriveled and were full of steel wool and if Taylor hadn't been propelling her along, she probably would have been the first to be eaten. She needed a few minutes simply to get her breath back. There was no time. Some of the zombies were dreadfully fast and came charging along at a tremendous pace.

In only a few minutes, it was obvious they weren't going to make it. "Go," Taylor growled, pushing a heavy pack into her arms and giving her a shove. It had been unexpected and she spun, flailing backwards and would have fallen if she hadn't slammed into a six-foot fence. She wished she had gone face-first. The sight behind her was enough to make her want to scream. There were so many of the dead coming after them that they were crawling over one another like spiders.

"I said, go!" Taylor yelled. He stood alone in a small gap between two of the houses, raised his rifle and began firing. With death staring him right in the face, his aim was magnificent, and the creatures fell one after another.

With her head reeling, Katherine clawed frantically for the gate in the fence, threw it back and careened into the backyard.

She almost ran into Thuy and Axelrod, who were both coming back to help. Before Katherine could suck in enough air to say a word, Axelrod pulled her behind him, saying, "Go. Get out of here." He ran for the gate, while Thuy ran for the house.

Katherine stumbled away, in no shape to help anyone, not even herself. She had no idea how she was going to get over the fence. Everyone except for a crazy-eyed and sweating Sergeant Carlton had already climbed over. Somewhat heroically—he was almost pissing himself in a most non-heroic manner—he was waiting to help her over.

In his fear, he practically heaved her over and onto her head. She barely held onto to the top of the fence where she had a perfect view of Taylor a second from being thrown down and eaten.

He was firing quickly and efficiently, but there were so many of them; hundreds now. Before he died, General Axelrod stormed through the gate, grabbed Taylor by the back of the vest and pulled him through the gate. He then shouldered the wooden gate shut.

Almost immediately, the gate was attacked, the top of the slats breaking off as if they were made of styrofoam. "Now shoot them, damn it!" Axelrod ordered. From point blank range, Taylor began shooting every face that appeared. He killed five of them when the night was suddenly lit by a rush of flame. Thuy had run to the patio where an outdoor grill sat under a neat weatherproof cover. She ripped it off and began digging in the cabinet below it. Just as she had hoped, it held a nearly full bottle of lighter fluid and a long-tipped lighter.

Since the house was brick, she doused the fence with half the bottle before lighting it up. The old, dry wood burned wonderfully and the wall of fire finally stopped the zombies who were became mesmerized. "This will keep them busy," Thuy remarked, pretending not to notice the colonel's shaking hands. She added more lighter fluid in a line across the rest of the fence and the fire spread eagerly after it. "Come on. Don't just stand there."

The fire enveloped the wooden slats and the bushes on either side. The zombies that managed to bash their way through the fence did so as walking torches with their clothes and hair on fire. If their eyes hadn't been melted out of their sockets, they were night blind and went in circles, frequently setting more of the yard ablaze. It wasn't long before the house caught fire and after that, the remainder of their trip to the research facility was relatively simple.

With the zombies flocking to the blaze, the little group crossed through the neighborhood, passed through a shopping center, hurried across a deserted highway and were at the R&K Building in next to no time.

The building was locked, dark and cold. "Wow, what a fucking surprise," Anna cried, yanking on the handles. "Tell me, General, how much research do you think we can do in the fucking dark?" He didn't have an answer for that besides glaring at her. "That's what I thought," she said, a smug look on her face. "The only reasonable thing to do; hell, the only smart thing to do is to send a few of your boys back to fetch the helicopter. It makes no sense to risk all of us, especially those of us who are extra valuable to the mission."

Colonel Taylor was red in the face. "Look lady, there's more than one mission here. We're all valuable."

"She isn't," Anna said, gesturing at Katherine, barely able to hide the sly smile that wanted to creep onto her face. Deep down, Anna worried that her pardon would be *extra*-conditional and that if Katherine was ever called on to testify against her, things would go very badly. It would be better if she never got the chance. "She could go with the fly boys. She's not just an FBI agent, she's a *Special Agent in Charge*. They don't give just anyone that sort of rank."

Katherine, who had finally gotten her breath back, didn't feel all that special. No, just then, she felt small and weak, and the last thing she wanted was to go back through the maze of undead once again.

Chapter 3
1-2:01 a.m.
Grafton, Massachusetts

An hour before, Sergeant Troy Ross had hit that point of exhaustion where death was beginning to seem like a fine alternative to the endless marching and fighting. Now he was in some sort of numb fugue where his body seemed to be doing its own thing, following along after the man in front of him. They could be walking straight into the Atlantic for all he knew.

The thought had just crossed his mind when he splashed knee-deep into a long strip of black water. The sudden cold goosed him into a semi-state of consciousness and he gazed around at the night forest. There was a ubiquitous nature to the mossy trees standing guard over the river and he felt he could have been anywhere from Mississippi to Maine.

The men around him were of a very average sort. Interspersed with the soldiers were civilians in a mishmash of grungy denim jeans and camouflage coats. They were ragged and hollow-eyed, most looking even more exhausted than Ross. He couldn't summon any energy for compassion. After all, most of these men had been his enemy only hours before. Now they were part of his company. "I think," he mumbled. None of them looked familiar in the least. As far as he knew, he had stumbled into another formation.

Checking his watch, he saw that it had only been twenty-three minutes since their last line had crumbled away under the screaming, howling attacks of the dead. "Twenty-three? That's it?" It seemed like it had been at least an hour since they had run pell-mell through the dark forest, chased by the shrieks of the wounded they had left behind.

Ross shook his head to try to clear it and as he did, one of the men in the stream knocked into him and gave him a bleary, "Sorry," before continuing on.

"Yeah," Ross answered. He took a deep, shaky breath before wading across the stream along with the rest.

At the far side of the stream, there was a bit of a hold-up as men struggled to mount the muddy bank. Ross pushed through the men, got to the bank and sighed at the lack of unit cohesion.

"What company is this?" he asked. He received shrugs in answer, which was no wonder since the men had been assigned to their companies by being tapped on the head by some unknown major saying: "You're Alpha. You're Bravo," and so on. Half of them went to where they were assigned, while the other half went with their friends or chose a company that they thought looked tougher than the others.

Ross had a reputation for winning and had twenty or thirty men over his allocated one hundred. When it came to fighting, he was happy with the number. When it came to resupply and getting chow, he figured he wouldn't be. So far neither had happened.

"What a cluster fuck!" he snarled. "This isn't so hard, people. One man goes up and helps the next in line and so on. You," he barked to a long, lanky scarecrow of a militiaman, "put out a damned hand."

Soon, the clump of men thinned and the formations began slugging through the river. Ross cut the line and let himself be pulled up by one of the burlier men. He was walking up the river when he came across some major he had never seen before, wearing a unit patch that was just as foreign.

"Are you Ross?"

If Ross could have willed himself to attention he would have. Instead, he laid one arm over a tree branch and sagged against it. "Yes, sir." He could barely keep his head up.

"You're being promoted, congratulations," the officer said with no more energy than Ross had demonstrated. He held out two plastic bags; one was filled with white pills, while the contents of the other wasn't obvious until Ross dug his hand in it and pulled out a staff sergeant insignia.

"Cool, thanks sir."

The major looked tiredly disgusted. "That's not for you. You're being bumped to first lieutenant. You're going to have to decide who gets the other patches. Don't screw it up."

First lieutenant! For a few seconds, Ross was stunned, unable to even count the number of pay grades he'd just been bumped…not that he ever expected to get an officer's actual pay. He knew the army well enough to know that *if* they managed to win, all he'd get was a little bit of ribbon for his Dress A uniform, a pat on the back, and a boot back down to E-5.

He found the little silver bars that denoted his new rank and sighed. Given the choice between the promotion and a full night's sleep, he would take the sleep. Lifting the other bag to his face, he gave it a little shake, asking, "So, what's with the pills? They some sort of vaccine or something?"

"They're caffeine pills. Give them to the men every six hours. They'll help for a little while."

"Will we get cocaine after that?" The major grunted out a laugh and looked like he was about to leave. Ross grabbed his arm. "Hold on, sir. What about resupply? We are stupid-low on ammo and no one's been fed since…I don't remember the last time we got chow." The only food he'd had that day was a peanut-butter and jelly sandwich and some cold left-over mac-n-cheese, liberated from one of the abandoned houses they had passed.

The major jerked his arm out of Ross's grip, and while he unbuttoned his fly, answered, "We're working on the ammo as fast as we can. Trust me, we know your situation is precarious. I don't know what to say about the food. It's on our to-do list, but it's kind of down the line. Right now, everything is screwed six ways from Sunday. Our communications are wrecked. Our chain of command is about to be…"

He stopped himself in midsentence as if he had been about to spill some state secret. "Let's just say we have challenges." Urine started to splash against a tree and he tilted his head back with his eyes closed. In a conversational tone, he said, "By the way Ross, don't ever grab a superior officer like that again. That's how you get shot."

Ross snorted. This guy wasn't going to shoot anyone and after fighting for his life for the last two days, the threat was utterly empty. "Yes sir. Hey, do we have orders yet? I've only been following Delta and I get the feeling they're going in circles."

"Yeah, we got you staked out defending a section of the Quinsigamond River."

"And where's that?" The major pointed at the stream they had just crossed; it was all of thirty yards from one side to the other, and only knee-deep. "That? Jeeze. Tell me we have some support, please. We haven't seen any birds since, hell, since we won at Webster."

The major cocked an eye at him—the odd patch on his sleeve meant he was Massachusetts National Guard, which meant that he had lost at Webster to the 101st. "We, uh we are working on that, too," he answered. "There's a fuel sitch that we're trying to untangle. We might be able to get some Apaches in the air soon."

There was no way the major was going to let slip that *all* air units had been diverted south and were busy decimating the northern stretches of Baltimore, rendering the landscape completely unrecognizable. Thousands of sorties had already been flown, and now the air was filled with ash and flames, while below, the earth was a desolation of craters and rubble.

It was over-kill on a tragic level and already the lack of air-support was being felt. Over the last six hours, the line holding back the zombies had fallen more times than Ross could count.

"Well, I guess Apaches are better than nothing," Ross muttered in disappointment. The major was still pissing and it seemed like he was going to be at it for a while longer. "If you got nothing else for me, I'll let you get on with your business." Dismissing himself wasn't exactly proper, but they were both too tired to care.

Ross headed up stream for half a mile before he found a butter bar with a clipboard. The man, small and fastidious, looked as though he was better suited conducting an IRS audit. After Ross introduced himself as *Lieutenant Ross* of Echo Company, the second lieutenant shone a red light at the clipboard. "You've gone too far. This is all Foxtrot." He pointed at the men settling down along the bank of the river. "You need to turn back. There's orange tape on a tree. You can't miss it. That's you. Fill your men in until you get to the next tape."

He was about to ask how much of the stream he would have to cover when there came a ragged burst of gunfire west of them. It was the 3rd Battalion acting as a rear guard. Their job was to slow the zombies down long enough for the rest of the brigade to get dug in. The 3rd had been lucky to get this long of a reprieve.

"How much am I supposed to cover?" Ross asked, one ear cocked, not just hoping the battle would go on for another hour, but also praying that it would.

"A little over a hundred yards."

This interrupted his prayer something quick. "Son of a bitch!" Ross exploded. "That's one man a yard. One man! Do you even know what you're doing? How do you expect us to fight thinned out like that? Have you seen them…" He stopped in mid-tirade. The young lieutenant was almost hiding behind his clipboard, while the men around him looked nervous. Part of the job of a commanding officer was to instill a fighting spirit in their men and his outburst was uselessly detracting from that.

The butter bar took the break to stammer out, "Al-Alpha Company w-will be acting in reserve. They'll reinforce any part of the line that gets in trouble."

And what happens if the entire line gets in trouble at once? It was best not to ask. Ross mumbled an apology about yelling, a second before he bawled, "Echo Company! On me. Let's go. We're moving back downstream." Even saying the word stream was particularly galling. The little trickle wasn't going to slow the demons down for a minute.

After a short walk, he found the tape and began assigning a hundred of his men along the line at random, giving each one a caffeine pill before moving on. He kept the remaining twenty-two men back as his own reserve force. This only took minutes and he was just finishing up the little task when the shooting to the west began to peter out. Half a minute went by and it was down to a few sporadic shots.

"No way," Ross whispered in angry shock. "How long was that? Was that even ten minutes?"

He wasn't the only one outraged. "Did they just give up?" someone in the dark demanded.

A soldier next to Ross hissed, "When it was us, we held for twenty-eight minutes. Twenty-eight! I timed it, start to finish, and that was against that big bunch. You guys remember that?"

"Pussies!" another man yelled. "All of you are a bunch of…" Someone threw a hat at him and another punched him. He was being loud and now that the undead were coming for them, everyone buttoned up.

"Okay, that's enough," Ross said, just loud enough to be heard. "You have your positions, so let's get to clearing the underbrush." As the men hurried to get battle ready, Ross went among them, promoting a dozen men to sergeant and another four to staff sergeant. He was understandably biased and every man who received the new insignia were, regular army, like him. Then he divvied up his company into four nearly equal platoons.

Once done, he walked the lines, looking for the weakest areas—as far as he could tell, it was all weak. Nothing had changed; the tune was the same. They would hold for as long as possible before pulling up stakes once again. His guess was that they wouldn't be able to hold for more than half an hour, depending on the concentration of the dead. Sometimes they came in small gaggles of twenty or thirty. At other times it was like being at the beach and they would come in long waves of a thousand or two. The worst was when they'd come as a flood. If ten thousand of them hit the little stream all at once, the fight would be over in a minute.

And that's why they needed airpower so desperately. A few properly aimed cluster bombs had proved capable of breaking up these huge throngs. Napalm was even better. One MK 77 could roast an amazing number of dead-heads. It would also give them light to shoot by. Shooting in the dark was particularly hellish. During the day, they had been able to make almost every bullet count. They could also kill at much greater ranges, something they couldn't do at night. In the dark, they had to wait until the creatures were practically in their laps.

"We need more flares," he said to himself, looking up at the empty sky. While he was searching in vain for a plane, he heard the first cry of: "Friendlies coming in! We're human so don't shoot."

"Shut the hell up for Christ's sake!" someone in the next company cried. The 3rd Battalion came staggering through the stream and were hit with a nasty whispering barrage of curses and accusations of cowardice.

Ross didn't have time to vent his frustration. He needed information. "How many were there?" he asked the first man across. Up close he discovered it was not a man at all, it was a boy of *maybe* fifteen. He was ghost-white and shivering. "It's alright, you're safe. Now, tell me, how many were there?"

"Millions," the kid whispered, his wide, terrified eyes unable to focus.

As much as Ross wanted to slap some sense into him, he refrained. "Alright. Good. Keep going." He asked the same question of the next few men and received the same sort of odd and unnerving answers.

Finally, he came across an officer who gave him the bad news. "A hell of a lot. They're sort of balled-up. Like a fist. Most of the line could have held for a while, but the center-left crumbled. We threw our reserves in, but it was too late. Too many of the men are on the verge of cracking." This last part came out in a creaky, secretive whisper.

"Too many of the men aren't even men," Ross said in reply. "Tell me, are they close?"

"We lit some fires to confuse them, but yeah. Maybe a few hundred yards back. Good luck, man."

He was gone. After him followed haggard soldiers, baby-faced farm boys, and city dwellers who were far out of their depth. After them came the dead. From afar it sounded as though some immense beast was *eating* the forest. The smaller trees were enveloped and crushed under the squirming bodies as branches snapped and bushes were ground under foot. Up close, the sound was a thousand times worse. Up close, Ross could hear the horde breathing; it made him want to run away screaming as fast as he could.

But he held his ground, hunkering low, refusing to move or even to swallow.

There was total silence along the entire line. No one wanted the horde to center on them and so, the long thin line huddled in fright, hoping and praying for some miracle that would turn the awful creatures away. Ross looked for his miracle in the heavens in the form of a flight of *B2 Spirits*. All it would take was just one to clear the other side of the river for a square mile.

Please God, he mouthed and was still searching the empty sky when a rifle fired. His first reaction was to breathe a sigh of relief. The shot had come from far up the line and as expected, the thousands of beasts suddenly swung in that direction.

Foxtrot was going to get it bad, but that didn't mean Ross' Echo Company was going to get off scot-free. There'd be a little overlap, though probably not something they couldn't handle. Already there was a splash to his left as one of the dead fell into the river. More followed. Still his soldiers didn't move. The lifeless monsters kept shifting north as more rifles began to *pop, pop, pop* upstream.

Why stop them? each of the soldiers was thinking. *Why not let them go on and kill someone else?*

Ross was thinking the same thing and had been all night when an unexpected answer filtered through his relief: *Because the line won't hold.* It wouldn't, he realized. No miracle was coming to save them and without one there'd be nothing to stop the zombies from overrunning the soldiers of Foxtrot, perhaps killing them all. And if that happened, then what?

"We'd have to run again," he whispered. "And again and again." And each time their numbers would be fewer and fewer. His stomach rolled over, nausea creeping through his guts like a huge oily slug. He knew what he had to do. "Son of a bitch," he muttered, fear gripping him hard. He had to take a deep, deep breath to spit out the next order.

"Rifles up, Echo! It's time to fight."

2-2:03 a.m.
New Rochelle, New York

The building was cold and forbidding, but not so cold and forbidding as the night, where there were howls and moans coming from almost every direction. Everyone was staring at Katherine Pennock and the three Blackhawk crew members.

It seemed unbelievable that they were being asked to go back through the deadly gauntlet they had just escaped from.

The pilot was a forty-year old reservist with a beak of a nose that jutted almost as far out as his Adam's apple, which was oddly sharp and looked like he'd gotten a clam stuck sideways in his throat. His name was Tim Bryan and he was as brave as the next man, but the idea of going back undercut him badly.

"Maybe we should all go. We can leave the gear here and I can land the bird right over there. The, uh, blonde chick is right; there's plenty of room." The words had run out of his mouth in one long stream and when it dried up, all he saw were heads shaking. He wasn't the only one who had been unnerved by the helter-skelter flight through the neighborhood.

General Axelrod looked at Bryan with disgust and even made something of an *ugh* sound as he turned from the nervous pilot. "I'm having trouble with this. Did we come all this way for nothing?" he demanded of Thuy. "I thought you were some sort of genius."

Thuy was lost in thought, her mind harkening back five days before when she had been trapped in a similar building. It had been a nightmare that she would never have gotten out of if it hadn't been for Deckard—and now that he was dead, she was wondering if she went inside, whether she would walk out again. She had been somewhat oblivious to the entire conversation until the word "genius" entered her consciousness.

Before she could open her mouth, Anna jumped in, "We're wasting valuable time. You have to make them get the helicopter, General. It's our only chance. And with the fire going, they should make it easy. If you're worried about the President, we can go north or..."

"No," Thuy said, her soft voice cutting across Anna. "Why on earth are any of you listening to her? She's a criminal. She's a murderer on a scale that dwarfs even Hitler."

"I have a pardon," Anna hissed. "And it wasn't even me who did all this. It was Eng, and you know that. But none of that changes the fact that this was a waste of a trip!"

Thuy snorted derisively and reached out her small hand, laying it on the dark glass wall. "This is a bio-research facility for a billion-dollar pharmaceutical company. Do you really think that a man like Stephan Kipling would forget something as elementary as having a back-up generator in case of a power failure?"

The thought really hadn't crossed Anna's mind, and judging how the others seemed to wilt in relief, they hadn't consider either. "Then what are we waiting for?" Sergeant Carlton asked, moving toward the door. "Let's get in there."

"Hold on," the colonel demanded, easily pulling the man back with one hand. "We have to think about defending this place. If we start smashing holes in the doors, it'll give the dead an easy ingress site. Is there roof access around back?"

Thuy, who had never been to the rear of the building, replied with a shrug. Anna did as well. She assumed that was where the garbage bins were and why on earth would she want to visit them?

The general sent out two teams to find a way inside and while they were gone, Thuy went and stood off to the side, staring across the parking lot. She should have been thinking of finding the cure, instead she couldn't stop thinking about that last gunshot of Deckard's. It had come down at an angle, probably from the third floor. Could he have fought his way clear from there? How many bullets had he had?

Deckard had started with seven magazines, but there was no way of knowing how many times he'd shot his weapon. He'd been firing far too quickly to count. She only knew that when he fired the shot that had stopped Eng, he had to have been scraping the bottom of the barrel, ammo wise.

She tried to convince herself that he had been able to hide from the huge mob of undead, except every time she closed her eyes, she could hear Jaimee Lynn Burke singing out in that sickly-sweet voice of hers: "Doctor Leeeee. I cun smell you, Dr. Lee. An' I cun smell that man, an' that woman. I cun smell all of you." As a zombie, little Jaimee Lynn was terrifying.

All alone, fighting against so many, Deckard hadn't had a chance in…

"Dr. Lee?" It was Sergeant Carlton taking her by the hand. "You're the lightest. You should be the top person. Come on. It'll be easy."

"Hmm? Top person? I'm sorry, I wasn't listening."

He pointed up at the second-floor window. "There's no way in without breaking a window so we decided we'll go in through that one. You're going to be the top of a human ladder."

Thuy's mouth fell open.

3–2:17 a.m.
The Walton Facility, New York

Jaimee Lynn Burke was far from satisfied. Hours before, she had gorged on the army girl until she began burping blood and chunks of tasty little gristle-like morsels that went down just as well the second time as they had the first. But that was before all the running around she had been forced to do. Setting up a moving trap in a partially collapsed building was not the easiest thing to do, especially when her only help were a bunch of zombies.

"They's worserer than a busload of kiddie-gartners," she said, sucking the marrow from the humerus of the man that had been killed in the west parking lot. If she had been told that man was her father, she would have angrily denied it. Her father most certainly had a face and hands, as well as two legs, and the ravaged corpse had none of those things.

Still, there had been something vaguely familiar about the body. There had been a southern dirt flavor to him that the man she had picked over on the third floor had lacked. *He* had been the biggest disappointment of all. She had done everything she could to get to him while he was still fighting, but there had been hundreds of the big, stupid zombies in her way and they had eaten him down to his boots.

And all the others had somehow gotten away. She stood in the parking lot, one end of the long bone stuck in her mouth, making it look strangely like a pipe. "Wut's that way?" she asked one of the zombies moaning by. "Hey, stoopid-head!" It kept going.

"He prolly didn't know nothin' no-how," she groused. "But that other one might." She wandered to where her little ones had treed Lieutenant Eng of the People's Liberation Army. She had eight little ones left, all of them horrible demons. They were a ragged, deformed lot, missing so many pieces of themselves that between them, they didn't make more than two and a half children.

At least they listened and had some smarts.

"Jammee, he smell," one told her.

"On top he do, but unner-neath, he gonna be good," Jaimee Lynn reassured her. "You just wait." She looked up at Eng, dying in the tree, her nose wrinkling at the smell of bleach. He had coated himself in it. "When y'all gonna drop on down, Chinaman? Ain't you tired yet?"

Eng wasn't tired. He was well past tired and was on whatever stage was two levels beyond exhaustion. His head swam and his right lung had begun to rattle when he tried to drag in futile sips of air; his left lung had already filled with blood. "Go away," he whispered.

"Okay, sure," Jaimee Lynn lied. "But first y'all gotta tell me what's that way. All them people went an' flew off that way." She pointed with the gnawed end of the bone to the south.

"I don't know. Just go away."

The Chinaman was being difficult. Jaimee Lynn decided to sweeten the bargain. "I'll send my friends away iffin you tell me. Y'all cun climb on down and scoot, you know? Y'all cun escape. How's that sound?"

It sounded to him like a bad lie. Then again, it also sounded like she was stuck on the question. With great difficulty, he lifted his head and stared off in the direction the Blackhawk had flown. As far as he could tell they had gone almost directly south.

Gasping, he told Jaimee Lynn, "They're going to New York. You should go, too. Lots of people. You could eat all of them."

Her black-demon eyes grew wide. "Is that close on by?"

In order to answer her, Eng had to drag air into his one lung as if he was sucking it from a straw with one end in the bottom of a nearly empty pool. "It's not far. Only a few miles away. You could…be there in no time." He drew in another long breath, picturing the city and the little apartment he had rented north of it when the Com-cell project had been located at the old R&K

research facility in New Rochelle. It struck him like a thunderbolt—that was where Dr. Lee was going.

Dying as he was, his mind had been sluggish and uncaring; now, it spooled-up, picking out the clues: the single helicopter, the utter lack of support, the fact that they had sent a useless hick like John Burke in with them. What did it all mean? Slowly, it dawned on him.

"They're on their own," he wheezed. "They're going to New Rochelle. To make a cure or a…" He was suddenly too dizzy to speak. As he lay on the branch gasping, he wondered why he cared. There was going to be no cure for his punctured lung and internal bleeding. He was going to drown in his own blood sometime in the next hour and there was nothing that would change that.

"Y'all almost done gonna fall?" Jaimee Lynn asked. "Y'all's takin' forever." Around her were the beastly half-children, many of them so mauled it was a wonder they could still stand. Seeing them gave Eng an awful, evil idea. There *was* a cure for a punctured lung, it came with a price, however.

Taking the deepest breath he could manage, he hugged the heavy branch with all his strength and let one of his legs dangle. The little beasts went nuts, leaping for his foot that hung just out of reach. They were all either too small or lacked the necessary muscles or limbs to jump.

Even lanky Jaimee Lynn couldn't reach the inviting flesh. After jumping to her highest, she stood back, a sneer on her blood-caked face. She needed a ladder, or a boost, or a step stool. The nasty sneer turned into an evil grin at the idea of a step-stool. She grabbed the nearest kid and threw him down on the ground. Two more were thrown on top of him and, once she was standing on the little pile, she could reach Eng's foot.

Beneath the strong stench of bleach was the sweet smell of flesh and clean blood. She attacked the foot, clawing at it with both hands and nearly managed to pull Eng down. He clawed the branch like a cat and held on, and when her hands slipped, he pulled himself up.

"Perfect," he whispered, feeling blood run down into his sock.

"Git on down here!" Jaimee Lynn raged, flinging her dad's humerus at him. Eng only smiled and held on, wondering how long it would be before the Com-cells started mending his lung.

He knew that he would be infectious in two hours and so struck with pain and inner fury that he wouldn't care about his wounds.

What he needed were painkillers. They'd keep him aware enough to find Thuy and make her cure him.

"You," he said to Jaimee Lynn. "Do you want blood? Real blood? Dr. Lee's blood? I can get her for you, but you have to help me."

For some reason, Jaimee Lynn harbored a strange hungering hate for Dr. Lee. She was a treat that was somehow always just out of reach. Sort of like the Chinaman's leg had been. "You know'd where she went?"

"Yes. A building. It's not far. Not more than thirty-five miles away." Jaimee Lynn's black eyes went to squints. She didn't know how far a mile was anymore, but she knew it was far. "It's okay," Eng went on, seeing the look. "I can drive us. I just need a few things first and then you'll have all the blood you want."

Chapter 4
1-3:09 a.m.
Grafton, Massachusetts

First Lieutenant Troy Ross decided on his own to make the fight for the little river the next great battle of the war. When his men hadn't budged, he simply picked out a target and fired his rifle. As expected, the undead creatures that had been slogging up the river immediately pivoted and came at him.

"You're in it now, boys," he shouted. "Let's make it count." Most of his men cursed under their breath, while a few whined, their spirit almost broken. "Shut your mouths and fight! The suburbs of Boston are only eighteen miles away. After that is the ocean and it's a long-ass swim to France. So, shoulder your rifles. We fight here and we fight now!"

Not bad for his first rah-rah speech as commander, he thought. His men continued to grumble, and that was okay; soldiers always complained. All he cared about was that his men did seem to be settling down and, as the dead started clawing at the muddy bank, they fired their guns, filling the stream with wretched bodies.

Ross was not content with the battle centering on a few companies. After telling one of his staff sergeants to hold the line until he got back, he jogged downstream, passing four companies of cowering men. There were zombies pushing past all four, heading right for his Echo Company.

"And," he raised his gun and fired at one that was practically on the eastern bank. "Now, they're not." Just like before, the surging beasts turned to the closest human sound.

"What the hell!" the commanding officer of the company hissed as he raced over. "Who fired their gun? Who was it?"

A hundred furious men pointed at Ross, who raised a hand. The C.O. was a captain, which was neither here nor there to Ross. With death threatening at every turn, the penalty for insubordination, or whatever the man would threaten him with, seemed inconsequential.

"How dare you! Your orders were to remain on the fucking line and to keep…wait, who are you?" He had just seen Ross' new silver bars, and he knew, sure as shit, that this dumb fuck wasn't one of his own officers.

"I'm Ross of Echo Company. We're doing something different: we're all going to fight from now on. No more hiding like little kiddies."

The captain's eyes flashed. He thumped into Ross chest first, demanding, "Are you calling me a coward?"

"No, I'm saying we all are. We have the enemy right in front of us and we are all hiding." Below them the captain's men were beginning to rip bullets into the dead. "Since you have a battle to win, I won't keep you." Ross pushed past the captain who sputtered curses after him. Ross jogged further down the stream for another two hundred yards to where the men were huddling behind bushes and trees. This time he didn't slow down as he shot at the zombies. What would be the point? More useless arguing with frightened officers? Or maybe he'd get fragged; that was a clear possibility.

There was, of course, another outburst of anger, but he was already on his way to the next company, where a dozen men whispered the same question at him: "Are we bugging out already?"

"No, we're staying put and fighting," was always his answer. He only went a little further before deciding to head back. He'd been gone for nine minutes and it felt like an eternity. After tromping down to the water's edge and killing a pair of zombies and causing another battle to erupt, he raced back towards his place in the line, fearing the worst. Had they already been overwhelmed? Or were they even now throwing their guns aside and running for Boston?

With his head filled with these thoughts, he nearly ran into a group of men, three of whom held leveled guns. *Was it going to be a good ol' fashioned fragging or a nuisance arrest?* he wondered.

"That's him," one of them growled.

"Yeah, it's me. I've got a company in the thick of it, so if you guys don't mind getting out of the way, that would be great."

A lieutenant colonel pushed to the front and stood with his hands on his hips. It seemed to Ross as if he were striking a pose like some sort of action figure or maybe a superhero; Ross had to suppress a smile. "Why don't you tell me what in fuck's sake you're doing?" the colonel demanded. "Because it feels a whole lot like you're trying to undermine our chances. We can shoot traitors, you know."

"I'm trying to win, sir." Ross quickly told him his idea, adding, "I would've run it past my C.O. if I knew who that was and if I had the time, which I don't. Actually, *WE* don't have a lot of time. Boston is getting close."

"Like I don't know that," the colonel snapped. "I know perfectly well where Boston is, just like I know perfectly well what our ammo situation is. Did it ever occur to you that we were letting the men bug-out for a reason?" It had not occurred to him. Feeling stupid, he shook his head and mumbled an apology.

The colonel made a rumbling sound in his throat at the barely heard, "Sorry." His anger was cooling quickly. It was hard to stay mad at an officer who wanted to fight; it was their job after all. And the man was right. They had been fighting a war of attrition, giving up ground to gain time to reorganize, reinforce and resupply.

It was a war within a war, and it was one they were losing. Boston was too close and its people were starting to panic. If that particular dam broke and they fled, there was no telling what would happen.

He didn't want to think about that and, thanks to Ross, he didn't have time to. The storm of gunfire shaking the leaves from the trees told him he had to get to his C.P. and get control of the situation. With a final glance up and down the line where his entire battalion was engaged at once, he growled, "Alright. Get back to your company and know this, Ross, this isn't over."

"Yes, sir." As far as Ross was concerned it was. He had a hundred and twenty-two men depending on him and he had better things to do besides being threatened. With a quick nod to the captain, who looked as if he had just swallowed something oily, Ross jogged away. After a few hundred yards, he began asking the men battling along the river: "Echo Company? You guys Echo Company?" Most of the people he ran into didn't know who they were attached to, which made sense since everything had been pure chaos for the last day and a half.

Eventually, he found his men, fighting the dead to a standstill, piling the river up with bodies. The heaps of corpses weren't yet at the level of the muddy bank, which was a relief. "What do we need?" Ross yelled, marching behind his men, making sure he was seen and heard. There was nothing worse for a soldier's moral than for his commanding officer to disappear when the fighting got thick.

The expected calls for more ammo came quick; no soldier ever thought he had enough. Ross bellowed for his staff sergeants to get an accurate ammo count and while the four of them went from man to man, he hurried to the next company in line simply to see how they were faring. The last thing he wanted was for a breakthrough to occur fifty yards away and not know it. The men of Charlie Company were fighting hard with no quit in them.

"So far, so good," Ross muttered as he strode back. The ammo count averaged fifty-three rounds a man, which he knew meant something closer to seventy-five a man. With an unknown number of zombies attacking them, it was a dangerously low number. He sent one of his men running to the colonel with a count of forty-five per man and urgent demands for more. It was how the game was played.

The ammo situation was bad, but what his men desperately needed was light. They could make every shot count if they just had enough…these thoughts were crossing through his mind when, at that exact moment, a blink of light caught his eye.

Feeling excitement burst in his chest, Ross ran up the hill to stand on a stump, watching as shards of brilliant light blazed out into the forest. It was like nothing he had ever seen and, unfortunately, whatever the source of the light was, it wasn't enough.

2-3:22 a.m. Eastern Standard Time
Yangtze River, China

It was after four in the afternoon when Xu Jingxing finally crossed the bridge as part of a massive refugee caravan that encompassed over three million peasants. The bridge that passed from the city of Jiujiang was only two lanes and most people opted to make the semi-swim. It was either that or chance a change in the wind, which for now, was sending the radiation raining down to the southeast. There had been rumors of a storm pushing up out of the South China Sea and if that happened, they were all going to die horribly.

To help the peasants cross through the river, ropes and buoys were strung somewhat haphazardly. There should have been three distinct lanes to cross; however, the engineer who had been tasked with setting it up had made excuses and fled while still in the initial stages. The workers, who were as equally frightened of the radiation, had sent out some buoys, connected a few ropes and left almost as fast.

There were wide gaps, leaving the peasants a short swim across. Those who weren't strong enough to swim with their belongings either left them behind or drowned. No one helped one way or the other and so far, nearly a thousand people had drowned.

Xu wasn't about to leave his heavy pack behind. Within it was his future: thirty-six pounds of looted gold. When he fled his home, the pack had been filled with clothes, some food and a laptop. He still had the food, though he hadn't felt like eating real human food since he'd been attacked nearly four hours before.

During those hours, he had convinced himself that the creature had been just a man suffering from radiation poisoning and not one of black-eyed demons. Those had all been nuked out of existence. Everyone knew that. The army had done what it had to and sacrifices had been made for the greater good. Xu clung to the idea. He was a middle-aged man with a bowl haircut, awful circulation that left him with swollen feet, a saggy belly and a tiny scratch on his calf. It was that scratch that scared him to no end.

At least it had.

Now, he was too angry to be afraid. He stomped along in a drug-controlled fury; the drugs coming from a tiny doctor, who like everyone else, was trying to hump his livelihood across half of China. Thinking he was a shrewd businessman, the doctor had demanded outrageous prices for the medicines he carried. When demand became too great, he started swapping his pills for pieces of jewelry, expensive watches and, of course, gold.

When he saw Xu's gold, he foolishly asked for a private meeting which was held behind a large, rusting silo.

"With your gold and my drugs, I think you and I can come out of this like kings. How much do you have?" His eyes were so filled with greed that he failed to note how dark Xu's had become. As the doctor was pawing through his pack, Xu picked up a rock and beat his brains in. For just a moment, he was overcome with a desire for something clean—the doctor's blood.

It looked so beautiful and red and delicious that his fingers were dipping into its warmth before he could stop himself. Drinking that blood would have been proof that he was one of *them*, and at that point, he had still been human enough to be disgusted by the thought.

Since then he swallowed pain pills almost like they were candy. They kept his body and his mind going for many miles and many hours until he was fairly breathing out Com-cells. On the packed bridge alone, he managed to infect thirty-six people. When he crossed to the other side, he pushed through the crowd, infecting even more.

Being so close to that much fresh blood was warping his mind. He could feel the all-consuming hunger overcoming him and he knew he had to get away before he did something terrible. But there was nothing on the other side of the bridge. The land was one rice-paddy after another. In the distance was a small town and like a lunatic, he ran, pushing through the crowd, thinking that if he could find an empty room in one of the buildings, he would lock himself in and ride out the madness.

"The pills will help. Five at a time and I'll be fine." To get to the town, he knocked through a highway choked with fifty thousand people, leaving Com-cells swirling in his wake.

The town was even more crowded than the highway. There were exhausted peasants everywhere. They were stretched out on the ground, their throats bare. Xu felt his pulse hammering violently throughout his body, but didn't notice the drool dripping from both sides of his mouth. Somehow, he gathered enough strength to turn away and found himself heading to the river that flowed alongside the highway.

There were docks and boats, but there were also soldiers guarding the way. That didn't stop Xu. He forced his way to the gate, caught sight of the officer in charge and held out a gold bar. Once more the gleam of gold was blinding and Xu was allowed through the gate. Another bar got him on board a squat barge that was brimming with people. A third bar bought him a small cabin.

In his short time on the dock, he had managed to infect thirteen people who would get on boats of their own, spreading the disease north to Nanjing, whose population of eight million had nearly doubled in the last two days. Xu would go on to Wuhan, in the heart of China.

On the way, the story of his gold reached the captain of the vessel—he left Xu's cabin with a gleaming bar of his own and a host of deadly Com-cells multiplying in his sinuses. He wasn't Xu's only visitor. After the captain, more than one woman came to visit him. Each were brutally killed, their blood drained and their pale, lifeless bodies hidden under a blanket next to his bed.

The hot blood was wonderful and yet his hunger only grew until it was a raging beast that the tiny cabin couldn't contain. It was dark when he came out to feed and in the dark, he ate his fill.

3- 3:27 a.m.
New Rochelle, New York

There was one problem with using Thuy as the top person on the human ladder: she was almost too weak to break the glass. Especially since she was given a rock as her only tool. Laughably, it was thought that it would be quieter than a gun.

Her first attempt ended with: *GONG!* Everyone winced as the sound carried through the night. She had barely scratched the window.

General Axelrod growled, "Hit it harder, damn it."

"Wow, what a great idea," Thuy muttered under her breath. Didn't he understand that she could only hit it so hard before her hand went through and she cut herself to ribbons? Scrunching up her pretty face and holding her breath, she swung again with even worse results than her first attempt. The brick-sized rock smashed into the heavy glass, but not only didn't break it, the brick made an even louder *GONG!!!* What was worse, the rock bounced out of her hands and went flying, nearly cracking Dave Carlton on the head.

Now everyone was cursing. "Get her down!" the general groused.

Thuy hadn't liked climbing up, using the relatively soft limbs of the men as hand and foot holds, now getting down only seemed worse. Light as she was, she still feared she would accidentally pull down the entire ridiculous structure. "Just give me the rock," she ordered.

It was passed upward and she tried again, this time aiming only to crack the glass. From there she would expand the crack until it became a hole. It took seven loud hits before the glass finally came down in a sudden grey sheet of rain. By that time zombies were lurching in their direction.

Axelrod was again less than helpful. "Get inside! Get in!" he cried, going so far as to point at the hole.

What did he think she was going to do? Climb down? Jump for joy? She scrambled in, doing her best to keep away from the jagged glass sticking up here and there. Once inside, she found the building was unsettlingly dark; it was also as quiet as a tomb; just what she was hoping for.

Keeping hold of the rock, she hurried through the company's legal section where, despite this being the computer age, there was a surprising amount of paper lying about in thick stacks or neatly arranged in filing cabinets of which there seemed to be at least one per cubicle. These stood grim and shadowy, like metal sentinels.

As she had no use for lawyers, she had never been in the legal section before. It was no matter. She knew the layout of the ten-story building with its central elevator bank and three staircases, and was soon in the east hall, jogging for the closest staircase where the dark was perfect in its blackness. Thuy paused for only a second, again listening for any sign of the dead.

The silence was as pure as the darkness. Thuy descended down into it, counting the stairs until she reached the first floor. Just as she reached the stairwell door there were two quick gunshots from the front. With her heart in her throat, Thuy sprinted for the lobby. Another gunshot rang out before she got to the doors. She threw them open and saw four or five shadowy beasts lumbering across the parking lot.

Anna almost bowled Thuy over trying to get inside. "Hold on!" Thuy said, pushing her back. "Someone needs to distract them, otherwise they'll go for the door." They all knew what would happen then—another battle they couldn't afford to fight. "Who's the fastest of you?" Thuy asked. It was a status that no one wanted to claim, and the younger men suddenly found the ground of great interest. She knew Carlton's name, so she picked him out.

"Me? I'm not the…" Next to Thuy, Axelrod frowned and, even in the dark, the expression carried enough force to cut his protest short. "What am I supposed to do? Just run around?"

"Get them to follow you around the building and then sprint back here and we'll let you in. Hurry! Go!"

With something of a whine, Carlton jogged reluctantly toward the zombies, waving his arms and, as he did, the others scooted inside. General Axelrod did not bother to watch the sergeant. Time was getting away from him and he feared that the army that had been shoved into his lap was already unraveling. "Dr. Lee and you," he said, sneering at Anna. "Get to work on the cure. You three." He gestured to Katherine, Warrant Officer Tim Bryan, and Specialist Russell Hoskins, the other crew member. "Set up a defensive perimeter here on the first floor. Everyone else with me, including you, Miss Shaw."

He took the lead, heading for the stairs. Ten stories was a long climb for a sixty-three-year old man and eventually he waved the younger men ahead, gasping, "Communications first...I need to...know what's...going on." The last couple of flights were murderous and he had to wait a full minute at the top to catch his breath and to let his head stop spinning before he strode onto the floor.

His team had chosen a south-facing office as the operations center and by the time he stepped through the door, the portable satellite was halfway ready, laptops were ginning up, and maps were being spread. His staff was trained for mobile warfare and would have everything up and ready in minutes.

Data was already coming in. Axelrod, his bald head glistening with sweat, stared down at it in disbelief. "Why?" he whispered. They were all asking themselves the same vague question. "He's moved all the air units. All of them. We're screwed." He was too shocked to even curse.

"And look at the northern line," a lieutenant colonel said, choking in indignation. "They're being reallocated."

"Find out to where," Axelrod ordered. He could see the *redeploy* symbol over the unit names as well as the colonel could. There were a lot of units with the same symbol. Unbelievably, many were holding the western section of the Zone. "He's taking units out of the line in the middle of a damned fight!" It wasn't unheard of as long as there were units to replace them; in this case it would take most of the day or even longer to get even the closest of the northern Guard units in place.

The trouble didn't end there.

A few hours earlier, Axelrod had scraped together a smattering of odd units— engineers, medical companies, a cyber protection battalion, and even a tank maintenance company— they were supposed to have been airlifted into Boston to reinforce the badly mauled 101st. Instead, it had been re-tasked to help hold Long Island. To make matters worse, they weren't flying. The units were currently marching a hundred and six miles from Lynchburg to Norfolk where they would board a boat.

"It'll take them three days to get there," Axelrod muttered. "This is insane. We…we need to stop this." Without any help, he didn't see how the line around Boston would hold and if it fell, not only would millions die, it would spell disaster for the rest of New England.

He turned to Courtney. "Can you get on the phone with the governors of Maine, Vermont and New Hampshire. Tell them that if they don't send everything they have to help in Massachusetts they'll be doomed. You should call Canada as well. Their border's going to be wide open in a matter of hours."

"What do you want me to do about this mixed bag near Lynchburg?" Colonel Taylor asked.

Axelrod rubbed his bald head back and forth for a few seconds before shrugging. "The only thing we can do; we turn them around. That goes with all of them. I don't care if they've marched for the last three hours straight, I want every unit back where they were. Tell their C.O.s that until they hear differently from my own mouth, I'm running the 7th Army, not the President."

Chapter 5
1-4:03 a.m.
Grafton, Massachusetts

Four hundred yards from where First Lieutenant Ross' Echo Company was killing the dead with grim efficiency, stoically waiting until the creatures were right on top of them before pulling their triggers, a half dozen lights blazed into the face of Governor Clarren and thirty-two other high-ranking members of his staff and his party.

Most of them looked ridiculous. For the most part, it appeared as though they were getting ready for an early morning duck hunt. The rest wore green garbage bags from head to toe, duct-taped at the wrists, ankles and neck. They might have looked more ridiculous than the rest, at the same time, many of the nearby soldiers stared enviously. The only items they had in the way of protection were handkerchiefs and strips of cloth which they wound around their faces.

The officious and frightened group was surprisingly well armed. Clarren, in his last act as Governor, had relieved the security staff of their weapons and dismissed them. With every camera left in the state rolling, and radio stations broadcasting, he had closed the State House, saying, "I am being arrested for treason because of the part I played in trying to protect my state. The punishment for this is death. I say that if my life is forfeit, I cannot see a better death than one given in service to my family and to the people of Massachusetts. I will not cower in some closet or try running away. I would rather die fighting our common enemy than in front of a firing squad. But if the President still wants to arrest me, let him come in person. He'll find me on the front lines."

There had been a good deal of cheering from the crowd. Word spread of what was happening and, as Clarren took questions from the press, unexpected volunteers began to trickle in. It hurt his heart to see how young they were. The twenty-year-olds were bad enough, but some couldn't have been more than fifteen.

Christopher Gore, wearing a camouflage uniform like he would a suit, and sweating through it as if he had run a marathon, whispered, "We can't take the kids. How do we know if they even have permission from their parents?"

"I don't think that matters now. If the children want to fight for their families and their state, I will not stop them."

This was caught by one of the news crews who announced that Clarren was leading a "Children's Crusade." For some reason this sparked even more of a surge in volunteers and before long, the ex-Governor was leading a three thousand strong army across the state. Trucks and cars were gathered in a huge caravan and the whole thing moved west down the Massachusetts turnpike, lights blazing, and horns blaring so that there was a parade-like atmosphere to it.

They found the desperate "Army of Southern New England," *east* of Worcester, something that killed the manic euphoria. Without air support, the strategic city had fallen an hour before and now the army of undead was practically on the front steps of Boston. For the moment, the only things holding back the main horde was the exhausted, half-panicked army of men and boys.

The panic would have been worse if the ragged army knew what sort of chaos was going on behind the lines. An hour before, a flight of Blackhawks had swooped down, not to strafe the zombies or to bring reinforcements, but to land a swarm of FBI agents. General Milt Platnik, as well as his entire staff, were arrested, shackled and whisked away to answer for their "crimes." Replacing them were fourteen generals from the Pentagon, who had been picked almost at random. They felt like they had been thrown into a blender. Still, they were professionals and the ranking officer sorted out the positions among his staff and they went to work trying to regain control of what felt like a lost cause.

As professional as they were, the forty "political" officers that accompanied them by order of the president were not.

None of the political officers had any military training at all; they were party officials, mainly junior staffers from the White House or Congress. Most of them had degrees in political science or environmental studies. They were worse than useless.

They had been told about the coup attempt against the president and warned not to trust anyone in green. The best among them were surly and suspicious. The worst were puffed up with self-importance, reminding anyone who looked at them sideways how they had the power to arrest anyone they pleased for treason. It was a very real threat and it cowed hardened officers who allowed themselves to be bullied.

Orders from on high had to be filtered down through these political officers and the worst among them frequently added their own spin, perceiving themselves to be Napoleons in training. Many also displayed aggressively possessive attitudes. Supplies were not to be shared with other units, they were to be hoarded. The same was true of reinforcements. Although the center was in no danger, nearly half of Clarren's young recruits were positioned there, uselessly crouching in the forest behind a six-mile long lake while the horde split and spilled over the far edges.

None of the political officers that he ran into knew what to do with Clarren. Since he had come to the front line to die, he laughed in the face of threats of arrest.

On his own, Clarren followed the sound of the gunfire along the Quinsigamond River. At least a thousand of the children came with him, but most of these were again nabbed by units along the way and barely a hundred reached the point of attack.

It hurt Clarren's heart to watch the teens go into the line, taking timid steps, looking ready to run at any second. He wouldn't have blamed them if they had. They just seemed too damned young to fight and for a moment, he doubted himself and the wisdom of bringing them. Then the hollowed-eyed veterans on the line began to thank him, some practically in tears.

"If they want to fight, we'll take 'em," was the prevailing wisdom.

Luckily, there were no political officers below the battalion level and so common sense prevailed. The kids were buddied with an adult and when there was time, quick instructions were given: "Whatever you do, don't waste ammo! Keep your finger off the trigger until you're ready to fire. Never fire from behind someone. And no matter what happens, don't panic."

Clarren's staff could have used some of those instructions. None of them were vets and, in keeping with the prevailing politics of the state, they'd all been virulently anti-gun a week before. Still, they and the newspeople were welcomed—at first. Clarren's media entourage had started with the same nine stations that had covered his speech in Boston, but as he had gotten closer to the actual fighting, they had dropped off one by one. Unsurprisingly, by the time he reached the front lines, only two stations were still with him. The little group consisted of six very nervous people who walked in a huddle.

The glaring lights for the cameras provided a welcome relief. The soldiers could finally see what they were shooting at and in no time, they had cleared the river in front of them.

A cheer went up and Clarren and his staff were thumped on the shoulder and high-fived until their hands hurt. Another wave of the dead were dispatched with the same alacrity and the men began to clown for the cameras, feeling they had reached some sort of turning point. They were still congratulating themselves when a thunderous roar swept the far bank.

The cameras had been on Clarren, who had fought with everyone else, but was still more politician than soldier. He paled at the sound and took a step back. Someone yelled for the lights to be pointed across the river and when they were, they saw that the forest seemed to have disappeared under a great shadowy mass that roiled and screeched. This was the true zombie army and it made the stoutest men quail.

"Keep the lights on them!" the battalion commander ordered at the top of his lungs. "Where's the reserve company? Captain Tate! Get your men on the line this instant. Mackon! Break out the 240s."

"What about the mortars?" Mackon asked, his unblinking eyes staring in horror at what lay across the river. "If ever there was a time to use them, I think it's now."

The commander nodded. "Yeah. Might as well give them everything." Mackon hurried off, screaming over the growing gunfire. It wasn't going to be enough. Nowhere close to enough, in fact. The commander dialed his boss, the brigade C.O. and calmly told him that he had "the entire goddamned zombie army right in his damned lap," and then begged him to send every available man his way before it was too late.

The political officer attached to the brigade HQ heard the panic in the lieutenant colonel's voice and jumped when the first of the high-explosive mortar rounds began to explode among the undead.

Sitting on the hood of a Stryker, looking unmoved by the urgency of the situation, was the brigade commander, Colonel Welling a lean, hunk of gristle with an iron-grey flattop. "Well?"

"What do you mean? What do we do?" the political officer asked. She was inside the command vehicle and had no intention of getting out.

"That's what I asked you. Do we throw in our reserves?"

Her eyes went to the map, which was crawling with symbols. "I-I can't make that sort of decision. It has to come from higher up." He glared at her until she reached for her sat-phone. She hated his judging eyes and she rolled up her window to make her call. Her boss was with the division H.Q. and he couldn't authorize the use of reserves either and the call was passed on again.

The moment Welling heard her talking, he whispered to his executive officer, "Get something moving, now. We can't have penetration so close to the water barrier. We staked everything on holding it."

His XO was a hard veteran of both Gulf Wars and knew the danger posed as well as his CO, and yet he went cold and shifted his grey eyes toward the back of the vehicle at the request. "But…"

Welling glared the man into silence. Just giving the order had been a court-martial offense. "I'm willing to risk it. If they come for me, I'll pull a Clarren and head for the lines. What about you?"

"Yes, sir."

The XO put in the call to the haggard third battalion and ordered them back into battle. It was a two-minute conversation that was secretly monitored and recorded by the US Army Intelligence and Security Command.

The operator hearing the conversation sighed and turned to the strident political officer. "We have another one."

2–4:14 a.m.
Washington D.C.

Despite the early hour, the atmosphere thrummed in the White House, turning the air electric. Normally, there was an air of quiet reserve about the building, then again normally the place was filled with senior staffers, Cabinet members and other high-ranking officials who knew the proper etiquette. These had either been fired, forced to quit, run off, or arrested.

As he didn't know who he could trust, the President had decided to get rid of the whole shebang.

For the most part, the chaos that was expected from this "massacre", as it was being called, did not materialize. Most of the cabinet-level departments had ceased operations two days before. Those that remained fully operational, such as the Department of Homeland Security, had a staggering amount of "upper management" and when the top layer was skimmed away, there were plenty of people ready to fill the void.

It was only the Department of Defense where things were horribly scattered. Had it not been for the President's interference, the situation would have been wrangled into some sort of order by then.

The war...the entire war, was a cluster-fuck of epic proportions. The only real good news was that the President had gone to bed. The moment he had, Matthew Dimalanta loosened the thin black tie he wore. His wife had told him it made him look like Malcom X, but a palatable Malcom X, one that white people would approve of. He was no Malcom X. Dimalanta was weak and the tie felt like it was strangling him. He had been the President's campaign manager and when Marty Aleman—and everyone he was associated with—had been arrested, Dimalanta had been ordered into the position of Chief of Staff.

He knew going in that it would be a thankless job, but he had no real idea just how bad it would be.

An undercurrent of paranoia rang through the White House, making everyone extra vigilant to carry out orders to the letter with absolutely no deviation. Exhausted troops who had gone the last two days without sleep, and in many cases without food, were ordered to shift hundreds of miles. The Air Force was being asked to relocate hundreds of planes to bases that couldn't handle the influx—hundred million-dollar fighters were being pushed out into the fields to make room for billion-dollar bombers.

No one had the guts to say anything. After the arrest of General Phillips, a number of generals tried to make a stand and were immediately arrested as well. Things became far worse when the interrogations began. The President wanted answers quickly, and after the FBI couldn't—or wouldn't—stoop to using torture, the CIA was called in.

The few officers on duty at that time of the morning were not the cloak and dagger types. They were analysts who knew nothing about torture and frankly didn't want to know. They rushed out of Langley, regardless, made threats, only to be laughed at by General Phillips and General Haider. Marty couldn't tell the difference and, in a haze of tears and sweat, spilled everything, explaining how it was only a three-person cabal and that they had the President's and the country's best interests in mind.

This wasn't good enough for the President. "I want the truth!" he had screamed into Marty's face three hours before. Marty had only cried harder.

Now, the heavyweights from the CIA were arriving. The first were the senior deputy directors with sleep in their eyes, who were there, not as interrogators, but to find out what the hell was going on. They also needed to make sure everyone knew that the CIA never tortured anyone—especially Americans.

Dimalanta knew that wouldn't fly. The President knew certain things for a fact, whether or not they were a fact at all. In his mind, half of everything the CIA did involved torture and, if they weren't going to torture for him, it could only mean they were against him. Dimalanta tried to convey this without actually saying it, hinting that the arrests would begin at the top.

"How many arrests have been made so far?" the Deputy Director of the Office of Advanced Analytics asked in something of a choked whisper. He was drab, balding and pudging in the middle, someone the eyes rarely lingered on. In other words, he was the perfect spook.

"Over eight hundred."

The deputy swayed in place. "But I only work in analytics. Did you get my assessment of the Chinese situation? Did the President see that? Did you see the estimate of a Russian nuclear strike on China? That was what my team has been…"

Dimalanta's dark scowl interrupted him. "We need confessions! If you guys can't do it, get one of your agents here asap, and I do mean asap. If the President wakes up and finds out you haven't been cooperating, then I won't be able to help you."

It was because of this conversation that David Kazakoff was now in the White House striding past the beautiful oil paintings and the magnificent marble busts and the finely carved crown molding. Although Dimalanta had expressly demanded a CIA agent, he was not one. The CIA did not have "agents." They had officers and in some cases operatives. Kazakoff was neither of these, either. He was an asset, one that did not like the idea of being paraded around in the damned White House. It put a damper on one's ability to remain incognito.

Technically, he did not work for the CIA. His paychecks came from a well-connected law firm that funneled money to various people for various reasons, all the while skimming a bit off the top for themselves. No one in the law firm had ever met Kazakoff and had no idea what he did, which was perfect for all involved.

His escort through the building was twenty-four-year old Trista Price, a young intern: pretty, thin, blonde, who had found herself promoted in the course of the night and was now assistant undersecretary of…something. She couldn't remember the title that had been thrown at her and she had been too shocked to ask for it to be repeated. She didn't even know exactly who she was working for; she only knew that it was the greatest honor she could think of.

This honor was sullied by having to be anywhere near Kazakoff. He was slightly taller than average, but far stronger, hiding the bulk of his muscles beneath his over-sized jacket. It was impossible to hide his scarred-over knuckles. He was handsome in a way that Trista tried not to notice: dark wavy hair, penetrating eyes, a firm jaw.

"Where is the subject?" His voice was soft, accentless, cold.

Trista wouldn't look at him as she answered, "Beneath the west wing." Visiting the labyrinth of rooms beneath the White House had been a thrill the first time she had been there; now she was feeling ill. Five of the rooms had been turned into makeshift cells, which had been bad enough. In a few minutes they were going to be torture chambers.

"Are the kitchens down there, too?" Her chin turned slightly towards him—*was he going to eat before he tortured them?* The idea was off-putting. She wished that was the case. "I'm going to need some equipment," he added, making her blanch.

"Of course," she said, unable to hide her sneer. "You should have said something sooner."

He smiled coldly into that sneer, erasing it from her face. Her chin dropped and she meekly turned around, heading for the kitchen.

Kazakoff fell in beside her, enjoying her discomfort. He was an excellent judge of character and this girl fairly reeked of privilege—it was a privilege that he and other hard men like him afforded her. Without them, her life would be much different. More than likely, she would be the equivalent of some wool-covered maiden in Bulgaria, trying to work her looks into a good marriage.

It had been hard men doing the tough things that had made the country what it was. They had fought the wars, subdued the savages, tamed the land, and now hunted evil around the world…only to be sneered at.

And when things were turning to shit, who do they call? Who do they beg for?

His smile widened as he watched Trista's flesh crawl, enjoying the fact that the world was unravelling her Ivy League education, unmasking it for the fraud that it was. She was in for a wake-up call and a part of him wished that he could be around when she was finally forced to see reality.

But he had work to do. There were renegade generals to break. History was replete with them, making and breaking kings, destroying stable governments for their own selfish desires, destroying lives at a whim. They were a common blight, except in America. There had never been an American Caesar and as long as Kazakoff was around, there never would be.

The smile vanished at the thought. He was grim and, in Trista's mind, terrifying as he barged into the kitchens. The staff in their white aprons and high, fancy hats were just starting to get into gear, readying for breakfast. The two were greeted by the assistant kitchen manager.

"Show me your freezers," Kazakoff instructed as he opened his wide, smiling mouth. There was something about the way he spoke that made the manager decide not to question the request. Fifteen years in the White House kitchens had taught him that sometimes it was best just to smile and nod.

The freezers, like everything else, sparkled in perfection. Inside the second one, Kazakoff found half a steer hanging from the ceiling. "I want that meat hook and chain," he ordered and then spun on his heel leaving Trista and the kitchen manager gaping at each other. From there, he went to the closest butcher station and picked out a number of tools and wickedly sharp knives, laying them on the table.

"Have these sent down. I'm also going to need a sturdy, high-backed chair, rope, a hammer, jumper cables, and a car battery. Also sewing needles, and a Bunsen burner."

Again, the two looked at each other. He walked between them, heading for the hallway, making Trista jog to catch up. She was morbidly curious but refused to ask what he was going to do with it all. In silence, they made their way to the elevators, where they were stopped by Secret Service agents.

"I'm going to need an all-access pass to this place," Kazakoff remarked. "I don't want to have to rely on escorts every time I want a sandwich…unless you plan on staying with me the whole time. You might learn something." He leered down at her with a wolf's grin and she shook her head.

"Good." The elevator opened with a whisper. "I work alone. It's best for everyone. That way you can lie to yourself and pretend you didn't really know what was going on. As far as the world will know, this will just be an interrogation. The car battery and the jumper cables will be our little secret." He gave her a little nudge with his elbow and a wink as if they were just two co-workers flirting in the elevator.

Her smile in return, an involuntary human reaction; was sour and weak. "Yeah, sure." More than anything she wanted the jumper cables to be their little secret, but they wouldn't be, she would have to request them. *But not in writing*, she told herself as the doors opened.

The important prisoners were being kept in a row of small offices that had been cleared out just for them. Each held nothing but a chair, a desk and a video camera. In the hall were two Secret Service agents and their credentials were once again checked. Kazakoff had been expected.

"Run along little Trista," he said, taking her by the shoulders and turning her back the way they had come. "It's time for the men to get to work." She bristled, hating him; she did so in silence. She wanted to get out of that basement as soon as possible.

"Which one's Phillips? I want him first." He would be the toughest to break and Kazakoff liked a challenge. A glance in the monitor that had been set-up, showed a black and white feed of an older man, sitting in the corner of the room, slumped over to the side and sleeping with his mouth open. Kazakoff frowned. "I want them all awake. No one sleeps unless I say so." He didn't wait for a response and marched into the room.

Phillips jerked awake and gazed blearily at Kazakoff with red eyes. "Hello General." He smiled down at Phillips, an evil gleam in his eye. "My name is David Kazakoff. I'm here to conduct your interview. Your *real* interview."

This got Phillips' attention. "Who are you with? CIA? NSA?"

"None of those. I'm with America. Come, have a seat. It's going to be a few minutes before my accoutrements are assembled and I figured we could talk…" Kazakoff leaned over and turned off the video camera, "off the record, so to speak."

"That's not needed," Phillips said. "I have nothing to hide. The President is dangerously unfit for office and if you were any sort of patriot you would kill him immediately."

"With what? A knife? My bare hands?" Phillips shrugged as best he could with his hands cuffed behind his back. "I find it strange that you would ask me, a total stranger, to do this when you had every opportunity to kill him yourself. You have hands, don't you? You could have bludgeoned him with a lamp or ordered a steak from the kitchens and stabbed him with your fancy silver cutlery. Yet you didn't. Why is that? Was he not dangerous before?"

Phillips sighed. "I was weak. And I thought he was weaker. But he's got a hard streak in him that I never suspected. You're proof of that. And I get the feeling you'll get to see that hard streak as well. In the end, he'll kill you. No loose ends. That's how these types work. But you know that already. Deep in your heart you know that."

"Here's what experience has taught me, General, snakes like you will say and do anything to save their hide. You are a cancer and the only way to stop cancer is to cut it out." There was a knock on the door and one of the Secret Service agents slipped in holding a wrapped towel. It thumped when he laid it on the table. Kazakoff grinned as he opened it. On top was a steak knife; he shrugged and set it aside, preferring a nine-inch deboning knife. "Beautiful ain't it?" he observed, holding it up, letting the light bounce off its edge.

3-4:26 a.m.
Smithfield, Ohio

"It's time," Heather Harris said to herself—lied to herself was closer to the truth. It was long past time to leave. Smithfield was a ghost town already. Only the funeral parlor over at the Nightingale Chapel still had its lights on. Seeing them gleam when everything else was so dreadfully dark had been the final straw.

But she couldn't leave without Mister Renfro. He had been missing all night. "Doing what and with who, God only knows! It's an embarrassment, especially at his age!" The only saving grace was that there hadn't been anyone around to be embarrassed in front of.

Smithfield lay only eleven miles from the Pennsylvania border and although the edge of the Quarantine Zone was a hundred and fifty miles further than that, it still felt too close and people were bugging out and heading west. Heather had a sister in Kansas City and once she found that ridiculous Mister Renfro, she'd be in her nearly fifteen-year old 4-Runner and heading out. Normally it was a day-trip, but she planned for three days on the road.

Losing her patience, she stomped out onto her back porch and hollered, "Damn it, Mister Renfro! Get your butt back home this instant!" She paused, listening, straining to hear an answer. "He better not be hiding down at that damned fishing hole."

She hoped not. If he was carousing, he may not listen to reason. With a weary sigh—she had been up all night—she started through her backyard, leaving tracks in the early morning dew. An arc of trees was the only thing that passed as a fence around her house, and she slipped through the trunks to a small path. It branched, one side heading to her neighbor's house and the other curving with a slope down to the fishing hole.

It was darker in the woods and she hesitated. Heather had lived on the property for over forty years and knew there wasn't anything in the woods that could hurt her. And yet, she didn't automatically take the branch of the path. "Mister Renfro?" she hissed. She wanted to pretend that she wasn't afraid, and that she was only irritated. They had a very long drive ahead of them.

"I'm going to give him a piece of my mind," she told herself, putting her hands on her plump hips. She was short and plump, and looked all the more plump because she was bundled in two cardigans. Despite them, a shiver took hold of her. "I'm being silly," she said and forced herself on.

He was at the little pond—she almost stepped on his lifeless body. Her foot came down right next to his head before she realized what it was. "Oh God!" she hissed, dropping to one knee, her cartilage popping as it always did. He had been torn open; his guts were simply gone.

His green eyes were missing as well and his big bottlebrush tail that he had always been so proud of had been nearly torn off.

Heather's chest began to flutter. "This is terrible. What got to you? Oh, you poor thing." She told herself that it had to be a fox, probably. There were a few that wandered in close to town and an old tom like Mister Renfro didn't stand a chance against one of them…and besides, the monsters weren't supposed to eat animals. She took off one her cardigans and, with tears in her eyes for her old friend, she wrapped him in it.

"You need a proper burial." *Funeral*…the word just popped into her head and for the first time in her life it had an evil undertone. She was just wondering why when she caught sight of something across from her by the water's edge. It looked like a squat boulder sitting halfway in the water, only there were no boulders down there. Then the thing stood.

It was a man staring silently at her, an air of burning menace surrounding him.

Smithtown was one of the friendliest places on the Earth and it was unheard of to find someone lurking like this without even the simplest of greetings. Even struck by a sudden, incomprehensible fear, she started to bring her hand up to give him a small wave. Her hand was at shoulder height when he charged with a terrible growl.

She let out a shriek and took off running up the path, her old legs wobbling her along the curve of the path, one arm out in front of her, the other carrying Mister Renfro in her arms like a football. In her shrunken heart she knew she would never make it home. The man was charging through the forest at a sprint, cutting her off.

Sucking in a huge gulp of air, she spurred herself on to her fastest—it still wasn't enough. He loomed in her periphery, a terrifying growling shadow. She knew it was madness to take her eyes from the path, but her eyes were drawn to his blackened face and, sure enough, she stumbled over a root and fell. Her mind tried to categorize the fiend bearing down on her. A week before she would have thought he had escaped from an asylum. Now, she thought he had escaped from hell. His clothes were in tatters and his flesh was torn in a dozen places. The scabs were as black as tar.

It's one of them! she realized. It was a creature from the news. And it was in Ohio. This was worse than any demon. The army couldn't stop them and if the army couldn't, what chance did sixty-eight year old Heather have? She froze, waiting for the inevitable, and watched as the man-beast ran itself onto a tree branch. Its momentum was so great that the branch went right through its neck almost dead center.

It should have been dead, only the thing had been dead to begin with, or that was what everyone said. Instead of "dying" it drove itself further onto the branch, its hands out reaching for Heather. It got intolerably close before she finally started kicking back away. Scrambling to her feet she began running again, this time determined to keep her eyes forward.

A hundred yards went by with aching slowness and all the while she dreaded hearing the monster coming up after her, its diseased breath hot on her sweating, wrinkled, old lady neck. Any second, she expected the beast to break the branch off, scream in rage and crash through the forest like a freight train, but she heard nothing like that. In fact, soon enough, the only thing she could hear was her own harsh wheezing and her heart thundering in her ears.

Her world shrank to the path and she plodded up it at barely a jog, her legs growing heavier and slower with every step. It seemed impossible that she was going to make it to her reliable old 4-Runner, yet there it was fully packed, the keys in the ignition.

As if she had been carrying a purse, she tossed the dead cat into the passenger seat and jumped in herself. There was no fumbling around like in every horror movie she had ever seen; her hands worked with precision. Her left locked the doors while the right turned the key, gunning the engine to life. She reversed in the hardest, fastest arc she had ever made in her life, causing her other five cats, scrunched in their little boxes, to hiss and yowl.

"Sorry, sorry," she said in a warbling voice. "We're gonna be…" What she saw illuminated in her headlights caused her to choke.

It had once been Dan Crenshaw. Where his wife was, he didn't know and he was beyond the capacity to care. His mind was a hive of hate and pain, and it was entirely focused on gasping, round-eyed Heather. He was so far gone that he didn't notice that he had torn a gaping hole in his own neck. The wound was nasty and there was black blood pouring in a torrent from it.

Heather stared at him in disbelief, her body frozen in shock, her heart seizing in her chest with a sudden spear of pain. She was having a minor heart attack and had no idea; her brain was as frozen as the rest of her.

The light flashing into Crenshaw's face had confused him, stopping him momentarily. It was a pause that could not last. Destiny and the disease were running hand in hand, and after a long slow blink, he charged the rumbling SUV. At the same time, Heather stomped the gas. Gravel spewed out behind as her worn tires dug for purchase and the 4-Runner sped forward.

It would have been best if she had plowed right through the zombie, mangling and crushing it, turning its bones to dust. Instead, she turned at the last second, giving it only a glancing blow and leaving a long black streak along the side of her vehicle.

Feeling as though she was either going to vomit or pass out, she raced out onto the main street and blazed west, her car covered in zombie blood and the carcass of a diseased cat sitting next to her.

"Oh, God. Oh, God. Oh, God," she panted, only just beginning to feel the pain of her heart attack. It was nothing compared to her fear. Her fear kept her juiced for good hour and by then it was her head that was the problem, not her heart. The headache was so bad that when she pulled into Columbus, Ohio with its population swollen to over a million people, her eyeballs were throbbing in their sockets.

A quick stop for some Extra Strength Tylenol doomed central Ohio, and then she was off again, hoping to make it to Cincinnati before the sun came up.

Chapter 6
1-5:12 a.m.
New Rochelle, New York

"Cannan, please," Axelrod begged. Begging sounded strange coming from his normally growly voice. Strange and pathetic in his ears. "Please, me and you go back to the Point. Remember Riyadh?"

"Yes, and I owe you for that, but we're talking about treason." Thomas Cannan's voice came through the sat-phone grainy with far too many clicks and whirls than Axelrod would have liked, making him worry that the spooks had already picked up on the call. With so many thousands of conversations running through the military net, he knew the chances were very slim. His luck had been running like crap.

He glanced to the window, wondering if even then a cruise missile was streaking towards him at Mach 2.

"We're talking about the fate of the country, Cannan. The President is bopping units here and there like they're checker pieces. He's damning us, Cannan. If we don't shore up the western zone, that's it. Game over. We need the 3rd ID. Harrisburg is on the fucking verge and if it falls…" Once more his eyes went to the map. The only things holding back a horde of some ten million zombies were the Susquehanna River and a patchwork army of farmers, out of shape reservists, and a hodgepodge of Army units that were being worn down to nothing.

"If we can't hold the center we're screwed. We'd have to fall back thirty miles to the Juniata River and that's halfway to fucking Pittsburgh. And do you even see the Juniata on the map, Cannan? It's a fucking stream!"

Axelrod realized he had been yelling. Taking a deep breath, he added one more "Please, Cannan."

Two-hundred miles to the south, Major General Thomas Cannan was riding in his command Humvee somewhere in the middle of a four-mile long convoy that held his entire twelve-thousand man division. In the Humvee directly behind his were six political officers who had joined the group an hour before. The lead P.O. made it clear that there would be no deviating from the planned route or the planned timetable.

If there was a change, Cannan would be arrested immediately. The same would be true of his successor and his successor, and so on. "We're not playing," the soft-faced P.O. threatened.

Cannan had wanted to smash his face in; however, thirty years of training held him in check. His job was to follow orders to the best of his ability and he could only hope that his superiors knew what they were doing. "Sorry, Rod," he said, and hung up on his friend.

On the tenth floor of the R&K Building, Axelrod set the phone aside. He had called in every favor he could and had been turned down one after another. His name was poison and General Phillips' idea of him leading the 7th Army in hiding had been undermined before he had even got off the ground.

He stood on shaking legs and left the little cubby he'd been using and wandered back to the palatial offices of Dr. Stephan Kipling, where the rest of his crew were busy trying to get some sort of understanding of the situation. It wasn't good. So many moves had been ordered from the White House without regard to what was happening on the ground that disaster was imminent.

In the north, two National Guard regiments had pulled up stakes, leaving a third made up of reservists supported by the local militia bogged down, in a battle that had flared up out of nowhere. It was in danger of being overrun, at least according to the commander on the ground. Air surveillance had been pulled and so there was no way of knowing what they were facing.

"He's going to have to retreat," said Axelrod, saying what they all knew. "Tell him to cross...what's that river?"

"The Mohawk, sir," Colonel Taylor informed him. "It's a perfect place to hold and it *was* their fallback position."

Axelrod didn't want to know, he just couldn't help himself. "Was?"

"Yes, sir. There are eight bridges and four wide crossing points that have to be manned in force. They can't do it alone, especially since both of their flanks will be hanging wide open."

The general cursed under his breath. "They have to retreat somewhere."

Taylor started shaking his head. "The official word from Washington..." Axelrod groaned and Taylor chuckled. "Yes, exactly. The official word is for them to disengage, head north to regroup and cut across the top of this big lake before swinging wide around and back south. They're hoping that Utica isn't compromised by then."

"They're giving up on New York entirely," someone remarked in a sneer.

"So, what do we do?" Axelrod demanded. "With all these fancy computers and phones, we know the problems we face. Now, how do we fix them?"

The officers exchanged looks, hoping to see ideas forming in someone else's eyes. Shrugging was normally frowned upon; Axelrod scowled as his officers could come up with nothing. "There are a few things we could do," Courtney Shaw announced. She had made her calls to the various governors and to the higher-ups in the Canadian government, all three of which had been so hungry for any sort of news that no one questioned her stated credentials. Since then she had been taking down names and frequencies, building a data base.

"We still have ways we can make a difference. A lot of these little battle groups haven't actually moved yet, especially the air units. Dulles and Reagan have planes everywhere. Even Richmond is filled. We still have assets in Pittsburgh, Shepherd Field and Niagara. They could be doing all sorts of bombings and stuff."

Axelrod smiled with more patience than he would have if the suggestion had come from one of his subordinates—at least she was giving him something to work with.

"Have you forgotten the political officers?" he asked her. "All orders have to go through them. No unit commander can make any decision without them."

"And have you forgotten that they have no idea what they're doing?" She had a little smirk going that seemed to drive the weariness from her home-town pretty face. "They have no concept of radio protocol at all. They have no trouble dropping names and blurting out information that we can use. Let me show you. What's the smartest place we can bomb right now?"

She expected Axelrod to point to some hot spot in one of the many battles that were going on at the moment, instead he turned a lap top around and pointed. "Here."

"Really? That's the most important?" She shrugged before pulling the computer closer so she could read the coordinates. "What sort of bombs do you want to use?"

Taylor told her, "I think six GBU-15s would suffice, but it'll never happen. That's right outside D.C."

"That'll make it easier," she told him. "You guys make some noise, talk or something, like we're in some sort of office."

They started talking, mostly about nothing, and for some reason they kept their eyes semi-averted as if they didn't want to be associated with something so crazy.

Courtney cleared her throat and dialed, when the line was picked up, she immediately began, "This is *Miz* Rachel Long, the political officer attached to General Stone. Who is this? Captain Lumburg? Good. We have a priority one mission." She covered the phone and whispered to the room, "They're all priority one."

She listened for a moment. "Two planes I think. What kind of bombs was that again, General?"

"GBU-15s," Axelrod said, pitching his voice low, afraid he'd be recognized and ruin the whole thing.

"GBU-15s," she repeated. "He thinks it'll only take six. Let me pass this on to Mr. Berry to make it official. Mr. Berry? This is *Miz* Long, we have a priority one airstrike at latitude: 38.968703, longitude: -77.179183." There was a long pause as he worked out where that was. When he did, he began to question the order. "We are aware of where that is. There are rumors of diseased individuals who have gotten through the Zone and the President is trying to isolate Washington. Make it happen." She turned off the phone with her thumb.

"There's no way this is going to work," Taylor said, shaking his bull of a head.

But even as he spoke, the order was being passed on to the airfield at Richmond, Virginia. It wasn't questioned. Too many insane things were happening at once to question them all.

Courtney had no idea how many bombs the "average" plane could carry. Whenever she saw an Air Force jet, they seemed to be sporting all sorts of missiles and such. In reality, the GBU-15 weighed two-thousand pounds apiece and even a sturdy platform like an F-15 Strike Eagle could only carry one at a time.

A flight of six was hastily prepared and sent up. Flight time was less than half an hour and the lead jet released its ordnance two miles from the target just as the sun cracked the horizon. As far as missions went, it was a cakewalk. The bomb's forward guidance section had to make only minor adjustments since it was practically impossible to miss such a broad, obvious target.

The warhead struck the American Legion Memorial Bridge dead center in the middle of the Potomac River, sending up a fireball two-hundred yards into the air and shaking the walls of houses for miles around. Two more explosions followed in quick succession sending the main bridge west of the nation's capital into the river. No more were needed.

General Axelrod listened to the pilot chatter in disbelief and embarrassment that the US military could be so easily compromised. The moment passed. There was too much work to do. His first job was to shore up the western portion of the zone. Once more, he called General Thomas Cannan. "Cannan, I think there's been a change of plans. Your route around the city has been compromised."

There was a moment of silence before Cannan came on. "What did you do?"

"What I had to do."

2-5:49 a.m.
Grafton, Massachusetts

Men went mad in the face of the horde and Lieutenant Ross couldn't blame them. A person could take only so much and what lay in front of the thin line guarding the shallow river was impossible for the mind to comprehend. Ross had been at this for what felt like days and he had finally reached the pinnacle of horror.

The camera lights had been a beacon to the dead. They came, not in endless waves, but in a storm, converging from every angle. The fight grew quick and hot. Soon everything was in short supply and the breakthrough Ross had worked so hard to stop was on the verge of happening.

He threw in his meager reserve platoon, screaming for his troops to hold their ground.

Twenty-two men were not enough and he could see his company wavering. It was then that the battalion mortars started thumping. Every man on the thirty-mile long line prayed they'd come down into the horde in front of them. There just weren't that many mortars. Still, the explosions turned the heads of the dead and relieved the pressure in key areas that were close to falling.

Echo Company's respite lasted only minutes, then the surge swept down the far bank. Ross grabbed the first man in reach. "Find the battalion commander! Tell him that we'll be out of ammo in five minutes! We need ammo and we need more men. Go!" He shoved the man up the hill behind them and took his place.

After four minutes, Ross' M4 felt like it had been pulled from a fire and all around him brass glittered in the morning light. Once more, they were down to it and he started craning his head back upstream, his pleading eyes looking for help.

"I'm out!" someone yelled, fear pitching his voice so high that he sounded like a rooster crowing. The man got up and started to back away from the line. He had his excuse to run away. How could he fight without bullets?

Ross was on him in a flash and threw him back to the bank of the river. It was cruel, but he knew that all it would take was for one person to run and then his entire company would crumble. If they faltered, the line would fall, and Boston would be next. "We all stay, damn it! We fight together as one."

For how much longer? he wondered, throwing some ammo toward the man. He had maybe ten rounds left, himself. There was no getting around the fact that they couldn't hold without help, and he was just looking for one of his staff sergeants to discuss some sort of orderly retreat when the runner came sprinting back, pointing over his shoulder.

Both the brigade commander and his executive officer had been arrested, but the order had gone out already and the 3rd Battalion was streaming forward in an uneven line. Unfortunately, they had been called on too many times to stand alone and when they saw what they were facing, the line wavered.

A colonel tried to scream them forward, but half broke and ran and the other half came forward skittishly, infecting the men on the river with a fever to take off. "They'll be back!" Ross yelled out the only encouragement he could think of. The saving grace came in the form of the heavy weapons company which pushed through to the front. Three M240 teams threw themselves down right on the little slope above Echo Company. The two-man crews set up their medium caliber machine guns in seconds and began working a tremendous slaughter among the undead.

As the guns fired only a couple of feet overhead, Ross scrambled around, grabbing the shaken reserves, and interspersing them among his men. "Spread the ammo around. No hoarding!"

The machine guns could only give his men a five-minute break and when the river directly in front of Echo Company was cleared, the machine gun teams popped up and moved on.

In the growing light, Ross could see that what had once been thirty yards of winding grey water, was now a hideous carpet of mutilated bodies five deep. Running in and around the corpses was a black sludge: a toxic stew of zombie blood and diseased body parts, mixed with just enough water to move it down stream.

Beyond the river, as far as the eye could see, was the army of undead. The shock of the mortars and machine guns seemed to have thrown them into a confused state. And when the sun broached the horizon, they fell back, repulsed by the searing light. This was only temporary. The mortars were already running out of munitions and the machine guns couldn't last much longer.

Ross felt naked without the guns and even with the reserves, he was still without enough ammo to hold against any real attack. He had no choice but to tell his people to hide in the scrub, "And pray," he added.

His men had been praying for days already but the words must have fallen on deaf ears. There were so many tens of thousands of zombies that the pressure from the rear pushed the entire mass forward. A huge grey wall surged over everything in its path, houses were demolished and trees were bent over until their trunks snapped or their roots exploded out of the ground.

Stunned and sickened, Ross stared at horde through binoculars. "We're not going to make it." In the face of the horror advancing on him retreat was the only option, but to where? With the reserves thrown in, they had no true fallback position and without one, the retreat would turn into a rout and there was no telling how far they would run.

Something had to be figured out or someone greater than himself had to see this. Once more he started looking around for the nearest staff sergeant, only to realize the man had run away sometime in the last hour. Ross' frustration mounted to a Vesuvian level and when he saw a soldier beginning to creep away, he erupted.

"Get back on the line, you fucking pussy!" he seethed.

The venom in his voice stopped the soldier, who crouched in the undergrowth. "I-I was just going t-to use the bathroom," the person whispered.

"There's a tree right next to you, piss on that."

"I-I can't." The answer was unbelievable to Ross and before he knew it, his rage got the better of him. He charged over and was about to throw the person down the bank and into the black bog when he realized that it was a girl he had by the shoulders, his nails digging into her coat and crushing down on her flesh.

She was a tiny thing in an over-sized hunting coat and the dark braids running along either side of her chin made her look shockingly young. *She's not even seventeen*, he thought and then quite forgot himself and quickly apologized—had she been a man, that would have never happened.

"Go if you need to," he added, thinking she was just making an excuse to run away.

Her name was Rita McCormick and she was only sixteen and felt like a terribly young and useless sixteen just then. "I do…and I'm coming back. I just can't, you know, with so many men around. I wasn't expecting it to be like this."

He was about to let her go when he realized something: if she needed privacy, she'd be halfway to the battalion headquarters by the time she found any. "Do what you have to do, but when you're done, run over to the HQ and tell whoever's in charge that I need to talk to them. We need to know where we're falling back to from here."

She nodded and was gone in a swirl of camouflage and braids. When he turned back to the river, he caught one of the men grinning at him. "Why didn't you just ask her out?"

"It's too late now," another whispered. "You're never going to see her again." But he was wrong.

Rita was pluckier than she seemed and did as she was told. Because of her lack of understanding concerning military procedures, she marched up to a circle of Humvees and looked for the oldest person among the men squatting over the maps and arguing into bulky sat-phones. Breathlessly, she gave the message and then asked for a bathroom.

"Was it Sergeant Ross?" the oldest of them asked. "Tell him he's in charge of 1st battalion now. Everyone at brigade's been arrested. I'm moving up and none of the company commanders have shown me dick in the way of initiative. Tell him it's him or no one." He reached into his pocket and fished out a little silver leaf and gave it to her.

"And tell him we're not falling back. This is it. The new governor is demanding that we make a stand." The colonel turned and spat.

Rita still had the echos of moans playing in her ears. "Can we say no to him?"

The colonel smiled without any humor. "Not unless we want a quick trip to the firing squad." She swayed at this, looking like she was about pass out. She was a baby in his eyes. "Here's what I want you to do, give Ross the message and then disappear. I'd go north if I was you. Forget about Boston and whatever you have there. Just go straight north."

Rita didn't want to run; it seemed beneath her. Ross, on the other hand, wanted to run the moment he accepted the new insignia and the orders from the colonel. He looked down at the silver leaf like a condemned man. The orders were the equivalent of a death sentence.

3-5:41 a.m.
The Walton Facility

The ungodly pain in Eng's head had eclipsed the pain of his gunshot wounds an hour before and as the sun came up, the hideous light had finally drove him down out of the tree. He no longer cared about being attacked by the demon children. They were little nothings compared to him now. What he wanted…no needed, was something or someone to vent his anger on.

He was sure that if someone came by he would have lost himself in an orgy of hate and fresh blood and would have forgotten all about who Lieutenant Eng was. But with no other target, his hate turned inward and hung on the memory of Dr. Lee.

"She did this to me," he snarled, pushing away one of the little half-creatures that had rushed up. It mewled petulantly when it smelled him and he turned aside to kick it.

Jaimee Lynn watched without emotion or comment. She too held a special hate in her black heart for Dr. Lee, but her hunger was beginning to override even that. "We's gonna git that truck, now? Hey, Mister Chinaman, wait up."

He didn't wait. He had long legs compared to her and he was striding off, heading for what was left of the hospital. All that time in the tree, he had kept his main goal squarely in the forefront of his mind. If he was going to get his cure, he needed to keep his mind functioning and there was only one way to do that. He had to get drugs—opiates to be precise.

"Ain't no truck in there, Mister Chinaman," Jaimee Lynn remarked crossly. Her memory of two hours before was fairly patchy, but she was pretty certain he had mentioned a truck. She liked the idea of riding in a truck. It made her think of something...something important. That something was just out of reach when they reached the building and she caught a familiar scent.

It was an odd mixture of sour sweat and old Walmart dungarees. Anyone else would have called it unpleasant; it reminded Jaimee Lynn of home. "My daidy. Wus he here? Hey, Mister Chinaman, wus my daidy here?"

Eng didn't answer. He was close to turning now. A filthy film had covered his eyes, and everything was shrouded in darkness and hate. The girl was a nuisance, easily ignored. The blood craving was full upon him and he even slowed his quick steps as the scent of John Burke's cold corpse struck him. The only thing he found unpleasant about the smell was the stench of zombies that hung over it like a cloud.

He paused for barely a second over the remains. There were only scraps. Furiously he went on, now single-mindedly. Years of stringent discipline carried him forward through the burned-out lobby and to the stairs, where he climbed mounds of bodies. At the second floor, he paused, his mind struggling to comprehend the devastation of the fire. Most of the third floor had collapsed onto the second and the mess and debris was amazing—and infuriating.

"Son of bitch!" he screamed. Where was the ward? Where was the nurses' station? Where was the mini-pharmacy? He gazed about in a growing fury that would soon end in his becoming one of *them*. Here and there were shambling, black-eyed beasts. More were scattered about, lying still, gaping holes in their heads.

Visible in the dim morning light streaming through the many broken windows was a great pile of bodies. Eng gazed across at it, a sneer on his twisted face. It was where Ryan Deckard had made his final stand, and also where he had shot Eng in the back, ruining everything. Eng was suddenly possessed with a violent desire to climb the pile and stomp what was left of Deckard into pieces, only there was nothing left of the man except for rags and cast-off bones.

Just like with Burke, Eng could smell Deckard's faint aroma, making his stomach growl. "No," he hissed, glaring down at his midsection. "We don't eat people." But he would if he couldn't find the pharmacy. "It was by the elevators."

Yes! He remembered now.

The elevator shafts were made of reinforced concrete. Buildings were frequently erected around them. They were sturdy and the floor closest to them were somewhat intact, including a few of the rooms. He eyed one with a blackened door. Unlike the other doors that were in view, it was not only still intact, it wasn't even warped.

"That's it," he growled, sounding like a cross between a Rottweiler and a cobra. He went straight for the elevator banks and clawed his way up through the rubble to get to the door. Of course, it was locked. With a new scream, he threw himself at it and shook it on its hinges; the door was sturdy, but the frame and walls around it were far less so, and before long, he managed to get his bleeding fingers around the frame.

He surprised even himself as he tore a chunk of a two-by-four out of the wall. In minutes, he was in the room, where everything was dark and the white labels practically unreadable. He had to pull each drawer out into the main atrium and squint at the tiny squiggles.

"Damn it!" he yelled tossing aside the first drawer. It felt as though someone had kicked over a nest of fire ants inside his brain, as if the squiggly letters had infected him somehow. He raked his temples with his broken fingers before going back inside and grabbing the next drawer. It fell, spilling pill bottles all over the floor.

The next fumbled out of his hands as well. Letting out an animal scream he grabbed the next drawer, only to have it unexpectedly resist coming out of its slot. He gaped at it, slowly realizing that there was a light cage over it and the rest of the drawers on that side. It was locked for a reason and his torpid mind slowly spun out the reason why: because there were Class 2 drugs inside. They were addictive, dangerous and exactly what he needed.

At that point, his clogged mind was beyond the ability to read the word *Ohmefentanyl* and couldn't have realized that he had hit the jackpot. He tore off the cage and smashed in the little door with his bare hands, grabbed one of the orange bottles and tore it open. Pills went everywhere, bouncing like tiny white marbles. In a flash, he was on his knees gobbling them up.

Twelve went down his gullet before he gave any thought to dosage. To be on the safe side, he took four more. He then stood to assess whether the pills were working. He swayed in place as the battle to retain the rational part of his mind raged. Minutes passed and still he only stood there, his black eyes swimming in and out of focus.

In the doorway were Jaimee Lynn and her pack of little creatures. They were bored and hungry. The pills and the crumbling building meant nothing to them. Finally, Jaimee Lynn asked, "What about the truck?"

The question triggered the clogged synapses in Eng's brain. He latched onto them as he remembered the idea of a truck and of driving. But to where? It clicked: *To kill Dr. Lee.* The idea of a cure was forgotten. Only revenge remained and he knew just where to find her.

Chapter 7
1-6:09 a.m. (9:09 p.m. local time)
Huanggang, China

The helicopters were a copy of an Airbus design and were not exactly formidable appearing despite the black paint and the soldiers practically spilling from the doors. There were seven Z-9s in the formation, their pilots sweating furiously in their rubber protective suits, ensuring that their masks were constantly fogging up.

It wasn't only the heat of their suits that had them sweating so badly. So far, their flight of seven helicopters had yet to lose a bird; they were the only ones. Flight A2 had two of their helicopters clip rotors with disastrous effect. One of the helicopters in the A-1 flight had an engine malfunction at eight-hundred feet and went down like a rock. Lastly, a bird in A-3 had its tail rotor get spiked by the jutting edge of a telephone pole and the next thing the pilot knew, his helicopter was spinning like a top. He tried to correct, but he spun right into the ground and burned to ashes along with nine people on board.

The pilots of A-4 wondered how long their luck would hold out. The last five days had strained the air arm of the People's Liberation Army Ground Force to the breaking point. After nearly a hundred hours of continuous operations, men and machines were breaking down at a frightening rate. A bleak morale made everything worse.

A fourth of the country's population lay dead in smoldering, radioactive ruins. Another third of their people were panicked refugees, flying west, and the remainder were nervously waiting for the next disaster to occur.

It was the job of team A-4 to cut off that disaster before it could form. They had been hopscotching all over the Hubei province investigating anyone acting strange. With fears running wild, "strange" was open to gross interpretation. The A-4 team had already detained four drunks, one lunatic and two ex-husbands.

Now they had a fresh body and a bloody one at that. The local police reported that it had taken fifteen shots to bring the man down. That sounded alarmingly strange.

If he twisted in his cramped cockpit, the lead pilot could just see a bit of the corpse over the lip of his mask. Not far away, a smoke grenade was pouring out a green fog and with the rotors whipping the air, the mission zone was cast in an eerie light.

There was barely enough room to hover the bird over the zone. "Sixty feet! Make it sixty feet!" he yelled into his mic to his crew chief. Because the closest place to land the helicopter in the teeming city was five blocks away, the team was going to fast-rope down. It wasn't an easy task dressed head to toe in rubber and carrying fifty pounds of equipment.

The length of the rope was adjusted and, after checking the altimeter a second time he yelled: "We are a go!"

One after another, the men raced down the line. Once on the ground, they fanned out, bringing their type 95 rifles up, making the local police step even further back. Five of the team members were soldiers, while the last two consisted of the team leader and an official scientific adviser named Zua Hehua. Zua was in deep over his head.

He had a scientific degree, and it was in microbiology, that was true, but for the last four years since he graduated, he had been studying bone density in paraplegics. This new disease was as foreign to him as it was to anyone. But at least he had been briefed on what to look for. There was no briefing in the world that could prepare him for stepping out of a helicopter three stories in the air.

Just as with the previous three insertions, Zua thought that his heart was going to explode as he reached out for the rope. The rubber gloves provided zero grip and it felt like the rope had been oiled as he shrieked down, his entire body clenched around it, holding on for dear life. His only saving grace was that he didn't have a microphone and so no one heard the girlish scream he let out, or the shuddering sigh that escaped him when he landed safely.

After a deep breath, he staggered over to the body and knelt next to it. When he looked down, his hood fell over his face; it was one-size fits all and that size seemed to be extra-large. He had to hold it back with one hand. The fug had already built up on the inside his mask and when that was combined with the dark of the dying day, he couldn't tell what in creation he was looking at.

"Uh, excuse me, officer? Can someone shine a light on him," he asked, his voice muffled and small. The only light on the scene came from the police cars that were parked far back. Their strobes were disorienting and gave the corpse alternating looks; one second it was pale and soft, the next, it was neon red and appeared semi-alive and was perhaps about to sit up and strangle Zua.

"It's sergeant," the team captain said, as if offended at being called an officer. He carried a small belt light which he fumbled at with his slick gloves while mumbling curses. Once he fetched it, he dropped to one knee across from Zua and blazed the light into the corpse's pale face. "What do you think? Is it one of them?"

Even with rubber gloves on, touching an infected body was pretty much the last thing Zua wanted to do. The rumors were all over the board when it came to the creatures and one of the most persistent ones was that they were ultimately unkillable. Was this one lying in wait, pretending to be dead? Would it tear into Zua like he was a rubber-coated treat?

Gingerly, he put out a finger and poked the corpse's face. The corpse felt unnatural and he gave it a second poke. The head flopped to the side and Zua pulled his finger back, quickly.

"Come on!" the sergeant growled. "The choppers can't stay up there all day." Unceremoniously, he pushed the head back toward Zua.

"Okay, don't rush me," he muttered under his breath. The first thing on the official checklist was to see whether the eyes were "dark." That was rather vague in his opinion; this was China, everyone had dark eyes. He pulled down the corpse's lids and leaned well over. Its eyes were blank, but no darker than anyone else's. Next, he checked the mouth, looking for broken teeth and black gums.

Right away he saw that the corpse was missing a lot of teeth and the teeth it had left were practically brown. He leaned back and continued his inspection almost at arm's length. The teeth suggested this was one of them, but the gums were pale red and the tongue almost white.

Next, he checked the hands; the fingernails were long and brittle, and slightly yellowed.

Zua's shoulder's slumped in relief. He was almost certain this wasn't one of the monsters. But how was he to explain the ugly teeth and the fact that it took so many bullets to kill him?

He sucked in his breath and whispered, "Bingdu!"

"Bingdu?" The sergeant shoved Zua back and leaned over the corpse, the mask hiding the sneer on his face. This was a meth-head. In the last few years, China had witnessed an exploding methamphetamine problem. It was so bad that apparently even an apocalypse wouldn't stop a junkie from getting high.

The sergeant pushed himself to his feet and gave the pilot the "all clear" sign. The leader of the flight relaxed in his chair, having felt like he had dodged another bullet.

"Find us an extraction point," he ordered his copilot, "preferably one with a bathroom and maybe a restaurant. I'm starving." The men could fast rope into a site, but they'd have to hump it out. The co-pilot's eyes skipped right over the Yangtze River—its banks were either crowded with buildings or trees—and he missed the derelict barge and the bodies lying in the water. And with the sound of the engines and the rotors slapping the air, no one heard the screams as Xu Jingxing and seven other zombies crept out of the dark hold of the barge where they had been gorging themselves on cold corpses.

They wanted fresh blood.

2-6:23 a.m.
New Rochelle, New York

Special Agent in Charge Katherine Pennock did not feel all that special at the moment. She cracked a bleary eye and found herself looking at Sergeant Dave Carlton's wide, slack face. He had his head canted well-over and if it hadn't been for his stiff ballistic vest, it would have been bent onto his shoulder. He was snoring gently as was Warrant Officer Bryan.

"Ahem."

Katherine jerked and looked around to see Anna Holloway smirking down at her. "Having a nice little nap?"

The others, except for Specialist Russell Hoskins, jerked awake. The specialist was completely out of it, splayed out on the carpet as if he were in a king-sized bed.

"Fuuuuck," Carlton groaned. "I feel like a truck hit me." He thought about kicking Hoskins awake, but didn't see the point. Their job had been to set up a defensive perimeter which, for all practical purposes was impossible with four people. Still, they had barricaded the entrances with pyramids of furniture and had basically sealed all of the stairwells with junk pulled from the second floor. They left only one stairwell open and even then, it was only partially open, with just enough room for one person to slip through sideways.

It was true one of them should have been on guard and Carlton gave Bryan a sheepish look.

"Did you want something?" Katherine asked, giving the collar of her ballistic vest a yank. It had been rubbing her neck raw.

"A word in private," Anna asked, shifting her eyes to the side. She walked about twenty feet away and was staring out at the rising sun when Katherine joined her. "Dr. Lee isn't doing anything," Anna whispered. "I caught her sleeping as well, but before that she was just staring into space. I tried to talk to her but she threw a stapler at me."

Katherine grunted, "After what you did, I'd say you were lucky she didn't throw a television at you."

Anna's face clouded with anger and she seethed, "You don't know how it was out there. It was survival of the fittest. And I don't have to answer to…" She stopped and forced a smile back onto her face, mastering herself. "None of that matters now. We, me and you, were supposed to find a cure. That was our mission. Lives depend on it. And we both know the President is on a short fuse."

"I get it." Katherine glanced out through the immense lobby windows, not seeing the sunrise, instead she pictured nuclear missiles raining down on them from above. Anna was right. They needed the cure and they needed it quickly. "I'll see what I can do. Wait here."

"But I'm supposed to be helping her. I'm the only one here with any background in pharmaceutical research and development."

Katherine held up her hand. "And you're the only one here who helped to cause the apocalypse in the first place, and you're the only one who helped kill Ryan Deckard. So, stay here and let me handle this."

Now, Anna's smile was a thin illusion covering her hate. She bobbed her head, as if allowing Katherine to leave.

It was three stories to the BSL labs where Dr. Lee had first perfected the Com-cells. Like the rest of the building, the third floor was dark, and Katherine paused, wondering where Thuy was. Then she heard the hum of a centrifuge. She followed the source of the sound and found the scientist leaning back in a chair with her eyes closed, a hugely thick book open on her lap.

In sleep, she was beautiful. Her features were elfin, small and perfect; her face was unlined by fear or worry, and her black hair streamed down her shoulders like a silken wave. How that could be, Katherine didn't know. Her own hair felt brittle from the constant application of bleach and she was sure that she would eventually have to cut it into a bob or risk losing it all.

She picked up a lank of her blonde hair and gave it an unhappy sniff. When she looked up, she found Thuy studying her. Embarrassed, Katherine let go of her hair. "I'm just worried about what all this bleach is doing to my hair. It's weird that your hair hasn't changed color."

"Actually, it would be weird if it did," Thuy replied. "People confuse the concept of the bleaching process with actual bleach, when the two have nothing to do with each other. Lightening the hair is done with products that are activated by hydrogen peroxide, not bleach."

"Ah." There was a long quiet moment between the two women before Katherine gestured to the whirring machine. "Is that the Com-cells? Will they be ready soon?"

Thuy nodded then sighed. "Yes, but I worry that they won't be effective in stopping the spread of the sabotaged Com-cells, what I am now designating as S-Com-cells. This will be especially true in advance cases. The Com-cells will be at a great numerical disadvantage, in many cases probably up to the sixth power. And this is assuming that the Com-cells would be able to compete against the S-Com-cells at all. Therapeutically, the Com-cells I designed are likely to be a dud."

Katherine felt her stomach drop. "That's unacceptable. The President is this close to going nuclear." She held her finger and thumb so closely together that almost no light could be seen between the two.

"Maybe that's for the best," Thuy answered softly.

"Believe me it's not. He's unstable. He may not know where to stop. Hell, he may not even know where to start. He might start with places that are still safe." The two women shared the exact thought then: *If there was any place that was still safe.* "Either way, our job is to try. It's all we can do."

Thuy let out a deeply weary sigh. "My problem stems from a lack of time. This alone will take two hours at a minimum."

That wasn't it, Katherine knew. Guilt and grief were crushing Thuy. Deckard had meant everything to her and now he was gone. Exhaustion had a good grip on her as well, and now that she was awake, ten years had been added to her face. But it was more than even that. Thuy couldn't look up as she said, "And I'm also going to need a batch of S-Com-cells to test."

"You don't have any?"

"No and there's only one way to get any." She lifted her chin towards the door. "Someone's going to have to go out and harvest some."

Katherine's nose wrinkled at the word harvest. The word just seemed overly scientific for…it suddenly struck her what the word really meant. "You mean someone's going to have to go back outside?" And it wasn't just going outside, whoever it was would have to go after one of *them*. The idea was enough to make her knees go weak.

"Yes, I'm sorry. It has to be fresh. Even a delay of twenty minutes may be enough to change too many variables. I would have said something sooner, but I wanted to make sure the base composition of the Com-cells was still viable."

"And are they?" It was a stupid question, Katherine would readily admit to that. Her mind was flailing because it made sense that whoever was going outside couldn't be mission critical. That ruled out Thuy and Anna—they were the only ones who knew anything about the Com-cells. It also ruled out all the bigwigs on the tenth floor—they were trying to save the 7th Army. Warrant Officer Bryan and Sergeant Carlton were needed to fly the helicopter.

That left Katherine, Courtney Shaw and Specialist Hoskins. It felt like she was going to be leading the "D" squad on a suicide mission. "I'll get the blood for you." She tried to put a little confidence into her voice but neither of them believed it.

"Sorry," Thuy said again.

"It'll be fine," Katherine said with a smile that failed as soon as she turned away. Dreading the prospect of going back out into the world, she went back to the stairs and started climbing with only the soft glow of the exit signs to light her way.

At the top, she could hear the murmur of voices even before she opened the door. The murmur grew louder with every step, until she found General Axelrod's group in a huge and quite beautiful office. Everyone seemed to be yammering into a phone —except for Courtney, who had two phones going at once.

"You!" Axelrod shouted. "I need you to check on the status of the cure and get back to me."

"I just came from the labs. Dr. Lee needs..." Katherine cast a disappointed look Courtney's way. It was clear that she was needed here; now the "D" team would be down to two people. "She needs time."

Axelrod's muddy eyes swung nervously to one of his two majors before coming back. "How much time? Wait. Hold on." He hurried her out of the room, shutting the door behind him.

"I'm not sure," Katherine answered honestly. "She's going to try something but it's going to take a few hours at least. Why?"

He looked like he had been punched in the gut. "A few hours? Is there any way she could hurry it along?" The question was ludicrous and he knew it. To begin with, a cure was a long shot, and to try to rush it would almost certainly render the whole exercise pointless. He waved away the question as stupid.

"Here's the thing, we've been sniffed out. We've managed to issue so many contradicting orders that someone caught on. Now we have a cyber unit all over us. Luckily, on the President's orders, they had been deemed nonessential and most of them were sent to the front lines. Still, they have the systems in place to find us eventually."

"I can help," Katherine said, jumping at the chance to avoid a trip outside and a confrontation with the dead. "I worked for the cyber criminal unit in the FBI. I know my way around computers."

"Good. Get with Major Palmburg. Right now, keeping one step ahead of cyber command is almost as important as getting the cure."

The word "almost" killed the sudden rush of relief. He was right, saving the world was more important than saving her hide. "I have to do something for Dr. Lee, first. Then I'll be back to help."

Axelrod gave her a sharp piercing eye, as if looking for cowardice. "Whatever you're doing for her had better be important," he said, lowering his voice. "The others have been kept out of the loop on this, but Major Palmburg doesn't know how long he can keep us hidden. He thinks for only a few hours."

"I'll be quick," she replied.

"You better be. If they find us, the only warning we'll have is when a cruise missile plants itself right here." He tapped the wall.

"A missile?"

He grunted a laugh while at the same time looking miserably over the top of her head and out the window. "Probably not one. Knowing this President, he'll send a dozen of them. He's all about overkill."

Chapter 8
1-7:00 a.m.
The White House, Washington D.C.

Perhaps the only person east of the Mississippi who could claim to have gotten a full night's sleep was the President. Before going to bed, he had rattled off a string of orders: arrest this person, move these troops, bomb this strip of Baltimore into oblivion.

Of course, he had added a threat to the end of the orders. Threats were his new thing. He liked them. He liked the way people grew suddenly meek around him. This was true power. It wasn't the mincing, wishy-washy, smile nice for the cameras crap that Marty Aleman had always tried to push on him. No. True power stemmed from an inner strength that the President had never known he'd had.

This was the source of his power, but what made him actually powerful was his will to wield it.

Just then, the most powerful man in the world was fast asleep, snoring lightly. As if the day was like any other—as if General Phillips wasn't sitting slumped over in a torture room, grinding his teeth together so he wouldn't scream—Emanuel Geometti, the President's butler, strode with silver coffee tray in hand through the West Sitting Hall of the Executive Residence and stopped precisely a foot from the President's bedroom.

And as always, a pair of Secret Service agents gave him a dull look as he tapped with a genteel knuckle on the door; the President didn't care for loud, incessant knocking, even if the world was on the verge of collapse. It made him high-strung and snappish.

Slowly, the President struggled up out of the warmth of a dream. At the same time, twenty-three miles north of the White House, eight-year old Jaiden was being shaken awake by her mother. The shake started softly but grew until her head slung back and forth. A great thundering ripple of explosions had woken Kimberly Calhoun seconds before. It had been the closest yet, maybe not even a mile away.

"Jai. Jaiden! Open your eyes! Mike, she's not…" The little girl's dark brown eyes cracked open. "There you are, Jai. Wake up. It's time to get up. Oh, Mike I don't like how she's acting."

"Sshe's jusst cold," he answered, sounding drunk. "She'll rev up. Trust me."

Kimberly didn't know if she trusted him, not anymore, at least not like she used to. Before all this, she had trusted him in what she had thought were important matters: she trusted him to hold down a job, and not run around on her, and to pick up his socks with a minimum of nagging on her part. Now, she needed an entirely different level of trust.

She had to trust him with their lives. Would he be able to protect her and Jaiden from the dead? What about from the roving gangs that were sweeping through the refugees? Would he be strong enough to steal food when theirs ran out? Would he slit someone's throat to keep Jaiden from freezing to death?

They had been on the road for the last three days, heading south from their upper middle-class home in Paramus, New Jersey. The traffic had been horrible; bumper to bumper, creeping along for more hours than they could count. Looking back, it was laughable how much bitching she had done. At one point, she had griped that it would be faster to get out and walk.

Ten hours later, their overloaded Expedition ran out of gas just outside of Philadelphia. "What do we do?" she had asked. "Do we stay with the car?" It was a grossly stupid question. Kimberly knew that now. The gas stations had been sucked dry and they had passed untold thousands of people, begging for even a drop of fuel. Those with gas also had guns, which they weren't afraid to point at anyone who looked at them cross-eyed.

Some of the people they passed sat on the top of their cars, holding cardboard signs with the word "HELP" written in marker. Some arrogantly claimed that walking was stupid, and that the government would never abandon them—they were tax-payers after all.

Yes, Kimberly knew better than to stay with the car and yet, it killed her to leave the last of their possessions behind. Her little three-person family packed all they could carry on their backs and walked through half the night until they were stumbling with exhaustion. At one in the morning, Jaiden was failing, her normally dark skin had turned dusky grey and she complained she couldn't feel her feet. Kimberly couldn't either.

They needed to stop, but they had never been campers. Unlike so many others, they were without sleeping bags or tents, and they only had one blanket between them. For miles around the highway, the houses were crowded with temporary squatters and every abandoned car had been broken into and was now crammed with sleepers.

Mike went from tent to tent begging for a spot for Jaiden. That night they had been lucky, and the little girl was allowed to crawl into a sleeping bag with another frail little child. Kimberly and her husband shivered under the single blanket. They started walking again at dawn with the world burning behind them. Hours dragged by; blisters formed, their muscles broke down, and their minds grew slow. It became an agony to force themselves on.

But there was no stopping. They were chased south all day, and not just by the sound of guns and bombs; the dead were coming on like a steamroller, destroying everything in their path.

Again, they drove themselves past the brink of exhaustion, and while the President slept in a bed that had been warmed by electric blankets to the exact temperature that he liked it, the three were begging once more for a place to sleep, this time in vain. The temperature dropped into the low forties and the one blanket wasn't enough. Jaiden's lips were now frighteningly pale.

"Get her up and moving," Mike said, as a fireball rose into the sky. Cold or not, they had to move. He pushed himself to his feet with a groan. "Where are we?"

The shoulders of the highway were strewn with refugees. One was just poking his head out of a tiny two-person tent. "Towson. We want to go…" A pair of F-18s roared by, four-hundred feet overhead. They were so loud that the sound seemed to crush Mike down and the earth shook. When the noise followed the jets north, the man went on, "We want to find 695 and go west."

The rumor had swept up the haggard line the night before that the FBI had closed off Baltimore. It was a bitter disappointment, made worse because they had struggled to within eyesight of the city.

"Come on, Jai," Kimberly whispered, standing the girl up and rubbing down her skinny legs. She would have to be carried soon, and that meant giving up some supplies. Food probably. Kimberly didn't want to think about that. "Where's this 695?"

2-7:30 a.m.
The White House, Washington D.C.

93

A dozen generals with three-hundred years of combined military experience, held their breath as the President eyed the monitors. They were hard-faced, formidable men, brought to bay by a man who hadn't wielded anything more fearsome than a steak knife in his entire life.

The silence in the Situation Room went on and on as little wisps of steam wafted up from the bone-china coffee cup sitting next to his right hand.

"I don't understand," he said at last. "Are my orders once more optional?"

"No, sir," the new Secretary of Defense answered. Up until the night before, he had been the President's National Economic Council Director. He knew nothing about the military, but he had been told that his was more of a go-between position. "There've been a few mix-ups and we believe that someone hacked into our computer systems. General Murphy?"

The hot potato had been passed. The National Security Advisor stood. "Our communications are in something of a disarray. We've undergone so many catastrophic changes in many of our leadership positions that there are some questions as to who outranks whom. We are striving to unravel the…"

"You're going to blame all of this on communication errors?" the President asked, his voice like silken ice.

"No sir. We're definitely being hacked. Someone who knows our codes and our systems are playing havoc with our chain of command. We strongly suspect it's General Mark Axelrod and we have two Predator drones in the air for when we find his position."

"Find him and kill him. That is a direct order." The President returned his gaze to the screen, shaking his head. The 3rd Infantry Division was completely out of position. Half of the division was already crossing the Potomac, but all the way to the west at Harper's Ferry. Even worse, from the President's point of view, the 1st and 2nd Armored Brigades were twenty miles northwest of that, crossing at Williamsport.

"Can anyone tell me why the hell the 3rd ID is spread out like a bunch of idiots?"

Every eye in the room switched back to the SECDEF, whose face began to twitch. "Um, sir, that was me. I authorized it, but only because someone in the Air Force…" He paused to shoot the Secretary of the Air Force a nasty look. "…screwed up and bombed these bridges." He went to the main screen and jabbed a finger at the bridges connecting Washington D.C. to Virginia.

"We considered sending the division around to the Woodrow Wilson Bridge, but the streets in that part of the city are jammed. It would take them days to get through. We thought this was smarter."

"Sit," the President ordered, softly. "I don't care what sort of hacking is going on. I want the pilots responsible for this arrested. They should have known better. In the meantime, get the 3rd ID here as fast as humanly possible."

The SECDEF sucked in his breath and then held it instead of speaking out. Next to him, the new Secretary of the Army, General Renee Smith muttered, "Say something." She was the first woman to ever hold this position and really wished she wasn't. She was pretty sure that she wouldn't last out the day.

Next to her, the SECDEF sat stony-faced. "You chicken-shit," she hissed before she stood up and announced, "That may be a mistake, sir. The danger to Washington is minimal, relatively speaking. However, the same can't be said for the western perimeter of the Zone."

She went to the main screen. And pointed out the obvious. "We lost Harrisburg at about three this morning. It means the entire right flank of the 2nd Corps is lost to Gettysburg, and that won't hold for long. Our only chance is to reinforce and try to stop the beasts here, in the Cumberland Valley. It's open enough for our tanks to be effective."

The President's initial response was to turn to one of his Secret Service agents. "I'll have my breakfast now." He then drummed his fingers, staring at the screen, his face twisted in disgust. "And we still have those three companies just sitting up there guarding nothing but Canada's back door. Another communications mishap?"

Although they were regiments and not companies, he received solemn nods in answer. "And look here. I asked for this entire area to be leveled." A wave of his hand traced I-695 on an arc across the suburbs of northern Baltimore.

"There were still refugees on it," the Secretary of the Air Force said in a small voice.

"And how many of them are infected!" the President screamed, slapping the table with the flat of his hand, making the coffee in his bone-china cup dance. "They are in the *Quarantine* Zone, Berry. Does the word have any fucking meaning to you? Listen, all of you. This is how things started yesterday. Insubordination, stupid excuses, lies and finally treason. And where did all of that get us? We lost practically the entire northeast. I won't have it. We are trying to protect America. All of it, or at least all that we can. To do that will mean making difficult decisions."

General Berrymore began nodding, and even went so far as to whisper, "Yes, sir," but he couldn't seem to be able bring himself to pick up the phone and give the order. The room was silent, waiting to see what he would do.

Twenty-three miles away, the Calhoun family began limping along the curve of the road in the direction of the outer beltway —I-695. They had walked fifty-five miles in the last two days, each carrying packs as heavy as they could possibly manage. Mike's was especially heavy and the straps bit cruelly into his shoulders.

Still, he took Jaiden's little pack as well as his own. "For just a little while," he told her and trudged toward the onramp, ignoring the new rumble of jets. All he could think about was getting close enough to see the next sign. It beckoned him, and it gave him hope.

There, just past the onramp—*Washington D.C. 22 Miles*— Mike breathed a sigh of relief. They'd be safe in Washington. In fact, he couldn't imagine anywhere safer in the country. And certainly, they would have refugee tents set up, with showers and food and cots. FEMA would be there and the Red Cross. Maybe even the Goodwill.

He paused, wondering if he could jettison some of the stuff he was carrying. Surely, they would get there by midafternoon and surely, they would have blankets and extra clothes.

"What are you doing, Mike," Kimberly asked as she came up to him. "We might need that stuff."

He pointed at the sign. "Naw. We're almost to the promised land."

The veritable king of Mike's promised land, the man both he and Kimberly had voted for, turned his back on his uneaten breakfast, the monitors and the Air Force general, who looked shattered as he hung up the phone. The President walked from the room saying, "Burn it down and you can move those armored companies anywhere you want to."

3-7:58 a.m.

New Rochelle, New York

The pair left the building from the loading docks, sneaking out like mice. They both wore body armor and they both thought it was useless weight. Their faces were uncovered, and the zombies always seemed to go for the eyes with their terrible claws.

Still, neither Katherine Pennock nor Specialist Hoskins considered ditching the gear for even a second.

Katherine already felt vulnerable enough just leaving the protection of the glass-walled building. It felt as though a thousand eyes were on her. Were there zombies lurking in the shadows, their stomachs grumbling at the prospect of another bloody meal? Was a satellite training its telescope down on her and was the President sitting back, laughing at her feeble attempts to blend in with the brick wall and the side of the dumpster? Was there a stealth drone orbiting high overhead and feeding coordinates to an incoming missile?

She was surprised just how timid she had become. When on the hunt for Eng and Anna, she had been fearless, but now that she was in the Zone, death seemed to be everywhere.

"You ready?" Hoskins asked. He had mottled grey eyes and stark-white skin, especially along the ridges of his knuckles; he was gripping his M4 so tightly that he was cutting off the circulation to his fingers.

"Yeah. All w-we need is just one of them," she said, to reassure them both. "We get one alone. Kill it, get its blood and get back." It sounded so simple, but when was there only just one? They usually traveled in packs and it was almost a guarantee that if one was spotted alone there would be a dozen more nearby.

Katherine was so undermined by fear that Hoskins was the first to move, jogging low through the back parking lot, which was empty save for a few company vans. Beyond the lot was a low hill that was studded with trees. Then they were back in another affluent neighborhood where the houses were tall and brick, and the zombies wore four-hundred dollar McAllister wingtip shoes and silk rags.

Six of them were in view and the pair shrunk down behind the lip of the hill. Hoskins gave Katherine a raised eyebrow that she read as: *What do you think?* "We're too close. If we have to run, they'll follow us right back to the building." It was the worst possible scenario since there were too few of them to withstand any sort of siege and all their efforts would've been in vain.

The pair scurried off to their left, to the end of the parking lot. They seemed far enough away to try to make it across the intervening street. To Katherine, the street seemed to be half a football field wide. By the time she made it to the side of the closest house, she was panting and sweating.

"I don't know what's wrong with me," said, embarrassed. "Everything feels worse in the daylight. You know, scarier."

"I know what you mean," Hoskins replied; he had sweat in his dark hair, too and his eyes flitted about. "It's because they can see us, that's why. And if they see us, they'll swarm."

It was then that Katherine's stomach began to ache. "All we need is one," she said again. She then nodded to Hoskins and followed him around the side of the house to the intersecting street. It was clear, as was the next, and the one after that. She didn't want to go any further. Already it seemed like the safety of the R&K Building was too far out of reach.

"This is good," she whispered, pulling him back as he was about to go on.

He looked relieved. "So how do you want to do this? We can maybe call out and see if only one comes sniffing around. What do you think?"

She pictured zombies bursting out of every house and from every shadow, charging down on them. It would be a mob scene and they'd be lucky to escape with their lives. Getting blood would be almost impossible. "We could, um…um…" She'd been going full-bore for two days and the pitiful bit of sleep that she had snatched earlier had left her slow and dopey. Simple plans were not popping into place like they should have.

Getting inside one of the houses was about the only thing that made sense. The desire also kicked off a quick idea that could work. "Here's something. All these doors look pretty sturdy. We call some of the dead over. We open the door for the first, kill it and slam the door on the others. Then escape out the back when we have the blood."

He grinned with relief. "That's good. That'll work. I know it."

The closest house seemed as good as any of the rest and, after making sure it was empty and there was a clear lane to run for the back door, Katherine took a deep breath. "You ready?"

"I need the syringes."

"Right. Sorry." Her hands shook as she held out the three capped syringes. He put them on a polished credenza next to a silver picture frame. The photo in the frame had been professionally done with an idyllic nature setting as a background. The family was young and perfectly blonde and perfectly happy; Katherine had to turn away, knowing they were probably dead.

She opened the front door and peeked out at the empty street before yelling, "Hello!" She paused to listen and then called out a second time, then a third. There was no response.

Hoskins had moved into the living room and was at the window, craning his head back and forth. "Go again." She was about to when he saw four of the beasts emerge from around the side of the house directly across the street. "Wait!" he hissed, hurrying back into the hall. "They're coming. Get ready."

She could see them now, racing right for her. The only sound they made was the slapping of their feet and their harsh breathing. They were faster than she thought possible. "Fuck," she whined, the corners of her mouth pulled down in a grimace. She ducked back behind the door, ready to slam it shut. At the same time, Hoskins took a few steps back and raised his gun. There was a thud and a screech from outside, and through the crack in the door, she saw the first of them stumbling up the porch.

As it fell, and the others scrambled over it, there was a sudden crash of glass behind them. The dining room window had exploded inwards and a naked grey-skinned man was flaying itself as it climbed inside. Spiked with panic, Hoskins turned and fired at the zombie, blasting off chunks of flesh and shattering its front teeth. The sound of the gun in the quiet morning was outrageous and a part of him wanted to fling it away, knowing that it was summoning every zombie within a mile.

When Hoskins turned back, it looked like the front door was being mobbed. They weren't coming one at a time; there were already two of them fighting to get in. Instead of letting them, which was their only chance of getting a sample, he fired once more. A perfect shot. The first beast dropped dead—completely dead this time—landing right in the doorway.

Another crawled over this one and again, instead of letting it in, he killed it with a clean shot. Its body added to the problem and threw their entire plan out the window. Katherine screamed as she saw what had happened and slammed her shoulder against the door.

"Kill them!" she yelled. It was their only chance. Hoskins leapt forward and fired six times and filling his head with numb echos. He thought he had got them all and turned to shoot again at the creature trying to get in through the dining room window. It was somehow still alive. He fired and fired.

Katherine was still straining to shut the door and even with her ears ringing from the gun blasts, she could hear a very close growl. "Hoskins!" she screamed just as he fired again, drowning out her voice.

A hideous grey-skinned creature pulled itself from the pile of corpses and slammed the door into Katherine sending her head crashing against the wall behind her. She was pinned and unable to defend herself, but the zombie ignored her and slammed into Hoskins, raking him with its diseased claws and tearing at his shoulder with its fangs.

The two went down with the credenza falling over them. Katherine squeezed out from behind the door and scrambled for her M4. She wanted to shoot the thing; however the fight was too wild and fast. They were rolling around so much that she was afraid she would hit Hoskins. Before she could get a good shot in, more zombies were flocking to the house. She knelt in the doorway and began firing, killing a pair of undead beasts with silver hair and black eyes, just as they were rushing for the door.

Finally, Hoskins got free enough to get his weapon around. He fired, blasting a gaping hole out of the top of its head. Black blood fountained up, hitting the ceiling before raining back down on him. It was dead, and so was Hoskins. He was scratched in eleven places and bitten in two. He was also drenched with black blood—he was infected. There was no question about that.

The mission was an abject failure. There was no time to harvest any blood, the syringes were nowhere in sight and the street was alive with zombies converging on the house in a shambling sprint.

"Go," Hoskins said, miserably to Katherine. His eyes wouldn't stop blinking and yet they remained completely unfocused. "I'll hold them off…for a while."

She knew what he was going to do. He would shoot a few of the monsters and then when she got away, he would kill himself. And maybe that was fine, except it would leave Katherine all alone and running for her life. Because of the horrible death he faced, she knew it wouldn't be right to try to stop him and yet, it wasn't just Katherine who was in need of him.

If there was going to be a cure, someone would have to be tested and what better person than someone who was already infected? It certainly would save Katherine another trip out into the world.

"Please," she begged, "I need you. *We* need you. Remember the cure, Hoskins!" Had he been thinking straight, he would have asked: *What cure?* So far, the cure consisted of little more than a bit of fungus and some molecules spinning in a centrifuge.

He wasn't thinking straight. The dull blinks turned to slow nods and he allowed her to pull him up. Together they raced through the house and out into the back yard just as the dead crashed through into the living room. It sounded like the monsters were destroying the house as they came on.

"Don't look back!" Katherine cried. She knew she wouldn't, afraid that if she did, she would become paralyzed with fear. Their only chance was to go as fast as they could for as long as they could.

The two of them tore through the grass to the tall fence at the back of the yard. It was slick and flat, and with their ballistic armor hampering their movement, neither made it up and over on the first try. He boosted her over, tossed his gun after and made another try. It would be his last try. Already there were nine of the creatures in the yard and some were terrifyingly fast. He backed up a few feet and made another run at the fence. His hands caught, and his feet kicked desperately on the wood, slowly gaining purchase. Far too slow. He had yet to get a leg over the top and the nearest zombie was only ten feet away when Katherine jammed her M4 through a crack in the fence and began firing.

Bam! Bam! Bam! Again, the gunshots sounded huge. They screamed their position to the world and the world was filled with the dead. Zombies were now coming at the fence from two sides.

Katherine yelled for him to hurry, only he had gone weak. A part of him had given up and it seemed to take forever before he dropped down next to her, panting and wild-eyed. Just as he struggled up, the fence was struck with terrific blows as the zombies plowed into it full force. The wood promptly cracked in two places. These cracks were attacked by the zombies bare-handed, and soon the fence was coming apart. By then Katherine and Hoskins were running towards the next house.

Before they could get to it, an upper floor window suddenly blasted out and, as Katherine watched in horror, a zombie fell three stories to land face-first on the patio. Impossibly, the thing sat up.

They ran past it. In front of them was a sliding glass door. There was no time to check to see if it was locked. Katherine fired a half-dozen bullets into it and it came down just at the two threw their bodies through it. They found themselves in a finished walkout basement. The house was so large that even the downstairs was something of a maze.

"Stairs, stairs, stairs," Hoskins kept repeating as they ran through door after door. They finally found the stairs leading up, while behind them zombies were everywhere, flooding the rooms and going in all directions. Thankfully, there was a sturdy door at the top of the stairs.

Katherine eased it quietly shut behind them. The house was surrounded, or very nearly so. Dozens of zombies were towards the backyard, streaming along either side of the house. Quickly, the two slunk down and practically crawled to the front door. Amazingly, the street was clear.

"Come on," Katherine hissed, and hurried out. Hoskins came along, almost reluctantly. He was slow, his feet wooden. Still, the zombies were entirely focused on tearing the house apart with great fury, which allowed the two of them to slink all the way back to the safety of the R&K Building.

He refused to go inside. He turned away, mumbling, "Just a moment."

She worried that he was going to kill himself and readied herself to tackle him before he could. Then she heard what sounded like a sniffle and she stepped back. He stood, half-hidden by the dumpster for a few minutes. "You're gonna have to kill me," he told her. "Eventually, I mean. There's never going to be a cure. Not in time for me, at least."

"You never know. Dr. Lee is very smart. I've seen her file. She's whatever it is that's beyond genius."

He grunted at her supposed genius. He knew that cures for anything, if they ever came about, were years in the making. Ripping a sleeve across his eyes, he turned back to Katherine. "We might as well do this. What's the worst that could happen?"

As they went inside and sprayed each other down, the question got under Katherine's skin. The infected became evil— terribly, terribly evil, and in truth, anything could happen. Anything at all.

When Emerald Storme slid the plate of eggs and bacon in front of him, Nicolas Read was struck by an intense feeling of déjà vu. He let it wash over him without dwelling on it as others might. Déjà vu was a daily occurrence with him. It was a familiar reassuring feeling.

He didn't make any claims to being psychic or clairvoyant or any of that nonsense. It was just that when a man lived in the same small town his entire life and went to the same diner every morning and ordered the same thing, déjà vu could be expected.

"Any news, Sheriff?" Emerald asked.

She didn't mean news from the day-old Indianapolis Star he had been re-reading. That morning's edition, if one had even been printed, hadn't come. It hadn't been a shock. The entire state had virtually closed up shop and about the only things moving out on the highway were family cars heading west, their roofs piled to the point of teetering with belongings. Emerald would've been one of them except she could no longer afford gas, which was currently selling at forty-five dollars a gallon and going up by the hour—and that was cash.

Although the machines still worked, no one was taking credit cards anymore. She hadn't mentioned that to Read yet. If he wasn't good for it, the county would be.

Being stranded in this pissant burg was the story of her life. She had once been a slip of a girl named Debbie Shultz with dreams of going to Hollywood and "making it big." Her journey to the good life had lasted only seventy-three miles before her Datsun up and died right on the highway within sight of the diner. Slowly, her dreams up and died as well.

The sheriff had just taken a heroic bite from his mounded-up fork and when he was done chewing, he answered, "Nothing that ain't been repeated seventy-five times an hour on the TV. 'Cept maybe that the governor is 'appropriating' the last of my deputies."

"Where they going? Indy?"

Because people were hoarding their cash, there was only one other patron in the diner and he was just about as far away from Sheriff Read as a man could get and still order an egg and waffles. Regardless, Read lowered his voice and said, "I-74."

Her penciled eyebrow shot up. "They closing the border? They tell you why?" She had good reason to be worried. Everyone was fairly certain that if Indiana closed their eastern border with Ohio, then Illinois was probably going to close their eastern border as well, which meant they'd be trapped if things went sideways.

"Yeah, the Governor's always calling me up to let me know his business," Read drawled, giving her a little smile before forking half an egg into his mouth. "I have my guesses, though. There's rumors flyin' around like you wouldn't believe and we get 'em all. Monsters here, zombies there. Hell, we even had a vampire sighting last night. Allegedly, I mean. I would say it was all nonsense if it weren't for the news."

"Is it true the mayor of Dayton shut down I-70? We had a trucker come through at the crack of dawn saying the CB was squawking about Dayton and Patterson Air Force Base throwing up road blocks."

Before he answered, another egg went down his gullet and then a slice of bacon went into his mouth like it was going into a grinder. He was in the process of licking his thumb when his sharp eyes caught something wrong. A smallish SUV had just rolled down from the highway, blasted through the barbed wire fence, and was trundling through a field of newly thinned corn.

He sighed and picked up a new piece of bacon. There was no sense getting up; the 4-Runner, he could see it plain as day now, was heading directly for the diner. If it stopped and the driver came in, well, they would have a talk. If it kept going, Sheriff Read would finish his breakfast and probably order a slice of pie as well because that was the mood he was in.

Fining the driver would be a waste of time and jailing him would be even worse. The courts were closed indefinitely, and he no longer had the manpower to lock people up for a bit of stupidity.

Read was hoping to finish his breakfast; however, the SUV crossed the field bounced down one curb and up the other before it began to slow. *Drunk, probably,* he was just thinking, when the driver went off the road, plowed into some bushes and turned slowly toward the diner, finally coming to a stop, bumping up against the single tree that had stood guarding the parking lot for as long as Read could remember.

He leaned over, his dirty blonde hair spilling over one ear, reminding him that he was past due for a haircut. "What is that?" The windows, front and back, were filthy. "Is that a woman?"

It had once been Heather Harris. Somehow, right up until she stepped out of the 4-Runner, she had held onto some scrap of her humanity. Starting from just outside of Cincinnati, it had been slowly tortured out of her and now the last bit of it hissed from her grey lips as she was hit with the glaring, brittle blue sky, and the piercing brightness of the sun.

She had to get out of sight of that terrible sun. That's all she cared about. The smell of fresh blood would have to wait. Heather bolted inside with her coat hauled up over her head and stood panting a few feet inside the diner. It was a long, narrow, low-ceilinged structure. Because of the tinted windows, it was dim inside, which allowed her to think.

Her first thought was of blood. She had never felt so dirty in her life and she needed blood to get the sickening taste from her mouth. There was no telling how she came to that conclusion; she just needed it so badly that she could barely stop herself.

"I'm hungry," she whispered, looking at Emerald through her straggling, sweaty hair. There was no missing the black eyes.

"Read?" she whispered, taking a step back. "Is that…"

His hand went to the butt of his gun, a Smith&Wesson M&P 9. Drawing it quickly wasn't going to be easy, sitting in the booth as he was. "It's okay," he announced to the diner. "There's no reason to get excited. Right, ma'am?"

It was too late not to get excited. Emerald had always worn her waitress uniform scandalously, at least as far as the local blue-hairs were concerned, and she showed a vast expanse of cleavage below her soft throat. Heather stared at the milky-white skin with more of an animal leer than any man who had ever graced the doors of the diner. She could see the blue veins coursing through Emerald's breasts and it drove the last of her humanity out of her head.

She barred her teeth and, with a scream, she charged.

That extra second was enough for Sheriff Read. He threw himself from the booth as he drew the M&P 9. His aim with the first shot was dead center and holed Heather's sternum without any outward effect. With all the rumors, he had not expected this to stop her. For this reason, he didn't let up on the trigger, walking his next two shots up Heather's plump, diseased body, hitting her in the throat and then in the bridge of the nose.

This last bullet traveled through her sinuses, into her brain and out the top of her head. She fell almost at Read's feet.

Heather was dead and yet Emerald backed away panting and pulling at her open uniform to haul the collar to her face. "That's one of them! Look at it!" She pointed and stared in rigid shock for all of a second before she darted for the kitchens, saying, "We gotta get out of here."

Read grabbed her by the arm. "No," he ordered. His voice was sharp; however, his insides were tilting in uncertainty. There were two voices balancing within him. The first asked: *What if they hadn't been infected yet? What if they were still clean? What if there was still a chance to escape alive?* This was his own voice, the Nicolas Read who liked to kick up his heels far out of his jurisdiction on a Saturday night.

The second voice was the voice of reason and responsibility. It was the voice of his badge. *What if they ran out and infected all of Indiana?* They were practically in the heart of America.

"No," he said again, holstering his gun. "We'll go in the back and put up whatever barriers we can…"

The man at the far end of the diner had stood up, his eyes shifting back and forth from the body to the door. His left hand was held up toward Read, palm up. His right was inching toward his coat pocket. He seemed like something of an inverted man. He was utterly bald and yet wore one of the thickest beards Read had ever seen. His coat was tailored wool, but his pants were ratty, washed-out denim with green stains at the cuffs. They were his lawn-mowing pants.

His name was Lancaster Holmes and normally he was as pretentious as his name, but that morning found Lancaster in a different frame of mind. The one-time frat-boy was on the verge of casting aside all societal restraints.

"I can leave," he said. "It's legal. I know my rights."

"A state of emergency has been declared," Read told him. "You don't have rights anymore. So, do yourself a favor and move your hand away from your pocket."

The hand didn't move. "I have basic human rights," Lancaster whispered, and now the hand inched closer, the tips of his fingers slipping inside.

"Stop!" Read dropped his hand to the butt of his gun. "Let's discuss this in the back where the air is clean. Every second we're out here, the worse our chances are. Get it? We still have a chance."

107

This was the wrong thing to say. Lancaster knew his only chance lay in getting outside as soon as possible. His hand slid easily into his pocket and found the grip of a Walther PPK he had bought after watching the latest James Bond movie. As far as pocket guns went, there were few better. It was compact enough to aim with a twist of his wrist. He had it aimed in his pocket while Read was still ripping his M&P 9 from its holster.

Lancaster fired, hitting Read in the chest; in his bullet resistant vest to be precise. The burning hunk of lead didn't penetrate the vest, but it did turn him sideways so that Lancaster's second shot deflected off the vest and buried itself in the booth behind him. By then, Read's gun was out and his arm extended. Having grown up in the sleepiest of sleepy towns, Read had never been in a shootout before. That didn't mean he hadn't prepared. He went to the range weekly, usually in the middle of the week when everyone else was at work, so they wouldn't see him practicing his quick draw. By his own standards, his draw had been achingly slow; in stark contrast, his aim was perfect, and he drilled Lancaster, knocking him back into his booth.

There was no need for a second shot as Lancaster began to gurgle and cough blood.

"Shit," Read said. His instinct was to go to the bald man and render what aid he could, but that would mean passing by the body of the woman. Her blood was everywhere, and he knew that he was pressing his luck already. He and Emerald backed away.

She wanted to run, and maybe on any other day she would have, but she was as afraid of Read as she was of getting the disease. She had known him all her life without ever realizing just how hard he really was. He had been shot and then killed the bald man without blinking and she got the feeling he wouldn't let her go, no matter how many free peeks at her bosom she had given him over the years.

In fact, he was already on the radio, dooming them both. "Mary, it's Read. Someone needs to contact the governor's office." He took a deep breath before he added, "And the CDC. I have identified a positive case of the plague."

"The real plague?" she asked in a whisper.

"Yes. I need all of Elnora on lock down."

2-8:48 a.m.
The White House, Washington D.C.

Elnora, Indiana was not yet on the radar during the President's morning security briefing. This was exceedingly lucky as he was mentally on the edge without hearing that the middle of the country had identified a positive case of the plague.

The rumors flying around Columbus and Cincinnati were bad enough and had him glancing at the weak-kneed major who had been stuck carrying the nuclear football that morning.

Matthew Dimalanta, the new Chief of Staff found himself in nearly exactly the same spot as Marty Aleman had been thirteen hours before. The President kept hinting at a nuclear option, while at the same time getting in the middle of and hampering a military solution. Dimalanta was being pulled from every side. FEMA was making outrageous and impossible demands concerning the nationwide refugee problem. DHS was begging for help trying to control borders. The military was pleading with him to distract the President for "just a few hours."

Then there was the FBI and the CDC, as well as ambassadors from thirty countries.

"And what about the press?" the president asked, interrupting Dimalanta's internal drowning.

The press was an entirely different story. Their access had been restricted, but did that stop them from wheedling into every situation? Hell, no! They seemed to know everything Dimalanta knew; despite that, they still felt the need to spring out from behind planters or columns to brace him with questions.

"They want to know about the current state of the insurrection." It was about the only thing they didn't have all the facts on and they were hungry. "They want to know if there's going to be actual trials, and if so, will they be televised? They're hinting that they won't be legitimate if they're not."

"They can hint all they want. You know, Matthew, Marty had it all wrong. The press can only break weak presidents. A strong president owns the press. Yes, that's the mind-set I want you to have. We own them. They have to come to us for crumbs and that's what I want you to give them. Tell them we have all the evidence needed to execute the top three conspirators right now. Tell them that these are military tribunals, not civilian ones.

The same rules that govern civilian courts do not apply since there are national security interests at stake."

He had Dimalanta repeat everything he'd just said back to him, gave him an overly friendly squeeze on the shoulder that caused the young man to wince, and then sent him off.

Yes, the press were his lap dogs and he would jail the first that nipped at his hand. Still, they could be trouble if they were not fed daily. Before the apocalypse the President had found that they were inherently lazy. Marty would have their talking points delivered by midday and these would be swallowed without question and regurgitated all evening long. Many times, they were repeated word for word.

But sometimes, usually when it came to some actual scandal in the opposition party, they would do their jobs and really dig. Watergate was like that. Compared to some of the shenanigans that he knew about, and had been a part of, Watergate had been child's play. It was the press that had destroyed Nixon, not the facts.

The same could happen to him, and if it did, he wouldn't be forced to resign. No, he was living by the sword now and if someone came after him, they would have to come with a bigger sword.

"But we won't let that happen," he muttered as he headed for the small meeting rooms where the prisoners were being held and interrogated. As he got closer, he shed staffers. He had six or seven in tow; men or women he treated with less consideration than he would a gaggle of servants. Normally, they were eager to carry out his bidding. Now, not one wanted to be anywhere close to the torture rooms.

And that was fine. The President wanted full control over the proceedings and the last thing he needed was someone to start whispering to the press.

As he turned the corner, he almost ran into Trista Price. There were hollows under her blue eyes and her pert lips were drawn back in a grimace. She jerked in surprise and then stood back, and bowed from the shoulders as if she were Japanese. It wasn't proper etiquette to display to an American president, but since he felt as though he were more of an American emperor, he liked it.

"Just the woman I wanted to see," he said, throwing an arm around her thin shoulders, and leading her back the way she had come, passing a pair of Secret Service agents whose job it was to restrict access to that little section of the sub-floor. "Do you have confessions for me?"

"Yes, Mr. President," she answered, this time, bowing from the neck. She held out a small, black rectangle. It was an external hard drive and looked sleek and vaguely evil. He pulled his hand back. *Fingerprints were forever,* Marty used to say.

He guided her to an empty room and suggested: "Why don't you just show me what you have?"

She gave him yet another, "Yes, Mr. President," before setting up a laptop and plugging in the hard drive. "Mister Kazakoff says this is a rough draft. He has to put it through a number of filters, though what these were, he didn't say."

The President watched as first Marty Aleman, followed by Generals Haider and Phillips baldly admitted to treason. The camera focused in close on their faces; they were red-eyed and had sallow bags, but were unmarked. In dry voices they each admitted to deliberately disobeying orders and forming a cabal to undermine their Commander in Chief.

"And do you know that the penalty for treason is death?" Kazakoff asked each at the end of their interviews. They each answered "Yes." Phillips and Haider did it with their chins held high. Marty whispered the word as if it were a secret.

"That's it?"

Trista had no idea how to answer the question. Wasn't it enough? Didn't that prove the President had been right to arrest them? Couldn't she go back to being just an aide? More than anything, she wanted to be in charge of getting the coffee. Haider's screams were still crawling around inside her mind. "It's all he gave me," she answered.

"It's not. I know it. Where's the spook? Show me." He was already at the door heading out. In the hall, he repeated the question and blew past a stiff Secret Service agent with Trista hurrying after. Inside the room he found Kazakoff calmly wiping down stainless-steel instruments as General Haider sat tied to a bloody chair, shivering uncontrollably.

"What's wrong with him?" the President asked. "Do you still have him hooked up to something?"

Kazakoff gave the general a glance. "No sir. It's the drugs in his system. They'll wear off eventually."

"About that. You're not quite through here. These *confessions,*" he said the word with his nose upturned, "only name each other. What about the rest? There's no way they could have kept their staff members out of the loop. And what about the Joint Chiefs and the different Secretaries? I can guarantee that the Secretary of the Army is in it up to his eyeballs."

"From what I gather," Kazakoff answered, "he purposely tried to stay out of the loop. I guess that he caught a whiff of what was going on and made himself scarce."

The President's eyes blazed. "I had him arrested, Kazakoff! I had him arrested for a reason…for cause." He tried to warp his face into a smile; however, it ended up resembling a toad's smile.

Now Kazakoff understood. The President wanted him to propagate a lie. The torturer had no qualms with that, after all it wasn't exactly a new concept. "I'll be most strenuous with the secretary and the others." David Kazakoff counted himself as a patriot and if a few soft politicians and some malcontents needed to be scapegoated for the war effort, then he was behind it a hundred percent.

Haider had been staring at the two, his head vibrating and shaking as if he were deep in the throes of Parkinson's disease. "If you expect me to turn on anyone who's innocent, then you're a bigger idiot than even I thought. And that's saying something."

The President looked down on him with contempt for a moment before turning back to Kazakoff. "We have his confession. You can do whatever you want with his face now."

Lost in all of this was Trista Price who, for the first time in her life, was happy that she was completely overlooked, standing in the corner of the room with a look of shock on her face.

Chapter 10
1-9:13 a.m.
Quinsigamond River, Massachusetts

The smoke was beginning to drift again, blown by a soft breeze and with a soft hiss. Some people muttered curses while most others whispered prayers. There was a lot of praying going on along the eastern bank of river.

"Please, no more wind," Troy Ross said under his breath, giving a quick glance up at the swirling grey blanket overhead. He could just make out the sun as a glaring round disk. Someone coughed and was immediately shushed by everyone within earshot. The last attack had nearly shattered the line and no one wanted a repeat of that.

The civilians, especially the recent ones, had been within seconds of breaking and running. Ross had thrown in his reserves and then begged for help. It had come in the form of smoke. He had asked for high explosive shells, but the last of these had been left behind when the forward ammunition supply point had been abandoned during one of the many wild flights the night before.

He had received smoke rounds which had confused the undead to such an extent that the attack had petered out. Since then his soldiers had been setting controlled fires using wet leaves and a grey pall hung over everything. But the wind was now pushing it eastward and soon his line was going to be exposed again.

And they weren't ready.

Leaving his battalion in the hands of a newly frocked captain he went straight to the division headquarters, in person. Once there, he stood in bewilderment watching the dreadfully inept workings of the new staff. Information and requests flowed sluggishly from one temporary shelter to another and then out to a Humvee and from there a runner was sent up the steps of the Grafton Public Library, where each matter was hashed out by the next higher-ups.

After a few minutes, if the request could be made by the local divisional PO, an order was given, and it went through the same slow process going back down the chain of command. Frequently there was a backup and delays. When that happened, people just stood around chatting, waiting their turn.

Ross was still gaping in astonishment when an MP asked him what he wanted. "I need smoke, now." Ross pointed back the way he had come. "I need it along the river from Pullard Road to Millbury Street. If we don't get it…that'll be it. We won't be able to stop them."

The MP snuck a look over his shoulder before he pointed out an empty table that had a sign which read DIV/ART. "Don't get caught," he warned before he turned quickly away and went to inspect some bushes without looking back.

"I'll just say I didn't know," Ross whispered as he went to the table. On it was a sat-phone, as well as a bulky SINCGARS —a Single Channel Ground and Airborne Radio System. The handset on the radio was a simple push to talk. "Panther 30, this is Able 30. I have a fire mission. I need smoke at the following…"

"Hold on. This is the FDC. What's your PO order number?"

Ross let out a long, "Uhhhhhh," as he stared around the table searching for anything that would resemble a PO number, whatever that was. "I am unable to locate that number at the moment, but this is a critical situation. The line is unstable and will fall. I repeat it will fall. I have the coordinates of the fire mission. They are…"

"Able 30, we cannot authorize a fire mission without a PO number from the brigade level or higher. Please stay off the net unless you have such authorization."

He was within an inch of screaming every obscenity he knew into the handset when the sat-phone buzzed. Hoping that he'd be able to talk directly with the artillery support element, he snatched it up. "Division artillery," he said, his voice cracking.

"PO authorization 3275," a woman said and then hung up.

Ross knew something clandestine had just happened and he felt the hackles on the back of his neck rise. *Am I being watched?* he wondered. *Or was it the radios? Were they bugged?* He almost dropped the handset as if it was coated in poison.

It didn't matter, he realized. What mattered was laying down the smoke as fast as he could. "I have PO authorization number 3275," he said into the handset. From there he fed the coordinates to the Fire Direction Center. He didn't wait around for the distant thumping of the guns. He would have to act as his own forward observer, so he took both the SINCGARS unit and the sat-phone, and quickly walked away.

At least this part of the military was working. Not thirty seconds later there came a single thump from miles to the rear. It was followed by a tearing sound and then a crumpled sort of explosion. Smoke erupted almost right on the river itself. With the soft wind, that was too close.

"FDC, this Able 30, can you walk that west one-hundred meters?" Another thump, another tear through the air. "Perfect FDC. Fire for effect."

Sixteen rounds were all that could be allotted, forcing Ross to scurry around as fast as he could to make sure his men were resupplied with the meager stores available. He then sprayed down everyone until there were half-choking on the stench of bleach, and then had them hide again.

Next, because he couldn't trust his newly frocked XO, he had to pull his reserve company from the line without leaving any gaps and distribute the frightened newbies who had been filtering down to him. And lastly, he had to "relocate" the people who were overheard complaining about headaches or who were seen to be rubbing their temples or the like.

The whispers concerning these people always got to him eventually. On average the battalion was losing eight people an hour, and somebody had to make the decision that would doom them. As acting C.O. Ross knew he couldn't pass the buck.

"Looking for Bravo," he called out in a low voice as he went north up the line. When he finally found the company, he pulled aside the commander, a jumped-up sergeant like himself. "Who's got the headache?"

"Over by that leanin' tree. The one sticking up out of the water. Don't know the guy's name. Careful, he started cursin' like five minutes ago. I mean like real loud."

It was a bad sign and a dangerous situation. If the man got too loud, he might bring down the horde on them and Ross' battalion had been bearing the brunt of the fighting for too many hours now to go on much longer. Ross hurried to the tree. With the smoke drifting over the cadavers and casting the sunlight in a green glow, everyone around the tree had something of an alien tinge.

"You guys doing alright over here?" he asked mildly. Although they wore camouflage, none of them were real soldiers. They were an older group. All eyes shifted to a man who looked a bit like one of Ross' uncles. His eyebrows pointed in and down, and his grey toothbrush mustache gave him both a peevish and a stodgy air. "Maybe you should come with me, sir." Ross' M4 was held loosely and at the same time ready to be yanked up at the least flinch.

"Maybe you should fuck off."

That was telling, and Ross' grip on his gun grew slightly tighter. He glanced to the others, all but one of whom averted their eyes. Ross chose the one that didn't. "You. Help your friend to the rear for evaluation. Then get your ass back here, pronto."

"That's not how you talk to your Governor," Christopher Gore snapped. "Have a little respect."

Ross gave the "Governor" a closer look; he was different. His eyes were a bit brighter, his clothes newer and cleaner. His hair was fancy, unlike Ross' high and tight. So this was Clarren. Ross wasn't impressed. "Listen, jackass, he's not my governor. Look at the patch." He jabbed a thumb at the Screaming Eagle sewn on his shoulder. "I'm with the 101st and you're the asshole that killed most of my division and who knows how many hundreds of thousands of others. And for what?"

"To protect his people," Gore shot back, heaving himself up. He squared his drooping shoulders, planted his flat feet and thrust his sagging belly into Ross.

Never one to back down, Ross stood his ground and demanded, "By sacrificing the people of Connecticut and Rhode Island!"

"They could have fought just like we did."

Their noses were so close to each other that they were practically fencing with them; Clarren put a hand between their faces. "Stop," he said softly. They both took a step back, each glaring at the other. "Stop, both of you. Whoever I was and whatever I did yesterday doesn't matter. Today I'm a soldier. If I have to apologize for anything, then I apologize. And if I have to make an act of contrition, then let this be it."

"Of course, sir," Gore said. "Well said, well said."

Ross had to agree. It had been so well said that he felt an immediate guilt for having brought up the past in the first place and dropped his eyes. They fell on the infected man with the toothbrush mustache and darkening eyes. Seeing him caused the guilt to dry up.

"You haven't even scratched the surface of contrition, *soldier*." To Ross, a civilian didn't become a soldier just by putting on someone else's uniform and picking up a gun. "To start, I want you to escort your friend to the rear and find the battalion head-quarters. You'll take a turn working there."

"Headquarters?" Clarren started to argue. "I'm not here to push papers around. I'm here to…"

Ross snapped his fingers in front of Clarren's face. "A real soldier follows orders. Do as you're told, Private. Besides, going to the rear and getting out of the smoke might just clear your head. The air is cleaner back there. Right?" This last, he had directed toward the infected man, who quickly agreed.

Clarren swallowed his argument, shouldered his rifle and said, "Come on, Joe. It looks like we can best serve the war effort by wielding a three-hole punch." He led Joe Kokolakis up the slope and through the clouds of smoke. Once on higher ground, the smoke dissipated, and he was surprised to see that the day was fine and clear. It was one of those mornings that made spring in Massachusetts perfect.

The two walked, strolled really, up a hill to a pleasant suburban street where the homes had been properly maintained. The yards had recently been mown, the bushes were trimmed, and the trees shaped by years of exact pruning. The only thing wrong with what felt like a reunion with the world was the smell. The acrid smell of the smoke shells had hidden the fetid stench of thousands of corpses.

Kokolakis didn't seem to mind it, but Clarren felt like gagging. The smell did not get better as they followed signs to a white-trimmed house with a long driveway that ended at a basketball hoop.

Directly beneath it, two men were arguing about oysters of all things. One was dressed in camo, the other looked overly warm in a heavy winter coat that hung down to his knees. They both wore blue masks and gloves.

"Battalion headquarters?" Clarren asked.

The oyster talk dried up in a second and the two eyed Clarren and Kokolakis suspiciously. "Yeah. Who's who?"

It was an odd question. "If that's some sort of password code, I don't know it. I'm supposed to work a shift here."

"And I'm clearin' my fuckin' head," Kokolakis said, his Boston accent picking up suddenly.

These answers seemed to suffice and the man with the heavy coat said, "Okay good. Let's go inside, but first leave your weapons. It's policy." Once they had left their weapons leaning against the garage, the man pointed to the door with his left hand; his right was stuffed deep into the pocket of the heavy coat. It was then that Clarren felt a shiver of fear.

When he hesitated, the man in the camouflage said, "Go," with a hard tone to his voice.

Clarren used to have nightmares just like this. Coming up as a Boston politician had meant meeting with some very unsavory types, and there had always been the possibility that some union thug would make a demand that he couldn't answer to and then…

"Go on. Inside."

Compared to the beautiful morning, the garage was dark, purposely so. There were black plastic bags covering the windows and more plastic underfoot. The air was saturated with a strange mixed aroma of motor oil and bleach.

Clarren's hands involuntarily raised to shoulder height as he stepped into the empty room. "I think this is a mistake. I want to fight. It's why I came in the first place. Hey, are you listening?"

One of the two men flicked on the overhead lights. These were a quartet of 400 watt bar-lights that caused Clarren to flinch from the brightness. He was about to go on when Kokolakis roared out, "Turn those fuckin' things off!" He was hiding behind both hands, cringing in pain.

"Step back," the man with the heavy coat said to Clarren. The gun that had been in his pocket was out now. "Do we have a positive?" he asked his camouflaged friend.

"We have a positive," the other man replied, his voice tight and high, sounding as though he were trying to hold his breath and speak at the same time.

The gun came up, pointing at the back of Kokolakis' head.

"Wait," Clarren cried, suddenly realizing the truth about what was happening.

"Wait for what?" the man in camo asked. "He's not going to get any better. From here it just gets bad."

Clarren was both numb and dumb, unable to say anything. He had known Joe Kokolakis since high school. They were, in fact third cousins. Kokolakis had once laid down a thousand-dollar bribe to get Clarren out of some serious shit. Shit that would have derailed his political life.

And yet, Clarren could do nothing but gape as his friend was shot in the head. The .25 caliber slug rattled around inside his head, killing him instantly, and he fell with a baleful thud onto the plastic-covered cement.

"Get gloves and a mask, then wrap him up. We'll help you bring him out back."

Clarren wore a slapped expression. His mouth was hanging open and when he spoke it felt like it was on a loose hinge. "What's outside?"

"The fire pit."

The ex-governor turned and vomited next to the corpse of his friend.

2-9:42 a.m.
Baltimore, Maryland

"Uh, hold on there, Stubby. You just blew through eight-hundred feet." The multirole F-15E Strike Eagle really hadn't blown through anything. With its twin Pratt & Whitney engines at full thrust, it could climb at a rate of 50,000 feet a minute, but just then he was taking it easy, almost gliding.

Tony "Stubby" Alvarez glanced at the altimeter. He was rising gently to two-thousand feet. "Okaaay," he replied, drawing the word out. "I'm not seeing that." The numbers registered on his brain, but they couldn't replace the images that were haunting him.

The blatant lie had his weapons systems officer frowning. He had four different methods to track the plane's exact position in the air and they all read the same. "Are you certain? Everything's in the green back here. Check your *Sniper*."

Tony didn't bother checking his targeting pod. Instead, he looked out the side of his cockpit and wished he could climb even higher. Even from this height, the figures running for cover along the highway still looked too much like real people. Because they were people. He could no longer fool himself.

On his last run, he had made the mistake of looking away from his instruments just as he had banked around. It was as if he had been looking through a telescope, and with perfect clarity he had seen a little girl. She wasn't a monster or a zombie, or whatever the grunts on the ground were fighting. It was a little girl with a pink ribbon in her thick black hair. She had dark skin, which made her eyes seem huge. She was staring right up at Tony when his cluster munitions exploded in a vast brilliant light.

He had murdered that little girl and countless others.

"The Sniper's bent," he heard himself whisper and pushed the throttles forward. The engines roared, and he was thrust back in his seat.

"Damn it, Stubby!" his weapons officer cried. "It's fine. There's nothing wrong with it. What are you doing? We are ten seconds from release. Eight. Stubby! Five…"

Tony banked hard to his right, swinging north. In one ear, he had his WSO barking at him and in his other he had control demanding to know what was going on. "Tango Zero One," Tony said, "this is Five Zero Five, I was spiked. Did you pick it up? Over."

Behind him, his WSO pulled away his mask and covered the mic with his hand. "We weren't pinged because there aren't any damned bogies out there, Stubbs. What's going on, really?"

"I-I heard it, I swear. The threat receiver just went off and I…" The excuse was the stuff a grade-schooler would attempt. "Maybe you're probably right. I must've misheard. We'll set up again. Or…or we could go back."

"With a full payload? Think that over for a second, Stubbs. It's one thing to have a uh, I don't know, a brain fart or whatever, but to *skip* a mission altogether? They'll ground you at a minimum. At a *minimum*, Stubbs! They could arrest you, you know. They arrested General Stanimar and they classified his entire staff as nonessential. I heard they were bussed to the front an hour ago."

Tony had heard the same thing. "Yeah. Okay. It was a brain fart. You were right." *I just won't look out the window*, he thought to himself as he began to pull the big bird around. Of course, the moment he thought it, his eyes strayed to the right and he found himself looking down on Highway 1. There was a crowd on it. They weren't running. In fact, they were barely walking.

"Look!" he cried, feeling a mania grab him. It was like a jolt of caffeine. "Look at all of them. That's who we should be bombing. Get it set up. Tango Zero One, this is Five Zero Five, we had a hiccup. Situation now normal. We have a visual on a large group of IPs heading southwest."

"Copy that Five Zero Five."

"Setting up a run." Tony was almost out of his turn and had dropped down to eight hundred feet. This was the sort of fight that he would gladly be a part of. He turned on the *Sniper Advanced Targeting Pod*. He almost didn't need it. His jet was cruising on a straight shot down the highway. Nothing could be simpler than a bombing run like this. And it was the right thing to do.

"Negative Five Zero Five. Return on a south bound. Target, two-six miles out."

Tony felt his stomach lurch and his hands go numb. He was only twenty-six miles from a fresh murder scene and in an F-15E that was barely half a minute away. How many innocent people had he already killed? How many more would die?

"None," he whispered as he over-shot the densest mass of zombies he had yet seen. Once more he hauled the bird around.

Behind him his WSO, First Lieutenant Matt Wolters covered the mic again. "They said negative, Stubby! Break off!"

"Shut up, Matt!" he raged. "We're doing this." Tony took a deep breath before drawling into the radio, "Enemy targets in view, Tango Zero One. Will return south bound. Roger."

"Five Zero Five, you are not authorized to engage at this time. Continue to your objective."

The center of the horde was coming up quickly and Tony had to make a decision. Was he going to drop his bombs as ordered and be patted on the back for murder or would he disobey orders and be arrested?

"Ten seconds," his WSO growled.

Again, numbness spread through his hands and crept up his arms. Before it got to his elbows, a woman broke in. "There are civilians within the mission's bombing zone. Do not engage. You are not authorized."

"Who is this? Stay off the net. Disregard…"

"Five Zero Five releasing!" The Eagle jumped a bit as the first CBU-87 combined effects munition dropped away. It immediately began to spin, releasing the 202 submunitions. Each of the yellow bomblets shot out so that when they landed, an entire section of the highway went up in flame and smoke.

Knowing he would never be able to come around for a second pass, Tony kept pickling off the CBUs one after another, leaving behind a long path of destruction.

"Holy fuck," Matt whispered. He was turned in his seat, his head cranked all the way around, gaping at the thousands of burnt and dismembered bodies. As far as bombing runs went, this one was epic.

"You heard that voice, right?" Tony asked him. "I told you there was a glitch. Tango Zero One, did you hear that?" He was sweating through his flight suit. "Was that authentic? It's hard enough up here without distractions."

There was a squawk of static before the radio crackled again. "This is Tango Zero One. Disregard any intrusion from here on out."

From here on out? Tony wilted into his seat at these words. He would cling to the woman's timely intervention and blame her for everything. She would keep him out of the stockade, at least for now. But what would he do on his next bombing run? Or the one after that?

Chapter 11
1-10:24 a.m.
Weldon, New York

Pretty much all the real monsters had dispersed, leaving only the broken ones, Jaimee Lynn Burke's pack and the ugly Chinaman, who was a huge disappointment. He had stuffed himself silly with pills and was lying there with his mouth hanging open, showing a disgusting white tongue set in black gums.

"He stink," one of the half-eaten little girls grumbled.

"How would y'all know?" Jaimee Lynn sniped. "Y'all don't even have a nose." The girl was missing an ear as well, though what that had to do with the price of gas Jaimee Lynn didn't know. That had been one of her daddy's favorite things to say. Somehow, everything had to do with the price of gas and given enough time John Burke could find the connection.

If he had been there, her daddy would have sussed it out in no time. The building and grounds were strange to Jaimee Lynn. Not because of the destruction, of course, or the pools of black blood and the corpses scattered all about carpeted by clouds of buzzing flies three inches deep. No, all that was normal stuff to her demon mind.

It was the whiff of her daddy she caught around every corner. She knew he had been there recently. It was why she hadn't left yet to find clean blood, though her belly was begging for more. But she couldn't stay there forever, and it seemed like half-past forever had come and gone while she waited on the stupid Chinaman to wake up.

She decided, without being able to pinpoint a rational cause, that perhaps more pills would be the answer. She picked pills at random and began poking them into his mouth and down his throat. It became something of a game to the other kids and before long, they had filled his mouth with so many pills that Jaimee Lynn couldn't even close his lips properly without some spilling onto the floor.

"He gotta swaller them," she explained to the others, and then "helped" him to swallow the pills by working his jaw up and down. The result was that the pills formed into a paste that had the consistency of spackle.

123

"Hmm," Jaimee Lynn said. The sound marked her attempt at thinking. It was slowly dawning on her that the spackle wasn't going to go down on its own. "Wut I need is a stick." Back in Arkansas, sticks had many uses and were the go-to tool of choice. You could write in the dirt with them, you could tie a string to them and fish, or you could whack a boy on the head with one if he got overly curious and tried to lift your church dress on a Sunday morning. Jaimee Lynn had done all those things.

Now, she was going to add force-feeding a Chinaman some pills to the list. Since she didn't want to go all the way outside, she used the hunk of bone she had been carrying around since dawn. Although she had sucked all the marrow out of it a while back, she had kept it, less as a souvenir and more as a sort of totem. This made sense as it was her father's arm bone.

She jabbed the pointy end of the bone down into Eng's gullet as if she were trying to unclog a toilet.

Unexpectedly, to her at least, he vomited up a ghastly combination of black bile and the mash of pills. Although Jaimee Lynn received a healthy spray, she wasn't all that put out. After all, she had crawled through sewers and had slithered through rivers of blood, and she had spent part of a night curled up in the disemboweled body of a woman a few nights before.

Eng started snoring, which gave her an idea. She tapped his forehead with the bone. "Y'all know wut he need? He need coffee. My daidy always drunk up coffee to wake hisself up." She sent her pack out in search of coffee. Some were clueless and mindlessly followed around after Jaimee Lynn. Some forgot what they were looking for within a minute and came back to her with familiar objects: a busted lamp, a shoe, half a mug.

"Close," Jaimee Lynn said of the mug. "But coffee is like all black 'n all. Y'all drink it."

The little boy came back with the same mug dripping partially congealed zombie blood.

Jaimee Lynn eventually found part of a coffee pot and when she hunted around in the debris beneath it, she discovered more mugs and a bag of actual coffee beans. The smell was right, but the look of the whole beans was off. Her daidy had used some sort of powder.

"Like chocolate milk powder, only nasty," she muttered. Nasty or not, the smell of the beans held a certain nostalgic mastery over Jaimee Lynn and she breathed them in for a minute before deciding to use them regardless of their lack of powdery-ness. "We'll just pop them in his mouth."

This time she went about the operation of force-feeding Eng with more circumspection. Not only did she sit him up, she only put the beans in one at a time, poking them deep and working his jaw and neck around until the beans disappeared one after another.

Some went into his lungs, which was a given. These he coughed out and Jaimee Lynn had a number dangling in her hair before she decided enough had gone down the right pipe to make things happen. She and her pack watched him, waiting for him to do something besides snore.

"Me hun-gee," one of them said.

"Me too," Jaimee Lynn said, crossly. She was just about sick of the Chinaman and could barely remember why she wanted him around in the first place. Standing, she went to put the bag of beans in her pocket when she realized that she was naked. "Who stoled my undies? And my britches!"

The obvious villain was the Chinaman and in a fit of rage, she stabbed him with the bone. It kicked off a rib and got stuck in some cartilage. When she yanked it out, the Chinaman unexpectedly opened his eyes. They were black with driblets of what looked like ink leaking from the corners.

"*Guan ta ne…*" He paused, worked his tongue around in his mouth and then spat out beans and bits of pills. "What the hell?" he repeated, this time in English.

"The hell is," Jaimee Lynn said pointing the bone at him, "Y'all made us a promise and we's all hungry." She could not remember the promise, though she was pretty sure it had to do with food. Her pack agreed, at least those who could follow the short conversation; they nodded solemnly and gripped their bellies, which were shrunken and sad.

"Oh, we'll eat," Eng said, feeling both famished and revolted as he imagined hot red blood dripping down his chin. "First, I need more pills." Already his head was aching worse than any hangover he'd ever had. It put him in an ugly mood and he cursed the children and shoved them out of the way as he went about scraping up the fallen pills. He filled his pockets and, as he'd been given baggy ACUs to wear, he had a lot of pockets.

Once he was ready, he barged past Jaimee Lynn and looked out over the crater that made up most of the interior of the building. "I need a gun," he muttered.

"I knowd where one is," Jaimee Lynn piped up. "That mean man what always hung around with Dr. Lee had one." Eng followed her to the mound of corpses Deckard had made during his final stand. The assault rifle, dripping blood and gore, was found cast off to the side by one of the pack. The boy carried it in two hands like it was an axe.

Its bolt was back and the magazine was empty. Eng glared. "What is this? Huh? I need one with fucking bullets! *She* will have bullets," he said, meaning Thuy. Picturing her sent a shock of rage through him and he cursed the gun and flung it away.

His fury washed right over Jaimee Lynn without affecting her in the least. "The army man had one." Her stomach rumbled as she remembered how he had fought to get at the M4 he had set aside. He'd had half a dozen little zombies crawling all over him, scratching and biting, all for nothing. Like some sort of malicious turtle, he'd been encased in metal that broke their teeth. And his heavy coat defied their claws.

Only when he stretched out for that gun was he vulnerable; his neck exposed. Jaimee Lynn had burrowed in on it and had struck the finest vein of blood imaginable.

"What army man?" Eng demanded.

"It's too late," Jaimee Lynn answered, sadly. "He's all ated up. There's nothin' left."

Eng realized that he was disappointed by this. He shook his head, trying not to think about the blood wasted on the little parasites. "Just show me where the gun is." Jaimee Lynn led the way to the helicopter that Eng had departed from hours before.

"Can y'all fly this here thing, Mister Chinaman?"

He wasn't listening. His mind was far away. Now that he had a gun and the pack of demons, he and Dr. Lee were on a level playing field, and he would force her to cure him or he vowed he would suck every ounce of blood right out of her. This time the idea of drinking human blood wasn't revolting in the least. It was wonderful.

2-10:41 a.m.
Springfield, Illinois

Standing at the top of the capital steps, behind a bulletproof podium, the governor spoke for an hour and twenty-eight minutes, most of it self-congratulatory pap that no one listened to. The only thing anyone really cared about came near the end of the speech. Two simple lines out of hundreds: "We are a nation that prides itself on its openness, from our speech to our borders. And just as we can't turn our back on immigrants seeking a better life, we can't turn our backs on our own refugees."

He went on for some time after that, sounding to the gathered press very much like a man running for higher office.

During the wrap-up and the handshaking that went on after, the lieutenant governor was asked whether she fully supported the governor. "Unequivocally," was her answer.

The same question was put to Major General Josh Lloyd, the Adjutant General of Illinois, the state's ranking officer. "One moment please," he told the reporter. He'd always liked a direct approach and frequently a visual was far more compelling than a simple yes or no.

With unhurried steps he walked over to the Governor, drew his Beretta, and shot the man in the back of the head. One leg kicked out as his body spazzed and he dropped onto his face, where someone earlier had spat something ugly up from the bottom of their lungs.

The crowd, which wasn't large and consisted of more reporters than constituents, let out a unified, but rather muted shriek and yet, they didn't take so much as a step back. They acted as if they were watching live theater rather than a coup attempt. No one so much as blinked as the general pivoted to his right, setting his gun sites on the lieutenant governor.

His hand was rock steady, as was his conviction that by ending two lives, he was saving millions. He fired before she could begin to beg. The bullet smashed through her breastbone and turned her heart inside out. She fell into her husband's arms, blood splashing on his grey Armani suit. She had picked it out for him that morning, telling him that it made him look "tough."

With his paunch a growing concern and twenty-two years since he had been in anything resembling a fight, he hadn't felt tough in years. Now, he felt rage. He laid his wife down and was about to get to his feet and charge the general, who was had holstered his piece and was turning toward the microphone.

"Don't do it, Earl." A strong hand came down on his shoulder. It was Illinois state trooper Morris Robinson—he was "their" state trooper. He was the man whose job it was to protect them whenever they were out in public like this. The trooper carried a Glock 22; it sat in its holster, his hand nowhere near it. None of the police were going for their guns.

"But...but...he just killed her."

Trooper Robinson nodded sadly, his dark face looking darker in his grief. He had really liked the lieutenant governor and he had personally voted for the governor on three separate occasions. Unfortunately, things had progressed beyond both politics and politicians.

Leaders were needed. It had taken some convincing for Morris Robinson to see that and it had taken two huge tumblers of Crown for him to walk up the capitol steps with the lieutenant governor, knowing what was going to happen. "She had been warned," he told her husband. The warning had been vague in its details to be sure, and yet the meaning was clear: *Do not stand with the governor on open borders.*

Now Morris had to give the same sort warning to Earl. "Stay here and mourn your wife. Things will end badly for you if you don't."

"Badly!" Earl cried, loud enough to make General Lloyd pause just as he was about to speak. "Badly? How can it end any worse?" Morris answered by fixing him with a steady cold as ice gaze. "So, they'll kill me?" he demanded, his voice both incredulous and furious.

"Yes."

"Let them try!" He staggered to his feet and began marching towards General Lloyd, passing right in front of John Stack, the Director of the State Police. John was carrying his sidearm for the first time in four years. He shot Earl in the back three times and had to fight the urge to turn the gun on himself.

General Lloyd sighed into the microphone. Cleared his throat twice, before starting. "I was going to begin my remarks by calling this a sad day. And it is, but more than that, this is a necessary day that will be filled with difficult but very necessary choices. It was impressed upon both the governor and the lieutenant governor the absolute need to close our border for the safety of our citizens. They were given clear evidence that the disease had made its way into Indiana and yet both chose, at the behest of the President, to ignore the evidence presented."

He turned and waved a hand at the bullet-ridden bodies. "This is a direct result of going against the will of the people. We must do everything in our power to prevent the disease from crossing our borders. To that end, we will not simply protect an imaginary line on a map. I have authorized the Illinois National Guard to advance to the Wabash River and to secure it all the way north to Attica."

"Attica?" a reporter called out. "That's in Indiana and so is the Wabash."

"It's a few miles into Indiana," Lloyd conceded. "The Wabash is the best natural boundary in the east."

Another reporter yelled out, "So you're saying we're invading Indiana? After what happened in Massachusetts, wouldn't you call that horribly irresponsible?"

Lloyd thought of the irony of the question as he stood within feet of an assassinated governor. He almost laughed and would have if he wasn't sick to his stomach. "The situation is not the same. Almost all of their forces are either guarding their eastern frontier or trying to move east to shore up the Quarantine Zone. A state of warfare is not imminent."

"You say they are moving east. Isn't it true that the Illinois National Guard was federalized two days ago? And isn't it true that the President ordered the 33rd Infantry Brigade Combat Team east as well?"

That was painfully true. "Yes, and we were in the process of transferring units east when we were made aware of the situation developing in Indiana. It made no sense to attempt to enforce one quarantine zone when we had one developing further west."

"What is the situation in Indiana?" someone cried out, the strident fear in their voice like an untuned violin.

3-10:56 a.m.
Elnora, Indiana

By all that was right and holy, Lancaster Holmes should have been dead. He had stopped breathing nearly three hours before. Blood had filled the pleural space between his left lung and the chest wall, eventually cutting off the airflow to his right lung. He stopped breathing and Sheriff Nicolas Read had assumed that he had died.

The Sheriff had reported Lancaster's death as well as that of the black-eyed old lady, and then, during his and Emerald's long wait, he had wrapped himself in guilt.

The guilt turned quickly to fear when he heard a sudden soggy hiss from the front of the diner. Read's grandfather had been a smoker all his life and on his deathbed, he had made that same sort of ugly, phlegmy sound. In this case, it was something like a death-rattle, but in reverse.

"Did you hear that?" Emerald asked, her great bosom heaving, her large dark eyes wide circles.

"Yep," Read answered, giving thought to his gun for the first time since he had fired it. He hadn't changed out the magazine and decided it was well past time he did.

As he was reaching for his holster, Emerald grabbed his arm. "We have to get out of here! I-I know what you said, but we're fine. Look at me. Do I look like a fuckin' zombie to you? Huh? Do I?"

"It's too late. You know that." There was no way they could leave now. All of Elnora was surrounded by elements of the 219th Battlefield Surveillance Brigade. These were not hardened veterans by any measure, but they had a lot of guns and were more than willing to use them. The diner, which sat on the edge of town, was something of a bubble within a bubble.

It had been taped off by the first state police units to arrive. Then, an hour later, the tape had been upgraded to barbed wire. Thirty minutes after men and women from the Indiana State Department of Health showed up wearing blue plastic suits and carrying drawn handguns.

"Do not attempt to leave the facility," one of them said, borrowing a nervous trooper's radio.

"It's a diner, not a facility," Read answered in a tired drawl. "We don't plan on leaving. Not yet. But it makes sense to move us, unless you want us to get infected."

"Which we do not. We are trying to set up an advanced quarantine staging area, but it may take some time. Just sit still and don't do anything stupid."

The threat had come across loud and clear, at least to Read. Emerald seemed to have forgotten it. "They'll shoot you if you try to leave," he whispered to her. She was starting to hyperventilate, and a certain madness had crept into her eyes. "Our best bet is to keep still and quiet. If that guy I shot is one of them, he'll probably see all the commotion and head outside."

"Just be quiet? That's...that's it?"

In her mind, that's all they had been doing since they'd foolishly locked themselves inside the diner. Read had duct-taped the cracks around the swinging doors that led from the front of house to the kitchens. Next, he had turned off the ventilation system to keep the air from mixing. As an added guard against the disease, they had cut swathes of cloth from the cleaner aprons and wore them like masks, when they were not eating, that is.

Other than worrying, there wasn't much to do besides eat. They had found themselves famished and they ate until they were bursting. When they couldn't find even a sliver of room left in their bellies, they poked around in their section of the diner, neither knowing what they were looking for exactly. Emerald discovered a battered old deck of cards in the manager's desk, but they couldn't concentrate long enough to finish a game of Go-fish.

All they could do was fret and when they weren't feeling phantom signs of becoming a zombie, they were seeing the symptoms in each other.

The re-awakening of Lancaster Holmes changed all that. A horrible wheeze came seconds after that first soggy breath and Read began to picture Lancaster as a bearded zombie with grey skin and mindless black eyes.

"Fuuuuck," Lancaster said in a long groan, proving he wasn't nearly as mindless as Read had assumed. He then hawked up something black, half the size of a rat, and spat it on the floor. "What the fuck is that? And what's with the fucking light?" He seemed to be getting louder and stronger with each breath. As he did, Emerald seemed to shrink, growing more and more clingy until finally, Read had to shake her off of him.

He put a finger to his lips and drew his Smith & Wesson M&P 9. He was just about to change out the magazine when Lancaster said, "I can smell you." Every inch of Read's flesh tented up in goosebumps and the hair on the back of his neck lifted straight out. "I can smell you and that bitch. You did this to me."

Something metal scraped on the linoleum out front. Read hoped it was a chair, but he feared that it wasn't. Lancaster had a gun.

The same realization struck Emerald an instant later and Read's shoulder was suddenly left cold as she pulled her bosom away and scrambled for the back door. Read tried to snatch her ankle, but she was too fast. Her panic had been escalating all morning and this was the final straw.

With a shriek, she burst from the backdoor. She fell straight down a set of three steps, landed in the dust and was up again in a flash. "It's alive!" she screamed as she ran at the yellow tape and the newly strung barbed wire. Someone yelled for her to get back inside.

Another yelled for her to stop and still someone else yelled, "They're running!" It was only Emerald running and she didn't hear anything. Her mind was a complete blank, save for the overarching fear that controlled her. She hit the wire and tried to tear it out of her way barehanded. She was a big woman and the nearest five-foot steel spear that had been driven into the ground came right up with a single heave.

There were more screams and yells. It was all a mishmash of noise to Read, who had not even tried to stand. He watched Emerald in horror as she threw down the wire and tried to cross the yellow tape. There was no call to fire. It wasn't needed. She was swept with bullets. In the first eight seconds, she was hit by no less than thirty rounds of all sorts of calibers. They staggered her, but she refused to fall. It took another twenty bullets before a huge 30-30 round cracked her frontal lobe and sprawled through her cranium, turning her brain to mush.

She fell in something of an oddly graceful pirouette, and as she spun, she was hit by another dozen bullets, and another dozen thumped into her when she finally face-planted in the dirt.

Someone bellowed for a cease-fire and, as the echoes of their gunfire rolled over the frightened little town, forty men stared at their handiwork: a bloody lump sprawled in the dirt that had once been a person. They waited behind their guns, ready to resume shooting if she so much as twitched. But she was no zombie. She had died as a woman without any sign of infection.

"Fuuuuck," Lancaster said. He was clutching the diner's bar to hold himself up. He felt angrily drunk, hellishly hungover, sick down into the pit of his stomach, and so furious that he thought he could rip the bar in half— all of these churned-up feelings were nothing compared to the evil hunger that was growing by the second.

It was a hunger to be clean again, but it was also a hunger for revenge and watching the chubby waitress get murdered Bonnie and Clyde style had brought a smile to his face.

"Did you see that?" he whispered to Sheriff Read. "That's what they gonna do to you. They gonna shoot you like a dog."

The man, if he was still even a man, which Read doubted, was correct. If he went out there for any reason, they would gun him down, no questions asked.

"Or…" Lancaster said, drawing the word out.

"Or what?" Read asked, pushing himself to his feet. As quietly as he could, he placed his M9 on the grill so he could re-tie the strip of cloth that had fallen from his face. His hands felt wooden, while his mind felt woolen, stuffed with the sound of all those gunshots. It had sounded like a battle, as if it had been two armies clashing instead of a lone, unarmed woman fleeing for her life.

When Lancaster didn't answer right away, he asked again, "Or what?" It felt strange to be asking a zombie for answers, but just then nothing was right in Read's world.

"It seems like you have three choices. Go out there and die. Stay where you are and eventually become like me. Or…" Again, he paused for effect and Read found himself leaning forward, waiting to hear his final choice. "You can come out here and finish what you started. Mano a mano. You and me. What do you say? Wanna dance?"

Read was slow to reply. The zombie had summed up his options succinctly. The level of fear demonstrated by those holding him captive in the diner would only mount as the day wore on. And if Read waited, eventually the zombie would try to come into the kitchen. Even if he managed to kill the zombie the disease had proven to be extra virulent and getting infected was almost a guarantee.

The choice Lancaster was offering was almost as bad: a gunfight in a narrow diner against an opponent who had already died once and who didn't seem to feel pain or fear. This didn't seem like a fight Read could win.

"Come on, *chicken*," Lancaster sneered. "What do you have to lose?"

Read had everything to lose and only one thing to possibly gain: time. "And maybe a chance to put a bullet into my own head," he whispered. Louder, he called out, "Step back from the door. In fact, go to your table. Put your gun on it and I'll holster mine. That'll make it fair."

"If you want it fair you'd take off your vest. Do it or I'll piss right under this fuckin' door. I know you got towels and shit along the crack, but I got me a broom, and in the great battle of broom verse towel, the broom wins every time, fuck-face. So, take off the vest and throw it out first."

"Shit!" Read hissed, wishing he hadn't used the word fair. He took off the brown uniform shirt and gazed wistfully down at the scarred vest. It had saved his life and now he was giving it up. He muttered another curse and stripped it off. Without it he felt small and weak.

"It's off, now move back. I want to hear you when you get to the table."

"I'm already here."

Taking a long knife, Read cut along the duct tape. He then yanked on the ends of the cloth around his face until his nose was bent sideways. "I'm coming out!" Cracking the door, he peeked down the length of the diner. Lancaster was sitting just as he had been when Read had walked into the diner hours before, only now there was a shiny silver pistol on the table in front of him. It sat inches from his right hand. His left hand was at his temple massaging it so fiercely that he was in danger of rubbing the flesh away from the bone.

Read tossed the vest onto the long counter, inadvertently knocking over a coffee mug which exploded on the old linoleum, causing Lancaster to wince.

"You did that on purpose," Lancaster seethed, his hand inching toward the gun.

He hadn't, but he wished he had. There had been a good second and a half when Read could have drawn his gun and fired. Now it was too late. He stood in the narrow lane between the counter and the crowded back wall—he was perfectly framed.

"You gonna do this sittin' down?" Read hoped he'd stand up. If the half-man made the attempt, Read would draw on him. It was completely unfair. Then again, nothing about the situation was fair.

Lancaster had ideas of his own. "You think I should die like a man? It's a little too late for that, don't you think?"

Read shrugged, mostly to loosen his shoulders. The muscles of his neck and shoulders were so stiff he didn't know if they would actually move when it came time to fight. He could picture himself freezing in place when the time came. He had seen enough dash-cam footage to know that it happened more than anyone cared to admit.

"It's never too late," Read told him. "Do the right thing."

Lancaster regarded Read with his black eyes. "And that is? Kill myself? Is that the right thing? Maybe you should kill yourself."

"If I was in your position, I would," he answered honestly. "Maybe it's too late for you. Probably it is. Come on. Stand up. Let's get this over with." Read knew it wouldn't be smart to draw the moment out any longer. His body felt like a spring; an old rusty, brittle spring.

"Okay," Lancaster said and began to heave himself up. As he did, his right hand shot out and grabbed the pistol.

Read was already reaching for his own. In a surprisingly fluid motion, the grip was in his hand and he was drawing the piece up from its holster. Unfortunately, the gun sat high on his hip, which didn't lend itself to a quick draw. Worse for Read, he had to haul his elbow up to almost shoulder height to clear the weapon and when he did, he cracked the back of his arm on the shelf that held the coffee machine which had been left on all morning.

Scalding coffee splashed across his arm just as the front sight caught on the edge of his holster. The gun dropped from his fumbling hand. Read was quick and dropped along with the gun, going to one knee and almost catching it in midair. It clacked loudly on the linoleum a split second before Lancaster fired his weapon.

The air blazed an inch over Read's head. Then the M9 was in his hand just as a bullet ripped through the meat of his right arm. The gun almost dropped from his hand a second time as his arm went limp and dangled uselessly from his shoulder.

He was in deep shit and knew it all too well. The narrow lane he was crouched in, seemed to channel every bullet right at him. He had to get out before Lancaster fired again. This was basically impossible as the half-man was already lining up another shot, a gleeful black grin on his face.

Read launched himself over the counter…mostly over the counter, that is. He landed on the far edge, a bullet missing the side of his head by millimeters. The high counter stools broke his fall somewhat. Four of these went over with him and he landed amidst a clatter of bouncing metal. He rolled left as a bullet *tinged* off one of the chairs.

Then he went back the way he had come as he realized his gun had fallen from his weak grasp. Left-handed, he grabbed it, flinched as sparks flew into his face from a bullet that scorched the linoleum and then fired at Lancaster with barely a nod towards actually aiming. Stretched out on the floor wasn't a good position for shooting, especially as he couldn't use his right arm for support. He couldn't raise the gun above waist height and when he jerked the trigger, the first four bullets went into the cushion next to Lancaster.

"They'll let anyone be a cop these days," Lancaster laughed, firing his gun again and missing high this time. Now that he was out from behind the counter, Read had become a much more difficult target. The hated sun was bouncing off the metal chairs and burning right into his eyes.

Lancaster's consecutive misses gave Read one second to pull himself together and with a grunt of pain, he rolled onto his right side and was able to aim the M9 down the length of his body, resting his left arm on his hip. With a stable platform, he was squeezed the trigger the way it was meant to be. His first shot hit Lancaster in the shoulder. His next two buried themselves in his chest without appearing to affect him in the least.

He adjusted slightly and punched Lancaster's ticket with a beauty of a headshot. Lancaster's head swung back, struck the cushion, rebounded, and then flopped forward to smash the table, leaving a black smear.

Read wilted onto the linoleum and after a few breaths, he felt tears come to his eyes. He laughed at them without understanding their nature. "Probably just blood loss." There was blood everywhere: up the side of the door, on the ceiling, across the counter, and finally, where he lay in a puddle of red.

It took him three attempts to sit up and, once his head stopped spinning, his first thoughts were on his arm. The wound was a through and through and already the bleeding was slowing. "That's good. Nothing big has been…" His words dried up as he realized that he'd been rolling around in the still tacky black blood that had come gushing out of the old lady he had shot earlier.

"No," he whispered, lifting his good left hand and seeing what looked like smears of tar. It was only then that he realized the cloth around his face had slipped again. He went to tighten it, only one arm wasn't working and the other was covered in diseased blood. Suddenly, his entire body began to feel itchy, as if the germs were the size of ants and were crawling all over him.

Dropping his gun, he went to the sink behind the counter and tried to wash one handed. It was impossible. He got his right arm clean enough; however, his left was dirty up to his bicep, where his shirt sleeve started. There was blood on that as well, and on his pants.

For just a few moments, he considered pulling off his clothes and trying to bathe in the dish sink. It was a stupid idea. If the back area wasn't already contaminated, it would become so the moment he went back there.

"Besides, it's already too late." He figured that if the disease could get to a dead guy, he didn't stand a chance. "There's only one thing to do," he whispered. Ten minutes later, with every ounce of oil he could find spread evenly throughout the diner, he lit a match and watched as the flame spread down the counter, poured down onto the floor and spread out.

In seconds, the heat was explosive. It baked into him, drying the blood even as it trickled from his wound. At first the heat was strangely comforting. It was right.

Then it hurt. It was time to be done.

"We have an in-bound *Sentinel!*" Colonel Taylor yelled over the room's seemingly endless chatter. "Stop transmitting!"

Courtney Shaw, who had been monitoring five aviation frequencies at once, and was feeding misinformation to three different regimental commanders, simultaneously, didn't understand Taylor. She covered her mic and turned to Major Justin Iler, the soldier closest to her and asked, "Did he say a sentinel? Isn't that a guard or something?"

"Damn it," General Axelrod groused, rubbing one of his large hands over his face. The liver-spots were just beginning to show on the back of them. "How far out?"

Taylor shrugged. "Five minutes maybe. It's hard to tell. I picked up transmission from a Sentry over Harrisburg that was clearing a lane for an east-bound flight out of BFE. Someone asked him if it was for heavies and his answer was that it was for *Hush-planes* out of Creech Air Force Base."

"What's all that mean?" Courtney demanded, suddenly nervous because everyone else was suddenly nervous.

"It means we're temporarily out of business," Axelrod said. "The only spy planes flying out of Creech is the RQ-170 *Sentinel*. It's a UAV, designed for stealth reconnaissance. It's up there, but we'll never know where exactly. Did we get any sort of heading from the AWAC?" Taylor shook his flat-topped head; Axelrod looked pained at the answer.

Boyish Major Clay Palmburg raised a soft hand. "It's not all bad, sir. We know the point of origin, and we know that only the 30th and the 44the Recon Squadrons fly the Sentinel. We just have to work out their communication path. If they're using JREAP-A protocols, we could saturate their network and gum everything up. In conjunction with that, we can hunt down where they refueled; it'll likely be in line with their destination. It could be Boston."

Major Iler didn't look convinced. "That'll only work if they are using a token passing protocol. You see, sir if they're using what's referred to as the *half-duplex method,* then there is a chance we might interfere, but if they..."

Axelrod, who didn't give a damn about protocols of any sort, stopped him. "Major Palmburg, you try the protocol thing. Major Iler do something else but do something! Everyone else, if you're not working on anything essential, shut down your computers."

Special Agent Katherine Pennock didn't look up from her computer. "I'm trying to hold off the NSA, the FBI and Army Cyber Command. If I can't keep ahead of them, we all might as well go home." There were at least a hundred different agents and officers searching through the mass of information that composed Link 16, the military's tactical data link network. Anything out of the ordinary was either being investigated by dedicated tactical teams swooping down in Blackhawks or simply obliterated by cruise missiles.

After Katherine's announcement, everyone else made claims that what they were doing was essential. All except Courtney Shaw. She was only saving lives by rerouting bombing runs, changing logistic paths to keep soldiers supplied, pulling reinforcements from less threatened areas, and sending them to places that were on the verge of being overrun—this was how Troy Ross was suddenly gifted with three platoons of Marines and was able to hold his section of the Black Blood Bog that had once been the Quinsigamond River.

Courtney took off her headset and shutdown her computer. It felt wrong. "So, does anyone need coffee?"

"Forget the coffee," Axelrod growled. "Those *Sentinels* are a bitch. We need to shut down any and all electronics that aren't being used. Also, we need to power down everything that's drawing power. We need our footprint as small as possible. Start with Dr. Lee's lab. And Courtney, you better hurry."

The way he said it was terribly ominous and she scurried out of the room without looking back. The stairs were poorly lit and yet they were free from obstruction and she took them three at a time, just as her thirteen-year-old self would have. Of course, her thirteen-year-old self would have been blubbering as she went, afraid that she was already too late and that a missile was, even then, homing in on the building.

Courtney from a week ago might also have been blubbering wreck. A lot had changed in her world in a very short time. She raced down to the third floor and once there, began turning off lights as she charged for the labs.

"We gotta shut every…" She started to say only to be confronted by a roar from the next room. Through the glass, she could see a zombie—it flung itself at her. Just as her thirteen-year-old self would have, she leapt back and let out a screech. The beast was brought up short. Its wrists were cuffed to the metal support post of a huge, twelve-foot wide stainless-steel cabinet.

"Oh, my God! That's Specialist Hoskins."

Anna Holloway looked up from the computer she'd been staring at. "Yeah. Pretty crappy, right? The 'Queen' over there doesn't want to mess up her findings by giving him any meds."

Courtney had to drag her eyes away from the creature. At the far end of the room, Thuy was simultaneously looking down into a microscope and jotting notes with a furious hand. "Meds?" Courtney asked Anna, hope leaping into her heart, before she remembered, "Right, the opiates. The stuff that makes them, like half-zombies."

"I'd rather be half a human than no human at all. So, anything going on upstairs? You guys need any help? I'm not doing anything here because Dr. Lee doesn't trust me, even though my ass is on the line just like hers."

Without looking up from the microscope, Thuy said, "When it's time to test a cure, you'll be the first person I call on, Anna."

There was no time for bickering. Courtney cut off Anna's retort. "We actually do have a situation. There's a drone of some sort heading our way and if it locates us we can expect a missile to follow within minutes."

Anna blanched, while Thuy only muttered, "Don't waste my time with 'ifs' when they don't immediately pertain to me."

"I'm afraid this one does. This drone can sniff out electronic, uh, noise, I guess is the right word. The general wants us to shut down everything that isn't needed."

Thuy shrugged. "The only thing that's not needed is Anna and whatever she's doing on that computer. Something treasonous, I have no doubt. All the rest of this is completely necessary."

"Maybe if we shut some of the stuff down temporarily."

"Impossible," Thuy stated.

Courtney wasn't easily stopped. "Certainly, you don't need both of your computers running simultaneously. And there's…"

Finally, Thuy turned her dark eyes from the microscope. "I said it was impossible. I have isolated both sets of Com-cells and am currently running eleven tests, simultaneously. Stopping now would ruin two hours' worth of work. We don't have minutes to waste, let alone hours. You will just have to think of something else."

"Like what?"

Thuy stuck her face back to the microscope, saying, "I have faith in you, Miss Shaw. You'll figure something out. Now, if you don't mind, I have my own work to do."

Anna made a point to turn off her computer with something of a flourish. She then gave Courtney a look that she read as: *Do you see what I have to put up with?* Courtney made no reply as she left. She hated when Thuy was like this. Only she saw Courtney's supposed genius. "Is it a girl power sort of thing with her?" she muttered as she hurried back up the many flights of stairs.

Courtney knew she was the dumbest one in the building. Among them were pilots, scientists, army officers who had to go through West Point, a school that was notoriously difficult, and finally an FBI Special Agent. "And all I ever did was drop out of college…community college, for fuck's sake!"

She was thoroughly dejected by the time she came huffing up to the tenth floor. There was no need to ask whether the drone was still coming. The men were sweating and Special Agent Pennock kept looking up from her computer to glance out the window. Courtney sighed before giving the bad news, "We're going to need to come up with a new plan. Dr. Lee won't budge. She says her experiments are in a critical phase and that she can't power down anything."

"Didn't you tell her about the damned drone?" Axelrod asked, his face growing brilliantly red.

"And I told her about the missile that's sure to follow." She had to hold her eyes steadily on his to keep from glancing out the window. "She thinks…she thinks *we* can come up with an idea to stop it. Do these drones have, like a self-destruct sequence on them?"

She knew right away that it was a stupid question. Axelrod rolled his eyes before heaving himself up. "I'll talk to her. In the meantime, find that damned frequency." Everyone went back to work. Everyone except Courtney, that is; she didn't know the first thing about network protocols or super-secret spy planes. Embarrassed, she dropped into her chair.

Colonel Taylor saw her not doing anything. "I could use your help. Why don't you get us some coffee? Black for me."

Coffee orders were yelled her way and, dejectedly she went in search of a break room, saying to herself, "This is about right."

2-11:39 a.m. Eastern Standard Time
Beijing, China

It was just after midnight in China as General Weilei, high commander of the People's Liberation Army Ground Force, made his way through the great double doors that towered twenty-five feet over his head. After a deep breath, he strode into the Great Hall of the People.

This was the first time he'd ever entered the building without feeling that wonderful patriotic fervor come over him. He had failed his people completely. Of course, he had his excuses: the unforeseeable nature of the event, the shocking quickness with which the virus spread, the mass panic, the complete breakdown in the societal structure in certain areas of the country, the insane refugee situation that was still clogging every road in the eastern half of the country…

The excuses were meaningless and embarrassing, and he would never utter them aloud, not even under torture. He would stick to the truth: he had not been prepared and thus he had not prepared his people properly.

He did not expect to live long enough to be tortured.

General Okini, Vice Chairman of the Central Military Commission, had been arrested earlier that day and had been shot in the back of the head in less than two hours. Weilei felt he deserved pretty much the same punishment.

Sucking in his breath, he marched into the beautiful auditorium and was surprised at how deserted it was. Two days before, it had been crowded with every heavy-weight party official within thirty miles of the capital; now it was less than a third full. Only three of the Politburo Standing Committee were present.

Embarrassed to be in the same room with me, Weilei figured. He came to attention, snapped off a salute to the General Secretary and waited on his judgment.

"You have heard about the fate of General Okini?" the General Secretary asked. Although it was, in form, a question, the General Secretary didn't wait for an answer. "Then you know his position is currently vacant. You have been chosen to succeed him."

Weilei blinked in surprise. "This is an honor I do not deserve and cannot accept. It would be a slap in the face to the people of China. If you will allow me to name a person that would be eminently more qualified…"

"Shut up," the Premier snapped, fire behind his narrow eyes. "You are right, this is an honor you do not deserve. That is something we can all agree on. But it is an honor you had better live up to. The future of China depends on you."

The General Secretary cleared his throat so that all eyes were on him again. "What my colleague means to say is that as the leader of our ground forces, you are preeminently qualified to take over the Vice Chairman's position. Your staff is already in place and you know the situation better than anyone."

Quickly, Weilei's look of surprise morphed, becoming the flat expressionless look of a card player trying to disguise a weak hand. They weren't in a "situation," they were in the midst of a catastrophe. The nukes had somehow failed to wipe out all of the zombies and now the creatures were mixed in with the refugees who were flying in every direction but east. His situational intelligence officer had estimated that the refugees numbered more than fifty million.

There was no way of knowing how many zombies were among them. The only estimate Weilei had of their numbers had been given by a trembling blank-eyed scientist; one of the embedded "experts." When forced to give a number, he had spat out, "Maybe seventy-five hundred. Maybe twenty thousand. There's no way to come to a number. Because of the virulence of the disease and the short incubation time, half of Wuhan may be infected."

And that hadn't even been the bad news. The expert was on much firmer footing when discussing the exponential growth in zombie numbers. With Shanghai as a model, he believed that the zombies would triple in numbers every hour. Weilei had met with the man three hours before and if his low guess of seventy-five hundred had been correct, they were currently facing over two-hundred thousand zombies in the heart of China. By morning that number would be in the tens of millions.

Containment had completely broken down and the chance of getting it back was essentially gone.

A third—the best third—of China's military had perished over the past three days. At least another fifth was mixed in with the refugees, meaning they were no longer considered viable. A stand had to be made somewhere and with every available soldier rushing helter skelter against the grain of the fleeing refugees, Weilei didn't think it would be more than a symbolic stand.

"The situation is...precarious," he lied to the committee.

"We all know that it's far worse than precarious," the General Secretary said. "Do you have plans to defend the capital?" Weilei said that he did. "And the rest of China?"

Before he could answer, the Premier snorted, "Of course he has plans. There's a plan for everything, perhaps even this. The only question that I want answered is: will you win?" The old man had cloudy eyes and yet seemed to look right through Weilei. "That's what I thought," the Premier whispered, sitting back in his chair. "We should clear the room."

A long sigh escaped the General Secretary before he agreed. With a nod, an aide began snapping his fingers and shooing the lesser officials out into hall beyond. In the hubbub, Weilei was gestured to come forward. He stood at attention before the three men, his spine straight and stiff as steel.

"I want you to be completely honest with us," the Premier said, softening his tone. "Do we have any chance of saving the capital?"

The mood in the streets was one of panic. It was no secret that the army had been defeated and that nukes had been used. And it wouldn't be long before it was leaked that there were still zombies on the loose. When that happened, Weilei suspected that there would be a complete break-down in civilization. It would be every man for himself.

"I believe it's doubtful. We haven't been able to rally the outlying provinces as we had earlier. The peasants are far more willing to risk the execution squads and, in a number of instances, they've turned on the squads themselves. Also, we have begun to see the first instances of Scenario 16, only in reverse, of course."

Scenario 16 was the theorized situation in which the pressure of overwhelming numbers of refugees led eventually to an unstoppable chain migration as the resources of each province were wiped out by ravaging waves of out of control peasants. The scenario envisioned a north to south path, kicked off by a Soviet invasion. In this case, the direction was on an opposite track.

"In response, we have fortified a number of rivers in the…"

"So, your answer is no, you can't save the capital," the Premier barked, cutting him off.

Ever the politician, the General Secretary patted the old man's hand. "He is trying his best." He gave Weilei a smile that didn't touch his dark eyes; they glittered like wet coal, a terrible secret behind them. "Would it be possible if nuclear weapons were involved?"

Weilei leaned back, suddenly nervous. "But we have shot our load, so to speak, in that regard. Even if we were to empty our reactors and use dirty bombs it would be too little, too late."

"We are not talking about dirty bombs," the General Secretary said. The smile was gone. "We are talking about full-use nuclear weapons. With these, could you protect the capital?"

All three men were staring intently at him. This wasn't a joke or a hypothetical, which begged the question: how many nuclear bombs did they have squirreled away? And where? After clearing his suddenly dry throat, he gave a measured response. "Yes. If enough of them were used. I should warn you that if other measures are used, lesser measures that is, saving the city would be only temporary."

"Explain," the Premier ordered.

"The menace is not only aimed at Beijing. The entire Yangtze watershed has been affected. Unless most of Hunan, Hubei, Jianxgi, and parts of Shandong providences are…" His throat was now so dry he could barely swallow—he was about to advocate killing upwards of four-hundred million people. "If these, uh lands are not similarly treated, then we can expect the capital will fall eventually."

With amazing indifference, the Premier asked, "And how many nuclear bombs would that take?"

Disgust finally weakened Weilei's rigid position and he turned his head to stare directly at the Premier. He answered glibly, "Depending on their size, fifteen hundred, give or take." It was an impossible number and yet the three old men didn't bat an eye. This made no sense because no one had that many nukes except…suddenly, Weilei understood where they were planning on getting their nukes from. "The Russians? You're going to ask the Russians to bomb us?"

"No," the Premier answered. "We would never do that. You are going to do it. This is the punishment for your failure. Draw up the plans and don't skimp on your estimate. This will be our only chance. You will meet with the Soviet...I mean the Russian Ambassador at six, sharp."

Weilei, soon to be the architect of the greatest mass murder in history, was dismissed and he left the room pale and trembling.

When the door shut, the General Secretary dropped his head for a moment, tired beyond his sixty-seven years. If China survived, she would be a shadow of her former self. She would be vulnerable and weak. Her greatest ports destroyed, her rivers boiling with radiation, the heart of her ripped out. How soon would it be before the hated Russians came to pick over her bones?

And what of the Japanese and the traitors on Taiwan? They would all swoop in and take a piece until there was nothing left but the scraps.

He turned to the one man who had yet to speak. Since he was only a minister, he did not officially belong at the table, but some matters of protocol were best ignored in time of crisis. His name was Jia Yun and he was the Minister of State Security. He was the Chinese equivalent of the head of the CIA.

The General Secretary explained what he wanted and then asked, "Can it be done?"

Yun had been a spy since the age of twelve. Cool beyond his years, he had got his step whispering information concerning Chairman Mao's fourth wife, Jiang Qing. What the General Secretary had in mind was child's play for him. "It will be my intense pleasure," he said, a sly fox's grin making his wisp of a mustache curl.

Chapter 13
1-12:23 p.m.
New Rochelle, New York

General Axelrod came back into the conference room, grumbling under his breath and slamming the door behind him. He glared around the room until his eyes fell on Courtney Shaw.

"Who does she think she is!" It wasn't a question, or if it was, he left no time for anyone to answer him. "Since when does a civilian have the brass balls to even think they can order about a three-star general?" Courtney got midway through a shrug—lifting her shoulders—before he went on, "She dismissed me! Me! Like I was some sort of servant."

In fact, it had been worse than that. The little slip of a woman had the audacity to actually suggest he "run along to the kitchens" and fetch her something to eat. Axelrod had turned red in the face and was so apoplectic that spit flew from his lips as he pointed to the ceiling. "We have drones hunting us and you want a fucking sandwich!"

"Or a salad," she had answered with unbelievable cool. "A Cobb salad would be nice."

He had exploded in a string of partial curses before he could manage to control his tongue. He then snarled, "What about her?"

Axelrod was referring to Anna, who had made a nest of sorts and was trying to sleep. Thuy went back to her notes, saying, "I would never put anything in my mouth if she's handled it. She's poisoned people before."

This took some of the steam out of the general, though he still wasn't going to play waiter even if a sandwich sounded good at the moment. Seeing Courtney sitting meekly at the tenth-floor conference room table, blowing on a mug of coffee, had brought the anger rising again.

"I-I'm sure she was busy," Courtney began. "It can't be easy. The cure rests squarely on her..."

"She told me to talk to you," Axelrod added, the glare making Courtney feel like a fly with a rolled-up newspaper looming over her. "She said you were going to come up with a plan."

Now everyone was staring at her. "I-I told her that I couldn't. I swear. There aren't even pilots to talk to."

"Sure, there are," Major Palmburg told her. "The drones have cameras and instruments the same as any plane. The pilots are probably sitting in fancy leather recliners out in Nevada. But they don't really matter if we can't intercept their signals. It's not like you'll be able to guilt a drone pilot. Trust me, his C.O. is probably sitting in the same room with him."

Courtney had a vision of a few scruffy guys in Cheeto-stained camo sitting around playing video games—these types couldn't be reasoned with. They were too far from the action. "But what about their boss?" Courtney asked. Just like Axelrod, she wasn't looking for an answer to her question. She dropped into her chair and fired up her laptop, tracing the chain of command for the 30th Reconnaissance Squadron—Lieutenant Colonel Lorber, to the 432d Air Expeditionary Wing—Colonel Bell, to the 12th Air Force—Major General McPeak, to Air Combat Command—General Doss. From there it was the Pentagon—General Berrymore, the Secretary of the Air Force.

Next, she checked the names against her compiled list of political officers and, as far as she could tell, Doss had one, Berrymore had three and the rest didn't have any.

"General, I'm going to need you to call this guy, Colonel Bell." Axelrod came around the long table and hunched over her laptop like a flat-headed bear. "You'll be the deputy…

"There it is," Colonel Taylor said, in a whisper that was somehow both loud and harsh. The room went dead silent as everyone stared out the long window. To Courtney, the jet-black *Sentinel* was far less frightening than she had anticipated. It looked like a much smaller version of a stealth bomber. It was maybe sixty feet long and was so compactly thin that it couldn't possibly hold any missiles or bombs. It didn't even have a machine gun as far as she could tell.

Still, there was something eerie and alien about it; something deadly. Perhaps because of the thickness of the glass, it seemed to glide past the R&K Building in effortless silence.

As if they were mice and it a hawk, no one moved as long as it was in sight. When it banked away, Courtney wilted back in her chair, sweat tingling along her scalp.

"Don't just sit there, damn it!" Taylor snapped. "They could be dialing up a missile any second."

"It's true," Major Palmburg said. "They aren't quiet about their Reapers. There are two loitering within about fifteen minutes of here."

She had no idea what a Reaper was, but it didn't sound pleasant. "Okay, then we have to work fast. General, I need you to be this guy, General Shunneson. He's the Deputy Commander of Air Combat Command. I'll call through to the 12th Air Force and if I can't get them to change the, uh, flight of these things, then I'll put you on. Try to act embarrassed."

"Why would I be embarrassed?" He felt like some dippy actor asking what his "motivation" was.

"Because you have to go through all this rigamarole. Tell them that you've been waiting on Doss' PO for half an hour and that we're in danger of losing the trail."

"Trail?" He was terrible at lying and now he was being asked to impersonate a junior officer as well. *Was that a crime?* he wondered.

Courtney was furiously clacking at her computer and for a moment she forgot she was talking to a general. "Yes, the trail! Us. They're after us, remember? You need to tell them that you have intel that we're in New York City. Okay, ready?" She didn't wait, and hit the send button on the phone.

"Hello, this is Marylin Kane, political officer for General Shunneson, Deputy Commander of Air Combat Command. I need Colonel Bell, asap. Hold? You have exactly one minute to get him on the line."

"Make it faster," Taylor hissed in that un-whisper of his. "The *Sentinel* is coming back!"

Axelrod started to look, but Courtney grabbed his arm and shook her head. She needed him focused. Holding up a finger, she snapped, "Finally. This is Marylin Kane, political officer for General Shunneson, Deputy Commander of Air Combat Command. I have PO number 6558, authenticated at 1143 hours. You need to shift all surveillance aircraft south of the New York City area, immediately."

She paused, listening, then repeated, "That's the 44th's search area?" She shrugged at Axelrod, not knowing exactly what to say. He held out a hand. "Hold for the General," she said, quickly and covered the mouthpiece.

Just then, Major Palmburg announced in an expressionless voice, "Someone just vectored a Reaper our way."

With his heart thumping madly in his chest, Axelrod took the phone. "Who is this? And don't tell me this is another political officer. Bell? Thank God. I feel like I'm being fucking babysat over here. The damn Pentagon is crawling with these officious pricks…"

"Langley," Courtney whispered. "He's at Langley."

"ETA on the Reaper is four minutes," Major Palmburg warned, adding to Axelrod's anxiety.

"And Langley's even worse," Axelrod said, quickly. "No one can make up their minds and when they do, they change 'em again five minutes later. And you know who has to scramble around like an idiot?" There was a pause and then Axelrod replied. "Yep, and here I am doing it again. The orders from on high have changed again." He didn't know his next line and had to pause while Courtney scribbled. He read over her shoulder: "The 44th is being shifted south, so we need you to pick up the slack. You'll be covering, covering a box encompassing Trenton, Wilmington, Lancaster, and Allentown."

Another pause. "Hell yeah, it's a big area. No, I can't authorize the release of any more *Sentinels*." Courtney could hear a tiny voice curse. "Sorry, Bell. Yes, immediately," Axelrod replied. "Cancel all current operations. Okay, I gotta go. My babysitter is glaring at me."

Actually, Courtney was chewing on a nail, looking like she was about to drop a litter of kittens in her chair. The moment Axelrod hung up, everyone turned to the window again.

"A Reaper at its cruising altitude could release its GBU-12 at any moment," Major Iler said. When Courtney craned her head up, he chuckled. "You'd never see it coming. It would be on a glide path and would take a minute or two to get here."

"Then we have at least a minute to keep working," Axelrod said. "Might as well make it count."

2-12:36 p.m.
Newville, Pennsylvania

The first elements of the 3rd Infantry Division swept along the entire three-mile width of Cumberland Valley. Over two hundred M1A1 Abrams came on in a line with the inevitability of the sun. Each of these monsters weighed 68 tons and were the most feared pieces of machinery on land. Along with their 120mm main gun, they sported a .50 caliber heavy machine gun and two 7.62mm medium machine guns. They could roar into battle at over forty miles an hour and were impervious to most anything short of a direct artillery strike.

Mixed in with the tanks were a few hundred infantry fighting vehicles: Strykers for the most part, but there were also six dozen Bradleys, which looked like smaller versions of tanks, sporting a nasty .30 caliber chain gun.

The division also had some stodgy old M113s, most with only the archaic and poky Browning M2 as their weapon. The M2 was nothing more than a scaled-up version of John Browning's M1917 .30 caliber machine gun developed in World War 1; they even used the same timing gauges as they had a hundred years before. Still the Browning M2 was reliable, accurate at a long range, and they had immense stopping power. A single bullet could tear through the breastbone of a zombie, rip out its heart and explode its spinal column.

Even a zombie would have trouble surviving that.

Interspersed among all these titans were a veritable swarm of Humvees. None of these were open or soft top and they all had some sort of weapon jutting from the roof. There were M2s, M240s, MK19grenade launchers, and even some with six-barrel miniguns.

And finally, draped on all these vehicles looking like camouflaged parasites, were hordes of soldiers each with fresh Georgia tans. All told, six-thousand men and women took up positions along the west side of the north-south running Centerville Road.

The other half of the division was spread thinly in the hills and forests to the east, guarding his right flank. His left flank, dug in along the face of the next valley over, was held by a Kentucky National Guard brigade that had been talked into joining the 3rd ID by the "Angel of the Airways," as many people had begun to refer to Courtney Shaw. On the Pentagon and White House battle maps, it was listed as Mil-BTL, making them believe it was a civilian force of battalion size and as such, it didn't even rate a political officer.

Judging by the recon photos, he didn't expect a giant surge of undead from that direction, but Major General Thomas Cannan had been studying the reports from the previous battles and knew he couldn't be too careful. Lancaster, Pennsylvania had been lost because a hundred or so zekes had managed to cross the Conestoga River and instead of dealing with the tiny breakthrough, a militia company had fled leaving a gaping hole in their flank.

"No. It's far better to be prepared," he muttered under his breath. "Like a filthy boy scout." His driver, a headquarters sergeant, who felt he had lucked into the cushiest job in the military, pretended not to hear, just as he had all day. "Where is Colonel Broadhurst?" This was another mumble. Somewhat unexpectedly, he threw open the door to his command Humvee. Mumbling wasn't the only bad habit the sergeant had to deal with. If they were going slow enough, the general would step right out of the Humvee without the least warning.

He enjoyed watching his useless political officer scramble to catch up. "Broadhurst, when will the Middle Spring line be ready?"

Colonel Kev Broadhurst was in the next Humvee and was prepared for the question he'd been dreading. "Not until four at the earliest, sir. The engineer companies are for shit. They're still off-loading their equipment. It's a complete cluster fuck."

"Do I relieve Heddles?" Cannan asked aloud.

"I wouldn't, at least not right now," Broadhurst answered. "His XO may also be inept. And besides, he might blossom under pressure. In Mosul…"

The division PO spoke over him in a shrill voice, "Firing people is not in either of your purviews. I decide who gets canned." The woman's name was Courtney Vertanen; she had been handpicked by the President to keep the 3rd ID in check. The President had even listened to her, concerning rank—unbelievably to Cannan, she was wearing a pair of pristine ACUs with three silver stars pinned to her collar.

By Presidential order, POs were now a rank *above* the officers they were supposed to be reporting on. In Cannan's view, it was a dangerous, dangerous situation.

"Sure, missy," Cannan said before walking back to his Humvee and telling the driver to get moving. He didn't move fast enough and the "three-star hunk of PO" as Cannan referred to Vertanen both in a mumbling tone and completely out loud, was able to jump in.

Vertanen began to fume at almost being left behind, again, only to be cut off by Cannan. "Your role here is not advisory and nor is it in any way a leadership position. You're something like a telephone wire. I speak in one end and you relay my message to the person I want answers from on the other. That's it. Now if…"

The first thump of artillery sent goosebumps across his flesh. It was always this way when he went into battle. He had been a wet-behind-the-ears lieutenant in the first Gulf War, racing his platoon of M1 Abrams across the sands and thinking nothing could touch him. Now, twenty-six years later, he had the same sensation.

"To the front!" The sensation was doubly pleasurable as he watched General PO's face go the color of chalk.

There wasn't much to see at the front. The artillery was landing three miles away—in truth none of the shells actually landed since they were fused for airburst to cause maximum casualties. Still, it was good for the men to see their commanding officer walking among them unafraid.

His normal jokes about food, sleep and broads wouldn't cut it now that battle was in the offing, so he made sure to find only compliments to give. Now was not the time to point out a zigzagging gig-line or a haircut that wasn't quite regulation. Now was the time to fire them up.

He spent an hour touring the line, which wasn't a line at all, as it didn't run along a linear path from one point to another. He wasn't a stickler for such simple things. What mattered to him was that his men had clear fields of fire. If the line had to loop around a barn or a little pocket of homes, then that was the way it was.

Of equal importance to him was that their avenue of retreat was clear. He had no plans to wreck his division for an empty town, a town of such little consequence that none of the residents had cared enough to stay and help defend it.

His soldiers were ready to fight, but what about the rest? At the end of the line, he turned and, as he expected, his Humvee was right there. Cannan was back on the phone, ignoring the PO completely as her voice rose almost to a screech concerning "priorities." He could care less what she felt was a priority. Just then it was precision logistics that was a priority; they would lose unless each man always had bullets to shoot, food in his belly, and gas in his tank.

From an officer's point of view, logistics came first, communication second and unit coordination third. Taken together, these things meant the difference between winning and losing. And they did not happen because one idiot in Washington wished it. These things happened because of constant training, attention to detail, and years of experience.

It was why the political officer's rank was so galling to Cannan. It wasn't just that those stars were an affront to everything he and his men had worked so hard for, they were also a sign that the snake was withering from the head down.

The PO, somehow making her camouflaged uniform look frumpy, glared as he rattled off orders. The glare was shaken out of her as a flight of Apaches roared overhead. Strange to Cannan, she looked nervous instead of thrilled. "Doesn't she understand this was the fun part of it all?" he muttered. "When I saw my first…" The sudden thundering appearance of thirty F-15 Strike Eagles made speech impossible.

The F-15s easily overtook the buzzing helicopters, passing over the top of them along the same line. *Brumm! Brumm! Brummmmmm!*

The valley shook with the violence left in the wake of the F-15s, which rocketed out of there, breaking into two elements. They curved away effortlessly into the sky and in seconds they were loitering at five-thousand feet, waiting as their next run was being plotted.

Now it was the Apaches turn. The helicopters stayed so low that they were hidden by the folds in the land. Gradually the explosions from their underwing missiles rippled back to the front line, going on for the next minute. Cannan grinned, reassured by the sound. "I say we go a little further," he said, and with one arm out the window, he smacked the side of the Humvee, making Vertanen jump.

"Wait, where are we going?"

"Just a little closer, you know, to see our enemy face to face."

Her face was the color of old cheese as the driver eased the Humvee between a pair of sharp-nosed Strykers, rolled down an embankment and set off across a fallow field. He glanced up as the Apaches came roaring back, barely fifty feet over their heads. Higher up, the first flight of four F-15s were banking around, setting up their next bombing run. Although his heart had begun to triphammer, the sergeant pretended not to even notice them.

"Shit," Vertanen whispered. She had her head craned up at an angle so she could see the F-15s swooping down like dragons. "What if they miss?"

Normally Cannan would have said something to reassure the woman; she was a civilian after all and he knew that his job, his one ultimate directive, was to protect the weak. Deep down this was the essence of a true American soldier. And this woman was terribly weak, and she represented the weakest president that had ever disgraced the Oval Office.

"Thank God I never voted for that dumb fuck," he muttered as the jets released their bombs and shot overhead, rocking the Humvee on its springs. "Green this, green that, pathetic. Diversity for the sake of diversity. What a bunch of miserable…" The valley in front of them was suddenly lit by brilliant explosions and when the sound pulsed over them, it came with a wave of heat. "What a bunch of bullshit," he finished loudly.

When they came to a rise, Cannan tapped the sergeant at the wheel on the shoulder. More bombs fell half a mile in front of them. The power of the cluster munitions was shocking and yet some of the zombies had managed to live through the holocaust. They were close enough that their horrible inhumanity could be both seen and felt on a gut level.

Beyond this first straggling line and beyond the fields of fire and smoke was a grey horizon—millions of zombies were swarming over the remains of Harrisburg, Mechanicsburg, and only a few miles away, Carlisle and the Army War College, where Cannan had been a guest speaker for three semesters.

"Dead on," Cannan muttered, nodding appreciably. "Those fancy little pilots know a thing or two about…" A new roar drowned him out and all three of them stared up as the F-15s made their final run straight at the horde, dropping lines of bombs, killing thousands. The millions simply marched over their burning bodies.

The closest of the dead were only the length of a football field away and Vertanen was eyeing them nervously. She pretended she wasn't afraid. She knew she was being tested. She knew that Cannan was trying to scare her off, but she had been appointed by the *President,* and no two-bit general—in her D.C. skewed mind there seemed to be more generals than there were privates—was going to make her sit in the corner like some wayward child.

"Diversity *is* our strength," she quoted the President's favorite line. "I heard what you said earlier. It's the thinking of a neanderthal."

The driver's eyebrows shot up and he had to bite the inside of his cheeks to keep from smiling. He had seen General Cannan rip into people before and it was always highly entertaining

"Is that so?" Cannan asked, rounding on Vertanen.

"It's common knowledge."

"Too bad it's also grade-school bullshit. You D.C. pussies are always desperate for polls and consensus. It's almost like you're afraid to have an idea that differs from anyone else." The driver nearly snorted. With his underlying tan, he was a shade of brick from the effort of holding back laughter.

The snort had been loud enough to catch the general's attention. "Sergeant Farnham, do you have a quarter I could borrow?"

The sergeant had to take a long, slow breath before he could answer the general and even then, it came out somewhat strangled, "Yes sir." He fished a quarter from the pile of dusty change in the cupholder and handed it back to his CO, making sure not to look at the PO.

Cannan held it up. "Do you know the Latin words on it, Farnham?"

"Yes sir; E Pluribus Unum. Out of many one."

"Exactly fucking right!" Cannan cried, slapping his hands together. "Diversity isn't a strength, it's a weakness. Unity is strength. A unity of purpose is strength. A unified people is strength. Look out the window, Vertanen. That ain't Washington where everyone bickers and backstabs. That's the real world where there are real consequences to being weak. Do you get that?"

Vertanen nodded, feeling the sand erode from beneath her feet. "I do, but…"

"There are no buts in this. There are no exceptions. Look at our 'union.' We have fifty states going in fifty different directions. It's pretty damned diverse out there, wouldn't you say? And look at our politics. It's every man for himself. Now, look at our military. Until a few days ago we were a well-oiled fighting machine. Now what are we?"

Before she could answer, Cannan said, "We're broken. I don't blame you and I don't really blame the President. Blame doesn't fix the problem. The only way to fix the problem is to move forward—together, as a unit. As one. I need you to do your job and when you really get down to it, there is only one fundamental reason you're here."

"To ensure that you don't undermine the presidency."

"Exactly. And what's my fundamental job?"

Vertanen hesitated for a moment, unsure if this was a trick question. "To win," she answered.

Now it was Cannan's turn to hide a smile, though his would have been a rueful one. He didn't know if they had a chance in hell of winning. He'd been following the events in China with particular attention and it had not come as a surprise to him that a static defense, no matter how spectacular the Grand Canal had been, would end in anything but failure.

But the fact that the nukes had not destroyed every last zombie, had hit home shockingly. Since the beginning of the apocalypse he had thought that if all else failed he could turn to a nuclear option. Now that seemed out the window and so was his complete confidence in his ability to actually win. But he would try. He would do everything in his power to win. It was the one reason he was a mile in front of his line, having a come to Jesus moment with his PO. Cannan needed the freedom to lead without everything being second-guessed along a chain of command that had no idea what the true tactical situation was.

"Exactly!" he cried. "My job is to win, and there's only one way we can win this battle and that's if I have a free hand. In war, seconds can mean the difference between victory and defeat. And you've seen how long decisions can take."

"But the rules…"

"Damn the rules! If you trust yourself and your instincts, your superiors will as well. Watch." His command vehicle was equipped with the latest tech in communications. With the punch of two buttons, he was able to reach a real three-star general, the 2nd Corps Commander, Lieutenant General Leonard.

"Sir, I have the enemy in front of me. My plan of battle is to destroy each and every one of them."

General Leonard had seen his divisions pulled apart as much by politics as by the dead; he had everything riding on the 3rd ID. If they failed, the entire western theatre would crumble. A part of him wanted to urge caution, only this was Thomas Cannan he was talking to. Suggesting caution would have resulted in laughter.

"Do whatever it takes to destroy them," Leonard said, heavily.

"I will, sir. I'll show the world what a fully prepared and fully independent American infantry division can do. And it will be glorious!" He hung up and turned to Vertanen. "See how simple that was? Now trust yourself and trust me. You know that you don't need to question every one of my orders. And you know I didn't drag my ass all the way up here to lose. We're here with the same purpose. Let's bury the past and start fresh."

He put out his hand, which in itself was a testament to how desperate he was to win.

She had been raised to distrust the military and that distrust had been deepened in college where she had delved into every conspiracy theory put forth. And yet, almost against her will, she shook the general's hand. They had a common enemy that didn't care one wit about ideology and fact-checkers, who was right four elections ago, and all the rest. Just then all of that felt like crap.

The handshake was strangely affectionate, especially since their common enemy was bearing down on them, eager to kill. It was affectionate because at that moment, they both remembered they were Americans first.

Chapter 14
1-1:09 p.m.
Grafton, Massachusetts

Lieutenant Colonel Troy Ross would have found General Cannan's idea that a static defense was untenable somewhat funny, since the ragged, bearded Army of Southern New England had clung to the sickly Quinsigamond River with a grim tenacity.

Win or lose, the river would never recover. It was a horrid desolation that the men had christened the *Black Bog*. The entire western bank was no longer a bank at all. It was an alien landscape made up of blood-filled craters. Corpses and parts of corpses by the tens of thousand were half-sunk and scattered as far as the eye could see in the man-made black marsh. The very air had been tortured by explosions and was filled with a nasty, unwholesome smoke.

Through it, the men stared out on the once pretty landscape. Gone were the fields of flowers that reminded so many of the of English meadows. Gone were the red-painted barns and the sad willows.

"I hate this," Clarren said to Ross. He couldn't tear his eyes from the scene. The craters, like tremendous bowls, were half-filled with black sludge. Their sides were so slick with blood that they acted like traps from which the zombies couldn't escape. Hundreds of the fiends were struggling in these pits and if ever one finally made it out, it would simply fall into the next. From a certain point of view, it was comical; no one laughed.

No one had the energy to laugh. For the time being, the battle had ended. With fake PO authorization numbers fed to him by Courtney Shaw, Ross had acted as the brigade's fire support team and directed the division's artillery with deadly precision. It was the only thing that kept the line from being overrun. But even with him using every available artillery shell within twenty miles, the fight had been a close one.

Many men had been down to their last few bullets before the tide turned and the wave of zombies had dried up. Exhausted, the soldiers fell asleep one by one. Ross had been in the middle of his own catnap when Clarren found him. He had come back from "Battalion Headquarters" a changed man. Not so much outwardly since he'd been quiet and drawn since coming to the line in the dark of the morning, but inwardly. It was one thing as Governor to order men to fight for their state and their families, knowing that many of them would die. It was quite another to do the killing personally.

It hurt. There was actual pain associated with executing a man, even one who was on the verge of changing over.

"Of course you hate this," Ross mumbled, pulling his ACU coat up to his chin and trying to find a more comfortable spot among the bramble. "What's there to like?"

"Nothing, I guess. Where am I supposed to be?" In the last few hours so much had changed that Clarren didn't know where he'd left his squad.

Ross cracked an eye. "It would be great if you could find some ammo for us. Oh, and wake me when the horde comes back our way."

Clarren squinted west at a column of smoke rising up in the distance. He could not have known it but the great mass undead was there, rampaging through the city of Worcester, four miles away.

A hundred or so patients hadn't been evacuated from Saint Vincent Hospital and for the last seven hours they had remained hidden on the third floor, watched over by four nurses who had refused to abandon them. Unfortunately, this dedication and selflessness on the part of the nurses was being accidentally undermined by some of the patients. A handful of them, led by the youngest of the patients, a gritty, determined woman named Dana Miller, were trying to make a break for freedom by taking an ambulance.

From the very start, Dana had decided that she wasn't going to be a victim in any of this. Full of piss and vinegar, she had gone south to defend her state, and for thirty hours, she had held her own, showing that she was as tough as any man. Then she'd been shot—pierced in all truth—by a huge hunk of depleted uranium, fired from the rotary canon of an A10 Thunderbolt. That same ugly plane had kept coming back time and again, looking as though it was breathing fire. It was low and slow, and everyone in sight shot at it. Lying there in a pool of blood, she could hear the whine of bullets bouncing off its thick titanium armor. In five passes, it had killed most of her company and sent the rest running.

Left for dead, it had taken her a day to crawl away from the border and now a day after that, she was sewn back together and barely able to walk. Her body felt like it was on the verge of coming apart, but she could think just fine and knew that the hospital was not a safe haven. The clear fact was that unless the zombies had some sort of expiration date and simply died on their own, everyone in the hospital would eventually be killed and eaten.

Dana wasn't going to go out that way. She would escape or die trying. With five others, none under seventy, they crept, and in Dana's case crawled down to the emergency room, found an ambulance, and made a mad getaway.

Since she could barely sit up, the driving was left to a man named Gene. Gene was recuperating from both a heart attack and a stroke. He had purple blotches running up and down his arms and a mid-line catheter tunneled through his chest and into the jugular vein in the neck.

But damn if he wasn't game. When the others held back, he stepped up.

In this case, although the mind was willing, the flesh was weak. The ambulance was something of a brute and far larger than anything Gene had driven in the last forty years. He misjudged how little room he had to work with and with a hellacious scream of metal, scraped the side of the bricked edge of the bay. The sound not only spooked a row of pigeons, which went winging away, it also caused every zombie within three blocks to turn and head their way.

"It's okay, Gene," Dana whispered, trying to reach over and pat his hand. "Just keep going. We can't stop."

He didn't have his hearing-aids in and was already stopping. "Oh, boy, this is no good. I have to straighten out. I got to get the angle just right. I had a station wagon once that was like tis. Long as a…"

"For fuck's sake, Gene!" another of the oldsters cried in thick Bostonian. "Yuh don't even hafta back up. Just point the fuckin' cah that way." He pointed through the windshield, and when Gene followed his hand, the first thing he saw was a walking corpse.

"It's one of them," Gene said in a useless stage whisper. In life, the zombie had been something of a stunted man. At just a few inches over five foot he'd had to endure three decades of bullying. As a zombie, it was terrifying. It charged up onto the canted hood of the ambulance and clung there like a deranged vampire.

161

Useless screams broke out in the ambulance. "Drive," Dana ordered. Gene did his best, which wasn't very good. He could barely see because of the zombie and decided to overcorrect his steering to keep from hitting the side of the bay a second time. Instead he ran up a curb and over a row of bushes. They hadn't been going very fast to begin with and now they were plowing along at a miserable four miles an hour.

Everyone was screaming the same thing: "Turn!" As though he were turning a tugboat, he went hand over fist and finally dropped down off the curb only to hit a car—his own car in fact. His wife had parked it near the emergency room four days before in the hope that Gene would be in and out of the hospital in time for her afternoon soaps.

It was just dawning on him that the 1999 Oldsmobile Cutlass was remarkably similar to his own, when the smallish zombie reared back a fist and starred the windshield.

"Christ almighty," Gene swore in frightened amazement, his heart giving a painful lurch in his chest.

"Back up!" everyone screamed.

These things used to be second nature to him, now it took some concentrating, especially since his heart was tweaking him something fierce with each beat, and he had broken out in a cold sweat that had nothing to do with the zombie. He peered down at the controls. The gear shifter was obvious, but where were the windshield wipers? Certainly getting smacked with windshield wipers would cream that monster's corn. There were four rows of buttons and toggles and he stared at them with little comprehension.

Dana grit her teeth, reached over and pulled the gear into reverse. She felt something give deep inside of her and when she tried to sit back up, she found she couldn't. Her strength left her and she slumped over the console.

"Go," she told him, but he was only starting to turn the wheel, while the zombie was raining blows on the windshield. Finally, he put his foot on the gas and the ambulance slewed backwards in a long curve, there were repeated and heavy thumps under the tires, each causing the console to leap up into Dana's chest. It pained her cruelly, and yet she did not regret it in the least.

We're getting away, she told herself. They weren't. Gene drove backwards in a wide, wide arc that took them in a complete half-circle and those thumps hadn't been more curbs as Dana guessed, they had been zombies.

When Gene finally tore his eyes from the scene playing itself out through his side window he squinted down and found the brake. The ambulance stopped, jarring them all back and forth. The little angry zombie had been flung off at some point; it was the only good news. In front of them were hundreds more. Gene began clicking his dentures. It was the only sound in the ambulance.

"What is it?" Dana asked, afraid that she already knew the answer. No one would answer her and she had to fight a wave of ghastly internal pain to sit up. "Oh God," she whispered at what was in front of them. "There's so many."

"Let us out!" one of the patients hissed banging the side of the ambulance.

"There's a door next to you, Gladys," Dana said. "Just pull the handle." She watched them pile out the back of the ambulance and crawl into some of the same sort of bushes that Gene had destroyed. Dana glanced over at Gene. He was grey in the face and sweating. "if you're going, you better hurry," she told him.

He shook his head. "I'm having another heart attack. It feels like I'm dying. What about you?"

"I can't run. I can't hardly even sit up. There is something we should do. For them and for the others." She pointed at the console to the toggle marked *Siren*. His eyes widened and then flicked away quickly. He was afraid of the zombies more than he had imagined he could be afraid of anything, and what she was suggesting could only end in the worst death imaginable. He didn't know if he could do it.

She understood his fear. "Look." She held up a scalpel she had taken from the crash-cart in her room. Next, she pulled aside a bandage on her upper chest. Beneath was a mid-line IV the same as his. "They said these go into my jugular. If I cut the tubes, it'll probably take about thirty seconds to bleed out."

Thirty seconds offered a glimmer of hope. If the windows and doors held up for that long, he'd be dead before he was even touched. "How far do you think we can get?"

"That's up to you. Just don't take your foot off the gas."

"I won't this time." He nodded at her, glanced at the scalpel, and then stabbed his foot down on the gas. At the same time, she flipped the siren on. The ambulance seemed to scream as it tore forward. For good measure, she tripped the lights. They were bright even in the midday sun.

The zombies in front of them cringed, moments before Gene plowed over them. "Faster!" Dana said in a shaky yell.

He was going as fast as he could. The converging zombies acted as speed bumps, causing the ambulance to buck like a bull, and slew left and right as if the tires were running through oil slicks. At one point, he started to go into a skid and they almost went over on its side.

Gene had lived in the northeast all his life and he knew how to fix a skid and he turned into it. This slowed their pace even more, which wasn't the worst thing since they were fast coming up on the ramp that led to the street. It curved down and around to the left.

"Hold on," he said to Dana, taking the turn as fast as he dared—it wasn't fast enough. At the bottom of the ramp was a mob of undead and there was nothing he could do but slam straight into them. He crushed the ones in front under his tires, and, as he did, the ambulance seemed to be climbing upward, and now the rear tires were spinning on rotting, grey flesh instead of concrete.

It killed their momentum as thoroughly as if they had run into pool of mud.

"Do it!" Gene cried in his tremoring old man's voice, as hands and fists began to tear at the ambulance and slam its windows.

"No! Keep going," she ordered.

He tried gunning the engine and hauling the wheels back and forth. Too late, he remembered that the vehicle had four-wheel drive. It took him a full six seconds of squinting around to find the switch and by then the rear doors were flung open.

"Dana!" He turned to her and nearly caught the scalpel in the eye. She was already coming at his mid-line IV.

"Hold still!" Her hands were weak and her first attempt at cutting the tubes failed. Gene had to guide her hands and help her saw through the line. His blood gushed out of the tube, pouring down the front of his hospital gown and strangely, he felt grateful.

She tried to cut through her own line, but the tubing was too thick. Behind them, thirty of the beasts were shoving themselves simultaneously through the open backdoor—she made the mistake of looking back, which drained what little strength she had.

"Gene, help me."

There'd be no help from Gene. His blood pressure was already bottoming out and he was gripped by what he thought was an odd malaise. Nothing seemed to matter and wasn't that strange when there were terrifying monsters fighting through the back of the ambulance?

They went for Gene first. His bright, clean blood was a lure that they couldn't resist. He was dragged out of his chair and pulled into the back and fought over. There was no struggle in him, or fear, or even much pain, except a dull echo as the fingers on his left hand were bitten off.

From the footwell of the passenger seat where she had slid in a last desperate attempt to hide, Dana heard him die and heard the beasts feasting on him. They would come for her next. Already the driver's side window had shattered and long grey arms were reaching in for her.

"Damn," she whispered, under the wail of the siren. She knew what she had to do and putting it off wouldn't make it any easier. After a deep breath, she closed her eyes and slit her own throat. Dana Miller did it right. There was no hesitation, no cringing, no second chances. The scalpel sliced through her carotid artery and the blood came fast and hot.

The wail of the siren did not let up and could be heard throughout the empty streets of Worcester. It called out to the undead and brought them flocking by the tens of thousands.

Seeing them coming was the final straw for the nurses trapped in the hospital. Collectively, their nerve broke and they too tried to make a dash for freedom. Sadly, they fared worse. One of them owned a Jeep Wrangler and because of its four-wheel drive, it was chosen as the getaway car. It didn't make it out of the parking lot. Compared to the ambulance, it was far too light and couldn't generate the same momentum.

The fourth zombie they hit nearly exploded the windshield. The safety glass held, even with half a body sticking through it. The fifth beast got caught up just under the grill and acted like a plow. The jeep no longer bounced over the dead, it built them up in front in a gory mound going slower and slower.

Seconds later, the nurses abandoned their escape and reversed back to the hospital, chased by hundreds of monsters. They fled inside and ran up to the third floor where they were trapped along with their patients. It was obvious that they wouldn't be trapped for long.

The zombies that had been attacking the Quinsigamond River, an estimated one million of them, were drawn to the hospital by the siren and soon they were assaulting the building itself. Doors were torn apart, windows were shattered; even the walls and bricks were attacked.

A Predator did a fly-by at one point and the pictures returned made even the toughest soldier shudder. Zombies buried the entire hospital. They looked like grey ants, undulating in a frenzied mound. Inside, the nurses did the only thing they could. Life support systems were shut off and mega-doses of drugs were given out like candy.

2-1:30 p.m.
The White House, Washington D.C.

Trista Price broke before either Heider or Phillips. She was a dragged-out, sniveling mess, and when Heider had his toes smashed with a hammer, she fled.

"For your sake, I'll edit that out," David Kazakoff said, pulling her into the next room. "Get yourself cleaned up before the President comes back. You know he hates weakness."

The President had changed a great deal in the last few days. Now, showing emotion, especially sympathy for those accused of treason, was considered a sign of affinity. If it went too far, collusion was thought to be a possibility. There was even talk of a double secret confederacy in which too little empathy would make one suspect.

The laughable "Face Crimes" proposed by George Orwell in *1984*, were no longer restricted to the realm of the fantastic. Everyone went about guarded, afraid that an errant smirk would be misconstrued.

"You need to stop," she whispered. "He's confessed over and over. That's all he's been doing."

"Yeah, but not to the right crimes." The President "knew" there was an overarching conspiracy with someone bigger than an ass-kissing nobody like Marty Aleman in charge. And because he "knew" it, proof had to be found. Heider, the old

Secretary of Defense, seemed like the right villain but when Kazakoff suggested it, the President waved the idea off.

There weren't too many people higher on the totem pole than Heider, at least that made sense.

"What about the Speaker of the House?" Kazakoff mused.

"You can't believe that!" Trista whispered. "She snuck out of town three days ago. Besides, she and the President go way back. They're in the same party, in case you've been living under a rock for the last five years."

Kazakoff laughed, gently. "I think the concept of parties is out the window and I couldn't be happier. All that in-fighting and hypocrisy made me sick."

"And this is better? He's gone crazy or he's getting there, and you're helping by feeding his paranoia. You should know better. You heard their confessions the same as me. The three of them kept everyone out of the loop."

The CIA asset gazed down at the girl; her tears had turned her almost into a child in his eyes. "Who would you replace him with? Like you said, the Speaker's bugged out. The Veep is even more of a pussy than the President. Do you want me to free Heider and let an admitted traitor take over the country? Trust me, once a general gets in power there's no getting them out again short of a civil war."

A part of her knew that he was right on one level, but on every other level he was dead wrong.

He reached out a hand to smooth down her blonde hair, saying, "No, we stick with the President. This is still America. If we win this thing, a president can be voted out. It'll be expected."

Trista didn't believe him, especially after Heider finally broke. It wasn't the torture that finally made him sign the confession the President wanted. Kazakoff eventually conceded that in Phillips and Heider, he was dealing with men of honor who would gladly accept any pain to retain that honor…as long it was themselves was being tortured.

When Kazakoff brought in their families, both broke immediately.

"All three of them implicated the Vice President," Kazakoff told the President, handing over the doctored video tapes and the signed confessions. His conversation with Trista had sprung the idea of using the VP as the scapegoat; the man was worthless otherwise.

"I knew it!" the President cried, his hands curled into fists, veins bulging on his neck. He turned to the David Blaise, Director of the FBI. "Find him. Find him and arrest him. I want him taken alive."

Blaise stood like a statue for a long moment, his mind rebelling against what was being asked of him. He knew deep down that there was no way the VP was part of this.

"Find him," the President repeated. "Or I'll find someone who will." The threat was clear and Blaise left, his face blank.

Kazakoff was thanked and then sent back into his torture chambers to extract more confessions; after all, there had been over eight hundred arrests so far and the number was growing by the hour, as the Political Officers began to feel their power.

Not long after this, Trista Price, made-up once again, was pulled aside by the man she worked for—she still couldn't remember his name or what her title was supposed to be. "I need you to do something important," he whispered. She didn't like how the sweat was beading up on his lip. "You've been working downstairs, right?" She nodded, already afraid of where this was going. "Good. Good. That's good. You should be used to all this by now. I'm going to need you to, uh oversee the uh, the first three executions."

Her mouth fell open.

"I already told the President and he's uh pleased as punch. So, okay we'll get this set up. Don't go anywhere."

Even if she wanted to refuse, it was too late. The President was… "Pleased as punch," she said in a strangled voice. Things, including executions, it seemed, were moving so quickly there was almost no time to even consider protesting.

A judge read the confessions, signed off on the death warrants and, before Trista could even find a suitable location, a squad of soldiers had been assembled. They were all younger than Trista; they looked like boys playing dress-up and she wondered if they would really pull the triggers when the time came.

If not, would she be blamed? Would she be suspected and arrested? Would she be the next one visited by Kazakoff?

She knew better than to do anything except what was ordered. There had been other interns who had come to the White House with her. Since coming up from the lower floor, she had already seen two of them in handcuffs.

Her mind was still spinning when Phillips, Heider and Marty Aleman were brought up. The two soldiers were bloody and bruised, but also defiant. Marty, although he seemed to have been hardly touched, whined, and cringed like an abused cur.

Trista began to argue that she wasn't ready and that she didn't even have a location yet. Inside the White House seemed horribly disrespectful and outside on the grounds was distasteful. A few vans could be found, she was sure, and driven to some remote location; a rusting old warehouse, empty save for the sinister rats and the dust, sprang to mind.

"It has to be now," her boss said, thrusting a tripod with a video camera attached at her. "The President is going to announce the executions during the two o'clock presser."

Down the hall, a hundred year old crystal-faced clock showed that it was eighteen minutes before two. "Shouldn't like a lawyer or someone from the Attorney General's office be doing this?"

Her boss had been somewhat handsome two days before. Now he was pinched and haggard. "You would think so, except most were either arrested or were fired for questioning the legality of this, so unless you want to join them, don't screw this up."

He ducked away before she could ask him where he wanted her to carry out the killing. There was a lot of ducking away going on. No one wanted to be a part of it; Trista most of all. She didn't have a choice.

"It has to be close and it has to out of sight. If the press finds out and follows us…" She didn't want to think about that. The only problem was that everything close to the White House was touristy. "But all the tourists have left!" Suddenly she knew where to go: The Smithsonian Museum. Many of the museums had below-ground galleries, and the closest of them, the Renwick, had a low basement. The year before, she'd been given a tour of the place by a randy guide who had hoped to score.

"Follow me," she ordered, handing over the tripod to one of the soldiers. Without looking at the prisoners, she set off through the West Wing in a rush. With his crushed toes, Heider couldn't keep up. He hobbled along and any insistence at hurrying was laughed at.

"Why on earth should I hurry?"

Trista couldn't think of a reason and so she ran ahead and yelled at the Secret Service agents gathered around the entrance until three black SUVs were brought around. It seemed like a waste since they only had a block and a half to travel. Time was against her. Eleven minutes left.

They were at the Renwick with a few minutes to spare. The execution squad let themselves inside the museum as one of the bigger soldiers shouldered in the front door, setting off an alarm that went ignored. Heider had to be carried down the stairs and Marty dragged, weeping. Phillips went down with his head held high, almost scraping the low ceiling of the basement. It was cold place with damp brick walls and less light than she remembered. Trista seemed more afraid than anyone, except for Marty, of course.

In the semi-dark Phillips face was carved by shadows so that he looked like his head belonged guarding a beach on Easter Island. "Your orders may be theoretically lawful," he said, moving to the closest of the walls, "but the man who's giving them is unhinged. Remember the 25th Amendment and do your duty." Only Trista knew what the 25th Amendment was. She dropped her eyes, knowing that he was right and worrying that fear would keep everyone from doing the right thing. Fear certainly controlled her. She had her excuses: her youth, her sex, her physical weakness. It was her moral weakness which was the real issue, and she knew it.

A check of her watch showed that she had only four minutes left. "I-I wish we had more time, you know, for last words or some sort of ceremony."

Heider was lifted to his feet. "Does it matter? Would any of you bother to remember what was said? Would you run the risk of recording it? I doubt it. You might as well just get it over with."

Marty Aleman had the opposite view of things and began to beg one of the soldiers who had a cigarette corked in his mouth. The soldier's head was held rigidly back and he was sucking so deeply on the Marlboro that Trista could see the outlines of his skull through his lean flesh.

"I'd like mine in the back of the head," Phillips said. When Heider agreed, Phillips helped his friend down, before dropping to his knees. Marty had to be thrown forward where he sat cross-legged, his back bowed, his hands over his face.

"I-I think a s-silent count of three should work," Trista said, "like this." She brought her hand down in a short chopping motion three times and on the last, shot a finger out.

There were seven soldiers. One worked the camera, while the others brought their weapons up, two aiming at each of the prisoners. "Safeties off," one said and they all checked their rifles.

"Ready?" Trista asked. They nodded and she began her quick count-down. On the third stroke, the guns went off and blood flew.

Two blocks away, a grim, solemn President stepped in front of his podium and sighed. "Before we get to the military briefing, I have to announce a grave situation that has been unfolding for the last few days. It saddens me to say that there has been a coup attempt made against my presidency by members of the military and led by the Vice President. Sadly, this entire, unfortunate situation was their brain child. These 'zombies' were a concoction developed by the military industrial complex."

A hundred questions were shouted at him at once. Rather than answering any of them, he said, "I have had the confessions of the three top conspirators emailed to each of you." The President hid his smile as the reporters danced to his tune and quickly unlimbered laptops or pulled out cellphones. They read the confessions and, as with most people, the reporters believed almost everything set down in writing. Marty Aleman would have been so proud as the reporters began to look up, eager for more.

Chapter 15
1-2:11 p.m.
Newville, Pennsylvania

Major General Thomas Cannan orchestrated his own dance. He had great and terrible weapons at his disposal, and he had to hold back on the eager desire to unleash them all in one great outpouring of volcanic rage. No, he had to husband his resources.

This war was one of attrition and if he had any chance of winning this particular battle, he had to make every shot count. His batteries of howitzers were twinned with small, hawk-sized battlefield drones that darted far in front of the lines searching out the largest concentrations of the dead. The positions were radioed to the howitzer crews and seconds later huge shells ripped through the sky overhead. The vast explosions tore great bloody swathes through the advancing zombie army.

Next came the A10s and the Apaches, cutting across the open valley at angles, blasting lanes through the beasts and further chopping up the army.

The gathered political officers watched the drone feeds, shook their heads and looked to Courtney Vertanen, who was sour-faced, her lips pursed as if she were sucking the seeds out of a lemon.

Cannan, who saw the looks, growled in that undertone way of his, "Fucking nervous nellies."

"We're not nervous," Vertanen lied. "These tactics just don't make sense." She pointed at one of the battle progression monitors. "Wouldn't it be smarter for those planes to cut across the *front* of the zombies? And the artillery is firing at parts of the zombie army that won't be here for half an hour."

"That's because in half an hour we'll still want to be here and fighting," he explained. "Remember, you were going to trust that I have a method to my madness? The warthogs and the gunships are doing exactly as I have asked them. We actually want to leave some of them unharmed. This division…*our* division, is a combined arms unit. We can engage and destroy the enemy coming and going, only as long as all the parts work together as a team and at their peak efficiency."

Cannan could see that although that sounded nice, none of the POs really believed it. They were all Washington ass-kissers, and their main goals had always been career advancement—they were self-oriented and couldn't see past the tips of their noses.

He tried again, "The idea is that if we purposely allow some zombies through each zone of the battlefield, they'll eventually hit the line in manageable numbers. We believe that the line will hold under the pressure of up to four thousand zombies per linear mile."

This admission had every one of the political officers glaring at Vertanen. "Four thousand at a time?" she asked, trying to keep up a casually brave appearance, and failing miserably. "That seems like way too many. Perhaps you should start with two-thousand."

"A little late for that, I think," Cannan answered. The defensive line bulged outward, almost in the exact center where a small community had been built up around Big Springs High School and Big Springs Middle School. The general had made sure to keep the monitors showing that section of the line turned away from the gaggle of political officers.

Now he put it on the largest monitor and they all saw the zombies bearing down on this salient.

"Have you ever seen a waltz?" he asked. "There's all these dancers turning and spinning, and you'd think they go crashing into each other, but they don't. This is just like a waltz. It's all about control. Trust me, every soldier out there wants to just start blasting away. Our job is to control them, and by doing so, we control the battle."

He pointed to the screen where the soldiers were waiting pensively, many of them chain smoking cigarettes right down to the filters.

When the beasts were seven hundred meters away, the mortars were cued and smaller explosions began to land among the undead. Although many were killed, the explosions had the added effect of causing eddies within the advancing army. Sometimes the undead would flock in towards where the explosion took place and at others they went in circles, chasing smoke.

At five hundred meters, the tank commanders finally got their turn. From the start, they had wanted to unleash their steel monsters into the horde, knowing that the Abrams could not be stopped by a thousand of the creatures or even ten thousand. But they could be stopped, Cannan knew.

173

"Go," Cannan relayed to his armored units. Most people thought of the M1A2 Abrams as a tank killer, first and foremost, but it was also deadly against infantry. The usual antitank M829A2 round that could be fired at ranges of up to 3,000 meters had been left behind. The tanks only carried M1028 canister rounds, which were anti-personnel/anti-helicopter munition that were packed with over 1,000 tungsten balls. These turned mobs of zombies into a field of black goo with one blast.

They were a hit among the infantry men who cheered and laughed as half an acre at a time were mowed down with each shot.

And still zombies got through by the thousands. At three hundred meters the fifty-caliber machine guns, firing in short bursts at head height, began to bring down their share; next were the M60s and M240s. And so on until at fifty meters the individual soldiers on the line got their turn.

The thin crackle of the M4s and M16A4s reached the command post seconds later. "And that is our waltz," Cannan said, "or at least the beginning of it. Logistics will be next and that's always something that needs to be worked out on the fly. In practice situations we know the roads like the back of our hands and they're always wide open. The reality is far different. Refugees clogging everything up; drivers getting lost or getting in accidents, bombs falling in the wrong places making craters. But it'll work out, if you trust me, Vertanen."

She snuck a peek back at the monitor where the line soldiers were taking well-aimed measured shots. Some fired from behind cars or fences and in some cases, sitting on rockers on the front porches of houses. At the moment, everything seemed just as the general had said: controlled.

"I trust you," she said, causing a few eyebrows to shoot up among the political officers gathered near her. Like a mother duck, she shooed her flock away from the circle of command vehicles. "We will trust them, but we'll also verify. Got it? We don't have to challenge every order, just the ones that don't make sense."

Vertanen released her minions, most of whom were under twenty-eight, to watch over men who had spent that long in uniform learning to command armies. They followed her command: trust but verify, and things moved along amazingly.

While the howitzers kept up a steady drumbeat of background thunder, the jets rumbled overhead, coming in intervals that a man could set his watch by. When the tanks let off their canisters of grape shot, there was a crackle like a hundred firecrackers going off at once. The fifty-cals sounded like jackhammers, making the M4s sound like toys.

Mixed in with this was the endless sound of trucks; the grinding of gears and growl of engines. The 3rd ID's supply train was forty miles long and stretched to Hagerstown, Maryland where the little airport boasted a seven-thousand foot runway.

Boeing C17s landed every five minutes, unloading 160,000 pounds of material per plane.

As every logistics officer knew, this was where the real dance occurred. The timing, from the off-loading, to the refueling, to the next take off had to be precise. Any breakdown in the system could be the deciding factor in battle, especially when there was no expected let-up in the fight. There would be no time for anyone to stop and catch their breath, at least not in the foreseeable future.

Thankfully, the support brigade's political officer was suffering from a migraine and was out of the loop. This allowed for the entire division to be fully provided for, no questions asked. No questions included the Kentucky guard brigade.

Cannan envied them. The brigade was headquartered just over the western hills in Blain, Pennsylvania and was tasked with holding Sherman's Valley. It was wide open farmland bracketed on the north and south by steep wooded ridges. Their battle consisted mainly of destroying the spillage of zombies pouring across the Susquehanna River around Harrisburg.

Whenever Cannan checked the drone feeds, it looked as though the Kentuckians were at the range getting in some practice, instead of fighting an actual battle.

And that was alright. It would allow the guardsmen to gain a feel for battle in a semi-controlled atmosphere. Cannan figured that they would be primed in eight hours or so, at which point he would switch them into the main line of battle to give his men a rest.

Even the engineer battalion had managed to pull their collective heads out of their asses and were in the process of creating a wonderfully straight fallback position. Bulldozers were, even then, flattening homesteads, silos and barns, while backhoes were digging a ditch three miles long across the valley.

Everything was going so swimmingly that Cannan didn't like it. He turned to his XO. "I don't want to rain on everyone's parade, but *something* is going to go wrong. Find out what. Find the weak link."

The XO had that same feeling, but try as he might, he couldn't see any thread that was coming unraveled.

His problem was that he wasn't looking in the right location. The problem lay a hundred miles away in Washington DC. The President sat looking at some of the same drone feeds that Cannan was watching. He drummed his manicured fingers on the gleaming tabletop, his eyes flicking from one monitor to the next. He was antsy, although exactly why eluded him.

According to the reports—the true reports, now—the lines seemed to have stabilized. Somehow Boston was hanging on, Long Island was being fortified and although upstate New York had been lost to the Mohawk River, no one cared about Albany anyway. Finally, and most importantly, Washington DC was safe at the cost of the total destruction of Baltimore and the quarter of a million people who'd been trapped there.

Those people had been a sacrifice he'd been willing to make.

Even the minor instances of rebellion had been reversed or were on the verge of being stomped out—supposedly. General what's-his-name in Illinois was less than a day away from discovering what being on the receiving end of an angry American infantry division was like.

The 4th ID out of Fort Carson Colorado had finally got on the move and had been pelting east. Springfield was only a slight detour. Once there, they were under orders to wipe out any opposition and arrest any surviving leaders. Easy-peasy. The President had been assured by all of his new military advisors that if there was a fight, it would be over in minutes.

After what had happened in Massachusetts, he didn't believe it. Those damned Bostonians had fought like devils, while his own soldiers had fought him almost as hard as they had fought the enemy. They were still fighting him. He knew it on a gut level. Why else would it take an infantry division…a mechanized infantry division, two days to go fewer than seven hundred miles? The 4th ID was dragging their feet. They were making excuses. General Cardenas claimed refugees and acts of sabotage were slowing him down and that, because they were picking up Guard and Reserve regiments as they steamed east, their logistics plan had gone out the window.

The President didn't give a damn about logistics. It was all mumbo jumbo, all smoke and mirrors designed to confuse him.

"A trillion dollars a year and they can't drive across three states!" he muttered. "They still don't respect me." That was the truth. He saw it in their eyes. With a snap of his fingers, his new Chief of Staff came running across the room where he'd been whispering with the generals in a little huddle. *Plotting, no doubt*, the President thought.

"My patience is wearing thin, Matthew."

Dimalanta began nodding, though he didn't know why exactly. He had learned the hard way not to throw out guesses. He waited, bobbing his head like an idiot until the President asked, "Where is Dr. Lee? Is she in custody yet?" Before Dimalanta could open his mouth, the President went on, "And where is Clarren? Has he been executed like I asked?"

"We are working on…"

"And why do I still see bombing runs being carried out in Pennsylvania? Is the Air Force going to tell me that their pilots got lost? Hmmm?"

"I-I-I…"

The President curled his lip and wished that he had a riding crop with him. He'd smack Dimalanta across the face with it. That would get his attention. "Get me General Berrymore, so I can ask him that very question." The only answers that the Secretary of the Air Force could possibly offer would point to either insubordination or ineptness. Unless he tried to lie.

"I'm also going to need a riding crop."

Dimalanta's dark face went grey. "A riding crop, sir?"

"Yes. A riding crop." His hand itched to have one, to smack down on the gleaming desk: *SWACK!* That would get their attention. "After that, find me a replacement for him. When I want the Air Force to bomb fucking Pennsylvania, I'll ask them to bomb fucking Pennsylvania. Things are slipping already, Matthew. The political officers need to step it up."

Dimalanta began nodding again and wished he could stop. Nodding was a lie. The political officers had been a terrible idea. They were slowing everything down and making the lives of…

"We'll start with them," the President said, jabbing an angry finger at the monitor which showed the tanks of the 3rd ID. They were just sitting there all in a row doing nothing. "They're doing nothing, Matthew. Why? Why on earth did we drag them all the way from Georgia just so they could sit in a ragged line like that, doing nothing at all?"

"We didn't," Dimalanta said. "They should be fighting, too." It's what the President wanted to hear. Or so he thought.

"No, they shouldn't be just fighting, they should be attacking!" God, how he wished he had a riding crop. "That had been my plan all along. Is anyone listening here?" He jumped up and went to the largest screen and slapped it with his open palm. "I said I wanted the 3rd and 4th Infantry Divisions to attack. You all said they were unstoppable. So, let's see it! I want to send the zombies reeling back. Bam, bam, like the old one-two."

He walked to the center of the room and planted his hands on his hips. "I want to start actually winning for a change."

2- 2:41 p.m.
North Highland, New York

"What the ever-loving fuck is all this?" Eng hissed in his native Mandarin as he wiped black gunk from his black eyes.

"Oinky-boinky chinking chonky," Jaimee Lynn mimicked, making two of her pack break out in hideous reptilian giggles.

He glared and she only grinned wickedly back at him. She wasn't afraid of him; far from it. She ran her pack like a vile little Nazi and the last time he hit her, they attacked him with teeth and claws. It hadn't hurt—he didn't really feel pain anymore—but he did want to preserve his face. He was going to be saved and he didn't want to look like a monster when he was.

The glare he gave her really wasn't all that different from the way his face was currently cast, anyway. The Com-cells had given him the headache to destroy all headaches. He had never felt this god-awful sick and yet, he had boundless energy. It seemed as though he could rip the steering wheel off the car if he wished. A good part of him wanted to.

In front of them the highway, the six-lane highway, was jam-packed with cars. And they weren't just on the street, there were cars, bumper to bumper on the shoulder and in the median, stretching out further than he could see. There was no way through.

He smashed the steering wheel and started turning the SUV around. With all the trash and empty cars with their doors flung open, it wasn't easy. More than once, the SUV was jolted as he smashed into things. The diseased little predators were flung about and that was good. It made him grin until he saw how black his gums were.

"China, I hungry," one of the kids remarked, tugging on his armored vest.

"What's new?" he asked. They were always hungry…and so was he. Never in his life had he ever been as hungry as he had been since he woke from his drug-induced coma. It wasn't anything like a normal human hunger. It was an infernal desire that was beyond his control. The only reason he wasn't feasting that very second was that there was no one around.

A shudder of desire ran up his back and he gripped the wheel harder. "I'll get better," he said, once more in Mandarin.

"Hey what's all this ching-chong?" Jaimee Lynn demanded. "Speak American and find us somethin' to eat."

"What we need to do is to find a way around this mess. Once we get to the facility, there'll be…stuff to eat."

This wasn't good enough for Jaimee Lynn and the pack. She clamped a hand on his arm, stared hard at him with her corrupt eyes and growled, "I says we's hungry, Chinaman. Find us some food." He glanced to his left just in time to see one of the more intact children slipping the gun from where he had stuck it between his seat and the door.

The kids, little gruesome half-eaten things, were vile and horrible, and also smart, in a cunning, sinister way. And they were getting smarter. The more they healed, the more he saw that nasty glint grow behind their eyes.

"Look, this is the Quarantine Zone. It's empty. There's no one here."

"Yeah, there is. Y'all cain't smell that?" Jaimee Lynn closed her eyes and breathed deeply, her nostrils flaring wide. "They's here. They's hiding like rats, covering they's smell with that white stuff."

Now that she had clued him in, he caught a whiff of something coppery. Just as she had, he breathed in deeply and smelled the earthy sweat of little children just off a baseball field. He smelled the wizened, rock-hard french fries under the back seats. He smelled the sharp copper smell of a woman in cycle. It was all ghostly and faint. They were the residual odors left behind by the people who had ridden in the SUV for years.

Ghostly or not, his stomach twisted and his heart began to hammer. He was almost sick with the suddenness of his hunger. The SUV skidded to a stop as he rolled down the window and once more breathed deeply. On the surface there were two clashing aromas: the perfectly wonderful smells of a beautiful spring day, and the dreadful stench of decaying bodies.

Three days before, North Highland had been the site of a bloody clash between those trying to keep containment of the Quarantine Zone and those trying to break out. The dead had been left to rot in the sun. Eng's lip curled at the stench. It wasn't fresh. It wasn't clean.

"You're smelling the car," he told the children.

Jaimee Lynn shook her head, causing little flakes of old blood to rain down onto her bare shoulders. "No, we ain't. They's there. Y'all cun smell their fear." The partial children all nodded, even the two that were nose-less; they snuffled through the holes in what used to be their faces.

Eng tried again, sniffing the breeze. "There's nothing, like I said before. We should…" He stopped in mid-explanation. Fear had its own smell. At a certain level, the emotive state of fear took on physical characteristics in individuals: increased heart rate, increased respirations, blood became more saturated with oxygen, the endocrine system opens up, specifically along the hypothalamic-pituitary-adrenal axis. All of this gave off a certain maddening odor—and it was in the air.

"You smell it now, China?" a little boy asked in a croaking voice. He was relatively intact. The only mark on him was an eight-inch gash across his throat where his mother had taken a kitchen knife and opened him up from ear to ear as the zombies tore down their front door. He had died and now he was alive and hungry.

"Yeah," he whispered, stepping out of the SUV. He turned in a circle, trying to get a bearing on the scent. It was everywhere, in every direction. As was the smell of bleach. It's what Jaimee Lynn had meant by "white stuff."

"They's hidin' good," she said, coming to stand next to him.

For the moment, Dr. Lee and her cure was driven from Eng's mind. "Get in. Maybe we can, uh, uh, uh." He had a word on the tip of his tongue, but it wouldn't come. With his two index fingers, he started pointing at a patch of nothing in front of his chest, making the same useless noise over and over as he struggled to find the word.

"Mayhap y'all need more of them pills," Jaimee Lynn suggested.

He growled a mandarin curse at her and followed that up by snapping, "I don't need any more pills. I just took some. What I need to do is…" He had been about to say *feed* which had such horrible animal overtones that he changed his wording. "I need to get something to eat."

"I hungry," one of the pack agreed.

Eng ignored her. The word he'd been searching for wouldn't come to him so he gave up on it and instead concentrated on the concept it represented: triangulation. He drove back the way they'd come for half a mile and then had Jaimee Lynn get out. "Is the smell stronger?"

"A smidge," she admitted.

"What's a smidge?"

She held up finger and thumb a half in apart. "It's what means teensy. How do y'all not know that word? Was you real dumb before?"

"Just get in the car," Eng griped, pushing her toward the SUV. Now he took the first right he could and drove another quarter of a mile. The scent of frightened human was just as strong, or just as weak. It was hard for either of them to tell. After circling as much of the town as they could, they hadn't gotten any closer to finding either a person or a way around the traffic jam. All the roads seemed to lead to nowhere.

"I hungry!" the same girl said, gripping her stomach with a hand that had only nubs for fingers. This got them all begging for food and growing angry.

"Everyone shut up!" he seethed, raising a threatening fist. This only got them louder, making Eng's head roar with hatred and pain. "Jaimee Lynn, shut them up so I can think." They listened to her and quieted; however their sullen, angry looks didn't leave, and Eng felt certain that if he didn't get them something to eat soon, they would turn on him.

With a moody sigh, he had to admit that going around in circles wasn't working. He had to find a new way to get to them. "They're hiding. They're afraid. But they're not running away. Why?"

"Cuz we'd eat them," Jaimee Lynn suggested, eagerly. She could picture a small crowd of survivors running away like frightened sheep, with her pack chasing, coming up right behind them, tripping them and lunging in to tear out throats and bellies.

"Right." Eng had been picturing pretty much the same thing and he found himself drooling. He shook his head to clear it, saying, "They are afraid to go on foot and they're out of gas, so they can't drive."

These were such obvious points that Jaimee Lynn began to frown again. "Yeah?" By this she meant: *Yeah, go on.*

Eng dug out another handful of pills. He had no idea what kind they were or what their strength was. His head wouldn't stop pounding. "Yeah and that means they're hiding. So how do we draw them out?" Since it was daylight, Jaimee Lynn didn't think that anyone would come to rescue any of her pack if they started crying out. Even she thought they were hideous.

Eng was trying to put himself in the shoes of someone hiding in a basement. "What would get me to come out?" They would definitely not come out for a black-eyed Asian man and a pack of monsters. "They'd have to want to come out. They wouldn't come out for food. They probably still have food and water. But would they come out for gas? Or a ride?"

A plan hatched, fully formed in his mind. People would come out if they thought there was a chance to escape the Zone. And yet, they would only go with someone they trusted. "Like the police."

He barked the kids back into the SUV and rushed back to the highway, guessing correctly that at the end of the jam he would find police cars. There were six of them, each riddled with bullets and splashed with old blood. They looked like wrecks, dented and smashed, but despite that, two of them were still drivable.

Eng chose the bigger of the two, a suburban that had a bloated, fly-blown body sitting behind the wheel. He didn't think twice about pulling it out and sitting in the still sticky seat. The pack sneered at the body, disliking even the thought of rancid meat.

"What's all these buttons do?" Jaimee Lynn asked, reaching for the control panel.

"Don't touch!" Eng swatted her hand away. He didn't want to give themselves away too soon. Besides, he didn't know. The words above each switch were terribly small and blurry. "First things first. We need to get into position." That meant getting back into town, something that was oddly easy from this direction. Just before the highway, he found a little gas station/minimart combo and pulled in behind it.

Picking up the radio mic, he started broadcasting on every channel. "Is anyone there? This is cruiser 16. Is anyone there? Over?"

After twenty minutes of this, the pack got bored and left to pick over the store. Jaimee Lynn stayed behind, not trusting Eng. Her once blue eyes shot wide when they finally got a hit.

"Hello? Is this the police?" a woman asked in a whisper.

"The state police," Eng corrected in the calmest voice he could manage. His hands were suddenly shaking. "We're looking for survivors. How many of you are there?"

"It's just me and my kids. We're in a house by the highway. We ran out of gas and my husband went for more, but that…that was two days ago and he never came back. He left…he left us and then the zombies came."

Eng's stomach let out a growl that was so loud that he covered the mic with both hands. "Are there zombies out there?" he asked. She said there wasn't and he smiled. "Good. Good. Now, where are you?"

She read an address off a piece of mail and then went one step further and gave him directions. It was less than a minute away.

"Be ready to run out when you see my lights," he told her.

"Okay, we will," she answered with nearly the same level of excitement that he was feeling.

He was so jazzed that he was reaching for the ignition when Jaimee Lynn smacked him in the back of the head. "Not without the others," she said, sounding like a squeaky-voiced general. "Hey, you guys! Git on over here. We got one!"

The pack piled into the Suburban, panting like dogs, their eyes wide and eager. Eng felt the same famished eagerness and knew he should've been trying to fight it. He was human, after all, and wasn't he on his way to find Dr. Lee to stay that way?

That had been the plan, but just then, the only thing he thought of when he pictured Dr. Lee was her elegant, bitable neck.

He stomped down on the gas and hit the siren. Jaimee Lynn found the lights before she sat forward in her chair, her clawed hands gripping the dash, while behind them, the pack was howling along with the siren. It was just about the stupidest way to go in and Eng didn't care a bit. He was beyond caring about anything other than feeding.

The family of three came racing out of the house while Eng was still halfway down the block. The woman saw the wreck of a SUV and stopped in the middle of the yard, knowing deep in her heart that something wasn't right. Just the fact that the cruiser was banged up wasn't what had her backing away. It was how the vehicle was slewing down the road, veering left and right for no reason.

She only had time to think: *Is the driver drunk?* before she saw Jaimee Lynn. The naked girl looked like she had just come crawling out of hell. Too late, the woman tried to grab her children's hands and run up to the house. Eng drove the Suburban right up onto the lawn and before it even stopped, the pack was out and racing like jackals.

The family was pulled down and eaten alive right on the porch with the perfect yellow sun beaming down on them.

Chapter 16
1-3:15 p.m.
Newville, Pennsylvania

General Cannan pulled the sat-phone from his ear and looked at it as if it had just bitten him. Slowly, he put it back up to his head. "Say again." He was talking to a Lieutenant General...the new commander of the 2nd Corps. Supposedly that is. There had been a lot of weird shit going on with people impersonating generals and senators and governors.

Cannan hoped to God this was the case.

"General Leonard has been relieved of his command and arrested for refusing a direct order. This is Lieutenant General Boggs, we were on General Lunder's staff together in Grafenwöhr."

"I remember," Cannan answered, forcing a touch of fake liveliness into his voice. He remembered Boggs as an ass-kisser even back then. "I'm sorry to hear about Leonard. He's a good man who knows the value of a free hand when it comes to his divisional commanders."

There was a lengthy pause before Boggs said, "He might have been a little too free. Your orders are changing. The 2nd Corps is no longer going to be standing on the defensive. The 3rd will be spearheading a drive to retake Pennsylvania."

Once more Cannan looked at the phone incredulously. "Sir, that's not a possibility just yet. Maybe when we get those units up from Fort Stewart and Fort Hood, that will be a consideration, until then..."

"Until then you will follow orders or be replaced," Boggs barked. "My God, if this is how Leonard ran things, it's no wonder he was arrested. Listen up, Cannan, the President has put up with as much shenanigans as he's going to, so follow orders or you can join Leonard in prison. You will be attacking and you will follow my timetable. It's as simple as that."

For a good half minute, Cannan was silent as he considered handing in his resignation. An attack at this point was outrageous. He had studied the lay of the land and, as far as he knew, there wasn't any objective that was worth giving up the defensive position he and his men had worked so hard to hold. It meant that the attack was either about Boggs' vanity—he probably had a train of reporters in tow and wanted to look like

185

the "man,"—or he was getting political pressure to do "something."

Either way, an attack was stupid and Cannan knew that eventually he would come out and say it was stupid, though he was sure that he would use a great deal more colorful language than that. He would likely refuse and would be fired or worse. It would probably be worse.

If a man like Leonard, a man who was as by the book as they came, could be jailed, then it would almost be a guarantee that Cannan would be as well. He knew his tongue and his pig-headedness would get him in trouble.

At the same time, could he lay this squarely on his XO's shoulders, knowing that Colonel Broadhurst was cut from the same cloth? Out of loyalty alone, it was almost a guarantee that he would laugh in Boggs' face and a betting man could make a mint putting money on how much spit would fly. Broadhurst had a fiery temper which had served him well in battle, but could now get him arrested.

It begged the question, who would Boggs bring in to lead the division when he was arrested as well? It was another sure bet that Boggs would choose an outsider. How long would it take him to get up to speed? An infantry division was a very complex animal and it could take as long as a week to get adjusted properly, and if an attack was in the offing, they didn't have minutes to spare let alone hours or days. And yet, it would most certainly be an outsider, probably a highly decorated paper-pusher like Boggs. It wouldn't sit well with the team Cannan had melded into a single fighting unit; there'd be anger and animosity, and, in the end, it would be the GIs on the line who would suffer the most.

Cannan loved his men too much to let them suffer or die without purpose.

"I'm your man," he said, softly, telling himself that he was not completely giving in. He looked at the move as buying time. "What's the plan of attack?" He secretly prayed that they were looking for some sort of limited gain that everyone could point to and say, "We're winning!" In his heart, he feared Boggs was about to unload such a pile of shit on him that it would test the limits of his composure, and he wasn't disappointed.

"I've uploaded the proposed plan of attack. It's encrypted through LCMC because of all the hacking going on." He sent a one-time code which allowed Cannan to open up the most bare-bones bit of assery he had ever seen. It might as well have been drawn in the dirt with a stick.

"What am I looking at?" It was a map of Pennsylvania, that much was obvious. What didn't make sense were the four colorful lines: one pointed up from Newville and was aimed at Harrisburg. Another ran from the dinky town of Blain and through Sherman's Valley. The final two poked like horns away from the hills on Cannan's flank.

He stared at the map with a lip curled. "Is this a concept plan that you want me to turn into an actual operational order?" he asked, eventually. This wasn't backyard football, after all. He understood that the arrows represented lines of attacks, but by what units? Were these regimental-sized attacks? How were they to be supported? What were the initial objectives? What were the timelines? What were the intelligence estimates of the zombie army in these areas? Had a reconnaissance, beyond the use of drones, been carried out? Where was the sustainment overlay? Were they going to receive proper air support for an actual attack?

The greatest question, of course, was once these objectives were reached, what then? He had no doubt whatsoever that his tanks could punch a lane through the undead and drive to Harrisburg at which point his force would be surrounded.

Boggs cleared his throat into the phone. "You're going to have to do that on the fly. I would do it, but Leonard's staff had to be replaced and my guys are still getting up to speed. Just a warning, we're on a time crunch. The President is pushing for a sixteen-hundred kick-off time."

Cannan looked at his watch and felt a wave of shock wash over him. "An hour? No, that's not even an hour! Sir, please. You know that we can't prep an assault of this magnitude in an hour. I'd need eight hours at a minimum. Hell, it would take three just to draw up the operational orders." And he'd have to do it while leading his division at the same time. "Jeeze-lou-fucking-wheeze," he muttered in that semi-heard, under the breath way of his.

"I didn't say you had to be in Harrisburg at four!" Boggs snapped. "You just have to be on the move by then. Drive them back. That's what the President wants. Our immediate goal is to retake the Susquehanna River."

187

"You want me to drive them back?" Cannan asked. He was too stunned for outrage. He could barely manage incredulity and it sounded like he was asking for the order to be repeated.

Boggs answered with a simple: "Yes," which had Cannan's head wagging back and forth, his mouth hanging wide open. It was insane. The order was beyond stupid. There was so much wrong with it that Cannan didn't know where to begin. He was just about to protest when Boggs said, "I'll be choppering in to watch the initial attack and rest assured that the President is very keen about this. He'll be watching the feeds."

Was that a warning?

Just then Cannan felt a prickling on the back of his neck. He turned and saw Vertanen, grey in the face, her makeup looking as if it had been painted on an old, dusty manikin. With her were four men in black suits that he had never seen before. They were hard men with uncaring eyes.

"Did you hear me, Cannan?"

"Yes sir," he answered in a whisper. "I heard you loud and clear."

2-3:28 p.m.
Creech AFB, Nevada

They were at war, but that was no reason to be late. The pilots had been flying nonstop for four hours and they both had to piss something wicked.

"It's your turn," the lieutenant said, "and it's been your turn for ten minutes. Are you just trying to run out the clock?"

Captain Rodrigo "Slick" Del Arroz's queen was trapped. He had brought her out too early and Lieutenant Schmidt had happily chased her into a corner. Perhaps worse than the loss of the queen, Del Arroz hadn't had time to develop any other piece except a damned horse.

"I'm not trying to run out the clock, I'm just in a situation." He gestured at the screen in front of him. "I'm dealing with *real* hazards here." His Sentinel the *Midnight Runner* was flying over Trenton which was still on fire, the smoke rising seven-hundred feet high in places. Schmidt's Sentinel was buzzing over Allentown where pigeons were the only things he had to worry about.

"Whoa, so scary. Maybe you should…"

He broke off as two men in black suits and dark glasses walked into the squadron's virtual cockpit. "Can I help you?" Del Arroz asked, glaring at them. They struck him as FBI and the FBI had no business interrupting pilots while they were in the middle of a mission.

This was especially true when the UAV in question was the RQ-170. It wasn't just a top-secret program, it was *compartmentalized*, meaning that only seven or eight people had access to the entire layout of the UAV. Even though he was the pilot, Del Arroz had no idea what the power plant in the RQ-170 was or what electronics were stored within its black body. He knew its ceiling, its weight, take-off and landing parameters, thrust-to-weight ratios and fuel consumption. Basically, he knew enough to fly it and that was all he needed to know.

"Yes, you may help us," the lead man said, coolly ignoring the glare. "Come to 20,000 feet and hold a steady northbound course."

Del Arroz shared a look with Schmidt before stabbing the button marked "radio." It was really something of a secure intercom. "Control, can you explain why I have two junior G-men in my cockpit? And maybe send for Colonel Bell while you're at it."

Like the cockpit, the control tower was virtual and located six doors down a stark white hallway. "The Colonel is aware of the situation, Slick." The operator's normally relaxed voice was pitched high. "The two men are authorized *Yankee White*. Follow their instructions without deviation." This caused Del Arroz to freeze at the stick. *Yankee White* meant that their authorization had come directly from either the President or the Vice President.

The lead agent smiled behind his dark glasses. "Like I said, come to 20,000 feet and hold a steady north-bound course. This will only take a minute."

It took fifteen minutes. "Think of it as a bug," the agent said when Del Arroz asked what the man was attaching inside the instrument panel of the cockpit. "It'll let us know exactly where these birds are. The President is getting tired of surprises and is going to do something about it."

"What surprises?" Del Arroz asked. "We are exactly where we are supposed to be."

"Actually, you're not. You're eighty-five miles off course. The good news is that it's not your fault. If it were…" He glanced at his partner and shared another ice-cold smile. "Maybe let's not think about that."

The two men left, going to the next cockpit. Schmidt waited until the door closed before he covered his mic and whispered, "That was messed up, Slick. I mean really messed up. This is billion-dollar equipment and that guy just stuck a LoJack on it for fuck's sake."

Del Arroz stuck a finger to his lips. It was possible that an actual bug had been installed as well as a virtual one. He cleared his throat and drawled in a close imitation to his own speaking voice, "Control, do you have a new heading for us?"

"Slick, this is Control. Continue on your current heading. You'll be going back to your previous hunting grounds. Someone's been playing games with us."

"Affirmative. ETA eighteen minutes. We have enough fuel to stay on station for maybe two hours before we're going to have to find a new home."

Control was quiet for a few minutes. "Negative, Slick. Saunter as needed until we get a tanker anchored. We'll be on station until further notice." The tower's next call was to the temporary Air Operations Center that had been set up at JFK airport in Queens, requesting hanger space for the six Sentinels in the area as well as mid-air tanker support.

Although the conversations that took place within the same building at Creech Air Force Base were sent over a secure line, the call to JFK was picked up by Major Palmburg at the R&K research facility.

"A tanker is being scrambled and sent our way," he stated in a choked voice. "It's being anchored over Paramus."

Everyone opened the map windows on their computers to check exactly where Paramus was. It was far too close; only ten miles to the west. Someone let out a long: "Fuuuuck." There was only one reason to have a flying fuel tanker loitering over a mostly deserted section of the Quarantine Zone.

Eyes shot from computers and to the windows, where they scanned for movement. For the moment, the skies were clear.

"Do we shut down?" the major asked. Just because they couldn't see the Sentinels, or the Predators, or even the E-3s, it didn't mean they weren't nearby listening, probing, sensing every little electromagnetic pulse.

"I can't," Colonel Taylor called out in a blaring voice. "I have nearly the entire 175th Infantry Regiment trapped in York,

PA. I'm this close to getting a squadron of B1s on site." He looked up and stared straight into General Axelrod's eyes. "It's eighteen planes, sir. You know what they can do. And you know what a full regiment could mean down there."

They all knew. They all had up to the moment access to the state of emergency going on along the entire border. The loss of Harrisburg and the Susquehanna River had unleashed a flood of zombies. Most had cooperated and were sweeping towards the 3rd ID, but nearly half a million of them were marching straight to the Maryland border which was being weakly held by a recruiting and retention battalion, the 290th Military Police Company, the 291st Digital Liaison Detachment, the 110th Information Operations Battalion, and similar 9 to 5 *remf* units.

Altogether, these quasi-military units numbered about four-thousand men and held twenty miles of rolling farmland and scrubby hills. The next twenty miles were being defended by the Virginia Defense Force. A week before, the full strength of this "unit" amounted to three-hundred weekend warriors with an average age of forty-seven. They held yearly drills and had potlucks and mostly bitched about their wives while dressed in camouflage.

Their numbers had surged in the last three days and now there were currently thirty-seven thousand men, women, and in some cases, children serving in impromptu companies under their own elected captains. They carried every sort of missile weapon, from crossbows to machine guns to reproductions of Kentucky muzzle loading flintlock rifles that used black powder straight from the horn and fired huge fifty caliber slugs.

About a third of these companies figured it was far better to fight the zombies in someone else's backyard instead of their own, and were nervously waiting the onslaught of the horde south of Gettysburg. No one figured they would last five minutes.

All of the borders were being precariously held, but just then the southwestern border of the zone was as fragile as an eggshell. The situation was only going to get worse if the 3rd ID actually attacked. It would leave huge gaps in the weak lines, and containment, what little containment they had, would go right out the window.

They had all been anxiously busy doing everything they could to stop the coming disaster.

"How long do you need?" Axelrod asked Taylor.

"Twenty minutes, maybe. It's hard to tell. There's channels within channels. But it won't be long, I promise."

Major Palmburg raised a hand. "A strong argument could be made that we don't have twenty minutes. We could be targeted right now and if we believe in Dr. Lee's work, we should not risk it." He wondered if anyone saw through this. Just at the moment, he didn't give a fig for Dr. Lee. He was afraid that they'd be dead in ten minutes if they didn't get out of the building.

"We don't have to shut down completely," Courtney suggested. "We could move to a different building every twenty or thirty minutes. How long does it take to like shoot a missile or a bomb?"

Three of the officers said: "Seconds," at once. To which she answered, "Oh." The question, feeble as it was, brought the absolute danger of their position to the forefront and each person looked over at the general. It was ultimately his decision. The choices before him were not good: on one hand, he risked getting evaporated in a blink of an eye, and on the other, he risked becoming zombie chow by running around in the Zone.

"We need a van or a truck," he said, quickly, deciding that as much as he feared getting eaten alive, he had full faith in the Air Force's ability to find a target and take it out in a blink. "We'll stick and move, staying in one place for only ten minutes. Agent Pennock, you'll be in charge of getting a vehicle. You can hotwire a car, right?"

This seemed like a rhetorical question and there was a scurry as everyone began shutting down their laptops and stowing them away. In the midst of this, she answered with a simple, "No, sorry. I was in the cybercrime division and really there isn't an agency-wide need for stealing cars. Besides, I'm not going with you. I still have a mission given to me by the President. I'm supposed to be bringing back a cure or, at the very least, the building blocks of one."

She decided not to bring up the fact that she also had an obligation to arrest, not just Dr. Lee, but all of them. It was an obligation that she could dodge, justifying letting them go because they were military. If questioned, she could point out that they had their own set of laws and courts, that they were operating under a declared emergency, and that they fell outside her jurisdiction.

"If anyone asks, I thought you guys were legit, okay? And I was just trying to help things run smoothly."

A few of them shrugged, confirming in an altogether listless way that they would…perhaps.

"I mean it. I could get in serious trouble," she insisted.

"Trust me, we won't be talking to anyone," Axelrod told her as he hiked his pack onto his broad shoulders. "The President had the damned Secretary of Defense executed for the crime of trying to save him from himself. What do you think he will do to us?"

She saw from their grim faces that they had already decided they weren't going to be taken alive. "I-I didn't know. Sorry."

It was something of a shock to Courtney Shaw, though it shouldn't have been. The airways were alive with chatter about the mass arrests, and the executions. They hadn't stopped with Heider, Phillips and Marty Aleman. Fourteen others had been killed for crimes far less serious than the ones Courtney had been perpetrating.

The consequence for what she'd been doing had always been in the back of her mind, but death by firing squad hadn't felt like a real thing…like a real thing that could happen to her, that is. Now that it was front and center, she couldn't look past it. "They're going to kill me," she whispered to Katherine as everyone rushed for the stairs.

"You can stay here with me and help Dr. Lee," Katherine suggested. "Once everyone leaves, we probably won't be targeted. Maybe."

Even with the weak "maybe" added, it sounded like a great idea to Courtney. She didn't know much about science, but she was a fast learner. *And besides*, she thought, *I've done my part to save the world*.

The only problem with this rationale was that the world wasn't saved yet. "No. People still need me." It took a lot out of her to walk away from the offer. She was in a bit of a daze and it was up to Colonel Taylor to take her by the hand and lead her down the stairs.

Stung by unexpected guilt, Katherine followed them to the lobby and even found the keys to the van parked in back. When they were all gone—the helicopter pilot and Sergeant Carlton had happily scurried into the van as well—the building felt completely empty and she was suddenly struck by the notion that when she went to the labs, she would find them deserted.

Looking up at the ceiling, she cocked her head, hoping to hear the hum of the generator or some sort of whir from one of the machines Thuy was using two floors overhead. The building was dead silent. The only noise that came to her was the rumble of an airplane. She froze, her body tense, wondering if there was a bomb in free fall hurtling towards her.

When a minute passed, she shook herself as if waking from a dream and then hurried up the stairs. She was greeted by Specialist Hoskins, screaming and spitting in rage from the clean room next door. His eyes were now coal black and wet. His flesh, what little she could see, was bruised, purple and blue, except around his wrists where the cuffs were digging deep and bringing up dark, dark red blood.

Dr. Lee glanced up. "Are we on the verge of being blown up again?"

Katherine was going to say no; however, she saw that Dr. Lee had every machine in sight running full bore. "Maybe. Any chance some of these can be powered down for a bit? The spy planes are coming back."

"And Miss Shaw can't reroute them?"

"Not for a bit. They...everyone's gone. They're going to try to move around to confuse the people flying the planes."

Thuy frowned at this. "Then I guess I don't understand why we would need to shut down anything at all."

"They're drones," Katherine explained, wondering if Thuy's head was stuffed more with theorems and formulas than with common sense. "They're unmanned. They don't care who is in a building. All they care about is making sure the bomb goes in the front door."

"A drone might not care, but surely its pilot does," Thuy replied, stepping over to the next workstation, and stepping over a sleeping Anna Holloway in the process. "If our military friends are gone, then a bomb would be a waste. I assume you are not a target and, as I am in your 'custody,' and Anna has her beloved pardon, we would not be either."

Katherine laughed at herself. "I guess not." She had retained a sat-phone, and as she began dialing the Deputy Director of the FBI, Matthew Bradbury, she gestured at Anna. "I bet things would go faster if you used her in some capacity."

"I would but her IQ is only slightly larger than her bust measurement."

"You're wrong about that," Katherine said, remembering the merry chase Anna had led the combined might of the FBI. She was anything but stupid. "You're letting your anger get in the way. Anna's smarter than you might th…" She suddenly held up a finger as the line was answered by a woman.

"This is Special Agent in Charge Katherine Pennock. I need to speak to Deputy Director Bradbury, asap."

There was a long pause before the woman whispered, "I'm afraid Deputy Director Bradbury has been arrested."

Katherine jerked in surprise, barely able to wrap her head around what she had just heard. How could the most senior law enforcement officer in the country be arrested? It made no sense. "And the Director?" she asked, already knowing the answer in her bones.

"Arrested, too," the woman said in an even lower voice.

This took the strength out of Katherine and she had to sit on a little spinning stool. "Then who…who…who's in charge?"

"John Alexander, Assistant Director for National Security. The old Assistant Director, I mean."

Relief washed over her. Alexander had been the one who'd sent into her into the Zone in the first place. "This is a priority one call. Tell him who I am and tell him it's about a cure."

This lit a fire under her and Alexander was on the phone in seconds. "Agent Pennock? I can't believe you're alive. We had a live feed going last night right up until we saw your chopper pilot get killed, then the President cut it. Where are you? Are you still in the Zone?"

"Yes, and I need your help. Eng was killed, but we found Dr. Lee. She's working on a cure right this second, but we have drones overhead and we think they might be targeting us. Is there any way for you to call them off? We're in the R & K research facility in New Rochelle." He started to say something, but she cut him off. "Sir, please. I'll explain everything just as soon as you get these drones away from us."

"That's what I was trying to say," he said, lowering his voice just as the secretary had. "I don't know if I can. Dr. Lee is on the kill list."

"The what?"

"There's a new list that's being circulated by the White House," he said so quietly that she had to crush the sat-phone into her ear. "The people on the list are to be killed on sight."

195

Chapter 17
1-4:00 p.m.
The White House, Washington DC

Each name on the kill list was accompanied by a "reason to kill" statement. One of the President's speech writers was employed full time to find the exact right syntax of these statements. It was harder than it looked since everyone was essentially guilty of the same crime: treason.

The most difficult to write were those of the junior staffers of some of the bigwigs. Their transgressions were always very vague and the actual fact of their guilt, even more so. Because of this, the writer found himself at his computer with a thesaurus on his lap, rearranging the same phrases over and over, so it didn't look like the President was after them simply due to their associations.

Dr. Lee was one step removed from the number one position on the list—that first rank belonged to the Vice President, who had fled into hiding. In part, Dr. Lee's read: "As she did knowingly construct a virus with the full intention of destroying America for all future generations..." Another line accused her of: "A deep-seated hatred towards, not just Caucasians, but also Hispanics, African Americans and Jews."

The President looked at that last word with something of disgust; his PC filters were still in place, but not as firmly as they had been. Marty would have advised him to have the word changed to "Jewish people," or better, "people of Jewish heritage." These were big campaign contributors, after all.

"Fuck him and them," he muttered, leaving the word in place. He had officially run his last campaign a year before, winning his second term. Legally, there couldn't be a third term, so he had decided, by presidential fiat, to simply extend his second term indefinitely.

It only made sense that elections in a time of emergency would have to be put on hold, and it was supposed that every other elected official's terms would be extended as well, but they wouldn't be. Whether they would be allowed to stay depended on how accommodating they were to the President. So far, he had more people on the naughty list than the nice list, and he had to restrain himself from moving people on his naughty list over to his kill list.

"Not yet," he muttered. The country was not yet his to command as a king might. It wouldn't be long, however. Fear was turning the people into sheep. They were begging for someone to protect them and he would be their savior. And he would save them; he had full faith in his powers as Commander in Chief—the war would be won, there was no doubt about that —before it ended; however, he was going to make some sweeping changes for the good of the country.

Clearly, the entire notion of state governors elected by a popular vote was antiquated and unwieldy. Instead, they would be handpicked by him and would swear fealty to him and not some piece of red and white striped cloth, again for the good of the nation, of course. That was going to be his bold mission statement: everything would be for the good of the nation.

The constitution would be rewritten, for the good of the nation.

The two parties would be abolished for the good of the nation.

Congressional candidates would be appointed by the governors for the good of the nation.

The freedom of the press would be untouched…except that all news stories would have to be examined and approved by a new Presidential board of "Public Programming," for the good of the nation.

And so on. And if there was the least bit of womanly hysteria over the eroding of rights, the President would be able to point at the zombie plague and say: "Is that what you want to go back to?"

He had glanced at the kill list simply because the new FBI Director was going on about a cure. A cure was a fine thing, but just then the President was supposed to be watching as *his* attack commenced. "Where are the bombers?" he asked the new Secretary of the Air Force, craning his head around Alexander.

"Just a minor delay," the Secretary answered before turning back to the phone and hissing frantically into his cupped hand.

The President glared furiously at him for a moment, his face bright red, right up to the tip of his ears. He then sneered once more at the name *Dr. Lee*, before tossing it aside and demanding of Alexander, "What are you going on about? What's this about a cure? I thought that was over and done with."

Alexander had been about to mention that Dr. Lee had been found but thought better of it. He forced a smile onto his face.

197

"That's the good news I wanted to give you, sir. Our agent is alive *and* she managed to get the pure Com-cells out of Walton."

"Okay," the President said, cautiously. A cure was all well and good as long as it fit within his timetable. In other words: not yet. "And those scientists with her, are they alive?"

"One of them is, and she's begun experimenting. Our agent has even managed to capture an infected person for testing purposes. There's just one problem, they're in the Quarantine Zone, in an area that is possibly being targeted by drones. I looked into it and there are illegal transmissions coming from a nearby source, but it's not the same building..."

The President cut across him. "What do you want? Just spit it out." He expected Alexander to ask for an extraction for his agent, which had been the plan from the beginning. But the President's plans had changed. A cure was a promise held in reserve for demonstrated good behavior, not something to be developed at great expense and then shelled out to undeserving masses.

"We need for the drones in the immediate area to be called off, and..."

"No," the President answered, flatly. "I understand perfectly what is meant by 'illegal transmissions.' It's your nice way of saying there are traitors operating in the area. Trust me, Alexander they will be hunted down and destroyed without mercy. All of them have to die, and if your agent happens to get killed in the process, her death will be for the good of the nation."

Alexander saw that the President was working himself into a fever and that he might just order a bombing run on a whim. "What about the specific building they're in? Can we protect that one? It's the R&K research facility in New Rochelle."

It was disconcerting seeing the President's eyes turn dark with paranoia. He stared up at Alexander. "The R&K research facility? How interesting. That's where this all started. Why would they want to go there, hmm? Are they after some other germ that's even worse than these zombies? Is that their plan? To kick us when we're down?"

"No sir," Alexander said, quickly. "They explained to me that the facility has all the equipment they need to develop a cure. It's a BSL-4 lab and has been strictly inspected and regulated by CDC officials. There are no bioweapons there, I promise. It's a cancer research facility."

"Oh." The suspicion in the President's eyes dropped away by degrees. "Maybe. I guess. A cure would be good. But, if we do this, I want a *Predator* orbiting over the building at all times and if they try to send even one message out, I want that building turned to dust, got it?"

Before Alexander could answer, the President basically dismissed him as he waved over a timid, brittle young blonde woman who looked as though she was on the verge of breaking into pieces.

"Where are we on apprehending the Vice President?"

The woman, Trista Price looked confused until she realized the question had been directed toward Alexander. "Still missing, sir," he answered curtly; the urgency to protect both his agent and their one shot at finding a cure made him short. "We've brought in his family as you asked."

"Good. Trista, tell Kazakoff to free up his schedule. Finding him is now his priority. Tell him he has a free hand with his questioning."

Trista Price's beautiful face looked like china that had been painted over to hide the cracks. Her eyes flicked to Alexander as if to ask for help, but he dropped his head. "Questioning? Do you mean with the wife?"

"With all of them," the President answered blithely, shooing her away with the back of his hand. "Where the hell are my damn bombers? Why isn't this happening yet? I have a full division waiting to attack, damn it!"

While the President ranted, Alexander and Trista stood there, both in a state of shock. The cracks in her face were now running like fault-lines through her makeup; she was being asked to send the Vice President's children down to be tortured by Kazakoff. The Vice President's youngest was seven.

"I don't think I can…" Trista started to say, but Alexander shook his head quickly and started to lead her off by the elbow. Since noon, he had seen three people frog-marched out of the room and sent to the new detention camps. Being right or moral wouldn't help her if she disobeyed a direct order from the President. He would demand that Alexander arrest her on the spot.

The situation made Alexander sick, especially since he was powerless to stop it. The President had his family in custody, just as he did everyone in the administration, as well as all the power people on the hill. They weren't in jail exactly, they were in something far more insidious. Under the cover of "protecting" the families, they had been transferred to supposedly safe and guarded hotels in Old Town Arlington, Virginia.

They were so safe and so guarded that they weren't allowed to leave unless they were dragged out in handcuffs, never to be seen again.

All because the President was a patchwork of paranoia, megalomania, and blossoming evil. He was unstoppable, not that anyone was trying to stop him. The American people were in the dark about what he was really like, and in fact were rallying around him as he stoked their fears and patriotism. The press, instead of reporting actual news was behaving like whipped dogs and accepting the spoonfuls of information without question.

"Don't do it," Alexander hissed to Trista. "Don't say anything. It won't do you any good. Just bide your…"

"Alexander!" the President barked. "Leave her alone. You have too much work to be doing to waste time flirting."

The Director of the FBI actually bowed towards the President. "Yes sir. Of course, sir." He felt like a waiter instead of an FBI agent with twenty-six years of experience.

He turned away but was recalled by the President. "Find out why we don't have Clarren in custody yet. I want you to make finding Clarren and the VP your number one priority."

Make useless political vengeance a priority over finding a cure? Alexander should have been shocked and he should have excoriated the President. Instead, he nodded and then hurried off like a little bitch. What was being asked of him was insane. Clarren was harmless now. From everything Alexander had found out, the man was intent on dying on the front lines fighting the zombies. And the Vice President had never been a man anyone could rally around. He wasn't an opposition leader. In truth, he got to where he was by grabbing onto every political fad under the sun.

And the President wanted Alexander to waste valuable resources on these two? With his stomach feeling like he had just swallowed a greasy turd sandwich, he watched Trista stumble away. She was going to fall apart soon. "Unless I find that putz first."

Alexander hurried to the operations room with a new purpose. "I have two priority one orders from the President," he said to the newly appointed Secretary of Political Operations.

She was *The* political officer of the White House and all orders, military or otherwise, went through her office. "The President wants the R&K Building in New Rochelle protected at all costs. The military can level the rest of the city, but that one building is to remain untouched."

She nodded to one of the fifteen subordinates she had working for her; the stern-faced, apple-cheeked, nazi-looking young man went right to work sending the order down the long, long chain of lesser political officers that stretched across the country. "And the second?" the woman asked.

"The FBI is to use its full force to find the Vice President and Governor Clarren." This was a huge exaggeration, but a necessary one. If he could find the Vice President, he could stop the torture of his children and save Trista from being sent to a detention camp for disloyalty. And if he sent a hundred agents to Massachusetts to dick around along the line, it would be a hundred fewer agents terrorizing people on the President's behalf.

The President wanted his people to be almost filled with religious mania when following his orders. Alexander would be the most maniacal of them all if it meant he could thwart the President's aims at the same time as protecting his family.

2-4:19 p.m.
Newville, Pennsylvania

The eighteen Rockwell B-1 Lancers slated to clear a path up the Cumberland Valley had somehow been re-routed to Gettysburg. The twelve thousand men of the 3rd ID craned their heads back and watched the procession of planes as they swept above them heading on the wrong tack. The grey planes looked old and slow, and seemed to be trudging across the sky rather than soaring, and it was no wonder since each was weighed down with over a hundred thousand pounds of bombs tucked inside them.

"Shit," Sergeant Farnham drawled in the front seat of the Humvee as the lead "Bone" began to drop its bombs. General Cannan grunted, but not in agreement. He knew about the trapped regiment and if he had been in charge of things, he would have sent those bombers in to help them five hours earlier.

For the next ten minutes, the battle in front of Newville was brought to a halt by the thunder and earth-shaking power of the bombs. The zombies were entranced at the sight and sound, while the soldiers took those precious free moments to reload and stockpile more ammo.

A mile to the rear of the line, Cannan's command Humvee rocked gently as smoke billowed higher and higher over the hills to their east. It was during the onslaught that General Boggs and his staff finally arrived. Their flight of thirteen Blackhawks swinging in from the southwest, had been forced into a wide detour to keep from being hit by an errant bomb.

"Look at all of them," Farnham muttered. "Thirteen helicopters, shit. What a waste. Does he have a staff or an entourage?"

This time Cannan's grunt was in complete agreement. A hundred-man staff to oversee the shattered remains of a single corps was ludicrous, especially since it was probably made up of old friends and Pentagon golfing buddies. Cannan could see them staring through the thick windows of the choppers, looking like tourists.

The only one who wasn't gaping was Boggs. He was scowling down at Cannan. It wasn't unexpected. The scowl only deepened as he marched out of the helicopter with his staff, his many political officers, and security detail swarming behind him. Boggs immediately began cursing, though most of what he had to say was drowned out by the Blackhawks which were loud even when they were idling.

Cannan waved Boggs away from the helicopters. "You were asking me a question, sir? I didn't quite make it out. I thought you called me a pussy and I'm sure I misunderstood."

"You heard me right. Why the hell hasn't your division moved out? You had explicit orders. Sixteen-hundred on the dot and it's now sixteen-twenty-three!"

"You told me that only some of my division had to be on the move and that I was to create an operational order. I've begun the attack by moving up some of my reserve units." Not far away a company of M6 Bradley Fighting Vehicles were moving toward the line that hadn't budged an inch forward or back.

General Boggs stared at the M6s, his head shaking in disbelief and anger. "Linebackers? You're going to open the attack with them? They're almost worthless."

He wasn't wrong. Cannan had wanted to leave them in Georgia but had been overruled by Lieutenant General Leonard, who said the President wanted the *full* power of the 3rd ID. "Really? Are we going to have flying zombies to deal with?" Cannan had asked, running right up to the edge of insubordination, something that was a monthly occurrence with him. Although the M6 Linebackers possessed a M242 Bushmaster turret-mounted 25-mm chain gun and a coaxial 7.62-mm machine gun, the M6s were mainly anti-aircraft platforms and could fire Sidewinders and Stinger surface-to-air missiles, both of which were useless against zombies.

Leonard had won him over by suggesting that what was happening in Massachusetts could spread to other states. That had been at the height of the short civil war and Cannan had reluctantly agreed to take them. Now, the M6s were finally making themselves useful by making Boggs' blood pressure skyrocket.

"They are just the beginning of the attack, I assure you." Behind them was an engineer battalion, their bulldozers and bucket loaders painted desert brown.

Boggs was not assured in the least. "The President is watching, damn it!" he said in a harsh whisper with a glance back at his political officer, whose uniform sported four gleaming stars, one more than Boggs possessed. The hyper-ranked PO stood glaring at Courtney Vertanen as she tried to explain the "trust" angle that Cannan had sold her on. Even from thirty yards, it was obvious the lead PO wasn't buying into its common sense.

"Oh God," Boggs whined. "There he goes with that damned phone again. Every time there's a damned hiccup, he calls the President. I warned you, Cannan. I warned you, damn it. Show me the orders you drew up. They had better be good."

For the last hour, Cannan had struggled over the orders. The idea of committing his men to an attack that he didn't believe in, that he was sure would end in the death of all of them, was not something he could ever put down on paper. It would have been impossible to. He saw the "battle" in his mind: the initial shock as the artillery rained explosions down in a wide path, the charge of the lead company of Abrams crushing the zombies under their treads, their machine guns spitting fire and their main guns blasting out grapeshot into the masses of undead, like they were fighting in Napoleonic times.

Then would come the Bradleys, the Strykers and the Humvees, all crammed with men; overflowing with men. There'd be soldiers clinging to every surface. Anything to keep from having to tread over the heaps of bodies. His division had already beaten off the attack of an estimated hundred thousand zombies, and their bodies carpeted the land for miles.

They would make it to Harrisburg, and there they'd be trapped, and there they'd die. It wouldn't be a heroic death, either. They would not be lionized like the three-hundred were in the Battle of Thermopylae. No, his men would be eaten alive. The hundred thousand they had killed was just the tip of the spear aimed at the heart of America.

That spear would impale his division and then drive through it to slay the country.

Cannan had agonized about writing the order, and he had agonized over not writing it. If he didn't write it, Boggs would find someone else to send them to their death, while Cannan, at best could expect a life sentence for cowardice, though with this President in charge, being executed was more likely. He and his division were in a lose-lose situation. They were doomed no matter what.

When that struck him, it did so with surprising gentleness. "If I am to die, it will be on my terms," he decided. It was then that he wrote his twenty-three page operational order. In his opinion it was some of his best work; twenty-three pages was amazingly succinct, especially as it contained six annexes and a half-page "personal" note. The entire operation rested squarely on the note which had been read to each of the companies twenty-four minutes previously.

Neither the order or the note mentioned attacking Harrisburg, Gettysburg or any other burg for that matter. It was a completely defensive order that supposed escalating attacks along the front lines as well as a growing threat from opposition forces from the southeast along the I-70 corridor—estimated at brigade strength. At the same time a separate force of regimental size which would likely be heading down from the northwest along the 522 Highway.

"What the hell is this?" Boggs demanded, holding the orders in a fist. "What brigade are you talking about? And this on airpower…" He flipped the order open to the seventh page, "this makes no sense at all."

"Sorry sir, but I think you blew right past the suppositions I had listed, and the third one down presupposes that the President will not observe the common sense of staying, at least for the time being, in a defensive posture. It's why I had the M6s brought up."

Boggs stared at him in complete amazement. It was so comical that if twelve-thousand lives weren't on the line, Cannan would have laughed. "I'm sure you understand that your order would necessarily end in the destruction of the 3rd ID and that…"

"Stop talking!" Boggs seethed.

"And that if we fall there is nothing, *nothing* standing between twenty million zombies and the heart of…"

"I said shut the hell up!" Boggs screamed, a cold light in his pale eyes. "You're disobeying a direct order." It wasn't a question; Cannan nodded. "You snake. You cowardly snake! Do you have any idea what you've done? I told you he was watching and now…of course you're under arrest." He paused and glanced upwards. "No, that's not enough. It can't be enough. Damn it, Tom, you've forced my hand."

Cannan nodded again, he was at the point where his own hand was about to be forced. "Do you not see the tactical situation here? Do you not see how it will become a strategic loss on an epic scale?"

"That's not the point."

"Just tell me if you see it or not!"

Boggs took a deep, deep breath, sucking air in as if it was the last on earth. When he let it out again, it was surprisingly controlled. Almost as if the air was strangling him, he choked out, "I don't see it. Orders are to be followed without question. There's no other way an army can be run."

A heavy sigh escaped Cannan. "In that case, I relieve you of your command. You are egregiously incompetent and sycophantic to a dangerous degree." Boggs began sucking in another long breath and Cannan was sure that he would be covered in a wave of expletives when Boggs expelled it. He lifted a hand to forestall it. "You and your staff will be held on a temporary basis and released unharmed, possibly in the next day or two."

This time the pent-up breath exploded out of him in a scream. "Held! Who are *you* to hold *me*?" He actually looked as though he wanted an answer. Cannan was done talking. He nodded to his XO, who held up a single finger high over his head. With this, the line of M6s turned suddenly and converged on the group.

"What is this?" Boggs demanded in disbelief. "You've turned them? My God, Cannan. Cowardice is one thing, but this is mutiny. Your men won't stand for it. Your officers…"

"My officers and my soldiers are completely behind me, one hundred percent." This was not hyperbole. The personal note had laid bare the situation and, in the most unprecedented move in the history of American warfare, it had given each man the option to follow the President's order to attack or to stay with the doomed division. In plain language, Cannan made sure that his men understood that staying was no salvation. The President would not just brand them as cowards and traitors, he would, in all likelihood, find them guilty of treason and order them killed.

There was no middle ground offered. They couldn't abstain. Just like Cannan, they had to make a choice. Those that chose to attack were to march out of the lines as ordered and die with their honor intact. Those that stayed, would stay and fight, knowing full well that they'd be fighting both the zombies and their own countrymen.

It was not an easy decision for any of them. In the end, it came down to numbers and time. Cannan estimated that by attacking, the 3rd ID would destroy approximately 300,000 zombies before they were finally overwhelmed. By staying on the defensive, he calculated that he could hold out for three days and destroy over a million of them.

Those three days would also give the army time to bring up another division or two, so that when the last of his men went down fighting, there wouldn't be a gigantic hole in the lines.

Cannan didn't normally carry a weapon, but he felt it would send a strong message if he took Boggs and the others into custody personally. He slid an M4 off his shoulder and aimed it at his commanding officer's midsection. When he clicked off the safety, Boggs sneered, "You don't have the guts to shoot me."

All around the group, hard-faced men appeared between the line of Bradley Fighting Vehicles. "Actually, I do," Cannan answered, with the smallest of shrugs. "I'll be dead soon one way or another. I am without fear." Deep down, he was at peace with his decision and would carry it out to its logical conclusion.

The 2nd Corps commander, as well as his staff and the division's political officers, were taken into custody, stripped of their weapons and communications and herded into a tent that was marked with a red cross. One of the 3rd ID soldiers, joked, "Luckily for you, the President would *never* bomb a medical facility. He's just too honorable for anything like that." The gallows humor had the group looking upwards in fear. They knew the truth, even if they'd been lying to themselves for the last five days.

"Ironic isn't it," Cannan said, a ghost of a smile playing on his lips as he watched them squirm. "Pretty much your only chance is if some Air Force pilot disobeys a direct order. Maybe one or two might, but eventually one will cave and then… booooom." He spread his hands in a mini simulation. "You do have a choice, of course. It's the same choice I gave my men. If you believe in the correctness of attacking Harrisburg, then I will give you a weapon and allow you the chance to retake the city. Anyone want to try that?"

Except for the guards, who chortled and whispered to themselves, no one budged or said a word.

"I didn't think so," Cannan said. "There is a second option. You can join me and take up arms against the dead. Come fight with us. Make a difference. Do some good for a change while you can. It's either that or sit here and hope your king doesn't decide to wipe us all out. Those B1s don't discriminate because of right or wrong."

Cannan had little hope that any of them would join and was surprised when Courtney Vertanen raised her hand. "I'll fight."

This didn't instigate a flood exactly, but half the MPs assigned to Boggs' security detail joined, as did nine members of his staff. Cannan knew all of them on a first-name basis and at least two had once been genuine soldiers before being softened by too many wine and cheese parties in DC.

"I didn't think this was how I was going to go out," one said, coming to stand on Cannan's side of the tent.

"We're not dead yet, Charlie," Cannan said, giving him his M4. "Come on. Let's go do some damage while we still can."

Chapter 18
5:00 p.m. Eastern Standard Time
Beijing, China

A murky, grey-tinged sun was just making an appearance, rising over the capital when the Russian ambassador, Maxim Bodeski arrived in the Great Hall. He had been there dozens of times and had never seen it so empty or so depressed. The few soldiers or party men he passed wouldn't look up from the red carpet.

They're whipped, Maxim thought to himself. Had it been for any other reason, he would have found it difficult to hide a smirk. For the last fifteen-hundred years, Russians had held a simultaneous view of China. On one hand, they knew without question, that they were vastly superior to the little slant-eyed gnats, while on the other, they feared, deep in their cold hearts, the Mongol, the Golden Horde, the Uyghurs and the Timurids.

To them, China had always been either a dangerous neighbor or an uncertain and untrustworthy ally, that could turn on them at any moment.

But what was happening now changed everything. Maxim had seen the footage from the satellites and the spy planes that had been crossing through Chinese airspace without any challenge whatsoever. It was so frightening that no one had bothered to couch what was happening in any of the usual bureaucratic nonsense. The folder he carried was titled simply: *Зомби*.

The translation from Cyrillic was as straight-forward as it got, the word meant zombie. Someone's hokey nightmare had come true.

There were four others with Maxim; a translator, two high-ranking generals who had been flown in specifically for the meeting, and a senior member of the Foreign Intelligence Service named Daluvich. The Cyrillic translation for the spy agency was a tongue twister and everyone referred to the Foreign Intelligence Service simply as the CBP; it was the Russian equivalent of the CIA.

Maxim thought Daluvich might be the coldest, most ruthless person he had ever met. He had such dead eyes, that if he became infected with the zombie virus, Maxim didn't think that much would change with him.

When they entered the main chamber, Maxim expected the usual mass of Asians, staring at them in cold dislike, but there were only three men present in a tremendous room that could fit a thousand. He recognized the greying, crumpled man in the middle as the General Secretary; he had aged badly in the last few days.

The man standing slightly behind him was a translator and thus must have been a spy as well—all Russian translators were spies, so it was always safe to assume that other countries worked the same way.

He didn't recognize the last man and cleared his throat lightly, which was the CBP agent's cue. "He is General Weilei, the new Vice Chairman of the Central Military Commission. The previous vice chairman, Okini was executed for failure to perform."

"I dare say," Maxim replied.

Their steps echoed in the chamber in a fatalistic manner. It was as if theirs would be the last steps ever to be heard there. This dark note was reinforced when the three Asians bowed deeply to the Russians. Bowing had become rare in China and when it was done, it was usually restricted to a movement of the head and neck. This bow bent the General Secretary nearly in half. What was more, he held the bow for a three-count.

"Ambassador Bodeski," he said through the translator. "I am grateful that you would come at such a time as this. Where others flee, you remain steadfast to your duty and should be praised." Maxim only nodded and the General Secretary went on with his praise for over a minute. Maxim, who was used to this sort of meaningless flowery rhetoric, very nearly let it wash over him, only there was a marked difference this time. The words weren't just harmless prattle. The General Secretary was being almost servile in his desperation. He was practically flaunting his country's weakness and playing up the greatness of Russia.

Maxim was a little shocked when he realized that the General Secretary was on the verge of begging. As much as he liked watching the man squirm and writhe there were zombies pressing north and he was there for a reason. "Why don't we cut to the chase? How can the Russian people help our friends to the south?"

"I ask that which cannot be asked."

The two generals shared a look and both rocked on their heels in satisfaction. They had been expecting the Chinese to ask for military assistance and the Russians were prepared to bomb the fuck out of them, but they weren't going to risk a single man on the ground.

The General Secretary nodded to General Weilei. He was a neat, little man, wearing a uniform stripped of the usual cacophony of ribbons and medals. With shaking hands, he opened a map of China. A large chunk around Shanghai was shaded in black, while a five-hundred mile arc around that was shaded grey. Weilei gestured at the arc. "This is the furthest we've found any of the infected. This area and every living thing within it must be destroyed and it must be destroyed irrevocably."

"I see," Maxim replied. "You are asking us to use nuclear weapons against your people. This is a terrible, terrible thing you ask of us." He made sure to arrange his face into a mask of grave concern even though plans had already been put in place for exactly this. The Russian plan was much more extensive and would have laid waste to forty percent of China.

"It is terrible, and yet necessary to secure the safety of both our peoples," Weilei said, with his head bowed. "Decisive action is needed now. Every hour that passes produces more of these creatures and it will not be long before we reach the tipping point where even nuclear weapons will not be enough."

Maxim sighed, spreading his hands as if helpless. "You ask too much. We do not possess nearly as many of these sorts of weapons as you suppose, and if we were to use them like this, well, you would leave us vulnerable, unable to defend ourselves. And what do we get in return? We would be looked on as pariahs. The world would shun us and rightly so. The Russian people are a peace-loving people. Our weapons are designed to be deterrents from western aggression, not to be used to commit genocide. Nyet, nyet, sorry. Maybe you should ask the Americans."

The General Secretary had already done exactly that, but the Americans were dealing with their own apocalypse and his call had been left unreturned. He assumed that Maxim knew that and was angling for something, and would very likely get it since China was in no state to play hardball.

"Perhaps if we offered a gift to the Russian people…"

"We don't want a gift," Maxim said, angrily cutting off the interpreter. "We want security from these demons, and even if we use our weapons—all of our weapons, it's no guarantee.

Have you not bombed your own people? And what has it given you? Nothing. We need more than a *gift*." He practically spat the word from his thick Slavic lips.

It was unnatural for the General Secretary to have his arm twisted so blatantly and not be able to do anything about it. "What do you propose?"

Maxim gave a glance toward the generals and Daluvich; all three nodded, giving their permission for Maxim to make the full demands. "For security reasons only, we will need to take over the province of Xinjiang, to be used as a buffer zone against possible zombie incursions." Xinjiang was the furthest western province and, in sheer size, it was the largest Chinese province. It was a harsh desert climate that even zombies would find difficult to withstand.

Even though the request was expected, the General Secretary sighed. "It makes sense, Mister Ambassador. We can draw up a formal…"

"I'm not done," Maxim said, raising his voice, slightly. The General Secretary cast an embarrassed look at Weilei, before nodding for Maxim to go on. "We will also need Inner Manchuria as well as Inner Mongolia for the same reasons." These two areas encompassed both a fifth of China's population as well as its land mass.

The General Secretary had been wrong about the Russians trying to rape them. No, this was far worse. The Russians were trying to cripple them for all time.

And yet, they had no other option. The General Secretary dropped his eyes. "I can't agree to any more."

Maxim hid a smile. "We don't want more. We only want a formal declaration on your behalf before the first missile is fired."

"Give me anything to sign and I will sign it. Give me something to read on television and I will read it," the General Secretary said abjectly, bending into another longer bow. With his face turned downward, none of the Russians could see the anger boiling across his features. It was gone when he straightened, hidden behind the mask he had perfected. It wasn't just his anger that was hidden. The knowledge that his revenge was already in motion was buried just as deeply.

2-5:30 p.m.

211

The White House, Washington DC

The Russian-Chinese treaty was written up and signed with indecent speed, and was set in the harshest of terms. Although the words "slave labor" were not written out per se, it was understood by all parties that the ethnic Chinese populations of the three provinces were to be given zero rights.

In fact, they were to be taken "possession of" by the Russian government. One line read: *All items, objects, resources, technology, existing infrastructure and human persons within the newly created buffer zones are the sole property of the Russian Federation and are hereby legally possessed.*

The Chinese Secretary General looked as though he'd been kicked in the balls as he signed the treaty. On the other hand, Maxim Bodeski could barely contain himself. He was overseeing what might be the greatest day in Russian history. Not only were the Americans imploding, the Chinese had just begged him to reduce their country to a pauper state. And they were going to pay the Russians to do it!

The minute the signing was completed, Maxim made his call to the Russian President saying, "We have won," in a greedy whisper. Just like that, the wheels of a completely one-sided nuclear war began to turn.

On the Chinese side, the Secretary General offered a quick goodbye without either a bow or a handshake. He strode to his inner office which, unlike the Great Hall, was teeming with people.

General Weilei was first to greet him, standing stiffly, he said, "They've begun fueling their rockets. We should remove you to safety, sir. We believe that it's almost certain they will target us by way of an 'accident' in guidance."

"One moment," the Secretary General said, before going to a secure phone. "I have to even the playing field, first." The phone rang once and was picked up without greeting or acknowledgement. "You may begin," was all he said before hanging up the phone and leaving as quickly as he arrived.

Half a world away, the American president, sat with his fingers steepled in front of his face. He had seen the translated broadcast and was frankly jealous. The Russians knew how to play the game. They knew how to get power and how to wield it.

"And look at me," he whispered, spreading his soft, manicured hands. "Supposedly the most powerful man in the world and everyone disrespects me at every turn. I'm a laughingstock." He hated to look at his "big" map. It mocked him.

The 4th ID was slogging through Kansas, their way impeded by destroyed bridges, and nails scattered across the highways from one end of the state to the other. Missouri, Indiana, and Kentucky had closed their borders in direct violation of his decrees. And something was happening in Ohio, but no one knew what.

Closer to home, he had *just* found out that the 3rd ID was staging a mutiny and not only wasn't attacking, its commanding officer had arrested its political officers. Of course, the President had ordered every unit in the area to attack them and instead of bullets and bombs, he got excuses—the militias were too ill-equipped and too inexperienced to fight frontline troops—the Air Force jets were all loaded down with antipersonnel bombs and couldn't go into a hostile environment without first suppressing the enemy's air defenses—the zombie threat was too great and every unit was needed to contain it.

"Fucking excuses!" he snarled, slamming a fist down on the table. "I don't hear the fucking Russians making excuses."

The Situation Room had been humming along quietly, no one was brave enough to raise their voice and be noticed. Now it went dead silent. "Pathetic," the President muttered, raking the assembled officers with his gaze. He picked out two of them huddled to the side; one held the "nuclear football." Since he was in a perfectly fine command center, the "football" wasn't needed. Still, the great man liked it nearby.

"You two! I need the plan adapted to take out those fucks. If they want to play, they're going to find out the hard way who they're dealing with."

"Yes sir," one said in something of a squeak. It was a little too easy to call the National Military Command Center and make the request. They were getting used to hearing from the White House, since the President had added to Emergency Response Plan #951 every hour that day. #951 called for a nuclear strike on American soil, something that was becoming more and more likely.

The President was watching the ranking officer closely to make sure his order was carried out when he caught sight of Trista Price standing a few feet away. He had forgotten that he had called for her. "Do we have the VP yet? No? It's been a fucking hour! Don't tell me Kazakoff hasn't been able to break Sheila. Trust me, she doesn't love Ron that much."

"No sir. He's barely started. He was still with the Attorney General. I mean the ex-Attorney General. And you were right. There has been talk about the 25th Amendment."

The President's eyes glittered in shallow victory. "I knew it! Tell him I want a list of everyone that Jew bastard talked to."

"Of course, sir." She bowed from the shoulders and was about to turn away when he made a secretive gesture for her to come closer.

"Tell me, what do you think about Kazakoff? I ask because he's delving into secrets that not everyone is fit to hear. Can he be trusted?"

She hated him with every ounce of her. The man was a human pit-bull…an abused human pit-bull. The only one who could possibly trust him was its master and even then, there was always a chance he could turn on him and tear his face off. Still, Kazakoff seemed to have a thing for Trista and, crazy as it seemed, it was possible he was her only ally in a building full of turncoats and snitches.

"Yes, I think so," she admitted, honestly. "He genuinely thinks you are the only man for the job."

"Good, good," the President said, sitting back and gazing up at the map. "Tell him 'thank you' for me. Then get him cracking on Sheila. She'll cave in no time. Remember, save her face."

Trista's throat tried to close itself off. She bowed again just to give herself a moment to collect herself. "Of course, sir," she managed to say without giving away her revulsion and terror of the man. Holding her head high, she hurried through the low-ceilinged maze to where the CIA was interrogating the President's suspects. Some of their suspects, that is.

Over eighty prisoners had been flown in from Boston to face the crimes of insurrection and treason. Another forty had come from the debacle at Harrisburg to face questions of gross incompetence. More than a hundred had been shuttled out of New York, including the governor, who had already been found guilty of malfeasance. It was basically a catch-all term that lumped in such things as lying to the American people, military fraud and collusion.

These numbers paled in comparison to the number of people who had been imprisoned in the DC area. Anyone who had ever looked cross-eyed at the President had been brought in. It was basically a death sentence even to question what he had been doing as commander in Chief.

It was why Trista was especially careful to keep her face set neutrally at all times; or almost at all times. Her carefully controlled visage broke when she saw that the Vice President's family was no longer sitting with the others in the back storeroom.

"No, no, no," she whispered running back along the corridors, peeking into each room until she found Kazakoff with the seven-year-old. The little girl was shaking and crying. Kazakoff was smiling.

"No, Kaz. This is wrong. At least start with the mom," Trista hissed, pulling him away from his video equipment.

He allowed himself to be pulled practically into her weak arms. "I did," he said, arching an eyebrow at their proximity, but not doing anything about it. Their noses were only inches apart. "She says she doesn't know where he is. But I think she's lying. I'm pretty sure this will get her to tell the truth."

Trista could feel her own tears welling in her eyes. She couldn't look at the girl; she would fall completely to pieces if she did. "Don't please. It's not worth it. The Vice President is a nobody. He's not a danger. It's all in the President's…"

Before she could go on, he crushed his hand across her face, bruising her lips. "Are you sure you want to finish that sentence?" he whispered so softly into her ear that it felt like a butterfly kiss. "If he hears, you'll be in the hot seat next." Her back shivered at this and he smiled, enjoying the effect.

Sickened by how close he was, she pushed past him and turned off the camera. That had been close. Her legs shook and her blouse was plastered to her skin. "Please Kaz. Maybe let this one go. We could tell him that he slipped out of town with the refugees."

"And what happens when he turns up hiding in the basement of the Capital Building? Don't be an idiot, Trista. The way to get through this rough patch is to roll with the punches."

"If that means torturing a little girl then no. No, I won't roll with that. I can't and neither should…" She bit off her words. There was no sense trying to find a soft spot inside *him*. Perhaps an appeal to his own safety would work. "Kaz, listen, the President is thinking about using nukes."

"Good," was his blithe answer. "It's about time. You've seen the maps. Don't tell me you haven't. Shit, every time I go in there, I wonder what he's waiting for."

"Maybe he's waiting for people to get to safety! Maybe he doesn't want to set off nuclear winter. Maybe he doesn't want to poison the entire eastern seaboard for all time. Have you ever thought about that?"

"No, but I will when I'm carving my initials into this girl's ass or when I'm raping her sister."

With anyone else, she would have thought they were being bombastic, or being purposely mean to get a rise out of her. That wasn't his style. He really would do those things. Trista started blinking rapidly, tears burning her eyes. "Y-You can't do that. Kaz! You can't do that to her. And, and her, her, her sister's only eleven. You can't do that."

"I can and I will. Rape is torture, if it's done right." He was smiling again and she was sure she had never seen anything so evil.

She stumbled from the room, her stomach rolling over. With tears in her eyes, she stared hard at the Secret Service agents, hoping to find a hero in one of them. Instead she saw cowardice. They'd had their chance to be heroes when General Phillips had been brought in, or when Haider was having his toes crushed with a hammer, or when Marty Aleman had been bawling worse than the seven-year-old girl who was, even then, screeching.

They had hidden behind excuses and parts of oaths and now they were ruined as men. She could see it in the way they refused to look at her.

"This is crazy," Trista hissed, uncaring if she was heard or who saw the hot tears. She felt like a weakling, but she still knew right and wrong. It felt like she was the only one who did. "Let me through," she challenged, as she came to the room where the Second Lady was being held, handcuffed to a chair.

So far, she hadn't been much abused and looked more angry than frightened, but not by much, and the fear in her began to ratchet up when she saw Trista, wild-eyed, panting, tears running down her face.

"You have to tell them where he is!" Trista begged, dropping down to her knees next to her.

"I know my rights. I demand to see a lawyer and a…"

Trista grabbed her with such force that her nails bit through the woman's shirt. "No! There are no more lawyers. Don't you understand anything? There's no more lawyers because there's no more laws." Trista lowered her voice and stared straight into the older woman's shocked eyes. "They're doing things to your daughters," she whispered with such honest force that the woman sat back, understanding finally creeping through the lies she had been telling herself.

The lies that nothing had changed and that America was still the land of freedom and truth had been her shield. Now, Sheila Patterson, the Second Lady of the United States saw her lies for what they were. She'd been hiding behind them. "Please, don't let them do anything to my children. I'll…I'll tell them everything, okay? I'll tell them where he is if they let us go."

"I don't know if they'll let you go, but I promise that if you tell me where he is I'll save your daughters. I promise that."

As much as Sheila loved her husband, she was a mother first and a wife second. "He's hiding with a friend of the family. His name is Gus Barkley and he lives in Falls Church. I don't know the address."

"We'll get it, don't worry. And don't worry about your daughters." Trista hopped up, nodded once to the woman, again almost a bow, and then ran from the room, only to be caught by a grinning David Kazakoff.

"That was perfect," he said. "I couldn't have staged that better if I'd tried. You and me make a great team."

Trista's head spun. "You-you weren't going to hurt that girl? You were lying the whole time?"

"Of course, I was going to hurt her, and I still might. Pain is simply a tool like any other. Like you. You're a tool. And I'm a tool, as well." He leaned in close to her once more, and again, she shivered. He whispered gently into her ear like a lover would. "You should be afraid, my sweet little tool. I want you to think about something. You need to realize that we only keep tools around as long as they remain useful. I had a pair pliers once that would pinch my palm every time I used them. And you know what I did with them?"

"You got rid of them," she said, understanding dawning in her mind.

"Shhhh," he said, blowing into her ear. "Not so loud. You wouldn't want someone to overhear you, because I think you now know what the President will do with you if he thinks you might hurt him in any way."

He was warning her yet again.

"But this isn't right."

A shrug lifted his shoulders. "Sure isn't. Come here, let me show you something." He pulled her to one of the rooms. It hadn't been used yet, which meant there wasn't blood on the floor or sweat stains on the arms of the chair. There was a folding table with some of the terrible tools Kazakoff had liberated from the kitchens: meat hooks and knives; there was even a bone saw that Trista couldn't stop staring at.

"I'm saving this room for you," Kazakoff told her, picking up a viciously sharp-looking knife. She couldn't have known it, but it was a Sakai Takayuki Aogami—a fancy peeling knife from Japan. It cost over a thousand dollars and had an edge that was sharper than any razor. "You'll be sitting right there soon enough, if you can't control yourself."

3-5:41 p.m.
Grafton, Massachusetts

At any point in the previous four hours, Ex-Governor Clarren could have been found with ease. The great eastern army of the dead had chased some magical willow-o'-wisp in a circle giving the defensive lines that were desperately trying to keep Boston safe, the slightest breather. The mass of undead was still frighteningly dangerous. It was millions strong and it moved with no rhyme or reason. Without apparent cause, it would cast off seemingly inconsequential tens of thousands in this direction or that.

One such minor horde, a bare fifteen thousand, threw itself into the two-mile gap between the Wachusett Reservoir and Lake Quinsigamond, north of Lieutenant Colonel Ross's regiment.

Defensively speaking, the area was a jewel; there was a wide open 18-hole golf course, two deep quarries, three ponds and a "transmission highway" that ran right down the length. This last was simply a long lane cut through the existing forest and neighborhoods to allow for power lines. It wasn't perfect, but fifty yards of open terrain was better than nothing.

The hour-long fight was a nice break for Ross' 1st Battalion, and while it went on in a great storm of flying metal and burning explosions, Ross slept easily. He had found in Clarren the makings of a great executive officer. The ex-governor paced the lines, making sure that what little ammo they had was distributed evenly. Not long after he had the ammo sorted out, a mass shipment of sandwiches arrived. They were brought in by a pickup truck driven by a woman with arms thick as hams and a vocabulary that was almost entirely composed of inventive curse words.

When she bawled, "I don't give a monkey's puckered-ass who ya were, ya ain't gettin' no more samiches!" at Clarren for daring to ask for more, it had the men crying with laughter.

The ruckus woke Ross, who thought they were being attacked again. When he found out what was going on, he tried sweet talking the woman into letting him take seconds for his men.

"Only for a kiss, honey," she said in her guttural Bostonian accent. She made fish lips at him, which made him rethink the first sandwich.

"I'll do it," he warned.

"What are ya waitin' for? Climb on up here prune-dick, I won't bite."

When Ross hesitated, Clarren smoothed back his dark hair and put out his arms. "Whadya say, doll?" She shrugged and was given a longer kiss than Ross would have attempted with a woman half as ugly for twice as many sandwiches.

The men cheered the kiss and slapped Clarren on the back for "Taking one for the team," as they collected their extra sandwiches. Ross was surprised to discover that he liked Clarren, and not just because his stomach was full for the first time since he had heard that zombies were real. They had been mortal enemies only the day before, and Ross would have punched his ticket without hesitation. Now they were on the same side, and Ross found himself admiring the man's raw courage. This courage was all the more impressive since he was not just a soft civilian, he was a pampered politician.

They were sharing their sandwiches when a Humvee filled with MPs came tearing up. The driver was a vaguely familiar butter bar with sweat on his upper lip. He stared out over the battlefield where the black bog stretched for hundreds of yards. Out in the middle of it were a few thousand grey beasts that seemed uncertain what to do; zombies were weird like that sometimes.

219

Without taking his eyes from them, the lieutenant said, "Hey, sergeant, I'm looking for Colonel Ross."

"You got him."

"Ha-ha. No really."

Ross looked down at himself and saw that somewhere in the last six hours of fighting, he had lost the little bits of silver that meant he could order men to their deaths. "I was bumped up. What's going on?"

The lieutenant gave him a closer look and then shrugged. "Division is looking for Dean Clarren. He was the governor; they're going to arrest him."

"Wasn't he the governor of this shitty little state?" Ross asked. "That's not something to brag about if you ask me. What do they want him for? Not paying his taxes? He get caught with the maid? The maid and her rottweiler?"

Clarren had been sitting stiffly next to him, but now he began to laugh out bits of turkey sandwich.

"No, they want to kill him. Well, they want to take him back to DC, but you know what's going to happen there." The young man put a finger gun to the side of his head and pulled the trigger. "Pow. Anyway, they said he was with you guys. This is 1st Battalion, right?"

"Yeah, but I don't friggin' know every swinging dick around here. Wait. He was that fancy-pants fudge-packer. Sort of swishy, right?" Next to him, Clarren was turning red, tears streaming from his eyes. Ross refused to look at him as he started to nod. "Now, I remember him. He took off a while ago. Said he had salsa lessons or was getting a facial or something. Sorry kid. Hey, tell those morons up at division that its's safe to come down here. They're no longer in danger of being fragged because we're out of fucking ammo. I'm not kidding. Use those exact words."

The lieutenant gave him a it's-your-funeral look and went back to the Humvee. When he was plowing back up the road as if the entire zombie army only cared about eating him in particular, Ross turned to Clarren, who had sobered up fast. "You better take off. I know you want to fight, but you don't have to do it here."

"No," Clarren said, wiping the tears from his eyes. "I can't run, not even from them. And I can't have people thinking that I have. I know I'm not governor anymore and I know a lot of people hate me…"

"I'd use loathe. Is that a good word? Maybe try despise."

Clarren elbowed him. "All those are fine words. They can hate me, but I don't want them to ever doubt my commitment to my state. If they kill me, fine. I'll even let them drag me out of here, but I won't go voluntarily. I don't want to toot my own horn, it's just I think it'll hurt morale if it looks like I'm chickening out, and that's already dangerously low."

Morale was actually high with the 1st Battalion. Ross had shown real leadership and Clarren's good will, courage and his stunt with the beefy truck driver had cemented his position as a favorite among the soldiers, especially among the guardsmen and militia. The few men of the 101st still in the battalion had a grudging respect for him since running away had been an option most politicians would have taken.

After finishing what had either been a very late breakfast or an early dinner, Ross made a tour of the line. It would be dark in two hours and he didn't know if he could expect flares. While it was quiet, he had the men work on making hedges of spears. Everyone knew that they wouldn't stop the undead. They could only hope to slow the beasts down long enough to get a bullet into their heads.

As he was heading back to his place in the center, he heard the rumble of engines. He hoped for an ammo run, instead he got a Major General with a stiff bottlebrush mustache, his Brigade Commander, looking like he'd been pulled out of bed after a three-minute nap. Along with him was a gaggle of political officers in BDUs that still had creases in them, and twenty MPs. It was obvious what this was about. Ross grabbed a soldier from the line. "Run and get the reserve company. Run! The rest of you, come with me. Come on, let's go."

Two platoons of dirty men trudged after Ross as he made his way up the little hill to where he sometimes came to take a leak against a tree. It was his version of a command post—he preferred to command on the go.

"What can I do for you, sir?" he said, coming to attention. Behind him the guardsmen stood straighter though none was particularly stiff. The militia men looked on casually, one quite flagrantly picking his nose.

"You have a person of interest among your men, Ross. Governor Dean Clarren. He's a traitor to the government."

Ross glanced back at his men. "We don't have any traitors here, sir. These are all patriots. They're all risking their lives…

for our *nation*." Clarren had been terribly wrong about closing his border and fighting the US Army, but the news was getting out about how the President was handling things—Courtney Shaw was seeing to that. She had made it her mission to let everyone know the insane nature of the orders that were being sent out.

When Ross had heard about what was happening in Pennsylvania, he had mentioned to Clarren, and a number of others, that he would have told the President to go fuck himself. It was big talk that he didn't think he'd ever have to back up with action, and yet here he was, more or less stuck in the same position.

The general's eyes drew down into angry little slits. "I'm sure they're all great men and I admire loyalty, but this is going to happen one way or another, Ross. Go get Clarren up here or I'll be forced to send my own men to get him. And if that's the way this is going to go down, he won't be the only one we'll be taking away with us."

Ross was regular army and it felt distinctly, perhaps even genetically wrong to even consider going against a direct order. He took a shaky breath and managed to say, "I'm sorry sir, but I need every man that I can get on the line. Your orders, as lawful as they are, do not take precedence over my duty to protect the people of Boston."

It felt like he had just put his head in a noose.

The general grew red in the face. He took two oddly large steps forward, almost as if he were some sort of robot. "We are not going have a fucking repeat of what's going on in Pennsylvania. Bring me the traitor, or else." He growled out these words, barely opening his mouth, his teeth grinding as if he were chewing on each word before spitting them out.

"With all due respect, sir, the answer is no. Chances are he'll die fighting the dead and that will be punishment enough."

"Don't listen to him, General," the ranking PO ordered. "If he dies on the line, he'll be lionized as a hero. That is unacceptable. And it's also unacceptable the way he's talking to you or how he spoke to our representative earlier. He basically threatened all of us."

Ross scoffed, "Your representative? This isn't a boardroom, jackass. The man was a second lieutenant and what I said was a joke. Trust me, we have enough bullets for a good ol' fashioned fragging." The general growled something in the back of his throat, while the political officer was beside himself with indignation. "It's nothing you have to worry about," Ross said to the PO. "Fragging involves the killing of a superior officer. I don't know what you are, but you aren't an officer and you aren't superior to anything."

"That does it!" the PO cried. "Arrest him! Arrest him right now!"

The MPs had been watching all of this with growing anxiety. At the beginning of the little altercation, they had about equal numbers with the platoon Ross had brought with him. Gradually, more and more soldiers had come from the line, and even more had come jogging up from behind, until now they were outnumbered three to one.

A staff sergeant in charge of the MP detail looked decidedly uncomfortable as he nudged two others and came forward.

Ross slid his rifle up to his shoulder and aimed it at the PO. "Keep coming and see what happens."

The political officer blanched, his face sour and pale. He looked over at the general, whose face was rigid but impassive. He then surveyed the men behind Ross; they wore sneers and their weapons were no longer carried casually.

"Fine. We'll leave. But I guarantee that when we come back things will be different. You'll see."

"Why? Because you have tanks?" Ross asked, still with the rifle at his shoulder. "Great. Bring them on. You can park them right here. We might be able to hold the line tonight if you do. And that's no joke, sir. My men are exhausted and on the verge of…" He stopped just short of saying they were on the verge of running. As true as it was, he wasn't going to disgrace his men by saying it aloud.

"All I'm saying is that tanks would be welcome," he said after the shortest of pauses. "You know what's not welcome? These Soviet-style political officers…sir."

Even though the general had been flown in from the Pentagon, he detested the political officers as well. But that didn't mean he was going to put up with this shit. "Take your *sir* and shove it up your ass, Ross. You've threatened a superior officer! Your days are numbered."

"I'm not too worried," Ross shot back. "If a million zombies can't kill me, I doubt a fat, brown-nosing general and his government appointed butt-buddy can even scratch me. Come back when you're ready to fight the real enemy, sir."

In a fury, the general and his people left and when they had turned their trucks and Humvees back the way they came, the little group of soldiers and wanna-be soldiers cheered.

Clarren suddenly appeared at Ross' side, sighing sadly. "I take it you've never read that book *How to Win Friends and Influence People*."

Ross shook his head, suddenly feeling sick to his stomach. "I'm not much of a reader." In a whisper, he added, "What have I done?"

Clarren considered the question. "Apart from becoming more of a criminal than I am? Well, for one you suggested that your commanding officer was gay, which probably wasn't helpful. It's weird. Soldiers seem to make a lot of homophobic jokes. You ever notice that?"

"Yeah, I noticed it. But I figure there's no reason to be a fag about it." Clarren chuckled; Ross only sighed, feeling low. "If they come for us, the line will fall and if the line falls, I don't see how Boston can stand for very long."

"You should've let them have me," Clarren answered.

"And lose the toughest rump-ranger this side of the Mississippi?" Ross replied, trying to smile. Clarren only rolled his eyes—Ross shook his head at this. "No, that's the wrong response. What you should've done was punch me in the arm and crack on how fat my mom is. What's with you Bostonians? You used to be tough. The founding of the revolution and all that."

This set Clarren in a reflective mood. "We've had our 'Bunker Hill' moment. Now we need a Lexington and Concord. This is April after all."

Ross had no idea what the month had to do with anything, and the same was true with Lexington and Concord. He knew they were Revolutionary War battles, but that was about it. "Meaning what, exactly? You had your own personal rebellion and it failed. I don't see how another will work."

"But now we have the illustrious Colonel Troy Ross on our side. You may not know it, but you're kind of famous out here. You're the reason we're still holding the line. That's what I hear. The artillery, the air strikes; everyone thinks that was your doing. If you lead them, men will follow you."

"Not against tanks they won't. And where do you think they would follow me to?"

Clarren grinned. "To arrest those fucking political officers. Once they're gone, we can win this, Ross. Everyone knows they're screwing things up. If you take them out, even the tanks will follow you. Trust me."

Chapter 19
6:20 p.m. Eastern Standard Time
Moscow, Russia

The Sukhoi Superjet 100 touched down twenty-eight minutes ahead of schedule. With China convulsing in its death throes behind them, and the launch of nuclear weapons reportedly only minutes away, the pilot pushed the SS100s cruising speed to its maximum. The last Russian officials to leave the country weren't going to complain, and neither would anyone at Aeroflot airlines. They wanted their plane back as fast as possible.

It wasn't germs they feared. They had scrubbed the jet from top to bottom and had forced the passengers and crew to sit through a four-hour quarantine before being allowed to board.

No, they were worried about their jet flying through a wall of radiation forty-thousand feet high.

Not that they were blind to the possibility of bringing the plague into Russia. There were two government officials on board watching the passengers with piercing eyes. Each carried compact pistols, rubber gloves, masks and spray bottles filled with bleach. Thankfully, no one showed even the least sign of a headache even now after the long flight.

When it landed, they were all glad to get away from the plane, but none more so than Svetlana Melnikova. She'd had a plastic tube shoved up her ass for the last five hours and couldn't wait to get the thing out of there.

After passing through security she went straight to the bathroom, as always, thankful that Aeroflot employees rated private stalls. Two minutes later, she sighed in relief and slid the tube, now smelling strongly of ethyl alcohol, into a plastic bag, which in turn was thrust into Svetlana's knock-off *Chanel* purse. Now that she had her ass uncorked, she strolled out of the bathroom and through the main terminal, careful to keep from hurrying.

Without being able to explain why, she thought that hurrying would only make her look guilty. In truth, she really didn't have much to worry about. Practically everyone was crowded about the many airport screens televising the countdown to the nuclear strike. Svetlana could have turned cartwheels through the airport and not be noticed. Still, she thought of herself as a professional spy and maintained her poise until she came to the parking garage.

Here the air was sharply cold and the quiet was, well, it was too quiet. After three days in China, a land of nearly one and a half billion people, she felt startlingly alone. Her pace picked up as she looked left and right for the drop signal. The signal was nothing more than a line of chalk scratched across the back of one of the parking spaces on the way to her car.

If it wasn't there, she'd go home and wait for a second signal: a single ring on her phone. That would require her to take a long boring walk around a park, which would suck because she was tired and wanted to be done with the assignment as fast as possible.

Thankfully, the chalk was there and she breathed another sigh of relief. Had she any idea what she was carrying or who she was really working for she would've cried with relief to be rid of the vial. At a million rubles per job—which came out to about $15,000—she didn't care about the who or the what. Svetlana liked to think she was working for the CBP, as a secret agent, but in her heart, she worried that she was working for the *Bratva*: the Russian mafia. The man who had brought her in, her "handler," was cool, handsome, rich beyond reason and coldly Russian.

The one time she had asked what she was smuggling in and out of China, his eyes had assumed a dead sort of look and he had replied, "Don't ask that. Never ask, and don't think about it. Do your job and hope the seal on the tube is never broken, because…" He ended the threat with a little shrug of one shoulder, and a small what-can-you-do smile.

The message was perfectly clear, they would kill her. It was something both the CBP and the Bratva were known to do.

It was also something operatives of China's Ministry of State Security(MSS) would do without batting an eye. The fact of the matter was that Svetlana had been working for a fabulously wealthy Chinese businessman who was openly tied to the Communist Party, and secretly to members of the MSS.

If she had known this, it would have made her sick to her stomach, and if she had known she was carrying a vial of infected zombie blood up her ass, she would have quite literally shit herself.

When she saw the chalk mark, she went into her normal routine of making a show of fumbling through her purse. It would be dropped and the bag with the vial in it would be brushed under the next car; just another piece of litter in a city that was slowly filling with garbage. This was not a normal drop, however. Nowhere close.

As she came up to her cramped little box of a car, she caught the whiff of a cigarette, an American one. Glancing to her right, she saw a Chinese man leaning against a white van. "Don't drop the purse," he said in choppy Russian.

"Huh?"

"Your purse." He pointed with his cigarette. "You normally drop it. This time, don't."

The knock-off *Channel* wasn't going anywhere. She had a firm grip on it as if the Chinese man was far more formidable than he appeared. With her three-inch heels, Svetlana towered over the paunchy little man. "Who are you?"

"Just a link in the chain," he lied. He was usually the last link, but with this drop, he thought it better to cut out the others. There was no need for layers of security, now. His identity…his entire life, at least as it had been, was soon to be over. "I'll take the vial if you please."

It did not please and she backed away. He sighed out a cone of blue smoke. "Svetlana, don't make me kill you." As she watched, he pulled out a small black pistol and held it loosely, easily. "Nothing is different about this drop except that instead of leaving the vial beneath a car, you're going to hand it to me. Be cool."

He knew her name and he knew the protocol. It had to mean he was legit, she told herself. And he had a gun. What could she do? Nothing. That's what she would tell her handler, if she was being set up. Slowly, she lifted her hand with the purse in it, but couldn't bring herself to walk across the intervening fifteen feet.

The Chinese man cocked the cigarette into the corner of his mouth and looked up and down the parking garage before he crossed over to take the purse from her. Plunking it down on the trunk of her car, he dug through it without taking his dark eyes from her. He found the vial by feel and when he did, he surprised Svetlana: his body spasmed as he stuck it deep into an inner pocket of his jacket and when he sucked on the last of the cigarette, his hand shook.

He paused for several long seconds looking up at the girl. Amazingly, he found himself struggling over the idea of telling her to leave the city. It was wrong and stupid, but she was young and pretty, and had been a reliable mule for three years. Hadn't he sent his other agents off with warnings not to look back?

They had been different. Seven of them were Chinese and two Lithuanian.

This girl was Russian. He had been raised to hate and fear the Russians. They couldn't ever be trusted. And Svetlana was no different, he decided.

He patted his pocket, said, "Good day to you," and turned to his car: a five-year-old Lada Largus. The Russian-built subcompact was about as dull and nondescript as a vehicle could get. Svetlana eyed it with distaste, thinking it wasn't the kind of car a real spy would drive. She couldn't be more wrong. The Asian got in and within minutes virtually disappeared into the city.

As he drove, he was hyper-aware of the vial. It felt huge beneath his coat, as if it was swelling. He wanted to check it, to measure it perhaps, or to make sure the seal hadn't been broken or was being dissolved by the plague within. With a strength of will, he put both hands on the wheel and kept them there until he was in the heart of Moscow. Pulling over to the side of the road, he dug out the vial and held it up so he could inspect the seal on the plastic. It was unbroken.

That was good and yet when he tried to swallow, his throat clenched like a dry fist. He stowed the vial away and once more patted his jacket.

Inside the tube would be a second vial. This one was also plastic but with a rubber stopper. It held 30ccs of diseased blood, more than enough to wipe out *Mother Russia*.

It would also kill Chen Qi.

Chen was the station chief's real name. It was a name only a handful of people knew. He had seven other aliases and seven different passports, none of which would save him. Chen had been picked for both the position of station chief, as well as for this particular job for a reason: his loyalty was beyond question and utterly unshakable. It would need to be. Nothing could be left to chance.

His phone buzzed with a text message: *Pick up bread on the way home*. Another spasm racked Chen. The message meant that the ICBMs had been launched; China was an hour from being virtually destroyed.

Taking a deep breath, he stuck the Luga in gear and headed for the Kazansky railway station. In a startlingly clean bathroom stall, he opened the first tube, revealing the deadly second one. It was whole and clean, the rubber stopper set down in it snuggly. Chen brought out his needle and syringe and, although his chest was fluttering, his hands were now steady as he drew out 10ccs. His plan to infect the train station was simple: he placed a drop of the blood on the corner of a stack of rubles.

They were 200-ruble notes. Because of inflation, it was the lowest denomination still used in bill form. Chen spread them around, spending them at every kiosk, newsstand, restaurant and food cart he came across. In all, he handed out seventy-seven of the bills, which were in turn handed out as change to fifty other people, who boarded nineteen different trains.

It took one hour and forty-eight minutes to spend the money. Halfway through, Chen paused along with the rest of the station to watch as satellites recorded the detonation of the first dozen nuclear weapons. People looked at him strangely after that. They wouldn't look him in the eye—it made killing them easier.

When Chen had gone through his first stack of bills, he was still feeling like himself and not some sort of monster. He got back into his Luga and headed cross town to the Kursky railway terminal, the next busiest train station in the city. This one connected three major metro lines that shot trains around Moscow. As well, it ran lines towards the western sections of the country. A number of its trains went to the Ukraine and beyond.

Chen's headache was just beginning when he left the bathroom stall with a wad of newly bloodied bills. The headache was expected and he swallowed five white pills. These helped long enough for him to spread his bills far and wide, infecting people on a further twenty-two trains. He was now out of money and the smuggled vial was empty, but he wasn't done. There was still a source of zombie blood available to him. It was burning through his veins and making his head rage.

After dry-swallowing seven more pills, he used the needle from his syringe to cut his left wrist. It wasn't a major laceration, just a cut big enough to leave blood smears from the ticket windows to the 319 train to Volgograd, what used to be known as Stalingrad. It was six-hour trip, but he only stayed on the train long enough to stagger from one end to the next, dripping blood. Forty-four people were infected before he went to the caboose, climbed up on the rail and ended his pain with a single bullet to the head.

He toppled away into the darkness, leaving behind a train that would never make it to Volgograd. It would make it only as far as Borisoglebsk, where it would jump the track and keel over on its side. No one died in the crash because the only ones left on board were the undead.

By then, a third of China was burning in a nuclear holocaust. It was a horror, but at least the zombies were dead—the Chinese zombies that is. In Russia, there were now close to three-thousand infected people scattered throughout every major city west of the Volga, an area encompassing over 350,000 square miles with a population of ninety million people.

Chen had done his job. Three-thousand became ten-thousand before Svetlana Melnikova lay down to sleep, and that ten-thousand became twenty before the first military units were sent racing in ten different directions, trying to contain a multiplying plague that was in many ways the equivalent of the mythological Hydra. As soon as they cast a perimeter around one outbreak, two more would spring up.

Still the police and the army fought on, not realizing that Russia was already doomed.

2-6:23 p.m.
Newville, Pennsylvania

The F-15E Strike Eagle was so close to the ground that its huge Pratt & Whitney engines sent the pines wagging back and forth after it roared by. Tony "Stubby" Alvarez was playing the Wild Weasel game of *Here, kitty kitty*.

It was a simple game, for Alvarez that is. His wingman on the other hand, had the dangerous part. He was twenty miles northeast of Alvarez flying nap-of-the-earth(NOE), at 500 knots, but doing so like a scrub right out of the academy. When he "hopped his hedges" instead of scraping over the hills, he would pop up sometimes as much as a hundred meters at a time. And when he cleared a valley, he would ease around as if he were out sightseeing.

The whole idea behind this pathetic display was to get the SAM radars focused on him, leaving Alvarez free to come up undetected and release his AGM-88s. These were High-speed Anti-radiation Missiles(HARM) designed to home in on electronic transmissions coming from surface-to-air radar systems.

Of course, the 3rd ID's anti-aircraft teams knew all about the kind of weasel games that the Air Force was likely going to play. There was a good chance that Alvarez had just shot right over the top of some kid with a shoulder-mounted Stinger. These could lock in on the immense heat signature of the F-15's engines and blot him out of the sky in a second.

"You getting anything, Matt?"

His backseat weapons officer answered quickly, "Not a blip. What are you up to on the ol' PF range?"

Alvarez's pucker factor had just edged past a six on the usual one-to-ten scale. "Nominal," he lied. The 3rd ID knew they were coming and they possessed the most advanced anti-aircraft missiles in the world. They were playing it so cool that it had Alvarez sweating.

He was the lead for a flight of fourteen planes and if he couldn't identify and knock out a few of the SAM sites, it was going to spell trouble for those behind him. He might have been conflicted over killing civilians, but this was warfare that he understood. These people would kill him if he didn't kill them first. Yes, it was terrible that these were American soldiers, but that didn't mean he could look the other way while they committed treason.

"Cove Gap in thirty seconds," Matt warned.

"I see it." At 460 knots the gap in the hills looked like the size of a thumb nail. It was on him in a blink as he banked hard to the right, cutting into the gap. At this speed, he knew he would shoot out of it in four seconds. Almost on faith, he banked hard left on the count of four and now he was rushing up the valley.

"I got nothing!" Matt practically shouted.

Shit! Their role in the game of *Here, kitty kitty* was about to be reversed. Alvarez was sure that they would be painted any second—his pucker factor was now at an eight. "Roger that. Switching to GBU15s. Give me a target, Matt." They would be on top of the SAM sites too quickly to set up a HARM strike.

"Flight Five Zero out of Langley, your targets are three miles west of Newville," a woman...*the* woman said. It was the same woman that had spoken directly to Alvarez earlier that morning. It was the woman who some called the Angel of the Airwaves and others bitterly called Pennsylvania Rose. "As the men of the 3rd Infantry Division are not your enemies, the M6s are unmanned. You may destroy them if you wish."

"This is Tango Zero One," the radio barked, "disregard the previous broadcast. Proceed to the target."

Courtney sighed into the radio microphone. "It will be a waste of your bombs. And not only that, it will make it harder for the men on the ground to fight off the zombies. You can see the zombies, can't you? There's millions of them and every bomb you drop means there's less…"

"Ignore her!" Tango Zero One cried into the radio.

Alvarez froze at the stick, indecision gripping him. He could see the zombies. He couldn't miss them since they stretched as far as the eye could see. They were no longer coming in controlled waves as they had been earlier, and the fight along the line was becoming fierce and desperate.

"Are we screwing up?" he asked, speaking to himself.

His WSO heard; however, and muttered, "Pull it together, Stubby! Our target is at our ten o'clock. Fox three, Stubby, let's go."

"It might be a trap," Alvarez said, and throttled the engines as he pulled back on the stick. His Eagle soared straight up, showing her underbelly to the world, becoming the perfect target.

"Stubby!"

Alvarez ignored his WSO and continued going straight up, ready to shuck and jive the instant he heard the shriek in his ear that told him a search radar had locked on to him. His pucker factor should have been off the charts, but he knew deep in his heart that no one was targeting him. Those were Americans down there, not rebels. They were fighting the undead, just like he should have been.

Up he soared, up and over in a glorious inverted loop. Had there been actual enemies below him, he could have been killed ten-times over. When he came out of the loop, he banked slightly, heading away from the line of M6s and towards the massive army bearing down on the 3rd ID.

"Tango Zero One, this is Five Zero Five. There is no SAM presence here. I'm changing targets."

"Negative Five Zero Five. Continue with mission as ordered."

Behind him his weapons officer actually kicked his chair. "I'm warning you, Stubby!"

Alvarez ignored him and spoke to the rest of the planes behind him. "Flight Five Zero, the SAM threat is neutralized. Engage high value targets. Follow my lead." Both Control and Matt began screaming at him, but he didn't care. Something had gone decidedly wrong with the military. It had been bad enough when they attacked Massachusetts, but now they were supposed to be bombing their own men? It was wrong. No, it was worse than wrong, it was insane. He saw that perfectly now.

From where Alvarez sat, he had a perfect view of the battlefield and he saw that it was clearly insane to expect the 3rd ID to attack in any direction. It was a wonder they weren't running away as fast as they could. They didn't deserve to die.

Feeling strangely calm, Alvarez drawled into his radio, "Control, those M6s aren't going anywhere and I have just about a jillion zombies right in front of me. Dropping on targets now." He brought his Eagle to eight-hundred feet, shot over the line of defenders like an avenging fury and began releasing his GBU15s one at a time.

He could hardly miss and the explosions thrummed and roiled the air behind him. When his load was jettisoned he casually remarked, "Going to guns," as he took a wide turn over the horde. He was banked far enough over that he could see behind him as the rest of his flight roared down the valley in wild confusion. Two planes were engaging the Bradleys; one with bombs, the other uselessly firing its AGM-88s. Without a radar to lock on, the two missiles soared off toward the setting sun.

The rest of his flight was split, with half engaging the zombies and the other half loitering, going in circles.

A hundred and fifty miles away, Courtney Shaw was monitoring the feeds from two different drones. She saw the hesitation of some of the pilots. "Flight Five Zero, if you believe there are two enemies down below you, kill the ones you think are the most danger to your families."

"That's enough, Courtney," Colonel Taylor warned. She had been broadcasting for too long in his opinion. They'd already had two close calls. Along with the *Sentinels*, there were two *Reapers* lurking somewhere above them. They could fly at 25,000 feet and launch their 500-pound, laser guided GBU-12 Paveways from miles away. In this case; however, since there was no danger from anti-aircraft weapons, they would probably get up close and personal to make sure of their kills.

General Axelrod agreed. "We should move again," he said, with a glance out the window. They were eleven stories above downtown New Rochelle, squatting in an abandoned apartment that smelled of old fried food. "Alright people, let's pack it up." It would be their third move in the last hour.

"Just a moment," Courtney answered. She cleared her throat, switched to the sat-phone and spoke in a sharp tone, "Flight Seven Seven, this is Tango Three Five, the SAM threat has been eliminated. Engage ground targets beyond Highway 233. Be aware there are friendlies on the ground."

"Tango Three Five say again. What friendlies?"

Major Clay Palmburg began snapping his fingers at Courtney. He had managed to reach a friend who had contacts in the Pentagon and who was somewhere along the chain of command that stretched from Washington to Nevada and then back out to New York. "A Sentinel's picked us up!"

All around Courtney there was a flurry of activity as the officers slammed their computers shut, yanked cords from walls and began stuffing everything into their packs. She was the only one not moving. She flipped away from the window she had open on her laptop that showed Tony Alvarez dropping his Eagle down so low it looked like he was going to try to land in the midst of the undead. He flew at head-height and began to blast away with his 20mm M61 Vulcan. The six-barreled Gatling gun, along with the huge jet roaring inches above the undead, cleared a path fifty feet wide and four-hundred yards long.

It was beautiful flying that Courtney missed as she brought up her unit map. "Flight Seven Seven, this is Tango Three Five; we have a newly arrived unit from Kentucky. It's the 149th Maneuver Enhancement Brigade out of Richmond. They are unaware of the situation and, until we can extricate them, they cannot be fired upon. Please acknowledge…"

Taylor shut her computer, nearly snapping her fingers in the process. He grabbed her bag as Major Palmburg took her by the arm and pulled her from the room at a run.

"Hey!" she cried. "Those guys need me."

"They need you alive," Axelrod yelled over his shoulder. It had been a surprise to him how true that had become. Courtney Shaw had an almost magical knack for finding the right person to talk to, or the right lie to concoct, or the right heart string to pull to get things done. Even with the full force of the government after her, she was making a mess of things for the President.

She was like a casting director from 21st Century Fox, handing out parts to each of them: "General, you're the junior senator from Virginia and you need to know what units are in the state and where—the muckety-mucks in the Pentagon will ask why. Just tell them you've seen soldiers with paratroop wings on their uniforms, and you're worried about traitors."

"Taylor, your name is Rene Papadopolis. You own the Athena Cantina right there outside of Langley. Call this number; it's the SP unit direct line. Tell them you saw someone with what looked like a bazooka slip into the woods west of the base. Yeah, I know no one would use a bazooka to shoot down a plane, but they'll think it's one of them Stingers."

"Major Palmburg, call this number. Tell them you're an *Eagle Keeper*, but you want to remain anonymous. Tell them the number two fuel tank is sparking again and that you told your PO. He didn't think it was a big deal, but you're worried it will blow."

Eagle Keeper was a slang term for a maintenance crew chief of an F-15, but how she knew it, Palmburg didn't know.

And she had her own roles: "Shepherd control tower? Great. This is Melinda Hildago, I'm a political officer with DHS. Is there a Colonel Roberts there? No, I don't want to talk to him. I need him arrested. Yeah, I don't know for sure why. I just get names and we let the CIA sort out all the answers."

This was why she was so valuable. She was almost singlehandedly keeping the 3rd ID from being destroyed and the Army of Southern New England supplied.

What she hadn't been able to do was crack the communications or chain of command of the drone pilots flying out of Nevada, and now the hunters were closing in.

Ahead of them, Major Palmburg held the elevator door open; it kept lurching into his back as its electronic brain demanded that it head down to the first floor. He leapt in the moment Courtney was thrust into the little box—as the door shut, they heard a distant rumble. Everyone stood with their heads cocked, as the elevator began descending.

"Was that a plane?" Courtney whispered.

"Yeah," Major said, feeling a touch of relief as the seconds ticked away and they weren't vaporized in a gigantic explosion. What he failed to realize was that the drone whooshing by was an unarmed *Sentinel* still in hunting mode. What they should have been more afraid of was the Predator that came sweeping in behind it, five-hundred pounds lighter.

The GBU-15 slammed into the building, striking an eighth-floor living room window, passing through the apartment, and blasting through the far wall, before its warhead detonated in the central hall. The explosion that followed blew out every window in the building in the blink of an eye, shivered the entire support system and opened huge cracks right through the foundation.

A second later, the building began to implode as the top floors caved in on one another. The weight of each crushed downwards, further and further, until the bottom floors were buried.

Then came the fires. What was left of the building would burn for many days.

3-6:49 p.m.
North Highland, New York

The explosion could be heard for miles, and in the dying light of the fifth day, the fire engulfing the building could be seen as a beacon twenty miles away in North Highland.

It brought Jaimee Lynn out of a lassitude so deep that it felt as though she'd been in a waking coma. And it roused in her, not hunger exactly, for she had eaten enough for two Thanksgivings, but the reminder that she'd be hungry again soon enough.

Eating the family had put her pack in a stupor that Eng had joined in, much to Jaimee's disgust. "Get up, China!" She kicked him in the kidney; he barely felt it and only growled at her. "Where's ya'll's pills?" They were in the pocket of his coat and as she dug them out, she realized for the third or fourth time that she was naked save for the old blood that coated her, as near as she could tell, from top to bottom.

"Eat these, China," she said and rudely shoved a small handful of pills into his mouth. He was almost all zombie now and just laid there with a blank look to his eyes and his mouth hanging open.

"Y'all so dumb," she griped, and began working his jaw up and down. Chalky grey drool seeped from the corners of his thin lips. She scooped it up with her cupped hand and shoved it back in. "Doctor's orders," she told him before grabbing a stick and using it to shove the mush deeper down his gullet.

When he bit down on the stick, she felt she had done enough, sure that he would come back from being a complete zombie. Once he did, they would get back into the truck and get going. In the meantime, she decided that she didn't want to be naked when she found Dr. Lee again. Jaimee Lynn didn't care what the scientist thought about anything, but the idea that her daddy would be with her made her want clothes.

"An' he wouldn't want me runnin' all over the place all necked." She wandered up to the house the little family had been hiding in and found that it had been a house for old people. All the clothes were too big for her scrawny little frame. Going back outside, she looked down at the remains of the people they had eaten. Two of them had been kids—my, how they had howled and screeched.

"They was like stuck pigs," Jaimee Lynn said with a little growl in her tummy. "Yummy stuck pigs." There was little left of the two kids, and the clothes that had been torn from their thrashing bodies were now only rags. Undeterred, she squinted up and down the block until she saw a house with a litter of toys in the front yard. Toys meant kids.

Again, her tummy growled. "Ain't no kids 'round here," she told her tummy. If there had been any, they would have run away during Jaimee Lynn's three course meal. She just hoped that they had left a proper outfit for her. In the dim light, she fumbled around in the house until she found the bedrooms. The first had been home to a creature far more malignant than she—it had been a boy's room, and she turned up her nose.

Next, she found a room painted in dusky pink. It was a proper little girl's room. Without much hope, she looked under the bed and in the closet, thinking that finding a tender young morsel would be a nice little snack. The house was empty. Disappointed, she gazed into the closet with her black eyes. The vibrant colors were lost on her. Everything was tinged grey.

She chose a canary-yellow dress that was two-sizes too big and hung on her like a gunny sack. She didn't care. With her fine blonde hair and her year-round tan, yellow used to look good on her and she figured it still did. She was wrong. The pretty dress made her look more like a monster than ever. Her hair was no longer blonde. It hung in thick black tangles with pieces of human flesh caught up in its knots. And the soft flesh of her face lacked its past perfection; she was coated in layers of dried blood. Her gums were black as were her eyes, which dribbled black tears.

Jaimee Lynn was such a horror that Eng, who was a monster in his own right and could only think past his desire to feed when he was filled with pills, gazed at her with a disgusted sneer as she came back to kick her pack awake.

"What's with the dress? It doesn't seem right." His head was spinning in confusion and pounding with hate. He fumbled at his bottle of pills and didn't have the sense to be shocked that they were mostly gone.

"For y'alls information, my daidy likes me in dresses. He says I's pretty. Like the spittin' image of my momma."

One of Jaimee's pack touched the dress and said that she wanted one, too. Jaimee Lynn pushed her away. "Dresses are only for little girls who still gots their daidies. Mine is with that Dr. Lee. She stoled him and did spear-i-ments on him. We's gonna kill her."

"And eat her?" the little creature asked, hopefully.

That was most obviously the plan and only a stupid Chinaman zombie would ruin it. "No, she's going to fix us, remember?" Eng told them. "She's going to make us normal again. And she's going to fix all of your mommies and daddies, too."

The pack liked the idea of their parents being fixed, although most of them equated that with being clean, and being clean meant they could eat them. Jaimee Lynn, superior in all ways to her minions, declared, "My daidy don't need fixin'. He's too strong to get sick. But I reckon, I could let Dr. Lee live for a whiles. Ya know, long enough to fix y'all's mommas and daidies."

With the plan a certainty in their minds, the pack piled into the SUV. The sun had set and in the twilight, Eng was blind. He had to turn on both the interior lights as well as the exterior ones to see anything at all. Compared to the darkness that filled the Quarantine Zone, they were a brilliant nova that attracted every eye.

Thousands of moaning creatures saw them and followed after in a gruesome parade that stretched for miles. And it was not just the dead who saw the police cruiser driving slowly southward. There were still living people in the Zone, hiding, afraid to do anything that might call attention to themselves.

239

There were also mechanical creatures that took notice of the vehicle. Its lights were picked up by one of the *Sentinels* circling New Rochelle while it was still miles away. The drone pilot kept track of the SUV as it weaved through stalled cars and around the remains of roadblocks.

"Holy shit," the pilot whispered, as zombies came charging at it from a church. He was sure he was about to witness a massacre, instead, after only a few seconds, the zombies simply just stood there, staring into the vehicle as it drove away. "What did I just see? Control!" he cried, leaning back in his chair.

The door to the "cockpit" was open and sometimes it was easier just to yell out instead of going through the usual back and forth. "Take a look at the last two minutes of my feed."

"Why? You got eyeballs on our targets?"

"Just do it." There was a long pause followed by a muttered curse. "You saw that too, didn't you? I'd send that to the colonel if I were you."

"No shit," the control officer yelled back down the hallway. "Just keep your cross on that SUV."

The pilot gave him a: "No shit," right back. He watched that SUV all the way into New Rochelle, marking each time it was attacked. The last of these strange events occurred just after Colonel Bell arrived, smelling of old sweat and stale cigars. He stared at the grainy video from a range of five inches.

"Are those children in there?" There were six others in the virtual cockpit, watching the feed in real time. They all agreed that the small figures were indeed children. "How the hell are they doing this? Do they have zombie repellent or something?"

The control officer pushed his glasses higher up on his nose and pointed to a different screen. "I don't think it's coincidence that they're heading for this particular building. It's been designated a non-action building." Colonel Bell was about to ask a question; however, the officer answered before he could spit it out. "That's the R & K research facility."

He had said this with a knowing look that was lost on everyone and was forced to explain, "That's where all this started. Or kinda started, I guess. That's where they developed the plague and then they moved it to Poughkeepsie, where it got out. So, it is possible they developed some sort of repellent."

Colonel Bell watched for a few minutes. "Can we get a better picture than this? The shadows are making everything…

weird." The children looked more than weird, they looked exactly like what they were: demonic.

"No sir," the pilot answered. "This is a filtered shot already. Their interior light is messing with our night lenses, and the surrounding darkness makes the natural light lens useless."

The colonel asked for a digital copy, which he sent up the chain of command. It was a slow wearisome chain that ended in a stack of papers over a foot in height that sat in front of the President.

The President was so afraid of traitors, saboteurs and provocateurs that he was trying to micro-manage every aspect of the war. It was an impossible task. Orders and decisions that only he could make were piling up. When he did make a decision, it was then triple checked by nervous generals and double checked by anxious, pale colonels, each afraid to make the smallest mistake.

It was grinding the war-effort almost to a halt, which seemed okay with the President. All he seemed to care about was punishing his perceived enemies. When he finally got to the envelope, he only gave it a second look because it was marked "Top Secret" and there was something heavier than a piece of paper within it; he was at the point that he was ready to burn the stack of paper on his desk. He asked for the Director of the FBI and when John Alexander showed up, he was immediately confronted with the video.

"Do you have anything you want to tell me about this little operation of yours?" the President asked, with an eyebrow cocked. He prided himself on being able to smell a rat and, in his mind, everything about R & K was extremely fishy.

Fear thrummed along Alexander's nerves, but he was a cool customer. "I don't know who those people are. But I'll find out. We'll get to the bottom of this."

"Yes, *we* will," the president said, patting the empty chair next to him. "And *we* will do it right here in front of everyone so there'll be no tricks. What do you think of that?"

I think I'm one wrong word away from going to the torture chambers, Alexander thought.

Special Agent in Charge, Katherine Pennock, her dark hair falling over her face, was going cross-eyed staring at the endless streams of numbers running down her computer screen—and she was used to raking through pages of data. This was much more mind numbing than anything she had ever done; she was looking for individual sequences of code hidden within a veritable waterfall of digits.

Behind her, Anna Holloway was doing the same thing, saying in an annoyingly girlish voice, "Nope, nope, nope," over and over again. Katherine wanted to punch her. She also wanted to punch Dr. Lee, but mostly because she was lining up even more tests.

As they had a nearly endless supply of zombie blood in the form of Specialist Russell Hoskins, Thuy was throwing everything she could at the mutated Com-cells, and she was coming up empty in a practical sense. They could, of course, be destroyed in all sorts of manners: bleach, fire, acid, but so far they hadn't found any way of killing them in a manner that didn't also kill their host.

Anti-viral medications were shrugged off; antibiotics were ignored; antibody therapy had been a waste of time, as had photodynamic therapy. The use of interferons and other cytokines to induce an immune response had been as useful as spraying the Com-cells with Holy Water. Dr. Lee had also tried hormonal therapy, providing both extra hormones as well as blocking certain hormones, with zero response one way or the other.

The numbers that Katherine were currently staring at were tracing the effect of an idea called synthetic lethality; it was a way of looking for deficiencies or weaknesses in the cells themselves. So far, there were none. During the last five years, Dr. Lee had managed to unlock the power of the stem-cell, or as Katherine thought of it: the *Anything* cell. Its ability to replicate itself into any cell in the human body was the miracle of creation, only now, it was the direct cause of their destruction.

If the Air Force didn't kill them first, that is. When the Reaper's 500-pound bomb had detonated a mile away, it had rattled the windows and set off an alarm somewhere in the building. Even Dr. Lee had stopped her experiments long enough to rush to the north end of the floor, where they could see a mushroom cloud of black smoke billowing up from a burning building.

"Do you think it was them?" Anna had asked.

She meant Courtney and the others. It was a question that couldn't be answered and shouldn't have been asked. Dr. Lee had glared her back to work. Since then they had been at it so hard that Katherine was oblivious to her phone.

"Is that you?" Anna asked her.

"Me what? Oh, the phone." She snatched it up and answered without looking at who was calling. "Agent Pennock."

There was a click and a hum before John Alexander came on. "Agent Pennock? I'm here with the President on speaker phone." This was rushed out in a spew. It was followed by a long pause to let the ramifications sink in.

She understood that caution was called for. "Hello sir. Hello Mr. President. It feels like a week since I was in the White House with you." This wasn't hyperbole on her part. Although it had only been thirty something hours, each of those hours had been a trial for her.

"Yes," was the President's cold reply. "What's going on up there? What sort of experiments are you running that involve children?"

"Children? We're not running experiments on children, sir. At least as far as I know of. Let me ask Dr. Lee if any of her experiments involve the tissue of children." She certainly hoped not. She put her hand over the phone and asked Dr. Lee point blank and received an honest no in reply. "She said that all the tissue is from…"

"Dr. Lee is with you?" the President thundered.

So much for caution. Katherine began to choke and stammer; she should have known better as his paranoia had been raging out of control the day before. She was sure it had to be so much worse with everything going on. "Yes, sir she is. I have taken her into custody." Dr. Lee raised a soft eyebrow as if to ask: *For what?* Katherine could only shrug in reply before going on. "She's working for us now."

"Is that right? And when can we expect a cure?" The President's voice fairly dripped skepticism.

The perfect eyebrow came crashing down. "Sir, this is Dr. Lee. I need to make sure you understand that we are in a

243

preliminary stage. This version of the Com-cell is almost like dealing with an advanced alien microbe. Currently, we are running a battery of tests to find a weakness within the cell itself."

"I note that you didn't answer my question," he replied, tartly. "And are you just going to pretend that you don't know anything about the children? Who are you working with? Huh?"

Thuy felt a prickle of fear as goosebumps flaring across her arms. "W-What children, sir? There are only the three of us here." There were actually four of them, if the raging Specialist Hoskins was counted. He was even then screaming his throat out in what had once been a clean room; it was now disgustingly filthy.

"The children who are right outside your building. I can see them plain as day. There's eight of them and there's a man with them. Your accomplice, I presume."

Katherine looked concerned by this and Anna was visibly nervous; they should have been scared right down to their cores, but neither had been hounded by Jaimee Lynn Burke quite like Thuy had been. They didn't know just how horribly cunning the girl could be. "Is the man Asian?" Thuy asked with a sinking feeling. She had seen Anna shoot Eng. She had seen it with her own two eyes—but she had not seen him die. Not really. Anna had shot him in the torso, and he'd been wearing a ballistic vest. Anna wasn't as tough as she liked to pretend she was. If she was, she would have shot him in the head. It would have been messy and dis...

"I can't tell," the President said. The man had left the SUV running and although the little crowd was illuminated by its headlights, the angle from above didn't lend itself to any sort of feature recognition. "It doesn't matter. Let me talk to the FBI agent. Pennock! Get this situation under control. I want answers and I want results. And I want them by morning or I'll pull the plug on this fiasco. There's no way we will even consider an extraction without a cure. So get one, fast."

Before Katherine could say a word, the sat-phone beeped once and went dead.

"What the hell?" Anna cried. "He wants a cure by morning? Is he an idiot, or what?"

"Yeah, I think he is," Katherine answered, with a glance towards the elevators. "Shouldn't we be more worried about these kids?"

"Of course, we should," Thuy started, "It's probably Eng and…"

Anna cut her off in something of a fury, a sneer contorting her pretty face. "You guys are really worried about them? Why? The situation isn't the same. Last night you led us right into a trap, *Special Agent*. This time is completely different. We have lights, we have a gun and the building is in one piece. Let those little fuckers come."

Katherine didn't believe her nonchalance. "You aren't afraid? I highly doubt that."

"What's there to be afraid of? A handful of kids and a stupid zombie? They don't have an army like last time. But I don't see that it matters. I say we blare the music and turn on every light on the floor and by the time they get up here, we'll be out the back and gone."

Thuy looked stunned. "What about all of this? What about finding a cure? What about your pardon?"

Anna laughed as she picked up the armored vest she had been given the night before and slid it on. "My pardon? Please. There won't be any pardon. The President is off his rocker. And he doesn't care about a cure, Thuy. If he did, he would have sent in a hundred helicopters last night, not just one."

Katherine laughed softly. "I hate to admit that she's right about the President. He's getting crazier by the minute, and when he says he'll pull the plug I think he means he'll pull *our* plugs, if you get my meaning."

"He'll kill us?" Thuy asked in astonishment. Anna rolled her eyes, while Katherine nodded. "That's…that's…" She found herself spluttering and took a moment to pull herself together. After a deep breath, she said, "What the President thinks or doesn't think shouldn't matter to us. Finding a cure is the most important thing anyone could be doing right now. Agent Pennock, I need you to stop the children. If there are just eight of them, it should be no problem. Take Anna with you and if you need to use her as bait, I'm willing to take that risk."

2-7:16 p.m.
Newville, Pennsylvania

245

Tony "Stubby" Alvarez took his F-15 Strike Eagle in a wide, wide racetrack, one that was much wider than was needed.

"Not again," his weapons officer, groaned, sounding bored. "Are you trying to get us killed or just arrested? Maybe it'll be both. You know they're doing that right? Arresting people and then killing them? I have a wife and two fucking kids, Stubby! But you know that. You know that and you just don't care."

"I care, Matt. But I also have to care about them." Below the jet, the 3rd ID was fighting for their lives in brilliant gouts of flame and thousands of tiny sparkles of light. The zombie army had coalesced and was now centered squarely on them. They were surging forward like a battering ram, throwing themselves at the tanks and soldiers. As they passed over the line, the shattering explosions rocked the jet as if they were flying straight through a thunderhead.

"Yeah, you care. That's fucking great, only we're out of ammo, Stubby. Did you happen to notice that? Huh? We're flying in circles. That's all we're doing, oh except for wasting fuel. We're also wasting a butt-load of fuel."

It wasn't all they were doing and Matt knew it. Stubby's wide circles were being timed to disrupt any attack runs being set up on the remaining M6s. Only seven of the original eighteen had been destroyed. They were valuable weapons and could be helpful in the fight against the dead.

"Can we at least turn the radio back on?" Matt asked. "It would be nice to know that we're not going to fly into another plane. Don't you think that would be smart?"

"They have our position." He was confident that they wouldn't hit anyone. Not only were there at least two drones circling the battlefield, lighting everything up, his wide circles were designed to make sure that no one was surprised. If someone missed him and his fifteen-ton Eagle, they probably shouldn't be flying.

"We only have a fuel load for another ten minutes," he told Matt. "Just sit back. You'll be fine. If anyone asks, I'll tell them that…" Alvarez jumped as something huge and dark appeared very close off his starboard wing. Matt began screaming his name and telling him to bank away. It was natural to want to edge away from another jet flying twenty feet from your wingtip, but Alvarez held his course.

A glance saw that the dark form would have appeared grey had not the night come crashing down not long before. It was an

F-16: a Fighting Falcon to his Eagle; a rapier to his bastard sword. Its pilot was gesturing furiously at him.

"I think he wants us to turn back," Matt yelled.

"Yeah, I think you're right." Air Force pilots don't use any sort of sign language and so when Alvarez held up a finger, he hoped that it would convey: *Just a minute.*

The pilot must have misread the sign because it suddenly slipped left, sliding under the Strike Eagle and disappearing. "What the fuck!" Matt cried, twisting in his seat to try to catch sight of the Falcon. "Holy crap! It's back there, Stubby. Turn us around, damn it."

"Why should I?" Alvarez asked himself.

"If you don't, I swear I will punch the fuck out!"

Alvarez nearly choked. "You wouldn't." He couldn't punch out alone. If he went, they would both go and that would be the death of his Eagle. It would be the equivalent of suicide. "Matt, this is a thirty-million dollar plane, damn it."

"If you care, then turn around."

Turning around meant huge trouble. He had broken just about every rule in the book, from ignoring comms to leading his flight against the wrong target. He had put his plane and his backseater in danger. He had disobeyed orders. But his orders were asinine and insane. The enemy below was not wearing green and anyone who thought so was allied with the real enemy. In his heart, he knew he was right.

And yet, his plane was his baby. He would never do anything to hurt her. "I'll explain to the tower this was on me."

"No! Just turn around."

"Tango Zero One, this is Five Zero Five," Alvarez announced, keying the mic for the first time since he called that he was switching to guns. At least four people began screaming at him, none of whom made any sense, each essentially saying: kill the humans and save the zombies. He ignored them. "Control, I have a Falcon acting aggressively. Please advise him that there are friendlies in the area."

"Shut the hell up, Stubby!" he knew the voice: it was Colonel Scott, the wing commander, a tough as balls veteran of two wars. This made it even more shocking that he wasn't siding with Alvarez. "You got two choices: Land your plane and face a court-martial, or get shot out of the sky."

The air seemed to leave his body and not return, and his hands went numb; he could only hope his plane was okay with flying herself for a little while. "Court martial for what?" It was a dumb question. There had been a number of pilots dragged away in the last few hours and the charge was always treason.

Sure enough, Colonel Scott answered in a low tone, "Mutiny, sedition, aiding the enemy…treason."

Although this had been expected, Alvarez still felt the numbness spread up his arms and into his chest. Those pilots who had been taken hadn't done anything close to what Alvarez had done. For the most part, they had faked weapons malfunctions or had purposely missed targets. Most had been locked up on base, but the worst offenders had been bundled off to a "camp" near Washington DC. They weren't expected to return.

"What did you think would happen, Tony?" Matt hissed from the backseat. "You had to know what would happen to you."

He did. Deep down he knew what was going to happen to him, but he had cracked. It had almost felt physical, as if there was a real crack inside of him, cutting him in two. On one side was his training, his sense of duty, his love of country; on the other was the fact that he wasn't just doing something wrong, he was doing something evil. The one side demanded that he meekly return to base and face the charges against him. The other side said: *Fuck it.*

This sounded very tough in his head, only just then the F-15's threat receiver began screeching in his ear. He had just been painted by two different radars. The sweat trickling down the back of his flight suit turned to ice—one of the radars was the F-16, that was obvious, but where was the other coming from? A drone? Was he being targeted by a *Reaper?*

The idea of a drone high above him with a missile ready to fire was more frightening than the thought of another Falcon with a lock on him. It made no sense, but he imparted a certain amount of cold perfection in the UAVs. He likened it to playing chess against a computer; there was no winning.

There's no winning, either way. This had come from the same part of him that had said: *Fuck it.* And it was right. There was no way he could win, but that didn't mean he had to just give up.

Just like that, he could feel his hands again. "Alright, turning around now," he lied with an amazingly calm voice. Instead of turning, his nimble fingers danced over the controls, hauling back on the throttle at the same time as hitting his air brake. Few people realize that an air brake is an actual thing. Most planes have a version of them, generally using relatively small flaps to create drag. The F-15's brake is far more dramatic and obvious. It sits just behind the dual cockpit and is nothing more than a fifteen-foot long, spine-mounted length of titanium that juts up at an angle when deployed.

It wasn't easy to see in the dark, especially from directly behind. The F-16 was a mile behind the Eagle, which was far too close when the planes were traveling at 600 miles an hour. Six seconds separated them at that speed.

In a blink, Alvarez cut his speed in half and then cut it again, by pulling the plane's nose up. He was nearly at stall speed with the Falcon roaring up on him with Matt screaming like mad. Almost casually, Alvarez launched a pair of flares before jerking the plane to the right.

The move was completely unexpected by the F-16 pilot. He knew that Alvarez was out of ammo for his Vulcan and that he had not gone up with a single air-to-air missile. Alvarez was essentially defenseless and the idea that he would do anything other than return to Langley with his tail between his legs was absurd. The only weapon Alvarez had left was his fifteen-ton aircraft, which seemed to come flying backwards at the Falcon. The flares shooting out of it made the F-16 pilot hesitate for a split second, just long enough for Alvarez to bank away.

Cursing, the pilot of the F-16 slammed his jet to the left, thinking he would circle around with his smaller, more maneuverable jet, and come up behind the Eagle again, but he did not take into account certain factors.

The F-16 was *usually* much lighter, which allowed for greater initial thrust, but his Falcon was loaded with missiles, 500-rounds of 20mm ammo, and a full tank of fuel, while the F-15 felt "zippy" under Alvarez's hand. He could have hit the after burners and shot out of there at 1,800 miles an hour, which was 500 miles an hour faster than the F-16's best rate of speed which only came at "altitude."

With that second radar lighting him up, Alvarez couldn't do that. He had to stick close to the F-16. After that initial jerk to the right, he turned so hard to port that his load warning sensors began to beep in his ear. The beeping was unnecessary since he could feel the G-forces building up. Once more his hands went numb as his internal blood pressure couldn't overcome the force that his aircraft was putting on his small frame.

For just a second, he thought he was going to black out, then the F-16 swung upward, cutting in front of him before banking back the other way. It was a typical dogfight maneuver, something Alvarez had seen a hundred times.

"What are you doing?" Matt demanded from his backseat. "No. Forget it. I'm punching out."

"Wait!" Alvarez yelled. "Look out the damned window first." He took the Eagle through a slow barrel roll. They were over the top of the zombie army. "You see now?"

Matt let out a stunned, "Yeah."

"I'll let you know when you can punch us...shit! Where'd he go?" Alvarez had come out of the roll at a slight upward angle that the pilot of the F-16 exploited. He shot down and away, turning too fast for the Eagle, disappearing below him hidden by the dark and the background clutter.

Almost immediately, there was a new tone in his ear—missile lock! "Countermeasures," Alvarez ordered through gritted teeth as he lit off flares and turned as fast and as hard as he dared. Behind him, Matt's first reaction had been to look for an incoming missile.

"They launched!" the WSO cried.

"Where? Damn it, Matt, where?"

Matt finally tore his eyes from the bolt of flame racing at them, to look down at his instrument panel. "Eight o'clock high! Range five miles. Speed...shit 2,800!" The death that was hurling at them came in the form of an AIM-120 Advanced Medium-Range Air-to-Air Missile; at Mach 4, it could easily outrace them and had a range of eighty miles to do so.

"Counter!" Alvarez yelled, turning again and letting off more flares. Matt turned on the Eagle's AN/ALQ-131—it was the bird's electronic counter measures pod. Among other things, the ECM mimicked the radar echo bouncing off the Eagle, making it seem larger and closer so as to fool the incoming missile into blowing up early.

The missile's built-in computer brain was smarter than this and countered the countermeasure. When its radar image went off kilter, it switched to a command data link stream, picked up a circling drone's heavier radar image pulse, and kept coming. Next, Alvarez released two canisters of chaff, waited for a three-second count before sitting the Eagle on its tail and blasting upwards.

Matt turned around backwards in his chair and watched as the missile approached the snow shower made from thousands of aluminum bits swirling in the air.

"Take it, bitch. Take it, bitch. Take the bait!" he whispered in a begging voice. The missile seemed to shudder as it passed through the chaff. Then it came on, even faster than before, its tail glowing brilliantly white. "It didn't work! Three miles!"

Cold realization struck Alvarez then: he couldn't outrun the missile, and nor could he turn circles tight enough to avoid it. If by some chance he managed to make it miss, he would be a sitting duck for the next missile or the one after that. It dawned on him that his death was a foregone conclusion.

"Fuck it," he muttered and gunned the Eagle forward as fast as it could go. He was pinned to his seat as Matt began giving him the proximity of the missile in hundreds of meters, his voice growing higher and higher.

"Do something, Stubbs!"

Gently, Alvarez eased the bird upward on an easy arc. At three-thousand feet, he throttled down. "There's only one thing we can do. Are you ready?"

"Yeah," Matt answered in a whisper, sounding as if he was at the whim of fate.

Alvarez understood completely. Death was a very great possibility. They were currently traveling at 800 miles an hour. This was simply too fast to eject. It would be suicide. And if they did happen to live through the ejection, they still wouldn't be safe. The defensive line of the 3rd ID was a mile away; they'd be landing in the very middle of a giant horde of zombies.

"This is your fault, Stubby."

"Nope. I'm just a cog, Matt. I'm not going to take the blame for doing the right thing."

"Five-hundred meters and fuck you, Stubs. You could…oh, shit!" Matt's cry was pure fear.

Alvarez craned his head around and saw to his horror that the sky was impossibly filled with missiles. Dozens and dozens of sleek white darts, sixty feet long with blazing tails of white fire. Alvarez gaped, unable to comprehend the reason for such overkill on the part of the Air Force. Did they hate him that much?

"Too bad for them," he muttered. "They can only kill me once." He pulled the ejection handle and there was an explosion of sound and wind that was so immense that his eardrums ruptured. He was struck by orange flames, invisible ice, and unbelievable shooting lights. His body was spun and bent and twisted by forces that it could not withstand, and the pain was so intense that his mind couldn't handle it. Everything went mercifully black.

He was dead before his parachute opened, and it was a ravaged, broken corpse that floated over the battlefield; a grim angel of death with exploded orbs for eyes, unable to bear witness, as the great mass of missiles descended out of the sky. They had never been meant for Tony Alvarez. They were meant for General Cannan, the 3rd Infantry Division and anyone else who had the temerity to stand up to the President.

3-7:43 p.m.
Grafton, Massachusetts

As the day's light fell along the line, a deeper fear set in and the same men who'd been cracking jokes an hour before retreated into themselves, becoming smaller. The entire seventy mile line became stiff and brittle, and it seemed as though it would crumble at the least bit of pressure.

No one believed that they could hold through the night. Things were just too wrong. The steady influx of new recruits was offset by the number of people who took to their heels and ran. There was a pervasive fear that the masks and the bleach weren't working as a dozen men an hour began to rave and were sent to the rear for "treatment," which everyone knew was just a bullet to the back of the head.

The consensus was that there were too few real soldiers among them, not enough supplies, and no real plan to win. The time was ripe for someone to do something. Unfortunately, doing something meant risking everything. Lieutenant Colonel Ross knew this better than anyone. He was a wanted man. "I thought it would feel different knowing that the government was after you," he remarked. "You know, maybe more terrifying or whatever."

"You get used to it," Clarren replied. "But compared to this," he waved a hand toward the horrid, stinking bog of corpses where hundreds of zombies were struggling toward them, "It's not so bad."

"It's annoying, is what it is," Ross griped. He stood and stared out over the bog without seeing the shadowy creatures coming to kill him. "You know it won't be enough to simply take down the division bigwigs. It'll just bring the rest of the army down on our heads. Sure, maybe we can count on our battalion, but what about the brigade or even the rest of the division? Will they fight for us? Are they willing to go through this again?"

Clarren insisted that they would.

"But if they don't, it'll be just us," Ross said. His regiment was the most ragged, the most ill-equipped and the worst supplied battalion in the entire Army of Southern New England. Despite this, it had been expected to hold the vital center of the line, and it would still have to, no matter the outcome of any internal fighting. That meant the head of the snake had to be lopped off in one quick blow, something that was practically impossible since the command post was guarded by a battalion of Marines, their fifty tanks, and a company of Army MPs.

"Believe me, Ross, real soldiers hate what's going on. Even that general you bitched at was disgusted by the political officer."

"Do you believe it enough to put your money where your mouth is?" Clarren had nothing to lose and said he did. "Good. Someone has to find out if we can count on the other battalions. Take a platoon with you and be careful."

Clarren felt like he was being fed to the wolves. "You know if they aren't on board, they'll try to arrest me. What happened to me being your ranger-rumper or whatever?"

"It's rump-ranger, and you'll be fine as long as the platoon is with you." Ross shooed him away. He lacked Clarren's faith in his fellow commanding officers. All of them had lived through the nightmare of fighting one enemy while having another attacking from behind. He didn't think they would do it again.

Ross had another idea in mind to lop the head off the snake, one that was far easier. It was also cowardly and nothing short of dishonorable. The idea was so heinous that Ross didn't want

Clarren around as he tried to set it up; this was the real reason he had sent the ex-politician away on what felt like a fool's errand.

His plan was to perform a high-tech fragging. If he could somehow get a cruise missile to "stray" off course, he could end the threat to himself and relieve the army of its terrible leadership in one blow. Sergeant Ross never thought he would ever stoop so low—on the other hand, *Colonel* Ross had a thousand men counting on him, and with no hesitation, he dialed the sat-phone in the hope of getting a hold of Courtney Shaw. If anyone could make this happen, it was her. Unfortunately, the phone only rang and rang in his ear. It was a bitter disappointment.

He would not be so easily defeated and tried to orchestrate the missile attack himself. The Navy claimed to be "out" of cruise missiles, while the Air Force said that its missions were now only coordinated through the White House.

"That's the dumbest thing I ever heard," Ross groused. "If you want to lose the war, that's the best way."

"May I have your name and rank, sir? I will need them to properly denounce you."

It was more of a warning than a threat, and the airman was shocked when Ross laughed easily and gave up his name without worry. "Denounce away, and tell the President he can go fuck himself. Be a doll and use those exact words." He hung up and brooded for a few minutes as his battalion began to fire into the oncoming zombies. A glance showed him that the main host was still some distance away. He still had time.

"And there's another way to skin a cat," he told himself as he called up divisional artillery. Putting as much authority into his voice, he did everything he could to talk them into firing a mile short of the lines. After his third attempt, a political officer barked into the radio, "Who is this?"

"Yo mama," was Ross' reply before he turned off the radio.

"Really?" Clarren said. He had been standing there for some time. "Yo mama? You're slipping, Ross. And what are you trying to do? Get them with friendly fire?"

A shrug was all Ross was willing to commit to. "How'd your mission go?" he asked, hoping to change the subject.

"Poorly," Clarren admitted. "Apparently we don't stand a chance. We both know it would be easier if I turned myself in to the…"

Ross cut him off. "Your ego is bigger than your ass and that's saying something. This isn't about you anymore. This is about all of us. They are a danger to all of us."

"That's what I tried to tell them and they all agreed that the idea of throwing off the yoke of the political officers was completely necessary. But logic and truth were not strong enough factors to overcome fear."

The thin crackle of rifle fire began to pick up and Ross glanced toward it, if only to hide his disappointment. The dead were surging forward again. They were out there in the dark, their awful moans growing louder and louder. After days of this, Ross knew that they were coming in numbers that his men could handle.

It was a different story a few miles south of them. The blaze of rifle fire became a roar that gradually drifted further and further eastward. "Fuck!" Ross knew the sound and what it meant: the line had fallen. In more of a habitual move rather than a considered one, he called division headquarters for an update, only to be told that he and his battalion were considered to be in open rebellion and that no answers, supplies or reinforcements were going to be given to him.

"Then what the hell are we fighting for?" he demanded.

"I'm sure I don't know," was the snide reply.

"Here's what I know: you can go fuck yourself," Ross barked into the radio before he hauled back and sent it spiraling into the black bog. "Did you hear that? Son of a bitch! Son of a mother-fucking bitch! I swear if I…"

Behind them someone was crashing through the woods, hissing his name over and over. It was a moment before he realized it was in fact a girl and that she was calling out what he felt was closer to his true name: "Sergeant Ross? Hey, does anyone know where Sergeant Ross is?"

Ross whistled her over and recognized the dark braids and the spray of freckles across the girl's nose. It was Rita McCormick. She fell against a tree, gasping for breath and he felt an odd desire to hug her. Her youth, her sudden youth at that terrible moment, reminded him of his own. That he was only twenty-three had been forgotten in the endless battle. He had felt like some sort of craggy old man for the last couple of days.

"I thought you had run off," he said. That seemed rude and he quickly added, "I'm glad you didn't, though."

"I didn't run, but…" She pointed back the way she had come. "They're sending the tanks. I was running messages for HQ and they made me go to the Marines. I wasn't supposed to read the message but there were all these rumors about you and the Governor, and so I did. I read the message. They're sending the whole Marine army this way. I couldn't find you at first and they're…"

She stopped as a distant rumble crept through the growing darkness. It was the sound of mechanical monsters coming for Ross and his men. "This is insane," he said, feeling that aged weariness descend upon him again. "As if they don't have anything better to do." He was even crabbing like an old man.

"Do you have a few minutes," he asked her. "Can you run along the river and send my company commanders back here?"

"Yeah. Anything for y…to help I mean." Like a deer she shot away and Ross wasted moments staring after her.

Clarren caught him staring and grinned. "Despite being so focused on men, I'm starting to think you're not gay after all."

Ross was suddenly young again and felt heat creep into his ears. "Sorry to disappoint you," he said, gruffly, fooling no one.

Rita's frightened urgency set a fire under everyone and in minutes Ross had six jumped-up captains huffing and puffing in front of him. "I'm afraid we're fucked. I was just on the line with Division and it seems the *entire* battalion is now considered to be in a state of revolt." He paused to let his company commanders stamp and curse. "Yeah, but it's worse than that. You hear that? They're sending that Marine battalion to arrest us."

Clarren raised a hand. "Maybe they'll arrest us. With these political officers it might be shoot first and ask questions later, so we're all in this now."

"Fuck 'em," the CO of Bravo Company spat. "I fuckin' volunteered for this shit and as of now, I'm un-volunteering." Heads bobbed, and all of them muttered, "Fuck 'em," in agreement.

"I wish it was that easy," Ross said. "These POs are on power trips. They're not going to respect someone trying to pull a conscientious objector status this late in the game. They're going to arrest the lot of us, shoot everyone E-5 and up as a warning, and then send everyone back to fight."

One of the commanders asked, "So the plan is to get out of Dodge, right?"

Again, there was head bobbing; this time it was enthusiastic head bobbing. Only Ross shook his head. "Not yet. We have to make sure the line is stabilized and then we'll all run."

The CO of Bravo Company held up a large flat, dirty palm. "Fuck the line. It don't sound like it's holding anyways. I say the only thing we have time for is to get the fuck out of here."

"No, we have just enough time to light a few fires," Ross said, his wicked smile gleaming in the night. He told them what he wanted and sent the captains running back to their units faster than they had come. This left only Rita and Clarren, who had been standing back a few feet, not wanting to interfere.

Clarren wore a look of tired resignation and Ross knew what he was going to say and beat him to it. "Stay and get executed if you want to, but it won't matter in the end. The only thing that will happen is that the President will win again. Trust me, the moment you die, he'll rewrite history and they'll say they found you hiding in an old folks home under the skirts of some poor old granny."

"A granny? Who's going to believe that? And running seems just as bad if you ask me."

"We won't be running far," Ross said and dropped to the ground. He opened a map, and clicked on a flashlight, uncaring that he was making himself a prime target. *If there were snipers let them shoot,* he thought. "This is where the Marine unit was stationed and you can hear them coming right down this road." He pointed to a road that was slanting diagonally toward them. "See this road here? We can scoot right up it. What does that say? Bruce Street?"

"It does," Rita agreed quickly with a smile that gleamed in the darkness. She thought that he was easily the best soldier in the army, and maybe the handsomest as well. "It's a good road," she gushed. "There's trees and bushes and no one will see us."

"If it has Rita's stamp of approval, then we'll take it." Ross jumped up, trying and failing to fold the map along its original lines. It ended up looking like a giant hunk of origami gone bad; maybe a cross between a swan and a pug. "Rita, you scout ahead. Make sure Bruce Street is empty. Clarren, you gather Alpha and Bravo and get them moving. I'll do the same with Charlie, Delta and Echo."

Youth again. He ran along the river, barking the men to their feet. There was confusion and fear, and also anger. "Are we running or fighting?" a soldier with a Screaming Eagle patch on his shoulder asked.

"Both," Ross answered grinning. He wasn't a chess player, but he knew a bad move when he saw it. The political officer he had baited was going after a pawn with his queen, and had left his king wide open for the taking.

Chapter 21
1-8:02 p.m.
New Rochelle, New York

"This is stupid," Anna hissed, grabbing Katherine's arm. After so many grinding hours wearing on them, the two women looked nothing like they had five days before. Anna's overt sexuality had been replaced by a savage will to live. She could no longer hide the conniving look in her hard, blue eyes. Katherine, who had always prided herself on a subtle and purposely semi-masked beauty was also in survival mode.

Her blonde hair had been tied back in a severely lashed ponytail and the planes of her face were now hard and unforgiving.

Neither of the two would ever admit it; however, they looked more like sisters than bitter enemies. Not only did they possess similar Nordic traits, they were both dressed in matching camouflage and wore the same sort of ballistic armor.

"We should be getting the hell out of here," Anna said, still speaking in something of a serpentine whisper. "I wasn't lying before, it really does take years to find a cure for anything. Years! Thuy is only doing this out of guilt. I caught her crying earlier. *Crying.*"

"So what? She's been through a lot. Didn't she lose a fiancé or something like that?"

"So what? This is Dr. Lee I'm talking about. She's a friggin' block of ice. You didn't know her before, and you haven't seen what she's like under pressure. She's like stone. So, to see her cry means there's trouble. It means she's cracking. I understand it. It makes sense, and sure, if we had time, I'd be right there with her, working as hard as anyone on a cure, but we don't have the time. You heard the President, didn't you?"

In the dark of the stairwell, Anna didn't see Katherine roll her eyes. "I'm not deaf, I heard him." She shook off the latex-covered hand and had to refrain from smashing Anna with the butt of her rifle.

"Then you agree that all we're doing is indulging her psychosis or guilt trip or whatever. The way I see it, if she wants to stay here and get fried by a nuke, that's her business. We still have a chance. Together we can make it back to the helicopter. All you FBI guys can fly helicopters, right?"

Anna had put out her hand again to touch Katherine, almost as if she needed to be reassured—or to make a grab for her rifle. Katherine smacked the hand away, saying, "Are you that big of an idiot? No, I can't fly a helicopter. And we aren't leaving Dr. Lee. There's still a chance."

Now it was Anna's turn to roll her eyes. "Yeah, a chance to die. Haven't you figured it out yet? Every second in the Zone gives you a whole new chance to die. And don't fall for the way Thuy talks, all cool and all. You saw those kids last night. They're monsters, and Eng...if that is Eng with them, then..." She trailed off, thinking that if it was a zombie version of Eng that the President had mentioned, they were in big trouble. Eng knew what drugs to take in order to retain a part of himself. It would be the most dangerous part, and Anna didn't want any part of a confrontation with him. He would be nearly invincible and driven by a voracious thirst for both blood and revenge.

But if Thuy and Katherine wanted to hang around and distract Eng, Jaimee Lynn and her pack, then great, more power to them. While they were busy getting eaten alive, Anna was going to light on out of there just as fast as her feet could carry her.

She didn't want to go empty-handed, however. "Hey, let me have one of your guns. I'll take the pistol if you want the rifle."

"Yeah, right. You're not getting a gun, and not only that, if you try to run, I will shoot you."

"Shoot me? Come on, we both know you're not shooting anyone. You're the good guy. You could have shot me so many times it's not funny. And I could have killed you if I wanted. Just a moment ago when you were peeking into the stairwell, I could have knocked you right in the back of the head, no problem. I didn't, though and you want to know why?"

"No," Katherine answered, flatly. "What I want is for you to shut up. I hear something down there." The two were only a flight up from the first-floor door; close enough to hear a thumping noise. It sounded like someone was tapping on a window. Katherine dropped her blue mask over her face and headed down. "Your one job is to watch my back. You don't need a gun for that."

Anna cursed at her under her breath—her shaky breath. With every step downward, her fear mounted, and the need to whine about the unfairness of not being armed grew in her. She felt extremely clingy, and had to fight the urge to grab Katherine again. The FBI agent would certainly smash her if she did, and Anna was tired of being hit and hurt, and tied up, and left defenseless and sneered at…and so on.

Oh yes, she was tired of all that bullshit. She had been treated as some sort of subhuman piece of garbage for too long, and so, was it any wonder that she would end up acting like one? Not in her way of thinking. Not in her *twisted* way of thinking. Unlike Eng, Anna needed excuses to kill and now that she had them firmly set in place, all she needed was a weapon and an opportunity.

This was definitely not an opportunity. There was no way of knowing what was on the other side of the door Katherine was about to—she opened it, staying back, her M4 held in one hand like a giant black pistol. The lobby looked just as it had: gleaming marble floors, twenty-foot high ceilings, and half of the long, wide room walled in glass. Piled in front of the lobby doors were soft leather couches, granite-topped tables and polished ash desks. It was just as she had last seen it, except that now shadows dominated everything.

Unnervingly dark shadows. Anything could be hiding in them.

"Do you see what's making that knocking sound?" Anna asked. The moment the door had opened, she had been cured of her clinginess and was now edging back towards the stairs.

"No. It's coming from down one of the halls." The building had two wings branching from the central bank of elevators. "The north hall, I think." Katherine started out of the stairwell, her weapon at the ready. Anna followed a few feet back, her steps were very light. She was ready to run at the first sign of trouble; she just didn't know where she'd run to, exactly. Nowhere was safe.

"This is a trap," she told Katherine. A derisive snort was the agent's answer. "No, I'm not kidding. They're smarter than they look."

"Just stop it. You're not getting a gun. *One* of them was sort of smart. She wasn't a genius or anything and if it hadn't been for you and Eng, we would have killed her, grabbed what we needed and wouldn't be in this situation." Anna opened her mouth to reply, but Katherine snapped her fingers under her nose and shut her up.

Katherine led the way through a heavy door that was marked *Personnel Division*. A long, dark corridor greeted them.

A dozen doors opened on the right, each leading to a small office. A few more offices were on the left before they came to a cubicled section where a number of the dividing walls were tilted far over and leaning on desks.

The tapping sound was clearer now: there was a sharpness to it, like metal on glass. Katherine refused to hurry. She eased forward, checking every corner; they were definitely walking into a trap, but she figured it would be obvious: they would try to corner her and then spring out to attack. To counter this, she didn't head directly towards the sound of the knocking; instead she took her first left and maneuvered through the cubicles.

Any moment she expected to come across a crouched child, trying to hide beneath a desk or behind a filing cabinet. Nothing. And there was nothing when she finally found where the tapping had been coming from. In the very corner office, far from the main hall, she found one of the windows was chipped as if someone had repeatedly smashed it with a hammer.

Anna had picked up a letter opener from one of the desks. She held it in her left hand, and in her right, she held a potted plant. "Where are they? They brought us here for a reason, right? They had to know you had a gun, right? They had to…" A crashing thud from behind them made them both jump. "That was one of the cubicle things," Anna cried in a hushed voice, darting to the side, raising her potted plant higher.

"Yes," Katherine said, going to the doorway and looking out. The halls were quiet again. Once more, she went into stalking mode, skirting the entire cubicle section, going around before entering what was essentially a maze.

In the center they found the wall that had been pushed over; there were small, black handprints on it. When Anna saw them, she spun too quickly and dropped her plant. Just as she picked it up, the sharp knocking began again.

"They're messing with us," Katherine muttered.

"No, it's a trap," Anna insisted, spinning, ready to hurl the plant at the first thing that moved. "You gotta give me a gun."

Katherine was just starting to get nervous, but not for herself. "This isn't a trap. They're just running us around. They're trying to keep us busy."

"Why would they…" Anna bit off her words as she realized who the kids were really after. Her head tilted back as if she could see through the floors between her and Dr. Lee, who stood frozen in front of one of the seven computers that she had running.

She had just heard the giggle of a child. In no way was it a normal giggle. No, this was a vile, evil sound.

2-8:19 p.m.
Grafton, Massachusetts

Twenty-five minutes before, the battalion had close to a thousand men. Now, without even a shot being fired, there were not even seven-hundred. Ross didn't blame the deserters. He knew full well that it was one thing to corner a small group of political officers and a few ill-prepared MPs, it was quite another to try to take on the full might of the army.

"They have tanks, sir," one of his sergeants had said in a whisper when Ross caught him trying to sneak off. "I would join you; I really would, but…" A shrug. "Ain't the zombies enough?"

There was no time to explain the "bigger picture" to the deserters. He let them go without recrimination. Those that stayed were eager to move. The tanks were indeed coming. They were coming slowly, at least compared to how fast they could travel through open country. Their speed was hampered by the amount of trash and broken-down vehicles that littered the streets.

Still, they were coming on at a steady fifteen miles an hour. Interspersed among them were a small fleet of Humvees and trucks laden down with Marines who had been held out of the fight for exactly this ignoble reason. Right down to the lowest jarhead, the Marines hated the political officers with fiery passion. About the only thing they hated more was a traitor.

They came roaring down North Street with their lights blaring. They had been warned about the danger from the zombies, but they wanted the dumb as shit militiamen to know they were coming. Each Marine figured the fight would be over before it started. Maybe a few heroes might take a few potshots; they'd be dealt with in a snap. The tanks came loaded for bear, and were ready with M1028 antipersonnel canister rounds.

"You seeing this sarge?" the driver of the lead Abrams asked.

"Friggin-A. What a bunch of morons." The tank commander flipped to the battalion net. "This is Six-one Alpha in lead. These cheese-dicks have lit off a bunch of fires along the river. Just a heads up, we're going to have bookoo IPs crawling all over the place real quick."

"Roger."

The tank commander glanced at his gunner with a raised eyebrow. "He gives me a 'roger.' What a pussy. The guy can't fart without permission from his PO." The gunner gave a grunt in agreement and then turned back to his periscope, flipping from the thermal night vision to day and then back again.

"The fires are messing with me, Sarge. I can't pick out any targets in close. All I get is a big blur."

"Me too. Friggin' cheese-dicks. There's our street. Turn left, Smitty." As they turned onto the frontage road, the gunner swung the monster 120mm gun so that it was aimed toward the black bog. He had his face crushed into his viewer, straining to see anything that was even vaguely human in shape—at least anything close in. Two-hundred yards away, he had a target-rich environment. There were so many zombies slogging towards them that even safe as he was in the belly of his steel beast, the gunner shivered.

Six-one Alpha rumbled along the road until the driver finally caught sight of a human. He was standing just off the side of the road, waving at the tank.

"Look at this cheese-dick," the driver said. "What do you think, sarge? Is he surrendering?"

"Dunno." Staff Sergeant JD Stronko pulled his M9 Beretta before opening the hatch directly over his head. He came up cautiously, the gun at the ready. "We're looking for Colonel Ross. You him?"

"Shit no. This is the 4th Battalion. You've gone too far. 1st Battalion was all back down that way." He pointed back the way they had come. As Stronko was looking back with a frown bending his bristly cheeks downward, the soldier went on, "I hope you do something about him. Look at those fires. He's been doing shit like this since we came on the line."

Stronko grunted, wondering how Ross had managed to hold the line this long. "All day? That's pretty fucked and he's pretty much fucked. Hold on a sec." He ducked back down and informed the battalion CO that he had reached the end of Ross' line. The gunner popped up out of his own hatch and watched as the rest of the tanks filled in along the line. Between them were the Humvees and 5-tons, the Marines pouring out of them and dropping along the road.

A hundred yards down, the battalion commander boomed out, "Colonel Ross!" His voice easily stretched out to reach the black bog, and beyond. The only answer he received was the growing moans of the dead. "Ross!"

The soldier was now casually leaning against the tread of Sergeant Stronko's Abrams. "Hey you know what?"

He paused for so long that Stronko had to ask, "What?"

"Yeah, about Ross and them, they all left." Again, the soldier just left this hanging in the air, as if there was no more that was needed to be added. No when, why or how, or even to where; they just left.

Sergeant Stronko felt himself swell in anger. "What? What the ever-lovin' fuck are you talking about? They left? When?"

The soldier was just a vague shadow. Stronko saw him cock his head as if something about the question was questionable. "Wellll," the soldier said in that frustratingly slow way of his, "I'm not the most knowledgeable about a great many things when it comes to the military. I mean, I just showed up the other day, you know, looking to do my part, and for whatever reason these high and mighty muckety-mucks, well they decided to put me in charge of things around here. Possibly because of my kindly disposition."

There was a thumpy kind of vein pulsing in Sergeant Stronko's forehead. It thumped along with his growing anger. "Kindly...!" he choked on the word. "Where the fuck is the 1st Battalion?"

"That's almost the question."

He paused, or so Stronko thought at first, but then the slow-talking cheese-dick never got to talking again. "If you don't answer me right this second, I will turn this gun on you and blast you into goo."

"Hmm, I wouldn't want that." The soldier tapped on the side of the tank, his knuckles barely making a thud. "Welllll, I didn't want to be overly officious. I find it doesn't answer as well as you'd think, but seeing as those muckety-mucks, in their vast but capricious wisdom, decided to make me an officer, and being officious pretty much comes with the territory. That being said, you've been talking to a ranking officer. As a sidebar, I

265

personally hate the concept of a 'superior' officer. It strikes an elitist note."

Sergeant Stronko didn't bother stifling a groan. He'd been talking to some useless militia officer. The ridiculously named Army of Southern New England was rife with them. They were all either voted into their positions by way of popularity polls or were given their ranks by having friends in high places.

"Sorry, *sir*," Stronko drawled. "I didn't see your rank. Could you tell me where Ross might have gone?"

The officer gave a dismissive wave with the back of his hand. "It being so dark and all, I really can't blame you, sergeant. These things happen all the time, I've no doubt. As for Colonel Ross, why I don't know where he plans on going. Perhaps Canada in the end. Who knows? He did scamper up that road not long ago."

"Thank you, *sir*." Stronko wasn't much into rolling his eyes, but this situation called for a big roll, which he coupled with a theatrical sigh as he thumbed the radio.

He had just taken a breath when the officer added, "You will of course stay and fight." It was the first definitive thing he had said. It almost sounded like an order.

"That'll be up to my CO, sir."

"Perhaps I should talk to him," he said, awkwardly climbing up on the tank. He held out his hand for the radio. As the officer, a lieutenant colonel "chatted" with his Marine counterpart, explaining that a retreat would be inevitable without the help of the Marine battalion. "Should I give the order to run away now or fire off a few meaningless shots? You know, as a way of saying something along the lines of *We tried, sorry Boston*. By the by, the beasts are practically right in front of us and you, as well. I can see them perfectly. What about you?"

Illuminated by the hundreds of fires that Ross had started, the horde couldn't be missed.

As slow talking as he had been, the officer was quick to go on, "I dare say you can. Perhaps a volley from these great steel creatures of yours would be in order. I know it would do wonders for morale. So many of the men talk about how you aren't Marines at all, and that you're just dressed-up MPs, afraid to fight a real enemy. But who listens to rumors, no matter how many times you hear them going up and down the line? Am I right?"

"We are Marines and we…"

"Really? How fantastic. So, you do plan on fighting... eventually. Will it be when we retreat back to Boston or maybe sometime after that? I heard that Marines fight from the shores. Do you also fight as you back up into it? Because it seems to me..."

The Marine CO butted in. "Enough! Get off the net. Let me talk to Sergeant Stronko." One minute later, the tanks roared out in a rippling broadside that lit the night and shredded hundreds of zombies. There was a cheer from the line, but it was short-lived. The roar of the guns had brought on the next great test as thousands of zombies charged the river.

Ross heard the *boom* of the guns and smiled. It was exactly the sort of distraction he needed. His battalion had surrounded a middle-school two miles from the front line. Here was the headquarters of the army. It was now guarded by only a hundred MPs, just thirty of whom were on duty.

Instead of swarming in like attacking soldiers, Ross ordered his men to form into units of fifty; he then marched them straight to the school from all directions. In a few places they had to jump a low fence or dart around bushes, but the effect was the same. There seemed to be an endless number of them. Without firing a shot, the MPs gave up and in less than a minute, Ross and his men stormed into the command tent itself.

"Who the hell are you?" a lieutenant general demanded. His hand had strayed to the Beretta he kept holstered at his hip. He barely brushed the butt and as he did, Ross cocked an eyebrow and pivoted his rifle toward the general's belly.

"I'm the man you were going to execute. Having an execution hanging over one's head is sorta liberating. It kinda makes me feel like I have nothing to lose. You get me? Like I can do whatever I want. Like I can *kill* whoever I want."

The general's hand slid away from the gun. Ross practically beamed. "In case anyone doesn't know who I am, my name is Troy Ross and I'm the new commander of this army and you are all under arrest."

3-8:58 p.m.
The White House, Washington DC

It didn't take long for the change in command of the Army of Southern New England to reach the President. As he had been for most of the day, he was sitting at the head of the enormous and, quite frankly, ludicrously long table in the Situation Room.

In front of him was a half-eaten piece of toast and a cup of coffee. This was the only thing he had eaten since four that afternoon when he had snuck away for a hot roast beef sandwich and an arugula salad. He had announced that since so many people were going without food, dinners were no longer going to be served in the Situation Room. In his mind, it was an amazing sacrifice.

"A coup, you say? Well, I can't say as I'm surprised." He took a sip of his coffee and set it down without saying more. He only stared at his Secretary of the Army, watching her age. General Renee Smith's practiced look of studious wisdom that got her to the top of her profession had been replaced by a slagged, wrinkled grey mask.

She had to wonder if this was the last straw for her. The Secretary of the Air Force—Renee couldn't even remember his name—had been fired earlier that day for being unable to control his pilots. At least he hadn't been arrested. At one point, the room had been bustling with Cabinet members, administration executives and generals of all sorts. Gradually, many of them snuck away, were fired or managed to say the wrong thing and were arrested.

After this latest fiasco, Renee didn't think it would be long before they came for her. She didn't even like looking at the huge TV, hanging over, and dominating the room. It was a map that essentially showed precisely where the army was screwing up. The 3rd ID was in revolt. The 4th ID was held up at the Mississippi River, unable to cross until a mile-long pontoon bridge could be constructed. The 6th Army was straggling out of Texas in complete disarray; its logistics a shocking, unravelable mess with half of everything being stripped from the division and flown north in support of the southern command surrounding Washington DC.

It didn't end there. Even with the western zombie army centered on the 3rd ID, Pennsylvania was in a state of wild panic and strange fluctuations. Something, no one knew what exactly, was happening in Ohio. Everyone, including government officials, the police and anyone with any sense with a car and a tank of gas had already fled for the nearest border, leaving behind the elderly and the indigent. Satellite photos showed Cincinnati, Columbus and Cleveland in flames.

There were definitely zombies in Indiana. So far, this news was being kept from the press but with Indianapolis surrounded by every swinging dick with a gun waiting for the dam to burst, it wouldn't be for long.

Among all these disasters, there were a few highlights. Somehow three regiments and a smattering of plaid-covered mountain men were holding the entire northern part of the Zone in up-state New York; a line that stretched for a hundred and forty miles. More amazing still, Long Island had not fallen despite everyone agreeing that it had no chance.

Best of all, the capital wasn't seriously threatened. Renee didn't want to think how things would be going if it had.

She smoothed down her uniform, took a breath and nodded. "Yes, sir. As per your orders, the FBI tracked down Ex-Governor Clarren. He was fighting with the Massachusetts National Guard. They moved in to arrest him; however, the PO overseeing the army in that sector decided to make the arrest himself. From the little that's been reported, there was a delay and during that time, Clarren and some militia men took over the headquarters area, arresting everyone on sight."

The President sat looking at her, drumming his fingers on the table top. "And? What are they doing now? Have they given us their demands, yet?"

"No, no demands have been given. They aren't doing anything out of the ordinary just yet." She held her breath, wondering if he could see through her lie. In actuality, they were doing something out of the ordinary, they were fighting smart. Every political officer from every unit had been rounded up and arrested. Hoarded ammunition was being properly distributed, and reinforcements were being allocated based on need rather than cowardice.

She would never say this, however. No way. Renee was no idiot. She held her tongue as the President pushed his chair back and went to stand beneath the immense screen. He shocked her by not exploding in outrage.

"Well," he said, in something of a whisper. "Well, well, well. Clear the room. Where's the DNI? Trista!" Trista Price had just been stopped at the door, and was waiting to go through the newly installed metal detector; the President's paranoia was growing at an alarming rate. He no longer trusted much of his own staff. "Forget all that and find the DNI."

"Excuse me ma'am?" she said to Renee, who was hurrying out, looking green. "Or sir? I'm sorry, I don't know which is correct. What's a DNI?"

At first, Renee recoiled from Trista, thinking that she was one of the ghouls in the basement torturing people— torturing her friends and colleagues. Then she saw the frightened, timid look in Trista's eyes. "It's the Director of National Intelligence. His name is Newsome, and the last time I saw him he was using the Treaty Room as an office."

"The Director of Intelligence? Oh, okay, thanks."

Renee hesitated. The frightening rumor was that the President and the Director of National Intelligence were planning a nuclear strike on US soil. The thought scared her down to her soul and she knew she should say or do something and yet, if she did, and she said the wrong thing to the wrong person…her courage failed her.

"Good luck," she said, and immediately wished she hadn't. Why would she need luck? She tried to force a smile onto her lips, only it came out thin and crooked. "I, uh, meant good luck finding him. Newsome is…" Quick? Elusive? Invisible? "He's just, uh, hard to find."

Trista wasn't really listening. She was dealing with her own issues. The torture chambers had been going full tilt since the break of dawn, and she thought she was on the verge of cracking under the strain. Ten minutes before, she had burst into tears while eating a sandwich. There had been no reason for the tears; no specific reason that she could point to. The tears had just come out of the blue, splashing down on her fries. She had cried the whole time while she ate and as soon as she was done, the tears stopped.

It wasn't right. It was mental and dangerous. And maybe it was why she had been sent to find the Director of National Intelligence. He was the head spy. The mastermind that ran the CIA and the NSA and all the other nefarious little agencies that did terrible things in the name of freedom.

Feeling gutted, Trista made a creditable job of faking a smile. "Thanks," she said to the general and left, walking with her shoulders back and her head held high. It was the walk of a woman who didn't have anything to hide. In her mind, it was very important to appear that way.

Although she was looking for a wicked, evil man, who was probably even then coming back from tossing kittens in the

Potomac or hosting a Klan rally, she discovered that Newsome looked more like a church deacon being asked to give the homily for the first time. He was old and white, and burped constantly behind a withered, wrinkled hand.

The Treaty Room was full of people Trista's age. They were all pale and pinched, their eyes red from staring at computer screens without let up. Newsome was going from one to the next, leaning over their shoulders and making a comment or asking a question.

"The President wants to see you in the Situation…"

"Already? Damn it." He reached into an inner pocket and produced a blue bottle, which he drank from. He bustled Trista from the room, asking her, "What kind of mood is he in?"

"Okay, I guess. I didn't really talk to him."

Newsome took another swig from the bottle and then wiped sweat from his forehead. "Good. His moods have been…" He caught himself and gave Trista a quick distrusting look from the corner of his eye. "You're new. Where are you working?"

"In the basement."

Although the torture chambers were on the same floor as the Situation Room, Newsome understood. His eyebrows came up slightly. "Sorry," he said, embarrassed. This stalled any more conversation between the two and they entered the Situation Room in silence. The room itself was just as silent. Only the President remained, staring up at the main screen.

"Let's see what you have on the Chinese solution," he said, right away. Newsome nodded, burped behind a hand, and went to one of the keyboards. As he did, Trista hesitated in the doorway. She had come to see the President for a reason, one that seemed extremely foolish just then. He caught her still in the room and his eyes went to slits. "What?"

"I have a question about the Second Lady and her family, sir." She was surprised how strong her voice was even though the President's sharp look hadn't changed a hair. "Once she discovered how duplicitous her husband was, she has fully cooperated and has been our finest witness against him." She was the only witness against the Vice President; Trista kept that little tidbit to herself.

The President shrugged. "You said you had a question?"

"I would like to release her and her family, under Secret Service 'protection' back to their home. We are having serious holding space issues and they can't possibly give us any more information. They've damned the Vice President coming and going. And…and I believe it will send the right message, sir."

"And that is?"

"That cooperation and uh, patriotism will be rewarded. The Second Lady is a perfect spokeswoman for that."

A rumble of satisfaction crept up his throat. "Not bad, Trista. I'm glad I kept you around. A great man sometimes needs a soft woman around to mellow him a bit. In fact, stick around for a few minutes. I want to you to hear this. Debbie can wait. Go ahead. Newsome. We'll start with what's happening in China."

"Of course, sir." He let out another soft burp and pushed the side of his fist into his chest before pointing at the screen. "Here is a thermal view of eastern China. As you can see, the Russians created a thirty-mile wide band of radiation, stretching in an arc from the providence of Guandong, here by the South China Sea, through Hubei and then to Jindan. We have repositioned satellites to monitor this arc. So far, nothing has come out of the radiation belt."

"And that? Is that the capital?"

Newsome changed the view, bringing the city of Beijing into focus. "Yes, sir. It appears the Russians had their revenge. It also seems that they are fueling a good portion of their medium range land-based missiles." He changed to a different view that highlighted the Russian missile bases. "As you can see, their long-range sites such as Dombarovsky, where they are testing the Avangard missile, are not active."

"So Vlad's not lying." The President seemed almost disappointed. "Alright, good. What do you think their chance of containing the IPs are?"

"Their own estimates suggest fifty-fifty. I think it's a lot lower than that. And we can't discount the fact that at least one of the trains made it into the Ukraine. They say they stopped it, but so far we haven't been able to trust anything when it comes to the infection."

Trista was shaking her head in disbelief. "There are zombies in Russia, too? And the Ukraine? Where else are they?"

"As far as we know, that's it," Newsome replied.

"And now everyone is begging for our help," the President said with a great deal of satisfaction. "The same jackasses who were all for banning the bomb now want us to start shooting them off willy-nilly." At some point, the president seemed to have forgotten that he had carried a brightly drawn sign in a "No-Nuke" march only twenty years before. "We need to know we are safe first before going to Europe's rescue once again. Put up the layout we've been working on."

Newsome put up a map of America. "As you can see, now that Indiana and Ohio are included, the spread of the infection is now beyond our current nuclear capacity. Because of certain measures, we are down to only eleven hundred deployed warheads." Newsome wasn't about to mention that it was the President himself who had reduced the stockpile by a third in his first year in office. Some of the same people who had cheered his use of Executive Orders were just starting to turn stiff beneath an inexcusably thin layer of dirt not far from the White House.

"Yes," Newsome said, going on, "we can bathe the entire northeast in radiation, but our tests suggest that many of the IPs will live through it. Their power to heal is phenomenal, far beyond our own. It'll take extremely intense radiation to kill them."

"Meaning what?" the President demanded. He clearly didn't like any idea that smacked of a half-measure.

"We should do what the Russians did to the Chinese. We seal off the entire northeast. We lay down a triple row of overlapping nuclear explosions and fry everything in a twenty-mile belt running from Baltimore to Cleveland." He drew a thick line between the two cities; the line also encompassed Pittsburgh, a city without a single case of the infection—the President liked things simple and Newsome wasn't going to put his neck out for any reason. "I suggest that Akron and Canton be included within the belt to be on the safe side."

"So be it," the President agreed, dooming an extra million people to a fiery death. "But no half-measures. I want this stopped in one swoop, so be *generous* with the bombs."

It was an odd choice of words and it brought up a tremendous burp from Newsome, whose face twinged in pain. "Excuse me. Sorry. Of course, generous. We'll be, uh, very generous. W-we'll have to completely reduce Dayton, Columbus, Cincinnati, and Indianapolis. Maybe even Louisville. To be, uh, generous, and to be on the safe side, we'll want to start outside in the suburbs and work our way to the center of the cities, that way if we run out of nukes, we'll have at least sealed off the cities."

273

"Sure. What about New York City and all the rest? What will we have available for them?"

If he was going to be as "generous" as the President wanted, he wouldn't have much left over. "Not a lot, I'm afraid. Maybe a single line of bombs to begin containment. But that's just for now. We still have stockpiled nuclear weapons that are basically dismantled or retired and waiting to be reduced. It'll take them a few months to be readied for actual use. Or they can be made into dirty bombs. That'll take only a few hours."

"Then do that. We'll give the whole area a fine dusting. I want the bombs in the air as soon as possible. Take out those Ohio cities first. We have to stop the westward shift of the infection asap. Then do that band, that line. Start it in Baltimore, but make sure the wind is right. I don't want any of that radioactive shit raining down on me. After that…"

He used his interactive map to make little arcs around New York City, Buffalo, and Detroit. "Save these cities. Hmm, and I guess Boston, but make it tight. Use this arc here. I-495. What do you think, Trista?"

That you're an evil man. She couldn't say this, although he was flippantly throwing the lives of millions of people away, many of whom could be saved with just a little more effort or forethought. He had also clearly chosen I-495 because it would put the entire Army of Southern New England within the blast zone. And the radiation belt would run right through Hagerstown, cutting off and trapping the entire 3rd ID, giving them the option of dying by radiation poisoning or by being torn apart by a zombie horde.

"It's pretty awesome," Trista gushed. "I'm just glad it will all be over soon." He grinned and she grinned right back, amazed at how easily the lie had come. "You should come up with a catchy name for the radiation belt. Like the Freedom Line or something like that."

"Maybe you could do that for me," the President suggested, then his face fell. "Oh, that's right. You'll be too busy saving the less fortunate." She gave him an honestly confused look and he said, "You know, Debbie and the kids."

"Right. I completely forgot about them. I guess I was just too caught up with…" She swallowed the words that had almost shot out of her mouth: *I was just too caught up with the idea of killing you.* "With all of this," she said, instead. "It'll be a relief when the terror is over."

Chapter 22
1-9:02 p.m.
New Rochelle, New York

Over the sound of the whirring machines, the hum of the centrifuges, and the ever-present scream of Specialist Hoskins, the sound of the child's voice rang, sickly sweet, and totally evil, "Doctor Leeeeee?"

Thuy froze and closed her large, doe eyes. She even held her breath. It was Jaimee Lynn Burke hunting her. Somehow the little monster had gone from being a somewhat dull eight-year-old child, to a creature sitting high on the food chain. In fact, she was an apex predator. She was the hunter and Thuy was her prey.

"I cun smell you, Doctor Lee. I cun smell how y'all been washin' with that pink soap stuff. It ain't gonna work. I cun smell y'all's blood right through it. Why don't y'all come on out. I's jus wanna talk."

Jaimee Lynn's stomach wouldn't stop growling, making her a liar. Or at least a little bit of a liar. She did want to talk, just maybe after she ate off one of Dr. Lee's legs. "I wanna know what y'all did with my daidy. I don't smell him none. Where is he? Come on out and iffin' y'all tell me, I promise that I won't kill none of you."

With her were five of her pack. They were slunk down behind the desks, their greedy black eyes sparkling like midnight diamonds as they crawled along. They were simpletons compared to Jaimee Lynn, but they were cunning, horrible simpletons and knew a lie when they heard it. Jaimee Lynn hadn't said nothing about them killing the lady. One of them started to giggle and was kicked in the face by their leader.

"All y'all gotta do is tell me where he went. Hello? Doctor Lee?" A look of unrepentant fury swept over the girl before she forced the hideous black smile back into place. "Please, Doctor Lee. He's all I got left."

Jaimee Lynn sniffed suddenly, catching a stronger scent: the faint aroma of woman's sweat; Doctor Lee's sweat. It was coming from somewhere near the back of the long lab. Jaimee Lynn passed rows of work stations, following the smell until she came to a low series of cabinets under the last counter.

"Jus tell me where he went," Jaimee Lynn said with growing excitement. No sound, but the smell was strong. Like a dog, she went from one cabinet to the next until she found the one. She snatched it open, saying, "I got…" Except for some science stuff that looked complicated and breakable, there was only a dirty shirt in the cabinet. She grabbed it and breathed in deeply.

It fueled her hunger and her rage. "Doctor Lee! I know y'alls here!" The scream echoed throughout the building, reaching all the way to the first floor.

Too late, Katherine Pennock realized the trap was sprung. "Come on," she cried, and rushed towards the lobby. Anna paused for only a second, wondering if this was her chance to escape; there was no doubt in her head that she had to escape. A thump behind her told her this was not the right moment and it got her racing after the FBI agent all the while twisting her head around owl-like, looking behind her.

Shadows shifted, seeming to come alive. Anna let out a hissing cry, "Kat!" just as she ran into Katherine who had paused at the end of the cubicle maze. "They're behind us!" Anna whispered.

Katherine didn't believe it for a moment, and gave only a single glance past Anna before she charged on. "Ha!" she cried when she saw one of the children. In the dark it might have been a goblin or a hissing chimp. She shot it, her M4 sounding like a cannon in the quiet building. The zombie-child was flung back, flying over a desk, leaving a glistening smear across the top.

Instinctively, Katherine turned, knocked aside Anna, and saw another darting in at them from beneath one of the light cubicle walls that had fallen. She shot it and looked to pin it to the floor with the hot bullet. Another turn. Katherine was suddenly short of breath and was puffing behind her blue mask.

Anna's hands were on her again. Katherine knocked them aside. Her adrenaline was pumping through her system and she was on a spring trigger, hyper-aware. A scraping sound to her right—the first little zombie she had shot had disappeared, leaving behind a greasy black trail. She turned back in time to see the second one she had shot slip back under the wall.

Once more, instinct kicked in and she wasted three bullets punching holes in the cubicle wall. She only had twenty-one rounds left. Dashing forward, she heaved the wall over. The zombie was gone.

"Son of a bitch!" Without worrying whether Anna would follow her, Katherine ran for the door that led to the central part of the lobby; it was partially blocked with furniture. "They were trying to trap us. Shit. Clear it. I'll watch our back."

Anna had followed, and now she reluctantly went about pulling aside the furniture. Even with gloves on, she didn't want to touch a thing. And she was tired. Unlike Katherine who had been on the go for only thirty-six hours, Anna had been neck deep in the apocalypse for five days now. She was exhausted, and bruised, battered and broken; literally broken. Two of her fingers had been cruelly damaged from a fall and they still ached despite having been set and bandaged by an FBI medic.

On top of all of that, she wasn't exactly motivated to save Dr. Lee and so, she cleared the door but slowly. When it was finally done, she didn't volunteer to go through first.

"You are a piece of work," Katherine said, pushing past her and heading for the stairs. The fall of her black boots echoed in the lobby.

A moment later, Anna joined her, a plan percolating in her mind. If they went upstairs, the zombie children would follow and when they did, she would slip away, head out the back door and get the hell out of there. It made no sense at all to stay now. If there had ever been a chance at a cure, it was gone now that Eng and Jaimee Lynn had found them.

Up the stairs the two went, with Anna trailing a few steps down, listening intently for any sign that they were being followed. The door below had let out a pneumatic hiss when they had come through. The hiss had not repeated; they were alone.

At the third floor, Katherine cracked the door, just enough to look out; she wouldn't commit, however. She was listening, trying to hear beyond Specialist Hoskins, who was screaming his black lungs out.

It was time to run, Anna decided. *But why go empty-handed or unarmed?* she asked herself. Katherine was giving her a perfect opportunity, Anna just wished she had kept a hold of her potted plant. The slim, silver letter opener was a stupid weapon, especially against a person in ballistic armor. Besides, she didn't want to kill Katherine, she wanted to leave that to the zombie children.

Eating the FBI agent would be a fantastic distraction.

277

But how to accomplish this? Katherine was slightly taller, much stronger and trained to fight. She was armored and her heart was pumping. Going toe-to-toe with her would be idiotic, and Anna was no idiot. She was, however, a backstabbing bitch, although in this case, she wasn't going to stab anyone. Katherine was leaning too close to the edge of the door frame.

Anna came up fast and silent. She slammed Katherine's head into the side of the metal frame with an ugly thud. Anna tried to smash her a second time, but Katherine's legs had already buckled and she collapsed, falling limply to the painted cement. Anna was on her in a second, punching her in the face and further knocking the back of her head into the floor until stars flashed across her vision.

"I said we should leave," Anna whispered as she stripped Katherine of her pistol and rifle. "I told you. I *warned* you, and now look what's happened." She stood tall over the agent, appearing like some sort of yellow-haired titan from a blurry mythological past. She pulled out the letter opener and tossed it onto Katherine's armored chest. "Good luck."

Katherine could barely focus and the words had no meaning. They were a mumbled nothing compared to the pounding in her head. Then Anna yelled something that echoed in the stairwell as well as in Katherine's head, before she turned and leapt down the stairs. "What?" Katherine muttered, trying to make sense of what had just happened. "We-we're in here?" That's what Anna had cried out, but who was she talking to? "An' and w-why does my head hurt?" She thought her words sounded slushy as if it was impossible for words to be as unfocused as her vision.

With the world spinning and tilting up and down, she forced herself upright, putting her back to the wall. Far below her, the pneumatic serpentine hiss of the stairwell door shutting drifted up. "She ran away," Katherine said, suddenly realizing what had happened to her. Quick righteous anger dispelled a good bit of the woolly fog that had filled most of her mind. "She left us. That fucking whore! I'll…"

A small, but nasty, bloody-faced zombie interrupted her. It popped its brutally lumped head through the third-floor door and smiled wickedly at her, showing off rows of needle-sharp baby teeth.

"Holy crap!" she cried, feeling an electric shock of fear blast through her entire being. Just as the beast leapt full on her, its terrible little teeth digging for her throat, she spied the letter opener next to her leg. Her hand closed on it and in a silver flash she brought the dull blade around in a sharp, vicious arc, driving it into the creature's neck so hard that the point protruded out the other side.

The force of the blow knocked the child to the side. Katherine scrambled up just as the door opened and three more of the monsters charged into the darkened stairwell. Had they been ordinary kids, she would have been able to bend them over her knee and given them something to think about. These were the furthest things from normal.

They were fearless and amazingly strong. Before she could even ready her mind for the insanity she faced, she was bowled over by the force of the three and sent falling backwards down the stairs. It was too soon after getting her head smashed and before she knew it, she couldn't tell up from down. She was lucky that the zombies were in something of the same boat. Their brains were ineffectual to begin with, and they were equally slow at grasping where they were when they crashed into the landing at the bottom of the staircase.

Katherine recovered a hair quicker. She lashed out from her back with a kick that broke the nose and top row of teeth of one of the monsters. Next, she grabbed the second one and threw it face first into the wall, where it left a greasy black smear before it fell. She was reaching for the third when it bit down on her hip bone, just below the angle of her armor. It felt like a pitbull with iron teeth had chomped down on her. The pain was enough to make her scream.

Afraid that she was infected, she drove her elbow down with raging force, aiming for the thing's temple. The angle was bad and she hit it at the top of its jaw, dislocating it. The relief from the pain was immediate. "Oh god!" she gasped as she shoved the little zombie away; it was trying to bite her again, but without a working jaw it wasn't doing anything but pressing its face against her.

She was up in a flash, but fell again as the beast grabbed her ankle. "Get the fuck off of me!" With a yank, she pulled herself free, and was about to race down the stairs when the door to the second floor banged open below her.

"Anna?" Katherine called out, suddenly nervous.

"Nope. Guess again."

There was no need to guess. It was Eng. He had come back from the dead.

2-9:14 p.m.
R & K Research Facility

A moment before she heard that single, hideous giggle, Thuy felt a prickle of fear. Something small triggered a warning inside her; perhaps it was a change in air pressure made by the opening of a door, or the tiny vibration of running feet coming up through the linoleum. Either way, she was tense and ready when she heard the giggle.

It was all the warning she needed. In a quick move, she yanked off the shirt she'd been wearing over a white cami for the past few days, chucked it into one of the cabinets beneath her work station and then ducked through the closest door seconds before Jaimee Lynn and her pack entered the lab.

The door had been her only choice, but she regretted it immediately. She was trapped in the lab's dedicated cleanroom. Not only was the room relatively small, it was the least protected room in the building. The top half of the walls was glass. This also included the door which had no lock! To top it all off, she shared the room with a raging zombie.

Across from her was Specialist Hoskins, his eyes black as sin and dripping what looked like motor oil. His flesh was tinted grey all except the skin around his wrists, which were black and bleeding. He was cuffed to the vertical strut of a long, steel workstation that was bolted to the wall. In his madness, it looked as though he was about to tear his own hands off in order to get at her.

And if he did, what could she do about it? Save for her mask and gloves, Thuy was defenseless. She had no weapons and was completely untrained in any martial art. Even her brilliant mind was useless under the circumstances.

Her only option was to remain perfectly still, no matter what happened—no matter how close Jaimee Lynn came to finding her hiding place. Thuy crouched behind the door, wondering if she was strong enough to hold it closed against the combined strength of the children. They were small but hellishly strong.

The minutes dragged as Jaimee Lynn hunted her. There were moments of hope, such as when Katherine fired her M4 down on the first floor. The hope didn't last and faded along with the smattering of gunshots.

Then Jaimee Lynn was just on the other side of the door. She stood tall enough to see into the room, and for some reason, her presence made Hoskins especially furious. The creature screamed as though he were trying to tear his own throat out and spit it onto the floor. He pulled against his cuffs with such strength that he yanked a few of the bolts out of the wall and the entire cabinet screeched toward Thuy, its metal legs grinding across the floor in a high squeal.

Thuy still refused to move. She closed her eyes and listened to her heart race inside her, too afraid to even pray. Barehanded, she had no chance against the pack. Of course, she would fight back and run if she could, but she would lose one way or another. Infection was a guarantee and death through dismemberment very likely.

Dismemberment—was her sterile, clinical way of saying that she would be torn apart by the pack's feral little teeth. Deckard would have laughed at the word. He would have scoffed and grinned that unbearably handsome grin of his and said something like, *Maybe try a bigger a word; more letters might save you.*

A fleeting smile lit up her face…then the door knob wiggled. They had found her at last. She decided that she would hold the door as long as she could and force them to come through the glass. Realistically, this might add all of a minute to her life. After all, the glass was germ-proof, not bullet-proof.

Thuy's smile came back, warped now by a feeling of lunacy that made her want to laugh and cry at the same time. All that separated her from whatever doom was due her was a half-inch of brittle glass. It seemed about right, about par for the course her life had been taking.

A thump vibrated through the wall, making her jump. Another followed right after. Some of the smaller children couldn't see inside and were jumping up to grab the sill, their mangled feet kicking the wall. Thuy could feel the eyes of the pack peering into the room and she shrank into herself, squeezing her knees to her chest. She was sure they would attack the glass any second. Hissed orders were given, followed by Jaimee Lynn saying, "Go get 'em."

This is it, Thuy thought and then shocked herself as she jumped up, ready to fight. But no one was ready to fight her. The pack of demon children were charging through the stairwell doorway and Thuy just caught a glimpse of a bloody-faced Katherine Pennock before the pack swarmed her and the door slammed shut.

Only Jaimee Lynn was left and she turned cat-quick and caught Thuy standing there, gaping like an idiot.

The girl grinned. "I cun see you, Doctor Lee," Jaimee Lynn said through a wicked grin.

Thuy took a steadying breath. "I can see you, too, Jaimee Lynn. I like your dress." The yellow dress was pretty; the head sitting above it was a horror. Especially that triumphant, hungry grin. Thuy did her best to ignore it. "Are you wearing it for your father? I know where he is."

A new look crossed her inhuman features. It was desire, but a different sort of desire. This wasn't about feeding on fresh blood. Thuy was shocked to see that it was a desire for love. It wasn't by any means a look of pure goodness. No, behind it was a selfish infantile demand to be loved that was twisted by innate cruelty.

"Where? Where is he?" Jaimee Lynn pressed her black hands to the glass, smearing it with filth. "Please tell me."

"The tenth-floor conference room, just to the left of the elevators. He couldn't be here be-because he, um, he was already given the shot. He didn't want to throw off the results of our tests."

Only a week before, Jaimee Lynn had huge luminous blue eyes, now they were large, black and wet. They reminded Thuy of an insect's eyes. These insect eyes blinked in surprise. "That's a lie, Doctor Lee," she said, breathless, amazed and actually insulted. She stuck her hands on her hips, stamped a filthy bare foot and cried, "That's a dirty lie and y'all know it."

"I suppose it is," Thuy admitted. "In my defense, being threatened gives one a certain moral leeway in these things. Perhaps if you were to step back so that I didn't feel as though my life were in jeopardy, we could discuss…"

"We ain't discussing nothin," Jaimee Lynn seethed. "Where's my daidy? Y'all know where he at. I smelled y'all together. Now tell me!"

It was then that Katherine Pennock's fear-filled voice rang loud enough to be heard throughout the third floor. "Thuy, run! Run!"

Cold dread, cold enough to make her shiver, filled Thuy at the scream. Katherine had shown such consistent bravery that the fear in her voice could only be justified by something truly awful. Had Eng found her? Was it really him? Thuy had the gut feeling that it was. If so, he had to be infected...or he had purposefully infected himself to keep from dying.

The idea was horrible. Only someone terribly twisted or hell bent on revenge would even consider trying something so disgusting. She wouldn't put it past Eng. He was that evil, and yet she was sure that this new version of Eng would be far worse. It wasn't a stretch of the imagination to envision him as no longer the geeky wannabe spy. The Com-cells would have transformed him into something far more difficult to handle. He was probably armed and was certainly armored. He would be impervious to pain and nearly indestructible, and worse, he would be far more devious and cunning than Jaimee Lynn.

And Thuy couldn't even handle her.

The little girl snarled as cold fury swept aside the somewhat confusing miasma of "love" that had been wafting through her mind. She didn't trust Eng or her pack. They were probably all feeding right that second—without her! Forgetting her father for the moment, she launched herself at the door with a piercing shriek.

Thuy slammed her shoulder against it, barely able to hold it closed. "Jaimee, please. I'm sorry I lied about your father. The truth is we were friends. Your father was..." Gunshots boomed through the building from somewhere above them.

For some reason, these shots seemed to light a fire in Jaimee Lynn more than the earlier ones had. "Get her!" she screamed at Specialist Hoskins. Why her order would make any difference to Hoskins was lost on Thuy. Wasn't he already doing everything in his power to eat her? She had thought that was the case and yet his roaring grew in volume and his tendons nearly tore from the constraints of his flesh as he began pulling with the strength of four men. The workstation groaned as the entire wall seemed to be bending towards her.

"Oh God," Thuy whispered, backing to the door, unaware that Jaimee Lynn was no longer pushing on it. The first clue that she wasn't was when a metal stool crashed most of the way through the window to her left.

"Where's he at?" Jaimee Lynn screamed as she yanked the stool out and swung again, sending out a blast of tiny glass cubes skittering through the cleanroom. Thuy shied away from the hole only to flinch back again as a section of the ceiling and part of the wall collapsed onto Specialist Hoskins. He was tearing the room apart, and still his maddened strength seemed to be growing—incredibly, the metal strut his arms were chained around began to bend.

Before Thuy could wrap her head around that, more glass flew over her. Jaimee Lynn was battering her way through the glass window, which was coming down like sheets of ice.

Thuy was caught between two fires and didn't know which way to turn. Oddly, this thought gave her an idea. Inches from Hoskins' cuffed wrists was a fire extinguisher. To get to it, she would have to practically climb into his back pocket. But she was desperate enough to try it even if it meant getting within biting distance of him. The smell coming off of him was rancid. As nasty as the fecal odor was, it was the stench of concentrated urine that made her eyes water. What was worse than both of these was the evil fumes coming from his mouth. There was a decaying graveyard stink rising from within him.

It made Thuy waver as she stepped closer. She had one chance, and that was to play matador. She showed him her left hand and even let him snap his deadly gnashing teeth within inches of it, and while he did, she undid the strap of the fire extinguisher with her right. She was so close to him that if he turned from her snapping fingers, he would be able to tear out her throat in a second.

"Git her! Git her!" Jaimee Lynn screamed. But it was too late. Thuy had the fire extinguisher. She pulled the pin and shot a gout of white powdery smoke into the zombie girl's face. When the cloud cleared, it looked like Jaimee Lynn had been rolled in flour and, except for her huge black beetle eyes glistening from within her alabaster cheeks, her looks had been tremendously improved. She could almost pass for a child once more.

For one stunned second, Jaimee Lynn just stood there, then she coughed out a great mouthful of powder. She had breathed in enough of the stuff to put out a cub-scout campfire and her body reacted in a purely human manner; she bent over and started hacking up what looked like wet chalk. Her chest heaved and her lungs convulsed and while she was at it, Thuy conked her on the top of the head with the extinguisher, dropping her right in the doorway.

Thuy considered hitting her again and again until her black brains gushed out onto the white floor, only just then there were more gunshots coming from the floor above them—the shooter seemed to be moving farther away, perhaps heading to the south stairwell. The idea that she might be left among the zombies terrified Thuy. She leapt over Jaimee Lynn and raced down the hallway for the stairs, leaving behind hours worth of work, leaving behind so many possibilities.

It was all ruined. Almost all the experiments were time sensitive and those that weren't had other parameters that needed to be babysat: temperatures had to be within in certain ranges, pH values could only be allowed to ride or fall so much and some were even photosensitive; too much light would destroy controlling factors.

Any shot at a cure went out the window the moment she blazed through the door to the stairwell.

She stopped on the landing, uncertain which way to turn. Below her was the patter of small feet—many small feet; above her was the sound of someone leaping down the stairs five at a time; and then *BOOM!!!!* Another gunshot filled the staircase with a tremendous sound. It was huge and wide. Beneath it was a stinging whine as the bullet bounced from wall to wall.

Thuy blinked in shock as the last fragments of it and bits of fine cement sprayed her harmlessly. Two seconds later, Katherine Pennock landed almost on top of her. "Thuy! We have to..." She had begun pulling Thuy towards the next flight of stairs only to stop when she heard the gang of children heading up towards them.

"This way," Katherine cried, yanking Thuy back onto the third floor.

"We can't!" Thuy pulled back on the FBI agent. "Jaimee Lynn's here." The warning came too late. The zombie girl stood thirty yards down the hall, grinning through the powder; her mouth was a black pit, as dark as her eyes.

The two women were trapped, at least as far as Thuy saw things. Jaimee Lynn was a wicked creature, overflowing with disease. Katherine had to know it, so it was mystifying to Thuy when the agent charged, racing at the girl in a full sprint. Ten feet before the two collided, Katherine leapt. She didn't leap to one side or the other as Thuy would have, she leapt full into Jaimee Lynn, striking her with a crushing front kick and laying the girl out.

285

"Come on," Katherine ordered, running on without checking her speed. Thuy ran after her. For a delicate flower, an indoor, lab-grown flower, Thuy was surprisingly fast. Unencumbered by armor and driven by fear, she caught up with Katherine just as Eng burst out onto the floor.

He shouldered his rifle and fired in one motion, missing high and wide with his first shot. The bullet blasted out a glowing exit sign. Katherine darted under the remains of it a second later and shouldered her way through the doorway to the central stair. Thuy was a step behind, a bare foot and half. Eng's next shot passed through that small space.

The passage of the bullet so close to her belly, made Thuy choke on her next breath as she sucked it in sideways, or so it felt.

Katherine wasn't waiting for anything. She flew down the stairs like a billygoat and in no time, Thuy was far back, afraid that she would break an ankle if she went any faster. The door opening above her spurred her on, however. It was Eng.

"It's going to be your turn next, Doctor Lee," he called out, his voice shaking as he came down the stairs as fast as he could. When he tripped and fell, his gun went off with another BOOM. A chorus of evil, childish giggles followed the sound of the gunshot.

Jaimee Lynn's pack was after them as well. Thuy let out an uncharacteristic curse. "No, it's a good thing," Katherine told her. "With them all after us, there'll be no one guarding the exit. We're home free."

A second later, she banged out into the dark lobby, and a second after that, Thuy banged into her. They weren't home free. Far from it. The headlights of the battered police cruiser that Eng had driven down from North Highland were still going strong and, in their glare, the two women could see hundreds of zombies. The building was surrounded and Thuy was trapped yet again.

Chapter 23
1-10:04 p.m.
The White House, Washington DC

The world was flying towards its end and no one seemed to care. The Russians had launched their last missiles and a hundred million people were about to be turned to ash. It was a fucking TV event. The work in the White House stalled as everyone sat glued to the closest screen on hand. Many of the staffers, with bewildered expressions plastered on their faces, watched the blurry satellite feeds of what appeared to be incredibly tiny missiles. It was as if a part of them thought they were watching a movie and could avoid the fate of the world by simply changing the channel.

Here and there among the bewildered were those who had some sort of clue concerning the reality of the situation. They were pale-faced and haggard; draping themselves weakly on whatever furniture that was nearby. Some of them cried.

But did they really fucking care?

Trista Price didn't think so. The same damn thing was about to happen right here in America, and where was the outrage? Where were the tears for their own people? Where were the moderates crying: *Slow down now. Let's explore other options.* Where was the military? Could those overly-aggressive macho men have been cowed so easily and so quickly? Didn't they see that the President was nothing more than a bit of fluff? That he was basically an average old man with good hair and a polished approach to making speeches? Because that's all he was.

"It's all any of them are," she griped under her breath, glaring at a pair of senators. Together, the two had been in office for fifty years. Fifty years of wasting taxpayer money, of naming highways after themselves, and becoming multi-multi-millionaires while being paid an upper middle-class salary. For the first time in her life she saw politicians for what they really were: grifters, snake-oil salesmen, parasites who divided the country and fomented hate and then demanded the greatest respect for pointing out the very problems they had created.

"They're all useless," she muttered. "Every one of them."

Was she the only one who wanted to stop this? Was she the only one who saw that they still had a chance to win?

Couldn't they see the 3rd Infantry Division only slowly giving ground even with bombs falling from the sky on *them* and not the zombies? Couldn't they see how the farmers and pipe-fitters and scrounged up inner-city kids were fighting the zombies to a standstill in Massachusetts?

She wanted to scream: *We can still win!* Oh, but she couldn't. No, if she did, she would be arrested. That was the problem…no *HE* was the problem. The President was making everything worse, if not impossible. Someone had to get rid of him. Trista searched the faces of everyone she came across, looking for someone like her, someone angrier than they were afraid.

All she saw was fear and weakness. Anyone that had shown even a little strength had been "replaced." That's how the staffers put it—*Have you seen Bob? Uh, no. He's been replaced.* That was so much better than the truth. No one wanted to think about the idea that he was in the basement getting his balls kicked in because he had authorized a transfer of fuel to FEMA to save a thousand stranded refugees.

That was going to be Trista soon. Her anger was going to get the best of her and eventually it would show through. Then…poof—*Does anyone know where Trista is? No, that Shauna girl is the President's new assistant.*

Trista's position had morphed during the day and she was now basically the President's bitch. His servant. She was whatever he wanted her to be. Currently, she was briefing the remaining staffers, concerning the "Use of Strategic Weapons." She had volunteered for the job, hoping she'd be able to find a kindred spirit, someone with backbone.

She started brutally and to the point, hoping to smack some of them awake. "We anticipate very high casualties, numbering in the tens of millions. Those people that do survive will not be able to expect any assistance from the government for some time, as we don't have the resources available. They'll have to make it on their own for the foreseeable future."

There was no outrage at this. There was merely a bit of muttering and some of the bewildered looks deepened, so that befuddled was the more accurate term to describe them.

"The *attack* will happen as soon as possible," she went on, with a simpleton's smile on her face. It was the only expression she could manage that wasn't a perpetual furious grimace. Her face was not well-suited for any expression that didn't suggest a gentle contentment with her near-perfect life.

"We'll start with the submarines. The…" She had to pause to look at her notes, since she had no idea what sort of boats and planes the military had available. "We have eleven Ohio-class submarines within striking distance. These should be able to launch within the hour. Bombers and ICBMs will be next. As you see on the screen, the cities that will be directly attacked are circled in red. Those areas that will be exposed to lethal doses of radiation are shaded in grey."

The entire northeast was either red or grey.

There was stunned silence. The last remaining press official asked, "Are we allowed to put this out?"

It was a stupid question and Trista's smile dimmed, a little of her anger peeking out in the process. "The President doesn't see the need to make anyone's last minutes any more difficult than they are by causing a panic."

"What about family?" the congressional liaison asked. "We should be able to say something to them, right? It's only fair."

Trista gazed on the man hungrily. Was it his mom he wanted to save? His wife? His three kids? It didn't matter. His family was about to be vaporized, certainly she could count on him to make a stand for their sake. "I'm afraid not. It'll be treason if anyone leaks any of this." The man deflated and stared at the floor with such a dazed expression that Trista thought he might start drooling.

She finished her briefing quickly and cornered the man before he could wander away. "Is it your mom?" she asked. "Are you worried about her?"

His face sagged all along the edges like a Basset Hound. "No, it's my brothers and their families. I have…two nephews… and a niece. In Cleveland. Jon just moved there a few weeks ago." He was crying. The tears dripping down his face were large and perfectly clear. They were a child's tears and they cut through Trista's anger and at first, she remembered the sadness she had felt earlier. The tears kept coming and, after a couple of dozen had fallen, her lip curled in disgust. They were useless show-tears.

"There are missiles even now being aimed at your nieces and nephews," she said in a low voice, angling her face to see into his. "They are going to die. Do you understand that? Yeah? So, what are you going to do about it?"

"What can I do?" he asked, looking even more miserable.

Trista only stared at him, waiting for him to see the obvious solution. When he didn't, she went purple in the face. She wanted to scream at him and slap him, and make the sort of scene that only a woman could get away with making in public. She wanted to shame him for his weakness. But she couldn't. No, too many people would see and too many people would talk, and that talk would eventually get back to the President.

Instead, she let out a long breath, the color draining from her face. "Okay then," she said. "You have a nice night." She left him and went to find David Kazakoff. That morning she had considered him the vilest creature on the planet. Now, he was the only person who didn't seem to be afraid, which made him the only person she felt she could turn to.

His looks, just like her own, had faded over the course of the long day. His dark hair was no longer as wavy as it had been and his penetrating eyes had blue/black circles beneath them. He sat in the same nondescript conference room that the President took his meals in. It was quiet in the room, wonderfully quiet.

In front of him was a garden salad that was half-drowned in ranch dressing. "Where have you been for fuck's sake? I've had the Veep cooling his heels for an hour now. In case you didn't know, that's a mistake in my line of work. You never want to give them a moment of rest. If they gather their…"

"Will you shut up!" she whispered, her eyes darting to the door, then to the ceiling, looking for cameras. She didn't see any, but that didn't mean they weren't there. Trista moved in so close to Kazakoff that she could smell the day of sweat under his suit jacket. "I need to talk to you about something important."

"Sure, you can talk to me. Your secrets are my secrets."

It was his idea of a joke and yet it set off warning bells inside her head. She had to ignore them; time was getting away from her. "I need your help. We, everyone needs your help. The President…" Her throat clamped good and shut. She took a swig from his water bottle so she could go on, "He has authorized the release of nuclear weapons."

David sighed, forked a mouthful of salad into his mouth, and then shrugged. It was his entire rebuttal.

She shoved his plate away so that it skittered across the table and came dangerously close to sliding right off the edge. "He's bombing Ohio, Indiana, Pennsylvania." She ticked off the states holding up her fingers with each, finishing with Virginia, even though the "Line" only passed close to the state.

"I know what you're going to say: maybe he has to, but he doesn't!" Trista had grown loud, and he put a finger to his lips in warning. She hunched forward again. "He doesn't have to. We're winning! The lines have barely shifted all day, and that's with him hogging all the airpower to bomb Baltimore into pieces of nothing. There have been over four-thousand sorties against the city today alone."

Trista wasn't exactly sure what a sortie was, which didn't slow her outrage in the least. "If the war was fought in the right way, we wouldn't need nukes. Or if we did, we wouldn't need to bomb cities that are completely fine. Pittsburg, Canton, Akron. Look at this."

She slid out her laptop and showed him the day's fighting in a fifty-second encapsulated video. "See? They've reached their peak, but we haven't. Look how close those units from Texas and Oklahoma are. And these from Alabama, Mississippi, and Florida; there are over sixty-thousand of them. And there are more coming. Enough to stop them without destroying everything."

Her pleading did nothing to persuade him; the maps did, however. He had assumed, like everyone else in the DC echo chamber, that their doom was a foregone conclusion. The press echoed the President, the cable news shows echoed the press, and the President used the cable shows to cement his positions. It was a circular, incestuous relationship.

"You see?" Trista insisted. "You do, don't you. We can win if someone has the guts to do something. If not, he'll be dropping nuke after nuke, and when those run out, he'll start using dirty bombs. And it won't ever end."

For a long time, Kazakoff sat back, staring at the map. "And you want to kill him?" Actually, Trista wanted Kazakoff to kill him. She nodded and he asked, "Who would take his place?"

"The Vice President, I guess. He's next in line and he's shown he's got some backbone."

"Mmm, the Vice President? Pick someone else."

She looked shocked. "I don't get to pick people. It's not up to me, it's up to the Constitution. People will only follow that, not some dictator chosen by a nobody. The VP is next in line and then after that it's the Speaker of the House and she's as bad as the President. She has basically ceded all control to him and has run back to California."

"Then I can't help you." He stood, hesitating, not looking at her. "You seem to forget that I just tortured that guy for hours. Trust me, he's not likely going to forgive and forget."

He started to leave and she grabbed his arm, fiercely. "David, I need you. Your country needs you. Please, I'm begging you. We-we can make his release conditional. We'll make sure you'll get a pardon…and one for me, too. I've done bad things, too."

"Like threatening to rape his wife and children?" He gave her a brief, painful smile before his eyes slid away. "No. We both know he won't forgive me. You're on your own. I won't try to stop you, but I won't help you either."

Without a look back, he ghosted from the room. Trista fell into the still warm chair. She wanted to lash out at him for being such a coward. "Aren't I being just as bad?" A part of her wanted to hide behind the shield of being 'just a girl.' After all, the President was surrounded by armed Secret Service agents, metal detectors and cameras.

She would have to kill him with her bare hands, which meant she had no chance whatsoever.

"Excuse me?" It was a black woman in a black pantsuit with wide flaring white lapels; it was one of the housekeeping staff. She gave the discarded salad plate a nervous glance. "Was there a problem with Mr. Kazakoff's salad? I can fetch another." Word had spread about what sort of man he was, and she was afraid of him. A funny thing occurred to Trista: she was probably the only one in the White House who was not afraid of David Kazakoff.

"No," she said, perhaps a little too sharply, as she stood up. She noted that the small woman edged back from her. *Is she afraid of me, as well?* Trista wondered. To test the idea, she narrowed her blue eyes and took a quick step towards the woman—she took a sharp breath and lowered her eyes.

Suddenly, Trista understood. People had seen her and David together, and they had heard about her executing Haider, Phillips, and Marty Aleman. They were probably also aware how the President seemed to rely on her more and more. Yes, they had to be afraid of her.

It was a strange sensation. "Could you do me a favor? Any chance I can get something to eat sent down here? I don't want to deal with people just now."

"Of course, ma'am. Anything you want. I should warn you that the President has asked for this room for his snack. But that's not for another forty minutes."

"A snack? What sort of snack?"

"Ice cream, ma'am. He's particular about eating alone now, so maybe I can find another room for you?"

Trista suddenly had an idea. "No, I want to eat here. And no ice cream for me. I want a steak. Well done." She would eat, make a joke, drop her knife, and come up with it in the President's soft throat.

The housekeeper was no fool. She'd been on staff for eighteen years and had seen all sorts of craziness in her time. She knew something wasn't right with the pretty young thing in front of her, and it wasn't hard to guess what she was thinking.

"We'll have Gerard slice it for you before serving, if that's alright. Trust me, it'll be hot and delicious. And easier to eat." The two locked eyes and Trista's flickered, giving away what she wanted concealed.

"Yeah, sure," she whispered and dropped her head.

2-10:17 p.m.
New Rochelle, New York

Doctor Thuy Lee had been living without hope for the last twenty-two hours, ever since the man she loved had given his life for hers. She could admit now that it had been a terrible trade. He was the sort of rugged, take no prisoners kind of man who could have adapted to this new world. Adapted and prospered.

She was not like that. She was too small, too soft, too delicate. "I should've died," she whispered as she gazed at the host of grey bodies surrounding the building.

"Stop that!" Special Agent Katherine Pennock barked. "Come on. We'll try the back. Maybe it's clear." She didn't believe that it would be. Not for a second. From the moment she had crossed into the Quarantine Zone, her luck had been crap. She grabbed Thuy's tiny wrist and hauled her around the corner, racing for the admin section.

There were more cubicles here, all perfectly aligned, each with identical rolling chairs, each with twenty-inch monitors, staplers, whiteboards and all the rest. There were minor touches of personal flare in each cubicle: pictures of children, plants, little dolls, a double-strand of gold Mardi Gras beads, and in one case, a bikini calendar hidden behind a calendar of frolicking kittens.

The cubicles showed a sterilized version of humanity, which was still better than the malformed Salvador Dali versions that came charging out of the stairwell seconds later. To hear them sniffing the air like dogs sent Thuy and Katherine hurtling through the cubicles.

At the end of the main row was the staff break-room, where a seldom-used coat rack stood like a thin metal soldier. Katherine grabbed it and held it awkwardly as if it was a spear. Thuy thought it might be the silliest weapon ever, but she didn't say anything. It was good that Katherine hadn't given up hope yet.

"Is there a way out on this side of the building?" the FBI agent asked.

"I really don't know," Thuy answered. She had worked in the building for five years and had only ever used the front doors. Had she ever bothered to take part in the bi-annual fire drills, she might have known where the other exits were, but she had been too busy to waste minutes tromping up and down stairs just to prove she could be as mindlessly sheep-like as the next person.

Katherine, who couldn't understand the concept of *not* following the rules, gave her a sharp look, wondering whether Thuy was being honest or was still uselessly wallowing in depression. "There probably is one," Katherine declared. "It only makes sense."

The layout of the building was indeed sensible and they came within a few feet of actually seeing the exit; however, a *thing* that was only just humanoid in appearance blocked their way, stumbling from the foyer. Its flesh hung from it in grey tatters, even the flesh of its face. Bones and teeth, and something black and pulsing showed through where a face should have been.

Fearlessly, it charged and just as fearlessly Katherine attacked it with the base of the coat rack, smashing it in its partially eaten face. It stumbled from the blow and, as it struggled to stand, Katherine crushed its head. More zombies were coming, slowly pushing through a hole in an office window.

"This way." Once again, Katherine took Thuy by the wrist and ran down a different corridor, this one dim and unlit. On their left were offices with little plaques bearing the names of the people who had once spent eighty hours a week in them. On their right was a solid wall with scenic pictures of waterfalls and meadows hanging every few feet, a painful reminder to the workers of what they were missing.

They were only a quarter of the way down the hall when they were stopped by the appearance of a grubby, naked child with only half a face and a letter opener sticking out of the side of her neck. She hissed an angry something, causing black bubbles to dribble around the point of the letter opener.

She charged. "We should…" Thuy began, only once more Katherine charged as well. Her face was ordered fury and her hands gripped the coat rack in front of her, somewhat like a pole vaulter might. The two came together with a muted crash; the girl taking the rack in the chest and was smashed to the ground. Katherine raised the rack, thumped it loudly off the ceiling and then crushed the girl's head.

"Over here! I heard something," a small voice piped from around the corner of the hall.

Once again, Thuy found herself between two fires. She darted to the side, opened an office door and pulled Katherine in, a second before the first little zombie rushed around the corner.

"Shit!" Katherine whispered as she gazed around the small twelve-foot by twelve-foot office. It was lit by a single lamp and showed the awful truth: there were no doors and no windows. There was no dropdown ceiling that could be climbed through and the air vent was barely ten-inches high. They were trapped.

Thuy stuck a finger to her lips as the sound of feet rushed up to the door. "Look-it what happened to her," a child whispered.

"It was Dr. Lee," Eng said. "She's around here somewhere. We're going to find you, Thuy!"

"Will y'all hush-up, ya stupid Chinaman!" Jaimee Lynn hissed. "We don't wanna have to share. Go push them zombie-monsters back on outside. Ever-one else, check these doors." Just as the doorknob twitched, Thuy reached over and thumbed the lock. The two women waited in silence as the knob rattled. They expected the door to be attacked, but the zombie moved on.

Katherine spun, taking in the office: nice desk, soft, leather chair, a fake plant, a set of golf clubs, a family portrait. There was nothing that would help them to escape. She went to the golf bag, picked out a 9-iron for Thuy and a pitching wedge for herself, which she thrust down into a belt loop like sword.

"Maybe they'll leave," Katherine remarked, somewhat flippantly.

Thuy, who was gasping behind her mask, pulled it up on her head. "Not likely. We should come up with a plan B."

"I already have one. I lead the way with the coat rack. I smash a few down and then make a run for the back door. When they come after me, you make your escape. We'll meet at the helicopter."

"Katherine, look, I think it's time you stopped protecting me. The chance at a cure is gone. There's nothing left at Walton and soon, what we have here will be ruined. I think it's time I took the lead."

Someone small went running past the door, causing the two women to go stiff. Katherine held her breath until the sound retreated. "I wish I could let you, but I'm younger and stronger, and I have this fancy vest to protect me. Also," she paused, feeling the pain radiate up from her hip, "I was bitten a little while ago."

Afraid to actually see the wound, she twisted slightly, reluctantly and lifted the edge of her shirt with nervous, stiff hands. Her hip was bruised purple and black, and the teeth marks within them were clear and defined. She gasped, not from the pain, but from a spurt of excited relief that filled her, lifting her like she had become lighter than air. Her flesh was bruised but intact! Laughter suddenly bubbled up in her throat only to come out in a choking cough as she caught sight of something else.

Running across her ankle above her boot were three long, bloody gashes. Seeing them pulled up a flash of memory: the tumble down the stairs, the flailing arms, the kicking. She had fought to her feet and one of the little zombies had grabbed her. Instinctively, she had wrenched her foot away and hadn't noticed the quick burn as the thing's ragged infected nails had clawed her.

The marks were unnaturally inflamed and red and she knew they'd smell like the worst combination of fungus and shit. Thuy wanted to look at the bite, but Katherine pulled her shirt down, went behind the desk and plopped down into the chair.

"You can't change anything, Thuy. My life is on a timer now." The laughter she had choked on before came out now, rueful and harsh. "Hell, maybe all of ours have been from the beginning."

Guilt washed over Thuy. Katherine's was one more death adding to her burden, and the weight of it was tremendous, greater than anyone could realize. It made it hard to breathe. In fact, it made it hard to even care about breathing. Before this moment, she had the possibility of a cure to keep her going. Now, she had nothing.

"It wasn't fate that did this to you," she said in a low mutter.

"And it wasn't you, either, Thuy. Look, we need a way out of here and if you don't like my plan, then come up with your own."

Thuy glanced around as a door slammed down the hall. A chirpy little voice let out a string of curses that would have made a sailor blush. "China! Gimme a gun, now git where y'all suppose-ed to be. We gotta find her." Thuy and Katherine locked eyes for a second; Jaimee Lynn with a gun was a scary thought to both of them.

Another door banged open, this one was closer. The zombie children were racing back and forth. The door knob to their room jiggled again. If they went out, they'd be attacked and Katherine would die, her bravery unable to overcome her foolishness. Thuy's first thought was that it would be a waste of a life; her second was cold and unjust: Katherine was going to die one way or the other and so would she.

"But not yet and not like this," Thuy told herself. She might have given up hope, it didn't mean she was going to allow herself to be somebody's dinner. A quick look around showed Thuy that they didn't have much to work with in the way of tools, and that any escape attempt would be loud.

"Defense first," she stated and pointed at the desk. "Help me with this, please." When Thuy gave orders, manners were always perfunctory. The "please" might as well have been a period to end the sentence with. "When they hear us, they'll come through the door in short order, and we have to slow them down."

Katherine went to Thuy's side and together they began pushing. "You know…" she said, between grunts and gasps, "this will…give us…only a minute." Katherine didn't think she

297

had to remind Thuy that the child zombies were shockingly strong.

"I'm only getting us out of the room, Agent and for that, we should not require more than a minute." The desk thumped lightly against the door. "This is good enough. Now, grab your coat rack. We're going to make a hole in the far wall."

Now Katherine understood what Thuy had meant when she said, *When they hear us.* Knocking a hole in wall big enough to get through would make all sorts of noise, maybe enough noise to draw more zombies in from outside, which was about the last thing she wanted. How on earth would they be able to escape the building with the first floor flooded with the undead? "Wouldn't a fire or some sort of muffled explosion be better?"

"In a cramped room? You forget that we are far more fragile than they are. A good deal more fragile. Besides, a fire wouldn't get us out of the room and what do we have on hand to create an explosion?"

Katherine shrugged, pulling out the 9-iron from her belt loop. "I don't know I thought you were a scientist and that you could just whip something up. You know, from a paperclip and a lightbulb."

At first, Thuy thought she was serious about the explosion and joking about using the golf club. When she realized she had it backwards, she gave an insincere laugh and took the club from the woman's hands. "We'll use the coat rack but not here. You're in line with the door. If Jaimee Lynn shoots the bullet will likely strike you."

She moved Katherine to the side, and together they took up the coat rack and used it as a battering ram. The main stem of it was a sturdy aluminum alloy and not easily bent; the first of the four fancy, stylized jutting legs that made up the base, broke off after two swings. They were two crashing swings. In the normal course of events, they would have sounded like two odd thuds. In the nearly silent building, they were like the explosions that Katherine wanted.

"To the left," Katherine cried, "we're hitting metal!" Behind them, the door was being savagely attacked—savagely, but inefficiently. Little fists pummeled it, while one small boy shook the knob with all his might. Either way, the noise was frightening and spurred the two women on. They found the space between two metal studs and opened a ragged but narrow hole.

By then, all of the legs of the base had broken off and the coat rack was now only a pole and they still needed to bust through the wall of the room that adjoined theirs.

It was then that Jaimee Lynn realized that the gun she carried could be used for more than just killing people. Without flinching, she stuck the barrel to the center of the doorknob and blew the thing apart. The children heaved against the door and the desk began to grind backwards.

"Stop them!" Thuy yelled, yanking Katherine away from the coat rack. She had been doing "it" wrong anyway. Poking inch-wide holes in the next wall would take forever. Thuy shoved the tip of the pole through one of the holes, squatted under the other end and then heaved upward, driving a line through the drywall. She did the same with a hole ten inches to the right. In this way she carved out a jagged wound in the wall.

She started in, yelling over her shoulder, "Katherine! I'm..." A gunshot made Thuy jump and banged her head on the top of the hole. When she looked back, she saw Katherine lying on her side, bleeding into the carpet.

As if she were on ice, Thuy spun around and grabbed the woman by the collar of her vest, and started to haul her back to the hole. At first, Thuy was surprised at her own strength, then she realized that Katherine was kicking out with her feet, driving her weight back. "That little bitch shot me!" She gestured with her chin at her left bicep, which ran red.

"Yes," was all Thuy had time to say. The "little bitch" was gradually pushing the door back, a snarl on her brutish face. Thuy shoved Katherine through the hole, pushing her rear, legs, and then feet through before slithering through herself. Katherine was already at the door, her left arm dangling, the coat rack, now more spear than rack, in her right hand.

"There's a few of them out here. Big ones, I mean, and they're close. We're going to have to chance it." Katherine darted through the door before Thuy was even on her feet.

Thuy followed, keeping low, imitating the FBI agent as she either ran hunched over or half-slid, half-crawled along, ignoring her injured arm. They made it into the cubicle area when the little zombies suddenly appeared in front of them, cutting them off.

"Get to the stairs," Katherine commanded, shoving her away.

They both should have been running in Thuy's view. It made no sense to stay and fight, unless it was Katherine's way of dying quickly, of being shot before she had a chance to be eaten alive or of turning into a zombie. Thuy turned and was about to run just as Katherine hurled the pole at Jaimee Lynn. It turned slightly in midair and only kicked off the girl's arm harmlessly.

Still, Katherine didn't run, which meant that Thuy couldn't either, not in good conscience. And yet, she couldn't fight, not barehanded. She embraced a happy medium between offense and defense by charging at the closest cubicle wall and throwing her entire hundred and four pounds into it. Small as she was, she still had enough strength to send the cubicle wall crashing down right into the path of the charging zombies.

The beasts tripped and went sprawling over it. Katherine stomped one in the head as it landed practically at her feet.

"No, come on!" Thuy yelled, and raced for the stairs. She took two turns and there was the door, and there just beyond it was also the elevator open but only somewhat inviting. The ceiling lights had been smashed and in the glow of the police cruiser's headlights, a squinting Thuy Lee could see Anna Holloway gesturing at her.

"Doctor Lee!" Anna hissed, scooping the air with a beckoning arm. "This way!"

Thuy had been racing around so much that she had completely forgotten about Anna. She now assumed that Katherine had set her watching the elevators, perhaps for a fast getaway. Thuy ran for the elevator, gulping air.

As if she were playing some sort of video game, Anna repeatedly jabbed the button for the third floor. "There's no way out! We gotta get those army guys back here *with* their fucking helicopter. It's the only way…" The door started to close and Thuy stuck her hand out to stop it. Anna smacked it away. "What are you doing?"

Just then Katherine hurried inside. The two blonde women glared into each other's faces. "You!" Katherine started forward, her left hand bunching into a fist.

"Don't even think about it," Anna said. Thuy was slow to realize that Anna was armed. In her hand was the black pistol. "These vests are good, but they aren't perfect. I think Eng taught us both that. Damn it, Thuy. Stop staring and hit the door close button."

Thuy didn't need to; the door started to close on its own. The simple procedure was almost interrupted again as one of the child zombies came rushing up, its black eyes bright with anticipation, its horrible mouth wide open. Anna shot it below the left eye, knocking it back with a spray of black blood.

"Disgusting," she seethed. "Remind me to take a bleach bath when we get to the third floor."

"There's nothing for us there," Thuy told her. "You know that the simplest experiments I have running will take hours and no amount of hoping will induce them to bear fruit any faster."

Anna slid her blue mask down so it hung around her neck. "No shit, Sherlock. You act like I didn't do all this when I was with Dr. Milner. He wanted the cure so badly that he made us do the tests over and over. It was tedious as hell with him doing nothing but staring at my boobs all day long."

"Perhaps if you didn't have them hanging out all the time he wouldn't have stared so much. Now, I don't mean to be contradictory without reason, Anna, but you won't be able to hold out here for very long. Certainly not long enough for even the first test to be completed. It's impossible."

The elevator came to a halt and the door slid open with a gentle electronic *boop*. Anna waved Katherine out first. The FBI agent cautiously edged out. Thuy started to follow, but Anna held her back. "If you don't want me to use Miss FBI as a distraction, you'll keep the elevator from going anywhere. I'll be just a minute."

They were back in thirty seconds, out of breath, Katherine lugging a green backpack in her right hand which clinked and clanked.

Thuy, ever curious, took the pack and peered inside. "I used up all the base components that we picked up at Walton. What is…? The *Renway* experiments? What the hell, Anna? You know these are variable-dependent. As soon as the temperature increases, you'll see a corresponding increase in the growth factors…"

Anna reached in front of Thuy and punched the button marked: 10. "I know all that, Thuy." In truth, Dr. Milner had been a poor lead researcher and didn't like to share any information that he didn't have to. He had lived in fear of being one-upped by anyone, especially a gifted research assistant.

Anna knew enough to fake it, and she planned on doing just that. "We're going to tell the Army that we have a cure. They'll send a chopper to save us and then—oops, something went wrong. We'll say they took too long to get to us or that the base molecules were destroyed because they only sent one damned agent with us. Or whatever. What matters is that we are out of here. It wasn't right that they sent us in the way they did, so I say fuck 'em."

"I say, fuck you," Katherine snarled. "You are the reason we're in this mess. You and Eng."

"You know what I don't need right now?" Anna spat. "Is you."

Katherine smiled, wickedly. "Are you sure? Who do you plan on calling and how? I bet there's a working radio out in that police cruiser. We'll wait here for you while you run and get it. Good luck."

"I don't need luck when I have this." Anna held up a sat-phone. "I think you might have dropped this when you got that little bruise on your cheek. And look, it's tied into the military net, and here is the number to FBI HQ, and this one here is the White House."

"And you think they'll take your call?" Thuy asked. She hit the stop button and the elevator jerked to a halt. "Try it."

Anna made seven calls and grew increasingly frustrated with each. As well as she could manipulate people by using her looks, her voice was somewhat creaky and tense. Anger and hate seemed to be threaded into it, and it only got worse with each call until the last, when she told the person on the other end to: "Eat shit and die!"

She then stood seething, staring down at the phone, fighting the desire to smash it. "Okay, new plan. We call Courtney. We tell her that we have a cure and that it's time to get out of the Zone."

"Courtney is too…" Thuy had to hold back using the word *smart*. Courtney Shaw was no genius; however, she had a native wisdom that had grown rapidly during the last few days. She would see right through any lie that Anna might try to spin. "Courtney won't believe you."

"She'll believe you," Anna replied, holding out the phone, displaying her own version of intelligence: conniving, self-serving, cunning.

Thuy took the phone. "She'll believe me because I'll tell her the truth."

A second after the bomb detonated, the elevator had
dropped like a stone, hurtling down four floors before its brakes
kicked in, adding their metal shriek to the immense noise of the
explosion and the great thunder of the building collapsing
around them.

Courtney Shaw added a high, terrified scream to the mix
when the brakes only slowed them a little. The elevator shaft
itself was imploding. They fell straight down another four stories
before there were no longer actual stories left to the building. At
that point there was a ringing crash as the elevator went
sideways, the lights blinked out and everything went black. In
the darkness there was a new scream of metal and then a scream
of pain, and then there was a horrible wet, gushing sound which
Courtney would later find out was one of the soldiers being bent
in two as the elevator was partially crushed by fifty tons of
rubble.

That had been hours before. Her watch, a $19.99 Walmart
special, had a crack running through its blank face, but there was
an arm sticking out from beneath a black metal beam and on the
stiffening wrist was a big clunky steel watch that proudly ticked
away.

Courtney glanced at it a moment after General Axelrod took
his last gurgling breath. *Forty miles from the ocean, and he died
by drowning*, she thought. *Is that irony?* She didn't know. Irony
was one of those things few people really understood, and this
was a perfect example. He had died, drowning in blood; it had
nothing to do with the ocean.

There were only four of them left. Sergeant Carlton, who
had disappeared through a hole in the elevator seventy-two
minutes before. Colonel Taylor, who was a scabbed-over,
swollen mess, but who could stand if there was room to stand.
The elevator was on its side and canted down; it had been
crushed like a beer can and now they barely had room to sit
upright. Warrant Officer Tim Bryan was slumped over next to
Axelrod. He too was brutally swollen around the face. There
would be no standing for him as his left leg was limp and saggy.
The bones had been turned to jelly.

He moaned in a half-stupor as he had for the last couple of hours since Carlton and Colonel Taylor had pried a ginormous block of cement off of him. He seemed to be slowly dying and Courtney wondered if little bits of bone were floating up from his leg and were settling in his heart and lungs because his vital signs were dropping.

Comparatively, she wasn't doing so badly. She had huge lump on the side of her head, her left elbow was swollen to the size of a softball, and her back had random electric spasms from where the elevator door had slammed into her, but otherwise she couldn't complain.

She was in something of a doze when the sat-phone *brrrred* into life. "Shit!" she cried, jerking and feeling a sheet of pain run down her back. "Jeeze, I thought that was a snake or something."

"You gonna get that?" Taylor asked in a dry whisper.

"Yeah, I guess." She wasn't used to people calling her and she had the sinking suspicion that it was going to be a government official on the other end, maybe even one she had impersonated. "Hello?"

There was a pause. "Miss Shaw?"

"Doctor Lee? Oh, thank God." Courtney felt a foolish wave of relief wash over her. As they were miles deep into the Quarantine Zone, they hadn't tried to call anyone for help and for some reason that included Dr. Lee. "We were hit by a bomb or something and we're trapped in a building downtown. The Ge-General's d-dead and s-so is m-m-m…" Unexpected tears poured from her and her breath was suddenly light and difficult to catch.

"Calm down, Courtney," Thuy ordered, coming across harsher than she wished. She softened her tone. "It's going to be alright. We'll figure out something."

"Can you come? I hate to take you away from the cure, but we're really stuck. Sergeant Carlton is trying to find a way out, but he left ages ago and the building keeps making noises, you know, crashes and things like that." She was racing through her words again and had to take a shaky breath.

In the pause, Thuy broke the bad news to her. "I'm sorry but we're trapped as well." She gave a brief description of their predicament, including the end of her search for a cure.

Just after this, there was a strange crackling coming from the phone and Anna Holloway came on. "We can still turn this around, Courtney. All we have to do is tell the Army that we have a cure. Sure, it's a lie but look what you've been doing for the last five days. You haven't told the truth once. I'm not saying that's a bad thing, I'm just saying that you are a strong resourceful woman and we all need that right now."

"I lied to help people," Courtney growled, furiously.

"And that's exactly what you'd be doing now," Anna answered, not missing a beat. "I get that you wouldn't lie to save me, but what about Dr. Lee? Or Katherine? What about the men with you? What about yourself, Courtney? Don't you deserve to be finally free?"

Courtney wanted to be free more than anything. And she wasn't the only one. She glanced over at Colonel Taylor; he dropped his eyes without saying a word; without trying to argue against Anna. He knew the truth as well as she did. They had done all they could to save the 7th Army from the President's interference, and they had succeeded in the face of nearly impossible barriers.

But that time was gone. There was no longer any true structure to the building and what was left of it could fold in on itself at any moment. If it didn't spontaneously collapse, they still had to face the real, but remote possibility of being burned alive. There were fires in the remains of the building, but as Taylor explained in that uncompromising way of his, the fires would more than likely eat up the little pockets of oxygen left to them.

"We'll suffocate instead of roast," he had said. "So, we have that to look forward to."

This all went through Courtney's mind in a flash. "I'll get us out of here," she promised Anna and then hung up before Thuy could try to talk her out of it.

"Who are you going to try?" Taylor asked. "The Coast Guard? They're about the only ones we haven't tricked yet. Everyone else knows our voices by now."

Courtney tried without much hope. The Coast Guard's squadrons of Jayhawks, Dolphins, HC-130s and HC-144s had been grounded the night before because they were "wasteful," a word that had apparently undergone some sort of transition in its meaning, since the Coast Guard birds had been performing valuable services for days now.

As their fuel had been taken by the Air Force, Courtney had to change tactics. She set about hunting out Marine air units that they hadn't yet tricked and received an oddly cryptic reply from the first base she called: "We've been ordered by the White House to stand down for maintenance." Never one to give up, Courtney tried again and again with different units, but always got the same reply.

Worried that she was being played, she dialed the direct line to the HQ of the 3rd Infantry Division. "General Axelrod for General Cannan, please." She had played the secretary for Axelrod a few times in this same manner, but this was the first time there was hesitation. She was given a quick: "Hold please."

"This is Colonel Knowles. I'm acting commander of the 3rd." In the background was the sound of gunfire and engines, and someone yelling: "Move your asses, damn it!"

"What happened to Cannan?" Courtney asked, fearing the worst. "Was he arrested?"

"KIA. The Air Force couldn't trust their pilots so they sent like a hundred Tomahawks our way. Who is this?"

Courtney looked at the phone and came close to hanging up. She had never met Cannan but had spent hours trying to keep him and his men safe. His death struck her harder than Axelrod's and his corpse was an inch from her left foot. "I think you know," she eventually answered. "They've been coming after me, as well. Do you need anything?"

He laughed without joy. "Reinforcements. Or maybe an armored brigade if you have one handy. Other than that, no. You've done enough just calling off those jets. At least we can fight now."

"You have no air activity?" He told her that they hadn't heard even a rumble from up top in the last hour. His relief was evident, while her fear began to ramp up. She gave him a quick goodbye and dialed a stolen number—the only number she had stolen from a friend.

A sharp woman answered and Courtney began speaking in a stern voice: "Director Alexander, please. This is Special Agent Katherine Pennock. I have news about the cure. It's urgent." This brought on an intense flurry of activity in Courtney's ear: papers shuffled, people yelling back and forth, a phone buzzing.

It was only a minute though it felt longer. "You have a cure?" Alexander cried the second he picked up the phone. "Thank God! Oh, sweet Jesus, thank you! What do you need from us? A flight plan out of there? Ha! That'll be no problem since everything's grounded."

Courtney's fear ramped up even more. "Why is everything grounded?"

He hesitated before lying, "That doesn't matter."

"It does matter. We're trapped. We need helicopters, and this time some real support. We need a lot of men with guns, the whole nine yards." A long silence drew out between them and she asked again: "Why is everything grounded?"

His answer was completely expected and yet it still took her breath away. "The President is sending nukes. He's going to fry pretty much the entire zone."

Courtney began to cry again.

The President was seven minutes late for his mid-ish night snack; his "rejuvenation" as he called his ice cream. He had become big with euphemisms. It was so much better sounding to "take a moment to rejuvenate himself" than to have it passed about that he was off stuffing his face, especially when there were missiles being launched.

There'd be lots of missiles and most of them would take quite a while to hit home, and besides, he'd been present for the most important ones.

Five minutes earlier he had sat perfectly straight and perfectly still, his hands in fists on the table, his arms held just right. He had set his face at a precise angle, listening as the first submarine reported it was ready to launch its flight of nuclear weapons. "This is a horror for us, but it will be a greater horror for them." It was a prepared line that he gave with steely-eyed determination. "Fire when ready."

There was a pause before he turned to Matthew Dimalanta. "Was that good?"

His new Chief of Staff thought the line was bloated with self-importance and better suited for a movie and not a president about to destroy a quarter of his own country. Of course, Dimalanta said nothing of the sort. He put on his shit-eating grin, stepped around the camera and told the President what he wanted to hear.

"You were great, sir. A natural leader. The camera loves you."

"Good, now get these people out of here. I'll be back in a few minutes and I want essential people only." He pulled Dimalanta aside. "Make sure you get some footage showing the city as empty. Like Sunday morning footage. You ever see lower Manhattan on a Sunday? It's a ghost town. We'll give them the idea that it's only buildings we're bombing and not people."

Dimalanta knew there were still tens of thousands of people trapped in Manhattan and the Bronx, holed up in apartment buildings and skyscrapers. The President had just ordered their deaths and now he was off to eat his ice cream, leaving Dimalanta to scrub history clean of any guilt.

"Of course, sir," he choked out. The moment the President left the Situation Room, Dimalanta wilted into a chair. "No more filming, Rio. He wants you to find some footage of empty streets. We'll intersperse it with a bunch of graphs and some shots of the infected."

"It'll come across cold. People like people, Matthew. He's always trying to cut out the human angle."

Dimalanta sighed and glanced up at the giant screen. Four submarines had already launched their missiles. "There is no human angle in this, Rio. That's the point. It's just buildings and that's what we're going to show." And then it'll be empty fields and empty beaches.

The President was picturing the same thing as he strolled along, two Secret Service agents in tow. Casualty lists would be downplayed into manageable numbers. It would be as simple as finding "experts" who could be relied upon to explain how there were very few humans left in the Quarantine Zone. None maybe, especially if the infection rate was a hundred percent.

He nodded to himself as he entered the little out of the way room he used for his moments of rejuvenation.

"What is this?" he asked one of the staff. His ice cream was in its proper place, set directly in the middle of an eight-chair conference table. Next to it was a cloche covering a plate.

"The young lady said you wouldn't mind," the waiter said. "She made it seem like she was expected, sir. I can remove it if you wish."

Before he could ask: *What young lady?* Trista Price came in, her arms raised to the two agents as if she were surrendering to them. "Me, Mr. President. I haven't eaten since breakfast and I thought you wouldn't mind a little company. It's a New York Strip. You're welcome to some. Sixteen ounces is a lot. They already cut it up." She pointed at the silver covered plate just as one of the agents turned towards her.

"I was just talking with Kazakoff," she added significantly. She had just come from his torture room. They had said very little to each other.

I'm having dinner with the President.

Okay.

I just wanted to let you know.

They had locked eyes, his tray of "tools" between them, both wondering the exact same thing: did she want him to stop her or join her? The intense desire for either choice was in such perfect balance that neither knew which way to choose. He turned his back on her and yet did nothing when he heard the scrape of metal.

Now she had sweat dripping down her back. It was hidden by her stylish black jacket.

"I was talking to him about the Vice President," she added when the president failed to say anything. She took advantage of the lag and stepped past the agents, who didn't know whether she was staying or leaving. She uncovered the steak, showing them the pre-sliced meat, the innocent mashed potatoes and the spears of asparagus. Instead of handing the cloche to the waiter or setting it aside, she gave it to the closest agent.

"Yes, I guess that's fine, Trista," the President said. "Though I normally like to separate work from pleasure."

"Normally, I would agree," she replied, seating herself and taking up her fork. She heaped it with meat and potatoes. "But…" To get the bite into her mouth she had to practically unhinge her jaw. She gave her head a jerk towards the waiter and the agents.

He shooed them out the door, which he ordered shut behind them. Trista swallowed with a grimace; her throat was constricting and her hands began to shake, making her fork rattle against her plate. She set it aside, saying, "Thanks. I hate eating with them watching over me like a couple of vultures. I also agree with you about mixing business and pleasure."

"Especially our business of late." He shook his head and addressed his bowl of ice cream. "People can be so upsetting. So nasty."

Trista caught herself staring at him in such shocked disbelief that had he turned, he would have arrested her on the spot. Quickly, she arranged her face into a bland, neutral look; it was the best she could do. "Yes, it's true. So nasty." Unable to come up with anything else—her mind had suddenly gone blank—she took another bite, hoping that he would say something.

He commented on his ice cream and she mentioned her food, saying it was delicious, even though it tasted like cardboard. She was running out of time. Hanging on the wall opposite of them was another TV, this one with a colorful map of America. Red, arcing lines denoting the trajectories of the missiles fired from all the ballistic submarines within firing distance. It was strangely entrancing.

"I never thought it would be me," the President whispered. "I always thought it would be one of those war-mongering fools."

No, just an ordinary fool, Trista thought. *I have to do this now, before it's too late*. The steak knife—the one forgotten knife in Kazakoff's collection—was nestled, point down, in her bra. With her shirt buttoned extra high, the handle was hidden in her cleavage. She needed a good three seconds to unbutton her shirt and pull it.

"So…what's with that sub?" she asked, pointing at the TV. Thirty-two miles northeast of the Azores was a dot with the tiny words: *USS Wyoming* (SSBN-742) set next to it. It was sitting by itself doing nothing as far as they could tell.

The President's eyes narrowed. "I don't know." He reached for a phone.

At the same moment, Captain Alan Davidson stepped into the missile control center. With his rubber soled shoes, he walked softly, *Like a thief*, he thought. *No, an assassin was closer to the mark*.

Actually mass-murderer was the proper analogy. He tried not to think about it, but it remained, lurking in the back of his mind and kept bubbling up whenever he paused to catch his breath. He was strangely breathless. The same feeling had come over him on the day he had taken command of the *Wyoming*. He had gone down into the missile room and stood in the middle of the vertical silo-like tubes, absolutely staggered by the weight of responsibility. The boat…his boat, had been made with one purpose: the killing of humans on a tremendously grand scale; on a Godly scale.

And he was no god. Unlike the President, Captain Davidson knew he was only a man with a man's failings and weaknesses. He knew he was about to commit mass-murder, which was terrible even when it was applied to enemies, but the idea that he would be killing his own people felt a thousand times worse.

"Are we in the green?" he asked his executive officer.

Commander Sowell had sweat running down through what had once been laugh-lines; he didn't look as though he would ever laugh again. He held up a brass key. "Yes, sir. All systems are good as per protocols."

Davidson was sure that everything had been checked, and double checked as well. And Sowell hadn't been the only one going down the launch list. Every single person on the boat had been doing the same thing and most of them were hoping to find a problem.

A crack in just one of the solid-propellant missiles or perhaps an overlooked drop of nitrogen, or a short in one of the navigation systems could scrub the entire attack; and maybe that wasn't a bad thing.

There were one hundred and fifty-four souls on board, and by some weird quirk of fate a hundred and three of them were from the northeast. The *USS Wyoming* was being tasked with destroying their homes and perhaps their families. It was heart-rending for each of them and literally sickening for many.

Captain Davidson took another deep breath and slowly let it out, giving the powers that be, just one more second to change their minds. He couldn't stall another second. "Initiate launch sequence." It was almost entirely automated from this point. The on-board MARK 6 navigation systems had been activated long before and the specified mission trajectory for each Trident II (D5) UGM-133A missile had been loaded into their flight computers.

The sub was at the correct depth and the tubes flooded. Another deep breath. "Fire in sequence," he said, his voice dropping to a whisper.

A button was pressed and an explosive charge was ignited in the container beneath the first of the missiles. Water in the container was flash-vaporized to steam, creating a pressure spike strong enough to eject the missile out of the tube and give it enough momentum to reach the surface of the ocean. The sixty-five-ton missile popped up out of the water, hung suspended forty feet over the surface for what seemed like an impossibly long second before its first stage rocket ignited.

The *Wyoming* shuddered from the launch, rolling slightly before leveling a few seconds later. Every eye went to the status board—all green.

"Fire," Davidson said again.

It was the seventh Trident that was aimed at Mt Vernon, New York, two miles from New Rochelle and the R&K Research Facility. It was part of the President's plan to save what he could of New York City, namely: Long Island. Sixteen warheads were destined for Staten Island, Newark, Manhattan, the Bronx and on northward until White Plains. Nothing was expected to live.

"There it goes," the President said, when the first red arc stretched from the dot that represented the *Wyoming*. "Better late than never, I guess. I swear, if I get stabbed in the back by one more person, I don't know what I would do."

"Yeah?" Trista said, frozen in place. She had both hands clutched to her white button-up shirt. One on the handle of the steak knife, the other holding closed her shirt. In her rush, her shirt had practically flung itself open.

Seeing this, the President leaned back from her, his eyes widening in surprise. "Miss Price, I'm flattered. And I'm sure if the situation was different." He glanced back at the door, half-expecting it to be open a crack with a spying eye peeking in on them. "Well, you know. Maybe we could talk in the morning."

"Oh, right," she replied, not knowing what else to say. How could he think she would want him? He was wrinkly and old. And he was evil. The thought was repugnant and, if anything, made her want to kill him even more. "Sorry, I should go."

The President was old and slow. She was up and moving past him before he could turn. In fact, he had to turn the opposite way, to his right and by the time he got his head around, she had the steak knife out, holding it by its thousand-dollar springbok horn handle, its forged Sandvik steel blade glittering.

Only the best for the President of the United States, she thought, before she slammed the knife into his throat. The steel passed through the right carotid artery, the windpipe and sliced the left jugular. She was surprised how easily the blade went in. It was almost too easy. Was it a killing strike? Would he linger and cough, or call out for help? It was an odd thing, but that first strike only fed her fear and she yanked out the blade and slammed it home again with even more force.

This time there was a good deal more *crunch*. She had sheared through bone. The President's eyes bugged almost out of his head. They grew wider and wider, and as they did, hers did as well. And together they drew in a long, sucking breath. They were in sync for half a minute, then his eyes grew dim and his shoulders seemed to wilt back from his torso.

He died and she lived.

2-11:19 p.m.
New Rochelle, New York

Courtney Shaw was only two miles away and yet she came across small and tinny, as if she were speaking through a tube that stretched out to the bottom of the ocean.

You'll have to rescue us, she had said.

"Okay, of course. That's no problem," was Thuy's insane reply. They had both hung up in dead silence.

Thuy couldn't look Katherine in the eye and she refused to even glance at Anna. The elevator was stuck between the sixth and seventh floor. She pressed the button for the seventh floor. The machine whirred obediently and opened its door seconds later.

"What are you doing?" Anna demanded in a croaking voice.

Thuy ignored her and walked across to an east-facing window, wondering if they would be able to see the missile coming. Katherine came to stand next to her. "What did I tell you? We're all living on a timer. We just didn't know it."

"Stop talking like that!" Anna snapped. "Do something Thuy. Hey! I'm talking to you. Do something. Get us out of here." She shoved the point of the gun into Thuy's midsection.

"How could that possibly scare me, now?" Thuy pushed the bore away. "I'm smart, but I can't invent wings and fly away. I can't wish away a ballistic missile. I can't make a cure and spray it out onto them." Eighty feet below them, a mob of undead milled about, making the night shadows undulate and look like waves. There were probably four hundred in sight, which was four hundred more than she could handle.

Anna looked down, and even though she had known they were there, she still felt fear squeeze down on her chest. "We could still try. Come on, Thuy. We know where there's a helicopter. If we could get past them, we could be there in ten minutes. Yeah, none of us knows how to fly it, but I'd rather crash in the ocean than get blown up by a nuke. Come on, what do you say?"

"I say what I always say: you're an idiot. Have you forgotten Jaimee Lynn and Eng? Do you think they're just sitting around waiting for us? Have they ever done that before? No. Right now, they're blocking exits and they're filling the stairwells with zombies. We are trapped."

Katherine rubbed her eyes. They felt gritty even through her gloves. "I guess I don't need these anymore," she muttered and pulled them off with a snapping sound. "I'm with Dr. Lee on this. You are an idiot, Anna. Let's say we can get out of here alive, and somehow dig out Courtney and the others, and make it back to the helicopter. We'll never be able to learn to fly it before we get vaporized, and it would crash long before we got to the ocean. They're not like airplanes. Not that we would do better in one of them. What I'm saying is that they're very complicated. They tilt and yaw, and can fly up, down and backwards."

"No duh. They still have a pilot. Yeah, he's hurt but maybe he can suck it up long enough to fly us somewhere safe. Thuy, please. I know you can get us out of here, just like I know you can find a cure. You're the smartest person I know."

Thuy cackled at this, sounding a lot like her mother. She turned and leaned against the window, her arms folded across her chest. "Keep going. Tell me how great I am. Tell me something that'll make me disbelieve my own eyes, because what I see out there is…"

"Is all Eng's fault," Anna said. "You did something great and he ruined it. But you could fix it. You know everything there is to know about this stuff. And if we get nuked, this building and the labs and all the computers are going to be blown to bits. You see now why you have to live. You're the only chance of a cure."

Katherine frowned. "She's probably right. Crap."

"Crap?" Thuy asked.

"It's all pretty much too late for me and I was hoping to go easy. A bullet in the brain and then a long nap. But now…she's right. We can't just do nothing. I bet you could figure out something. Maybe we can rig a catapult on the roof. We can hurl some homemade bombs across the parking lot and get most of the zombies to chase them. Once clear, we haul ass for where Courtney is."

Anna grew excited and began to jabber on about what chemicals they could scrounge from different labs and how hot they would burn. Thuy tuned her out. The whole idea was preposterous in the short time they had left, especially since they still had to deal with Jaimee Lynn, her pack of diseased mongrels, and Eng. Where were they? What were they up to? What sort of plot were they hatching? Thuy could count on it to be both crude and effective.

"Could we take them head on?" Thuy wondered. "Anna, how many bullets do we have left?"

"We?" Anna stepped back, gripping the M4 tighter. "I'm not giving up my guns. I know what you two would do if I did."

Katherine was suddenly so furious that she appeared to swell in size, her blue eyes flashing. "What I would do? That's rich coming from you." Anna glared right back, holding the rifle —her equalizer—easily, perfectly prepared to blow holes in the FBI agent.

Three feet away, Thuy stood with an odd expression on her beautiful face. The vague beginning of an idea was stirring inside of her, looking to catch hold of something and gain traction.

"It's okay," Thuy said, softly without direction, so that neither of the two was certain who she was talking to. "We're all enemies, or at least we've all been enemies at one time. And we've all been allies. Circumstances have changed and twisted, so that the needles on our moral compasses are no longer as straight as we wish they were. They're like corkscrews."

"Do you have a point?" Anna asked, in her usual disagreeable manner.

The point almost drifted away and Thuy had to have silence to get it back. She snapped her fingers at Anna like she would at a cat that was nibbling on a fern. "Yes. Yes, the point is we've been acting out Lord Palmerston's vision of statesmanship. To wit: 'Nations have no permanent friends or allies, they only have permanent interests.' Is it the same among the zombies? Yes, of course! Anna, you allied yourself with Von Braun. What's there stopping us from doing the same with Jaimee Lynn and Eng?"

"The fact that they want to eat us?" Katherine suggested. "That and the fact Anna here tried to murder Eng."

"To save you two!" Anna cried.

"You are quite the hero," Thuy said as she began walking towards the central stairwell. "Who were you trying to save when you sucker punched Katherine? Hmm?"

Behind her Anna made a face as she pushed Katherine to follow. "Okay, that was a mistake and I'm sorry…" Katherine snorted. Anna ignored her. "Either way, what do you think they'll want? Eng's gonna want me, but there's no way I'm just going to give up. We all know that."

Thuy knew that all too well. "He may be after something else entirely. The cure perhaps? And I know that there's one thing that Jaimee Lynn wants as much as eating us and that's finding her father." She was at the main stairs. Low, crashing sounds echoed up at them. The stairs were being blocked; the traps were being set.

"Jaimee Lynn! This is Doctor Lee. We need to talk." Giggles floated out of the depths of the building, then nothing. "I have blood. Fresh, clean blooooood!" The giggles became whispers. There was a series of crashes, and then silence.

A minute later, Eng called from very close beneath them, "Well, well, well, Doctor Lee. You must be getting nervous if you want to talk to that little runt. I'm in charge, Thuy. Me. So, who are you giving up? Anna or the spook? It doesn't matter. I came here for the cure and if I don't get it, I'm going to personally tear off your head and suck you dry."

"I…" Thuy's chest hitched as deep in her subconscious she pictured, with dreadful clarity, the threat Eng had made. "I have the cure, but you…"

"Already?" Eng said, cutting across her. "I printed off the results in progress and there was nothing promising."

"It's a new idea," Thuy said, thinking fast. "I'm basing it off the-the-the structure and chemical composition of a child's brain as compared to an adults. As evidenced by Jaimee Lynn and others, children are less affected by the Com-cells. So…"

Although she had mentioned both structural and chemical differences, she had to choose one to present to Eng— structurally, children possess an amazing number of synapses that are slowly weeded out over time. These extra synapses could be physical ways in which the infected child's brain was re-routing mental functions around areas that were saturated by Com-cells. This wouldn't help Eng.

"So, I looked into the chemical differences and what jumped out at me was the fact that children's nerves cells have not completed the process of myelination. Myelin is the fatty sheath that covers each nerve cell and increases the speed at which information, encoded as an electrical signal, travels from one nerve cell body to another."

"I know what fucking myelin is! What's the cure?"

Half a dozen ideas popped into her head and she went with the one she felt would be the easiest for Eng to understand. "I believe injections of glycolipids in the cerebroside family will attract replicating Com-cells, thereby preventing them from attaching to cranial nerve cells as they would have."

For a few moments, she paused in amazement. She had struck on a perfectly plausible method for delaying, if not

317

outright halting the spread of the Com-cells. And if it wasn't the lipid that attracted the Com-cells, it could only be one of the glycoproteins.

A smile spread across her face and she whispered to Katherine, "It could work."

Eng had crept closer than she thought and he had heard. "Could? Could? You haven't tried it? Of course, you haven't. Where would you get glycolipids on such short notice? So, you lied. You fucking lied!" His voice boomed through the stairwell.

"Eng, listen to me. The possibilities are there. And they wouldn't be hard…"

"You liar!" he shrieked.

After the echoes died, there was silence in the stairwell. "They're firing nukes, Eng," Thuy said, hoping to get his mind refocused.

"Liar! That little shit you call president would never bomb his own country. No, you are a liar and you are going to pay right here, right now!"

The sound of his feet charging up the stairs came out of the dark. Thuy pushed Anna and Katherine through the door and slammed it shut. Seconds later, it shook as Eng crashed into it.

"What are we going to do?" Anna said, a quiver in her voice. She shrieked a second later when Eng fired through the door. The bullet passed an inch over Thuy's left shoulder and just beneath Anna's jaw. Anna fired her rifle, while at the same time falling into and onto Katherine. Again, Thuy was nearly struck. She dropped, putting her back to the door as Eng knocked into it once more.

"Go!" Thuy hissed to the two women as they untangled themselves and the door slid open a few inches. "Get between floors where it's safe."

Another gunshot, this time through the crack of the door. Katherine was almost hit as she floundered back. Because the door opened toward the two women, they had no choice but to flee with bullets following them. Thuy jumped up and ran the other way, speeding leopard-like around the corner and racing for the north stairwell.

She made it safely and stepped into the darkness, to where all safety ended.

"I cun smell y'all, Doctor Lee." The words drifted up low and surly.

3- 11:28 p.m.
New Rochelle, New York

Courtney Shaw had seen enough video clips and movies to know that when the nukes hit, what was left of the building was going to be vaporized and blasted away into dust. She'd be exposed like a bug after its rock had been pulled up. Fire would roll over the land in a great wave, incinerating the crust of the earth and turning it black.

Then the fallout would come raining down like brilliant orange sparks, searing anything left alive, and leaving the land glowing and shimmering, and at the same time grey and forever dead. It was a bleak outlook that had been both subtly slipped into her mind as well as bashed into her since childhood—she thought she was going to be sick.

"How long do we have?" Colonel Taylor asked, his eyes sharp once more, his heavy features crowding together in a deep scowl.

"Maybe a little over half an hour? He didn't know for certain. The rockets can go super-fast, but they may not have been programmed to. It might be that the sub captains are giving the President as much time as possible to change his mind."

Taylor spat. "That weenie? No, that would take moral courage that is far beyond him." The colonel groaned as he shifted to all fours. "Come on, Bryan. Hey, wake up! We're about to get nuked. We have to find a way out of here." Bryan moaned as he rolled over; his leg flopped sickeningly and he went ghost-white. Courtney started to shift as well, but Taylor stopped her. "No. Stay. You need to warn as many people as you can. Don't worry, we'll come back for you."

He said this so earnestly that Courtney decided to believe him even though there was no way they would have time to dig their way out, get to the helicopter, fly it back and pick her up. There was no possible way and yet she gave him a fat-lipped smile and picked up her phone.

Barely a hundred miles away, the man who had started the day as a buck sergeant glanced at his sat-phone and decided against picking it up. He was now "General" Troy Ross, a position that was both easier and far more difficult than he had imagined it would be. It was easier once he had pinned the four gold stars to his collar. From then on, everyone had acknowledged him as commander of the army. There hadn't been a single gripe, and that even included Colonel Noah Halsey, the Marine battalion commander who had been sent to arrest him an hour before.

"Someone had to take those political dipshits down," Halsey growled. "I hated them. I begged on my fucking knees to get my men on the line, but they kept telling me that a revolt could happen any second. Talk about a fucking self-inflicted prophecy."

Ross hoped his relief wasn't too obvious. For the last hour, he had been dreading the sound of approaching tanks. There was no possibility of winning a battle against them and he wouldn't have tried. Needless suffering was not his aim. Defeating the zombies in battle was what he was after and, so far, he had been succeeding where others had failed.

But Lordy, it was difficult. The last line of defense guarding Boston had been hanging by a thread—in some places fewer than twenty men, women and children held great stretches of open land and it was only by a miracle that the undead hordes passed them by. In another place, a thousand men were clumped on top of each other guarding a bridge that could have been held by seven men and two machine guns. Of course, this was one of the approaches to the headquarters.

The supply situation was worse. Generally, large numbers of soldiers could not be hidden, however bullets could be and they were greedily hoarded by everyone right down to the squad level.

Because of his administration background, Ross chose Clarren to untangle the logistical nightmare. He in turn had sent out brave little Rita McCormick and other girls like her to act as both spies and informants. Sergeants, lieutenants and even colonels could lie to Ross with a straight face, but none would turn away a desperate girl who was just looking for a few magazines to help the cause.

In this way, great stashes of ammunition were unearthed, literally so in a number of cases.

Colonel Halsey had just left when the sat-phone rang again. Ross snapped it up, his stress and heart rate dropping now that he wasn't in danger of facing an angry M1 Abrams, something few people lived through. "Hey!" he said with a grin when he realized who it was. "Let me just say that for the first time since this all started, I'm doing pretty well. Though I wouldn't say no to a few B2s. The horde is swelling again to about seven-hundred thousand and…"

"You're going to have to run," Courtney told him, her voice flat and tired. "Pull out and run, now. The President…"

"Run? Sorry, it's hard to hear you. It sounds like you're in a tunnel or something. I think you might have misunderstood. We can still hold for a while longer. Those seven-hundred thousand probably won't hit all at once. That's how it's been since…"

"I said run!" Courtney screamed. "The President is going nuclear. He says he's gonna protect Boston by laying down a string of nukes right on top of you guys. Do you hear me?"

Ross felt a flash of adrenaline followed by a strange numbness in his hands and a burning in his ears. "Nukes?" He wanted to ask why? He wanted to scream it; however, his mind and body seemed to be coming detached.

"Ross? Ross! Can you hear me?"

"Yeah," he heard himself say. Physically, he could sense that his eyes were blinking, his knees were buckling and there was a rushing noise in his ears. He saw the world give a spinning lurch, but he didn't realize that he had fainted for some time. Gradually, he came to possess his physical form once again. A moment of embarrassment gave way to a chest-rattling fear.

He scrambled for the phone and found it dead. "No!" he cried, glancing up at the stars. They blinked placidly down on him, just as they always had. "It was a joke. A bad joke. It had to be." He dialed the number to the woman people called the *Angel of the Airways.* She didn't answer; Courtney was busy calling every unit on her very long list and was currently telling Colonel Knowles of the 3rd Infantry Division the bad news.

Ross had taken the call a little ways from the middle-school, and now he staggered toward it, veering slightly to his left where he had a moonlit view of what had once been a pretty little stream. After a day of fighting, it was a fetid ooze-filled bog that stretched away, glistening with a hellish sheen.

"That was her," he told himself. "That means it's gotta be true. Right?" The night was silent, giving him no hint to the truth. It just didn't make sense. They had been winning for a change. "We could've held the line!" That's what didn't make sense and it was why he was second-guessing what his gut knew to be true. He turned from the bog, knowing that the stakes were too high to rely only on his gut.

If he pulled his men and there weren't nukes heading his way, he would doom not just his men, but also all of Boston. Millions of people were dependent on him making this one decision.

"Do I stay and maybe die in a great big fucking ball of fire? Do I run and maybe let the line fall for no reason?" He felt like flipping a coin and reached into his pocket. All he found was a small lollipop that he had scrounged from a bank the day before. He cursed and dialed the number again. It was busy. A string of curses burst out of him followed by a whispered, "I can't do this!"

More than anything, he wanted to rip off the golden stars. They mocked him and his inability to make a decision.

He was half-panicked and on the way to fainting once more. He dialed the number a third time. She picked up and his fear spiked so badly that his intestines suddenly knotted themselves. "Is it true?" he asked, in a rush.

She was as frantic as he was, and blurted out, "Yeah. You have to hurry, please. You don't have much time, maybe a half an hour at the most. I have to go."

Half an hour. So little time. Mad fury roiled up inside him at the insanity of sending nuclear bombs, but only for a second and then his stomach unknotted and he felt the stress roll off of him. His brief time as general was over, and maybe the war was as well. He would give the order to retreat and let the chips fall where they would. "Wait. What's your name?"

A pause before she answered softly, "Courtney."

"Okay, I trust you, Courtney." She hung up and a second later he was running for the school, glancing upwards as went. For now, the sky was clear.

The headquarters for the entire Army of Southern New England consisted of sixty-three people, most of whom were regular army. He hoped he could count on them. "We are about to be nuked!" he bellowed over the din of twenty conversations. Everyone gaped at him.

"Yes, I said nuked. We have thirty minutes, so we don't have time for anything fancy. Give out just two orders. The first is for the men to leave the lines immediately and head east at a run. The second: no vehicle will leave unless it is as packed with as many people as possible. Any questions?"

"Nuked? For real? How do you know?"

"It came from the White House. This is it people. I want every fucking company notified before we leave. Start with the Marines. I want a tank on every road stopping any vehicle that isn't full. Go! Make your calls."

The alarm was sounded and in seconds he could hear cries and a few gunshots. Not a minute later, a nearly empty deuce-and-a-half tried to rumble past. Ross and two MPs stopped it and, without recrimination, he ordered it detained. The driver was over thirty and Ross let him stay with the truck; however, the two men with him were young and hale. He sent them running east.

Despite the fact that his army consisted almost exclusively of ragged, exhausted untrained militia men, there were surprisingly few incidents like this. These were men who had already volunteered to fight and die. Their mettle had been tested and it didn't matter what they had been like in their previous lives, they had found an unexpected chivalry within themselves.

In most instances, orders were not even needed and the trucks were filled, with preferences given to the many frightened teens who had volunteered, men and women of a certain age, and the injured. Everyone else jogged along after them.

Clarren was old enough to have snagged a spot on a Humvee. In fact, when he heard the news of the inbound missiles, he felt as though he had aged twenty years, and was hit by such intense weariness that he collapsed onto a stump. People rushed about and the zombies grew eager and slogged through the bog, but he just sat there, those years weighing him down. Finally, he struggled up and went to find Ross.

He wasn't hard to find. Ross was the only person doing nothing but staring up into the sky.

"I really doubt you'll see it coming," Clarren told him. "Those missiles go up into space. Or almost into space. So, are you going to stay? Chances are you'll get eaten before you get vaporized. All this action has got the zombies on the move."

Ross didn't know what he wanted to do. It felt wrong of him to leave while there were still people pulling back from the line. "I need you to get ahead of all this," he told Clarren. "We need to set up a quarantine zone. Well, first a new defensive line of some sort, one that's just outside the city. Then we need what we'll call a quarantine buffer."

"I'm sure that you…"

In the middle of Clarren's sentence, Ross sucked in a violent breath and stepped back, his eyes wide, his mouth gaping. "Shiiiit!" Ross said, gagging slightly on the word. High above them in the night sky shot eight, nine, a dozen streaks of orange flame.

4-11:50 p.m.
The White House, Washington D.C.

With a wet gurgle and a soft, ineffectual hand clawing at her arm, the President died. He slumped to the side and his blood made a pattering sound as it dribbled out onto the carpet. Trista Price stepped back, her once delicate, refined lips now twisted downward in an ugly grimace, her face lined and pinched, her manicured nails lacquered in blood.

Her first response to murder was to erase the evidence coating her hands and she almost wiped them on her own jacket. She used a napkin instead, tossing it on the President's ice cream when she was done. Red and white mixed but did not become pink as it should have. It became something inedible and un-seeable. She turned away, took a deep breath and opened the door.

The two agents glanced at her. One blandly, the other cocking an eyebrow just a little. Otherwise they were expressionless.

"The President is dead. We have to release the Vice President so that he can…" Her next word was spun out of her as she found herself yanked around and slammed into the wall. In the span of that second, the other agent darted into the room and pulled the dead man back.

"I am pardoned!" Trista cried. "The Vice President is now the President and he will pardon me. We have to get to him and free him. He's the only one who can stop this."

"He's behind this?" one of the agents demanded.

Trista tried to shake her head, but couldn't with her cheek pinned to the wall. "No. I did it, but he will pardon me. He's the only one left to pass judgement, and he's the next in line to lead. Who else is there? Damn it. Take me to him or ten million deaths will be on your heads!"

The two agents shared a look. One shrugged and the other took a bewildered breath. "He is only three doors down and he is sort of the next in line."

"What about the director?" the first asked, feeling the weight of responsibility. "Shouldn't we get him involved?"

"There is no time!" Trista shouted. "We have minutes to stop this. The army is winning. We have to give them the time they need."

Another look and then Trista was yanked from the wall and marched down the hall. They took a single left turn and found a third agent sitting in an incongruously placed antique Louis XV style French Country chair that had been pulled from the storage room that the Vice President was currently being held in. The agent didn't move from the plush, purple cushion; he only gave the three of them a curious look.

"The President is dead," Trista declared. "We need to see the Vice President. He's now the Commander in Chief."

"It's true," one of the agents said.

Trista didn't have time for more explanations. She pulled away and stepped into the storage room. The Vice President, once a tall, waspish, vanilla politician who'd had the wonderful ability to tell everyone exactly what they wanted to hear, was now a shattered wreck. He sat huddled in on himself, shaking and crying. Blood seeped through a cheerfully robust quilt that someone had tossed over him.

"Sir," Trista said, going to one knee. "The President is dead. I killed him to save the country." His eyes focused and narrowed; disbelief and desire warring within them. "You can be the new president but only if you issue a blanket pardon for me. Will you do that?"

His eyes darted around, making him look like a weasel with a pack of foxes surrounding him. "Sure. Why not. You're pardoned. Am I free to go?"

She felt half a second of relief and Trista considered trying to get David Kazakoff a pardon as well, but she feared that this would turn the new President against her. "Yes. sir. We need you in the Situation Room. The Pres...the old president has launched..." She paused to snap at the Secret Service agents, "Get him up. We need to hurry. Sir, the old president has launched a nuclear strike against our own troops and against cities that haven't shown any sign of the infection."

"He's really dead?"

"Yes, sir." Two of the agents stood the new President up and he immediately crumbled back to his knees. "Carry him by his arms if you have to! Yes, sir, he's dead. I'll show you." She marched straight to the little room and pointed inside without looking. "He's dead and you are the new president. Now, let's get to the Situation Room."

One of the agents had disappeared and now there was a flurry of activity. People were running; there was an angry shout. "Hurry!" Trista demanded. They rounded a corner and were confronted by four different Secret Service agents, who froze in confusion. "Out of the way! The President is coming through." They moved aside and then followed after as Trista barged into the nearly vacant Situation Room.

The big screen was alive now with more red arcs. They practically obscured the map. Eight-hundred missiles were in the air and more were being launched. "He really did it," the new President gasped. "That bastard. That fucking bastard!" He tried to make a fist, but his broken fingers screamed in agony and he groaned at the pain.

"You can still stop it, can't you?" Trista asked. "You can abort the mission, right?" When he didn't answer right away, she pulled out her laptop. "Look. These are the quarantine lines. They haven't changed all day. We're winning, sir, and we have more units coming. Think about it, you can be the president who 'won the war.' But if you let those bombs explode, you'll be the president who killed millions of innocent, *uninfected* people."

She drew in a big breath to go on, but he stopped her. "How much time do I have until the first bomb goes off?"

A new screen overlapped the main map. This one added the detonation times to the missiles. They were all over the board. Warren, Ohio was five miles from Youngstown, but their detonations were an hour apart. She found the first. "Midnight. Seven minutes from now, here in Columbus."

"Jesus Christ," the new President whispered through bruised and swollen lips. "There are zombies all the way out in Columbus?"

Trista flicked to a different map. "The areas shaded in green have known infestations. Yellow are possible areas. And look," she drew a line from Hagerstown, through Pittsburgh and into the northeast section of Ohio, "this is all clear, and so is all of this area here." The western third of Pennsylvania was blank, as was a chunk of Ohio and a huge part of western New York.

"The current plan will trap or incinerate millions of innocent people. And in Massachusetts, the bombs are going to fall right on the Army's head. If we just gave them time, they could get out of the bomb blast radius. It's only logical and compassionate to put a pause on this, sir."

He shifted his gaze back to the main map. New purple arcs were coming from the west. They were B2s out of California launching AGM-86s—cruise missiles with nuclear warheads. The new President asked about them and their targets. He asked about reinforcements and supplies. He asked about the Navy and the Air Force, and all the while the seconds ticked, ticked, ticked by and the warheads began to rain down.

Chapter 25
1-Midnight
Columbus, Ohio

The bank in which Corrina Troost had worked for the last six years had a wonderful view: she could easily see the 600-foot high Rhodes Tower. A little to the west of that was the slightly smaller, but prettier, Leveque Tower, and in the background of both was the Green Building. For some reason she couldn't name, seeing them standing amid the smoke was a great relief to her.

Also, from her vantage in the bank, if she stood on tiptoe so that her wide, flaring nose broached the very edge of the high little window, she could see the dead prowling around the city. There were a great many of them and their numbers seemed to multiply every hour. Columbus was completely overrun.

Unlike in so many other places, the zombies weren't fanning out in search of fresh blood, and Corrina guessed that there had to be thousands of people holed-up just like her, waiting to be rescued. Rescue was her only hope since her truck, the same truck that had been giving her fits for the last five years, had been dead for a week now with a broken alternator and a million-pound battery that she couldn't lift.

The truck had been a bad idea from the start. Her boyfriend, Zach had been a worse one. He and his flashy BMW had disappeared the day before without even leaving a note. She hadn't been terribly surprised. Mentally and spiritually crushed, yes, but not surprised or heart broken. She had known from the beginning that he wasn't "the one," and this just proved it, yet again.

His ditching her had left her stranded and alone in the middle of Ohio. Too late, she had called her friends, but they were gone as well, speeding off west, along with half the state. "Maybe it'll be okay," she told herself the night before when the zombies were still in eastern Pennsylvania. *They are a long way away*, she told herself. *Hundreds of miles*, she told herself. *I have time*, she told herself.

With a will and a great deal of wishful thinking, she had barricaded her apartment.

Then at noon she heard the first gunshot and all the lies she had told herself crumbled to dust, as the truth of her situation blossomed in front of her: It wasn't going to be okay; the zombies weren't hundreds of miles away; she had run out of time; and her apartment, with its flimsy lock, hollow doors and thin, brittle windows weren't going to keep her safe for more than five minutes.

Oh, but the bank was another story. Unlike so many modern banks, with their tall windows, airy spaces and cold attention to money, the John C Reedy Bank was a squat, ugly little brick building; the only windows it had were high, narrow and nearly useless, even for letting in sunlight.

It was ugly but very definitely safe she decided. Summoning what courage she had left, she grabbed a bag of clothes, a sharp knife and a pillow, and hurried through the nearly empty late afternoon streets feeling dreadfully weak and pathetically vulnerable. She saw zombies in every shadow and wasn't wrong at least twice, or so she judged by the inhuman moans and sickening stench.

Once in the bank, she wasted no time and was soon telling herself more lies. "I'm probably as safe as anyone in America," was the first. This *seemed* like a fact. It couldn't be denied that the building was completely zombie proof. The high windows were one and a half inches thick, and composed of nine separate layers. Although the door to the foyer was only strong enough to stop a bullet or two, the second "front" door was massive. With its thick metal core, it was a throw-back to an earlier time.

"I can hold out in here for weeks," was the next lie she told herself as she puttered about, taking stock of her situation. Along with about a thousand lollipops, she had a refrigerator filled with the leftovers from a poorly planned and sparsely attended retirement party for the bank president, a penny-pinching grouch of a man whom no one liked.

The next lie was plausible as well: "They'll come for me." It was a mantra that she repeated seven or eight times an hour. It was almost a prayer and indeed she frequently said it with her hands clasped together under her chin. There was even some basis for her belief.

All afternoon and into the evening, the sound of fighting gradually increased. And there were bombs and explosions. Immense flashes of light lit the sky, followed by sharp bangs or the rolling grumble of thunder. To her, it sounded like the army had finally arrived, when in truth there were only a few thousand police and some National Guardsmen ringing the city. The

329

explosions she'd heard were the fuel tanks just south of the airport erupting one after another.

"I have time. I just have to be patient." Corrina did not have nearly as much time as she thought. This was the biggest lie by far.

Three states away, the new president, his body twisted from pain, was stuck in a terrible position: he had the fate of millions of people hanging on this one decision. Which way to turn? Was it cowardice to let the bombs fall? Was it wisdom to order the override system into effect?

"Sir?" Trista whispered, crouching next to his chair and staring up into his face. She tried to smile but her lips fell slack after each attempt. "You can save thousands of lives! You can be a hero. Just stop the bombs, please."

His mind veered and seesawed. "I don't know. What if you're wrong? What if the President was right? I-I have to believe he decided on the missiles as a last resort." He looked to the Secret Service agents, but they were plank-faced.

"He was paranoid," Trista insisted. "Dangerously paranoid. He wanted to have your daughters raped and he wanted to film it. Just to get to you. That's the kind of man he was. He only cared about himself, but I know you're not like that. Now, do the right thing and save lives!"

The new President sucked in a long breath, tuned out Trista, ignoring the darting, uncertain eyes of the junior staffers and the silent military officials, none of whom had been around the day before. He concentrated on the maps, the Army units in place and those rushing to help. He took in the estimates of the undead...and more moments slipped away.

While he procrastinated, Corrina Troost was beginning to feel a building anxiety within her. It was an unnamable fear that was worse than anything she'd yet experienced and she was just then dragging a chair over to one of the high windows so she could see the lights of the city better. They weren't as bright as usual, but she needed their comfort. In her modern American mind, electricity meant that things were still, if not hunky-dory, then at least manageable. The chair, once belonging to the penny-pinching grouch, was heavy and she had never been what anyone would call strong. She had to drag it like it was a body and it was when she was turned away that the entire city exploded in light that was so spectacular, that even though she was facing away, it struck her nearly blind.

"Christ! Oh, God! What was that?" she gasped. A part of her was afraid she knew. With a last heave, she had the chair close enough to the window to see outside. The night was gone, banished by a spectacular brilliance, the like of which she had never seen before. It was like looking into a hundred suns.

Squinting and shielding her eyes, she peered through her crossed fingers. Her mind was that of a deer with a car bearing down on it. She was stunned and shocked, frozen in place as the brilliance took on a fantastic purple hue. Within it she saw a shimmering, spectral wall of silver light heading right for her at a fantastic speed. It was fire unlike any fire ever created. It was a fire that consumed reality. As it came on, trees turned to ash, windows instantly crystalized into trillions of particles of dust, asphalt streets ran like black rivers and bricks began to burn.

Corrina shrieked in fear as she leapt off the chair and ran for the vault. It was all of ten paces away, but before she could fling herself inside, the hurricane of fire roared around the building with a noise so terrible that no mortal could withstand it. Her eardrums exploded and in complete mindless terror, she threw herself into the bank vault. Earlier, she had hauled the door practically closed, "just in case." Now, that "just in case" moment had come, but she lacked the wit and the strength to close the door. The air pressure, fluctuating madly, slammed it shut for her. The five-ton door might as well have been five ounces as it thundered closed with concussive force.

She was splayed out on the thick metal floor, shaking from more than just fear. The vibrations from the vault doors had not diminished, but were growing until she skittered like a bean on a hot skillet to the wall and when she touched it, her skin instantly blackened and turned to what looked like tar. Pain tore through her and yet it could not hold a candle to her fear and confusion. She had no idea what was happening.

Simply put, she was about to die. The bank sat two miles from where a 450-kiloton nuclear bomb had exploded. The temperature outside the vault door was an astonishing 6,000 degrees Kelvin or just a shade over 10,000 degrees Fahrenheit. The bank itself had already disintegrated around the vault and, had Corrina not been deaf, she would have heard a crackling sound as the reinforced concrete walls dissolved and the steel melted.

The vault withstood the effects of the blast for five and a half seconds. Unbelievable heat radiated over her, blistering her skin, setting her hair alight and shriveling her lungs in mid-scream. "Nooo…" A fraction of a second later, the air inside the vault ignited in a flash, killing her instantly and turning her to ash.

The new President knew nothing of this, and yet he felt a great pain inside of him that had nothing to do with his torture. Seconds passed and all he could do was stare at the clock on the computer screen as it flashed 0:00 at him. There was silence in the Situation Room until he was able to finally pull his eyes from the clock. He turned them on Trista and rasped out, "It's too bad for them that you found your courage two-hours too late."

"My courage!" Trista cried, jumping to her feet, her face flashing instantly red. She was grabbed by the nearest Secret Service agent, but ignored the pain as her arms were thrust behind her back. "You of all people know what I risked by saving you. And don't forget, I saved your wife and daughters. That was me. Now it's your turn to take a risk…sir!" She spat out the word as if it tasted of shit. "Stop this before anyone else has to die."

"I can't," he said, his eyes dropping away, but not before she saw the weak cowardice in them. "What if you're wrong? What if…Look, if I stop those missiles, they don't come back. If I stop them now, we lose them forever, and what if we need them later? What if tomorrow is even worse? Do you understand? What's done is done."

2-12:03 a.m.
Chambersburg, Pennsylvania

Sergeant Tony Sindt had been the gunner for an M1A2 Abrams; a glorious position, probably the best job in the army. There was nothing more exciting, more wonderful, more *manly* than firing that gun and blasting targets into smithereens. And the grape shot he had been using against the zekes? Like the world's best video game.

While in the tank, he had been impervious to the dead, and that included their infection. He could honestly say that the battle had been fun for him right up until the miserable Air Force pukes had started raining missiles down on their own side. One moment he was happily blasting the zekes, and the next he was upside down, blood pouring down his face, and sucking in smoke from a fire raging in the engine compartment. Had it not been for the automatic halon system kicking in, flooding the cabin with a mixture of carbon dioxide and bromine, he would've either burned up or blown up.

He was the only one to make it out of the tank alive and then, only partially alive. He was concussed, lacerated in three different spots, broken in two others: a wrist and his shin bone, and was bleeding like a spigot. There was no use complaining, however. The entire line was in such shambles that they were forced to retreat. Because he was wounded, he could have hitched a ride on one of the remaining tanks or Bradleys; he chose to limp in pain instead.

Everyone knew there'd be more missiles coming at them, and no one wanted to be anywhere near an Abrams if they could help it.

What artillery was left sent smoke rounds screaming down, and in the confusion, the 3rd ID fell back a little over a mile to a dinky place called Green Spring, where the hot place to hang out on a Saturday night was the local bowling alley. They held out for an hour and then the fucking Air Force came back in the form of great lumbering B52s that looked like black dragons. At least half the pilots risked a court martial and death by firing squad by dropping their bomb loads three seconds too late. The other half showed all the backbone of a snake and dropped right on their heads.

Untold thousands of bombs shattered the line and turned the sleepy little hamlet into a hell on earth. Sindt had never seen such misery and, in a rage, he screamed every obscenity, and every combination of obscenities he knew at the retreating planes.

The broken, dazed survivors of the carpet bombing fell back again, leaving behind those too wounded to walk. Sindt's heart tore itself to pieces as he heard men beg to be killed before the zombies came again.

Only a bloody, ragged portion of the 3rd ID made it to the next line, and only the sudden arrival of the Kentucky Brigade saved them from being overrun as the zekes poured through the smoking ruins and came on again. Shippensburg couldn't be held, even with the fresh reserves. More bombs came and, even though the men dug deep, the casualties mounted once again. The division was now a mob. Without orders, it retreated in a jumble to another of the pissant burgs, where they fell into positions that had been dug hours before.

They couldn't go on much longer. Like everyone else, Tony Sindt fought the zekes, but always with an eye cast upwards. He fired his M4 until he was numb and mostly deaf, and as he did, he prayed with all his might. And for a while, it seemed that his prayers had been answered. No more planes came and once more the soldiers battled with the courage and tenacity they were known for—but in reality, his prayers hadn't been answered. Sindt had been cursed instead. The flying fucks had backed off for a reason.

"We have incoming nukes," a pallid, jittery major said, coming down the line. "Every tenth man will stay and fight so the rest can escape." That was all the explanation he had time for and, without ceremony, he began to count off the men, one through ten. The tenth man always seemed to sink in on himself, while the rest took off at a jog heading south.

"Ten," the major said, tapping Sergeant Sindt on the top of his helmet.

"Yes sir," Sindt said, trying to stand. The major saw his injuries and wavered in indecision. It was only for a second; however, and then he was counting off the next group.

Sindt watched the others around him go. They were strangers to him and at the same time beloved comrades. "Sorry," some told him before running off into the darkness. A few wished him good luck, which he found laughable. What sort of luck would help against a fucking nuclear bomb?

"This fucking sucks," he said, miserably. He had been afraid before, but at least he'd had a chance then. Now he would just die. Unbelievably, he found himself crying. "Shit. Fuck."

The zekes were lurching and stumbling toward the thin line. They came in a broken wave; many had stopped to feast on the banquet provided by the Air Force. Sindt only saw them as shadows until they were up close and their full horror was revealed. They were demons. Their eyes shone with unholy light. Their white teeth gleamed in black mouths. They came for Sindt with outstretched claws, and he killed them one after another without any hope. He killed them with stiff movements, afraid that every moment would be his last.

Twenty-two minutes went by this way before the battlefield was lit by the first of the nuclear bombs.

It was something of a shock that it went off miles behind him. Still the light was a brilliant strobe that displayed the horde to its fullest; it was uncountable. The monsters went on, rank after rank, each of them staring fixedly at the great night sun that had erupted into being. Slowly, Sindt turned to look back and as he did, a second sun appeared and a third and a fourth. Despite their brilliance, they seemed far away. Seven or eight miles, at least.

"They didn't make it," he whispered, realizing that the 3rd Infantry Division was somewhere beneath those mountainous balls of fire. The counting hadn't mattered. None of it had. All the fighting, and the death, and the pain had been for nothing.

In the light of the new suns, he could see the earth lifting and moving like water...like a tidal wave. It was coming toward him and would sweep him under. "Fuck that," he said before turning the M4 around and pulling the trigger one last time.

3-12:08 a.m.
New Rochelle, New York

The stairwell was cold and quiet. "I cun smell y'all, Doctor Lee." Behind the words was a faint and fleeting echo of bare feet, slapping on cement. The little demon was coming at a run.

"I have a gun!" Thuy cried. The sound died away. "And I'll use it if I have to. But...but I don't want to, Jaimee Lynn. I w-want to be friends. I want you and me to be on the same side."

There was a dark pause as Jaimee Lynn tried to figure out what that meant. "Y'all wanna be like that there Chinaman? Y'all want me to bite y'all just a little?"

"No. I just want to be on the same side. Bombs are coming, Jaimee Lynn. The Air Force is coming to kill both of us. You know what bombs are, don't you?"

She had seen the effect of bombs on the zombies; they turned the monsters to black goo. "Yeah, I knows 'bout bombs. Ever-body does. But how do I knows y'all tellin' the truth? Y'all lied to me before."

"And I'm sorry about that. It was wrong to lie, and to show that you can trust me, I'll put down my gun and come down there and talk face to face. You're going to want to attack me, but don't. I'm the only one who can save you. I'm working on a cure, Jaimee Lynn. I can make you like you were before. Do you want that?"

Jaimee Lynn's memory of her life before was sketchy, filled with fleeting glimpses of her father and their grubby little rented house in Arkansas. She remembered laughing but didn't know what that was about, except it meant happiness.

She told Thuy, "I reckon so." This was about the best Thuy thought she was going to get. Slowly, she came down three floors until she and Jaimee Lynn were only seven steps apart. *I can still run*, the foolish, irrational part of her mind whispered. She could run, but it wouldn't save her. It would only postpone her death by a few minutes. No, if she wanted to live it would be going through Jaimee Lynn.

"I'm unarmed." Thuy lifted her arms and spun slowly. "The bombs really are coming. That's the truth. And I really will do everything I can to save you and to make you the way you were before. Do you believe me?"

"I guess so." But she also wanted to eat Dr. Lee very, very badly. Her stomach growled in agreement. And really was it her fault? Dr. Lee somehow retained a deliciously beautiful quality even after so many days of fighting. Unlike everyone else, her hair was still silky and black, her soft flesh a golden tan, her lips full and large.

A shiver of anticipation ran up Jaimee Lynn's back. Bombs were something of a distant threat. Her hunger was here and now.

Thuy saw the fiendish desire plainly. Still, she had no choice but to go on with her spur of the moment plan. "If you want to be saved, you're going to need to clear out the zombies. We need a straight path to the SUV out front. Can you do that, Jaimee Lynn? Because I won't come down until the zombies are away from here."

That was fine with Jaimee Lynn. *I won't have to share*, went through her mind and she had to fight a smile. "I cun do that, no problem. Y'all wait right here."

Thuy did not wait; there was no time. As quietly as she could, she followed Jaimee Lynn to the first floor. It was not easy since there was a pile of trash filling the lowest part of the stairwell. Jaimee Lynn went through it as only a fearless kid would, surfing across it without a care. Thuy went through it as if she were trying to cross a landfill. Midway across the imperfectly balanced heap, she was pleasantly surprised to see a set of golf clubs. Whether it was the same set she had taken a 9-iron from earlier, she didn't know. She had lost the club at some point and now replaced it with a 1-wood with a huge ball of a head and added a smaller putter.

Thuy alternated between holding the clubs like a Spanish fencer and an Alpine skier. Either way made her feel absurd.

At the bottom, she felt the irresistible urge to check her watch: Twenty-three minutes left. There was no time for fear. Boldly, she stepped out into the main lobby and saw Jaimee Lynn and three of the other children in front of the building, pushing around zombies far larger than they were.

"Git y'all's stupid heads outta here!" Jaimee bawled. "Go on! Git!" She treated them like cattle, smacking and kicking them. Once a few started away, the rest followed mindlessly. Thuy thought she was alone in the lobby and started to hurry toward the elevators, thinking she could pry back the doors and call to Katherine and Anna, but she was stopped short as another of the little creatures came sniffing around the corner. It was naked, blackened, mangled and hideous.

Thuy hefted the 1-wood in one hand, holding it high above her head, while holding the putter out in front of her. "Stay back!" Thuy ordered. "Jaimee Lynn's in charge and she said I wasn't to be touched. You have to do what she says."

"I hungee," the thing mewled, coming closer.

"That doesn't matter. Rules are rules."

It didn't care about rules and advanced on Thuy, who didn't know what to do. If she smacked the beast on the head, what would Jaimee Lynn say? And she wasn't about to offer a tasty morsel of her flesh to appease the thing either. The only thing she could think to do was jab the putter at the child to keep it at bay. It was faster and stronger than Thuy could have imagined, and it snatched the club from her hands and threw it aside, nearly hitting another of the children.

Now there were two of them. Thuy backed to the elevator and swung the 1-wood in wide arcs, *wuffing* the air. "Get back! Jaimee Lynn and I have a deal. We're going to save you guys. Okay?" It wasn't okay at all. The children's bellies were empty sacks that gnawed their insides painfully. They kept getting closer and Thuy was forced to give one of them a hearty smack over the head with the club.

The force of the blow drove the little thing to its knees, dented its cranium, and snapped the head off the club. It

337

suddenly felt light and useless. She jabbed it as she had the putter and, as before, the little thing grabbed the broken end. Thuy held on tighter this time and yanked it back, just as a gunshot filled the lobby.

Black blood sprayed from the child's extended arm as he was spun around. Thuy threw herself back as much to avoid the blood as to get out of the way of the next shot. She assumed that it was Anna who was coming to her rescue; it was Eng, and he fired at Thuy, barely missing her left eye. The bullet passed so close that she felt a whisper of hot air on her cheek.

"Don't shoot," Thuy begged, holding the broken club out. "Please, Eng, I wasn't lying about the missiles. They're coming, I swear. You can leave with us. You can escape."

"Liar!" he seethed. "There are no missiles and there's no cure. You're just trying to trick me." He held the gun low, at waist height, and when he fired again the bullet caromed off the elevator door next to Thuy's slim hip.

Run! her frightened mind screamed. She turned to sprint away but saw the shadows move. The two children that had tried to get at her were both very much "alive" and were skulking in the shadows to her left. In front of her, Jaimee Lynn and two of her pack could be seen slipping through the smashed-in front doors like jackals looking to snatch a carcass from a leopard.

She was trapped.

Drawing herself up, she cried: "Stop!" The children all froze, but Eng came swaggering closer, a terrible smile playing on his black lips.

"I don't think so, bitch. You are no longer the queen bee. You don't give the orders, I do." Behind him, Jaimee Lynn hissed and he pointed the gun in her direction. "Do you have something to say? Hmm? I didn't think so." The gun swung back to Thuy. "I came here for a cure, but if you don't have one, I'll take your blood."

"All for yourself, I imagine," Thuy said. There was already a divide between Eng and Jaimee Lynn, but one was as dangerous to Thuy as the other. She needed them fighting each other, not her. "You don't like to share, do you? Did you share Deckard's blood?"

Confusion blinked in and out of his black eyes, then, "Oh him. Your boy-toy. No, I never got to taste him. The others took all of his blood for themselves."

"Okay then, like Private Jackson? She was the crew member on the Blackhawk. You killed her, remember?" More confusion and fluid as dark and rich as oil dripped from his eyes. He remembered the sour-faced girl, but couldn't remember eating her. Ever since he'd become infected, his memory was hazy about minor things like killing strangers. As he began to shake his head, Thuy asked another question, "What about John Burke? You killed him, right?"

That he remembered. "Oh, yes. I killed him. When I told him he wasn't immune, the look on his dumb, slack-jawed hick-face was priceless. And then when he screamed as he died, that was something I'll never…"

He was jarred out of his reverie by a new scream. Jaimee Lynn's one clear memory of the world before her unquenchable hunger was of her father and she loved him with every bit of her now shriveled heart. "Kill him!" she shrieked, and charged Eng with her jaw stretched wide open.

Surprised at first, he shot too quickly and missed. His second shot struck her in the side and sent her sprawling. Eng's training kicked in and he pivoted smoothly, firing calmly, blasting the child zombies that were attacking from Thuy's left. Even with the dark and the small size of his targets, he didn't miss. Two shots dropped them. Then he turned the gun on Thuy and pulled the trigger, but the bolt was back.

His magazine was spent. He started to fumble in his pocket for another when he was struck from behind by a boy with needle-like fangs. Those fangs sunk deep into the back of Eng's left knee. It was an altogether painless bite. Eng glanced down in annoyance before driving the butt of his rifle into the boy's forehead. The boy was like a pitbull and his iron jaws refused to let go. A second crack with the rifle dashed in his brains, while at the same time tore out the tendons behind Eng's knee.

"You little shit!" Eng cried in Mandarin and hit the boy again. His mind was red with rage and he hit the boy once more, giving the two other children time to race in and clamp their dirty teeth down into his flesh. With only one properly working leg, he wavered, his arms flailing. Jaimee Lynn came flying at him, and the four went down in fury of blood and screams.

This was Thuy's chance to get away; she was forgotten by the zombies inside, and the zombies outside were only just starting to flood back to the building. The SUV called to her—

339

she could be in it and driving away in seconds. And what was stopping her?

Katherine was going to die one way or the other, and Anna…Anna deserved to die.

Truly, the only thing stopping her was guilt. It held her in place and, instead of running, she repeatedly jabbed the button for the elevator until she heard a distant *ding!* She stood with one hand on the door, listening for the sound of whirring machinery; however, Katherine and Anna were still in between floors with the emergency stop button pressed.

A high whine of fear escaped Thuy as she took the golf club and jabbed the broken end in between the elevator doors and began to work the metal up and down until there was just enough of a crack to shove the club further into it. Prying back the doors turned the whine into a grunt and when there was just enough room, she stuck her foot in the crevice and yelled up into the dark shaft: "Let's go! It's clear!"

Not fifteen feet away, Eng was still battling the three little creatures. He had one dangling from his left wrist by her teeth, another on his back, tearing his left ear off, while the third was in the process of getting up after being thrown. There were splashes of black blood everywhere.

It was Jaimee Lynn who had been thrown; Thuy only recognized her by the yellow dress, which was already torn and hanging off her in bloody tatters. The girl charged and was easily swatted aside, giving Eng time to punch the child shredding his wrist over and over again, until its jaw broke and it let go.

He was so much stronger than the children, and Thuy was sure he would win the fight, which left her in a strange position. Whichever side won would instantly turn on her and attack her next. She would be helpless against either.

"Katherine, get down here!" she screamed at the top of her lungs, never taking her eyes from the fight. It was ending quickly. Eng managed to grab two of the children, one in each hand, and with terrific force, he dashed their heads together. What might have killed a normal child only dazed the two and he smashed them together again and again until their heads cracked open and Thuy could see their brains swimming in black juice.

Seeing that she was all alone, Jaimee Lynn hesitated. She had a gaping hole in her stomach and the side of her face was puffed up; she knew she couldn't defeat Eng and yet, her anger was so great that she went at him one last time. With ease, he slipped her charge, grabbed her by the throat and slammed her down.

He leaned over her, his right hand crushing her larynx. "I killed your father because I didn't need him anymore. And now I don't need you." Her face was a brilliant red beneath the black blood. Her eyes bulged, but they never lost the intensity of their hatred. She was an evil little creature right to the end.

"Which is my fault," Thuy mumbled. Louder, she called out, "Eng!" He turned and as he did, she drove the broken club four inches into his right eye. Impossibly, he didn't die. He grabbed the club with his right hand and bent it in half, tearing open his eye socket as he did. Thuy stepped back in shock, her mouth beneath the blue mask hanging open.

"Christ," she whispered.

He laughed at her fear and began to struggle upwards, only he had forgotten about Jaimee Lynn. She was beneath him where his soft spots were exposed. Rearing up, she sunk her teeth into his throat and began viciously wrangling her head side to side. Blood gushed down her face in sickening torrents. He tried to pry her away but with her jaws clamped on him, all he managed to do was tear his own throat out. The blood surged from him until at last, he trembled, faltered and fell to his side.

Jaimee Lynn was not done with him. She began to tear out his innards, making such hideous glopping noises that Thuy had to turn away.

The door to the elevator had closed and so she banged on it, crying, "Katherine! Anna! Get down here, please."

The machinery began whirring a second later and Thuy felt an almost magical feeling of relief. She sagged against the door and stared at Jaimee Lynn, a gloved hand up to her masked face; she had never seen anything quite so horrible. The little girl glowered at her from the remains of Eng. She had torn him open from his throat down to his belly button and, as Thuy watched, she grunted and pulled something fat and black from his chest cavity; it might have been his heart.

"I really did try to save your father," Thuy said, in something of an apology.

A strange mixture of hate and sadness passed across Jaimee Lynn's face. What was even more odd was seeing her considering this. It was as if she was thinking like a real person. She tossed aside the heart. "Can y'all really save me?"

341

The elevator was coming, announcing itself with more machine noises. In five seconds, Thuy would be free and running for the police SUV. None of that mattered. "I will do everything I can."

The elevator door opened a second later with a blooming stench of bleach, and Anna shoved Katherine out, holding the M4 to the back of her head. "Is…is that Eng?" Anna asked, amazed.

"I kilt him," Jaimee Lynn said. "He wus evil and bad."

Thuy glanced at her watch and felt her stomach lurch: there were seventeen minutes left before the bombs hit. "Yes, you did well," she replied, evenly. "By the way, she's coming with us."

Behind her mask, Anna looked shocked and then angry. "The hell she is!"

"I'm not asking you, Anna," Thuy said. "I'm telling you. Now, do something useful with that gun and shoot out the window. We have seventeen minutes to get to the helicopter, and look out there!" The zombies were almost to the SUV.

"Holy shit!" Anna gasped, before hurrying to the lobby window and firing her gun four times. A portion of the glass fell in with a crash that had even more zombies heading at them. Thuy was unencumbered by armor and not sporting horrible wounds, so she was able to sprint ahead. She darted around two beasts, outran three others, and made it to the SUV, getting inside a split second before the zombies converged on her. The vehicle was instantly swarmed. One creature with an eyeball out of its socket and hanging by a red tether, banged a meaty arm on the window, while a second tried to bite the hood. Nails scritched over the paint, scraping divots, and fists pummeled the glass.

Thuy ignored everything and concentrated on the task at hand. She yanked the vehicle into drive, slammed a foot on the accelerator and shot forward, bouncing over bodies. There was only so much room between her and the building and before she really got any speed, she hit the brakes with a screech. She had given the others all of three seconds of grace to get into the car.

It *might* have been enough, but Anna, who was the slowest, wasn't going to take any chances. She saw that even if they all got into the SUV in time, it would be mobbed, and was Thuy a good enough driver to get them out of there? Anna doubted it. They needed a distraction.

Jaimee Lynn went for the rear driver's side door, while Katherine went for the front passenger. The doors opened towards them and as the FBI agent yanked it open, Anna smashed into her from behind, sending her sprawling right out in the open. The dead went for her, but Katherine was fast, faster than Anna thought possible, and even before Anna had climbed into the passenger seat, Katherine was on her feet and scrambling for the rear door.

The night was suddenly alive with sound and thrashing movement. Thuy screamed for Katherine to get in, while Anna was yelling for Thuy to drive, "While we still can!"

"No!" Thuy yelled right back over the hungry moans of dozens of zombies. One of the bigger ones slammed his way to the front and reached out, pulling Katherine partially away from the SUV. She used the room to give it a chest-caving sidekick, sending it stumbling into the others. Now, there was just enough time for her to get inside and to perhaps close the door behind her, but as she turned to jump inside, she was confronted by a black pistol aimed into her stomach.

"Don't…"

Anna pulled the trigger. Katherine didn't hear the gun go off and she didn't feel the bullet part her ballistic armor at an angle and slice up into her spleen. She did feel the shock of the impact. It was like getting hit with a sledgehammer, and she reeled back, one hand still holding the door.

Thuy stared in shocked horror, even as Anna turned the gun on her. "Drive! Now, or else."

"No…Why, why, why did you do that?" Mindlessly, Thuy tried to get out of the car to help Katherine, only the door wouldn't open. A pair of zombies had crashed into it and were crushing it closed. More were coming behind them. So many that Katherine didn't stand a chance. "Shit!" she cried. In a fury, she faced Anna, ready to fight her; however, just then Anna stuck the still smoking barrel to Thuy's throat.

"Drive. Now." Anna ordered. "Now, before it's too late."

It was too late for Katherine Pennock. A long, gangly zombie had managed to pull her from the SUV, while another smaller one, what had once been a teen girl with short, unbalanced and multi-colored hair, suddenly tripped her. The SUV was forgotten as the zombies fought each other for the chance to eat her.

Even Jaimee Lynn, who had been watching the entire affair with unfeeling eyes, started across to the other side of the car, only to have the door slam in her face.

The dead were all over the agent, grabbing her, biting her, clawing at every bit of exposed flesh. And there was nothing Thuy could do, except stare. Anna shoved the gun harder into her throat, and demanded again that Thuy drive. "No. Pull the trigger if…"

Somehow, Katherine suddenly popped up out of the scrum. She tore away from the gang of undead and for a second, her and Thuy locked eyes, fear and misery flowing through the connection. It was too much for Thuy and she went for the door again, but Katherine shook her head—and then started backing away, waving her arms. Dozens and dozens of zombies charged her and she limped back to the R & K Building just ahead of them. She was drawing the undead away from the SUV. She was sacrificing herself.

"Bitch. Bitch! BITCH!" Thuy screamed into Anna's face. "You didn't have to do that."

"Actually, I did." Anna was completely composed and looked at Thuy over the gun. "She would have told all sorts of lies about me. Just like you. Right? You'll yap away with your version of the truth. Who will they believe?" She let out a long breath, as if coming to an unwanted conclusion.

"Don't think you can scare me with the gun. You need me for your pardon. You need a working cure of some sort for your pardon."

Behind her mask, Anna grinned. "Oh, I have a cure. Remember the glycolipids? Do you think I don't know what those are? I'll get my pardon…without you. Sorry, Thuy. It's survival of the fittest. Now, get out."

Thuy didn't budge. It seemed death was coming for her one way or another, and she had a choice of being eaten alive, incinerated to ash, or shot in the head. "Or none of the above," she said, a mad grin on her face. She had no chance against the stronger, younger woman by herself, but she wasn't by herself. "Jaimee Lynn, you can eat her if you want."

Too late, Anna realized that Jaimee Lynn was right behind her. Two small hands shot out and gripped her by the throat. The hands were fiendishly strong and the nails dug deep into her flesh as her head was pulled back. Anna turned the gun and fired blindly, blasting a hole through the back window. She tried to twist her arm high across her chest to get a better angle, and that was when Thuy lurched across the space between them, taking an iron grip on Anna's gun hand.

Anna was torqued around at an odd angle; her left hand and arm were uselessly pinned, and her right hand was slowly being bent in towards her as Thuy exerted all her strength. "Please... no," Anna begged.

The barrel was now even with Anna's ear and the more severe the angle became, the harder it was for her to fight back. Thuy twisted the gun for all she was worth and when she had it pointed straight into Anna's face, they both knew she could kill her. But Thuy didn't. Thuy twisted the gun until it was pointed down into Anna's vest.

Only then Thuy fired. Anna was still alive when Jaimee Lynn dragged her into the back seat. Blood was better when it was fresh; that was just science.

4-12:09 a.m.
New Rochelle, New England

After five days, Courtney Shaw finally shut her laptop. She had done all that she could. Her last call had been to Sergeant Ross. He was a general now and that seemed about right.

His so-called Army of Southern New England was running helter-skelter east toward Boston, while he was riding on the top of an M1, the very last M1 to pull out of the line. With him was Governor Clarren, a man who would probably slug Courtney in the face if he ever had the chance. She asked Ross not to mention her. Ross began to answer with a question when there was a burst of static and the line cut off.

The first nukes surrounding Boston were detonating, filling the atmosphere with electromagnetic pulses and radiation; her sat-phone was now useless. She worried briefly about Ross and his army. He said he had made it to Framingham, seven miles from the line.

Was it far enough away? She didn't know and frankly, she was too emotionally done in to care. She could barely find the strength to care about saving her own life. With a sigh, she crawled down into the crevice which led off into a dark little

345

tunnel. On any other day she would've laughed at the idea of crawling through a passage that was only fit for a rat, but just then she didn't blink. Using the meager LED light from the sat-phone, she scrambled through nooks and crannies, and over broken walls and heaved-up chunks of cement.

At one point she found the tunnel was forked. More on impulse than anything else, she chose the right passage and crawled for only twenty feet or so before she caught sight of a pair of boots sticking out of the rubble ahead of her. Judging by their size, she guessed they belonged to Colonel Taylor. Squeamishly, she gave them a shake; they didn't move.

Backtracking, she took the left-hand tunnel and saw where it had been carved out in places. Either Carlton or Bryan must have been through there and she was able to scurry faster. Above her, the building shook and rumbled, sending dirt and dust sifting down. At one point the walls groaned around her, and she was sure she was one sneeze away from being crushed like Taylor had been.

Knowing her luck, Courtney figured she wouldn't die right away. She would only be trapped and have to discover the wonders of being eaten alive by rats and cockroaches.

Even that morbid thought couldn't scare her more than she already was. The countdown clock running in her head prodded her a little and she hurried through the underground maze until she finally came out into a strange twilight world. A few feet away, Bryan was sitting on a pile of debris. He had slit open his ballistic vest and was unhurriedly making a splint from the plates.

"One's gone off already," he said, pointing southwest. Twenty-three miles away, Newark, New Jersey was the site of the latest man-made inferno. Three-hundred kilotons made a light bright enough to read by. Bryan seemed unfazed by the explosion. "Where's Taylor?" he asked, grunting through the pain of wrapping his broken leg.

"Dead. Have you seen Carlton?" He shook his head. They both looked back at the tunnel. Carlton was either dead or lost under the building. A glance at her watch showed Courtney that there was no time to go back. "We have approximately twelve minutes left to get out of here. Is that enough time to get off the ground?"

He chuckled. "I can get us in the air in about one minute, if I had a bird to fly." He waved his arms around. "But there isn't one here, so it's sort of a moot point, don't you think?"

"Dr. Lee will make it. I'm sure of it. Wait, do you have a flare or something? Don't you guys carry those sorts of gadgets?" He dug out something that looked like an electric razor. It was an MS-2000 strobe and when he flicked it on, he nearly blinded her. Blinking back the blob of light floating in her vision, she grabbed the strobe from him and quickly mounted the pile of debris that had once been a building but was now a cairn, memorializing the dead trapped inside it.

Midway up, she turned on the strobe and instantly heard a long moan. There were zombies nearby and for the first time, she felt nothing. Not even a smidgen of fear. "There's nothing like a nuclear bomb to make a person prioritize their life," she muttered. She held the strobe up high as the minutes ticked away. Another nuke went off over Hackensack, New Jersey.

It was spectacular. It was horrifying.

She was still staring in sick wonder when a rattletrap SUV pulled up to the remains of the building. It gave a cheerful: *beep, beep*. Slightly less cheerful was the bloody body that spilled like limp, red noodles from the rear passenger side door as it opened. Seeing it didn't slow Courtney in the least, and she leapt from slab to slab, risking a broken neck without a thought.

Thuy stepped out of the driver's side. Calmly spraying herself with the bleach she had taken from Anna's pack, she advised that Courtney should hurry if she didn't want to be "flash-fried." She also added: "It's nasty back there, so wear masks and gloves, and spray yourselves down as we go."

Courtney glanced in the back seat of the SUV—it looked like a hog had been butchered in the third row where Jaimee Lynn sat, looking like a living terror. In fact she really wasn't a danger at the moment. She was torpid and slow-witted from gorging herself. Still, Courtney sat sideways in her seat and kept a close eye on her as she sprayed copious amounts of bleach all over herself and the car.

"Seven minutes," Bryan said, hopping on one foot to the car. He gave it a long look before getting in. He gave Jaimee Lynn an even longer one, as he settled in, but he didn't say a word. There was no time for arguing and barely enough time to spray himself down with the bleach bottle.

"Can you fly with your leg like that?" Thuy asked, eyeing him doubtfully. "If not, I can take instructions from you."

He laughed this off. "Stick to the science, Doc. I'll fly. The pedals only point the nose along the horizontal axis, and I should be able...there's the golf course! Ahhhh, crap!" Thuy bounced them right up the curb, through a waist-high fence and went rumbling down a fairway without even considering the brake.

"Where is it?" she cried, meaning the helicopter. Even with her high beams on and the light from the nukes turning the night into a psychedelic twilight, there was no sign of the Blackhawk.

Gritting his teeth from the pain as his leg was bounced around, Bryan yelled out, "Keep going! It was a par-5."

Thuy understood to keep going; the par-5 aspect was lost on her. During a long stretch, she checked her watch: four minutes left. She jammed her foot down as hard as it would go.

"There!" Courtney screeched. "To the right." Thuy saw the helicopter as well and she aimed for its side, pulling up within feet of it so that Bryan could hop over without wasting a moment. He had his door open before the SUV had even stopped. Just as he put his good foot down on the soft grass, the world lurched beneath them.

Bryan managed to hold on, but Thuy was thrown to the ground and Courtney fell out of the backseat.

"Was that it?" Courtney cried, staring around. She had to yell to be heard because the air was suddenly filled with a great roaring noise that almost, but not quite drowned out the blare of car alarms, the crashing of a million windows being blown out, roofs caving in and the huge snapping sounds as forests of trees toppled.

"Get in!" Thuy screamed. "Courtney in front! Jaimee Lynn in the back. Strap yourself down." The zombie child couldn't work the belt properly and Thuy had to kneel within biting range to get her secure.

In the cockpit, Bryan was flicking switches like mad. His normal startup checklist went out the window. Batteries were turned on first, then the generators, then the APU. Just as he was about to turn on the dual General Electric T700 engines, they were struck by a blast of howling wind. The air was blistering hot and churned-up within it was an insane assortment of debris: branches, body parts, rocks zipping as fast as bullets, flaming lawn furniture, squirrels spinning like plates and even a ten-speed bike.

The SUV took the brunt of the damage and was hit so hard by the powerful wind that it fell into the helicopter. As frightening as that was, it helped to pin the bird in place, otherwise, it too might have been thrown over. Inside the Blackhawk, Bryan threw the engine switches and the four rotors began to spin, slapping the turbulent air until they were invisible to the naked eye.

He paused as the bird took on a shudder. It almost felt like it was coming apart. "Please not yet," he said, begging under his breath. Louder, he bellowed, "Hold on!" and yanked back on the collective. The ten-ton metal beast jumped up off the ground with sparks flying. They were immediately hammered by the shrieking wind and turned nearly side-on to the ground. He had almost no control of the Blackhawk and thought for sure that they were going to fall out of the sky. But the wind had them in its clutches and they slewed around. Fighting the cyclic for all he was worth, Bryan was just able to yaw the helicopter back over.

"Jesus Christ!" he screamed, unheard. The Blackhawk shook and trembled around him as he turned her so that she was no longer fighting the wind. The moment he did, it felt like an enormous hand picked them up and threw them across the sky.

In the seat next to him, Courtney was staring out in shock. The last nuke had exploded a half mile over the Tappan Zee Bridge, melting it in a millisecond and evaporating two miles of the Hudson River. The mushroom cloud was blooming ever larger and looked as though it was going to swallow them whole. She screamed for Bryan to go faster.

He already had the Blackhawk pegged at the *Never Exceed Speed* of 222 mph. "Fuck it," he growled and gave her full throttle. She was going 261 mph when a W-88 turned Mt. Vernon into a desolation from which it would never recover.

When it went off, Katherine Pennock was standing on the top of the R & K Building, dripping red blood and willing the helicopter to fly faster. It was tiny now and growing smaller as the distance between them grew. How far away was it? Ten miles? Twelve? Whatever the distance, she knew in her heart that it would get away and she smiled knowing she had done something right, something actually good. The smile broadened just as an infinite pure light enveloped her from behind. The light was all-powerful and was so intense that it killed her, boiling the fluid from every cell in her body in an instant.

Epilogue
After

For all intents and purposes, the Apocalypse ended with Katherine's death. Hers was not the last, not by far. Over a billion people had died in those five days and as terrible as that was, another five billion would die over the next six years, mostly due to famine, disease and terribly bloody warfare. Many countries simply ceased to exist as they dissolved in sad civil strife or imploded under the strain brought on by the new reality.

Gone were the days of geo-politics. Countries that had the means built immense walls along their borders and turned inward. The poorer countries were generally decimated as mass migration became the norm. It was not uncommon for huge stretches of land to be overrun and raped by half a million starving nomads.

While European borders crystallized even further, the rest of the word saw the rise of the "city-state." Turkey became a desert, but Istanbul flourished. Sao Paulo grew into a cultural jewel at the same time Brazil became a by-word for cannibalism. In Mumbai, anything at all, from heroin to young boys, could be had for a price, while everything down to the last blade of grass had been devoured in Calcutta.

In North America, things were just as chaotic, although not nearly as bloody. While Russia and China ceased to exist for all time, the USA made a concerted stab at staying together. The country held together for eight years, until the President was assassinated and Texas broke off to form its own country(what became known as the Texas Unified Republic). After that, everything more or less fell apart.

California started the Pacific Coast League, which crumbled into eleven different countries within sixteen years. The southern states had more success, throwing up a huge wall along the Mason-Dixon line and founding the 2nd Confederate States of America. Without the slavery and the racism, it blossomed as a rural land and was one of the few countries that had the luxury to export food.

The Midwest, the mountain states and what was left of the Great Lakes region were essentially depopulated and immense areas reverted back to nature. The center of the country was dotted with city-states: Denver, Kansas City, Chicago and

Minneapolis. Out east Boston, Buffalo, Long Island City and Washington DC were all that were left.

In between these eastern cities were frightening lands simply called the Dead Zone. Every city and every country had laws against setting foot there and yet there were those called *Dead Eyes* who took the risk, but that is a story for another time.

Before it can be told, this saga has to have an ending of sorts. But how can it? The crusade against the undead did not have a neat and defining boundary. Every person who made it out alive had a story that continued on and, since each could fill a library in themselves, only a brief summary will be given:

Trista Price: Trista stayed on in the administration until the first election was postponed due to unspecified threats. There were no threats and everyone knew it. Knowing that the shit was going to hit the fan eventually, she skipped town with a sackful of credits and a new name. Two years later, she bought a ranch in Texas, south of Abilene, where she raised cattle and married a good man. Trista died sixty years after the Apocalypse, a great-grand mother three times over.

David Kazakoff: Just seconds ahead of arresting agents, Kazakoff fled the White House and the capital, eventually finding his way to Canada. During the 1st Quebec Revolution, he was hung as a spy by the government in Ottawa and buried in a mass grave.

Governor Dean Clarren: The ex-governor became Boston's first Premiere, a position he held for nine years until his death from pancreatic cancer. His wife, as well as more than a hundred thousand others, followed him to the grave the next year with the same disease. Relentless in his outlook, Clarren rebuilt and reordered Boston, and was known as the "First Father of Boston."

General Troy Ross: The general headed the works project that built the "Forever Wall" around Boston. Later he was elected as Boston's fourth Premiere, and served for twenty-three years. The "Second" father of Boston built a strong and prosperous city which sadly did not last. Within twenty years of his death, corruption took its toll and the city started to fall into ruin. Boston went from being a shining example of a city-state to a slum-state as the first underground sweatshops opened up a decade later and not long after, the term "serf" came into use once again.

Courtney Shaw: Arrested briefly after escaping the zone, she became a "king-maker" and was the woman behind many successful political campaigns in the over-crowded city-state of Long Island City. She became rich by the standards of the day simply by knowing who to call if there was something that was desperately needed. She married twice, each time for love, and gave up both husbands and two of her five children to cancer. Still, she died happy, knowing that she had done all that she could with her days.

Dr. Thuy Lee: Arrested briefly after escaping the zone, she gave birth to a son, Ryan Deckard Jr, while still in prison. She created the *Semi-vax* for the zombie virus. It was neither a cure nor a vaccine. It was a serum that could only mitigate the symptoms of the disease and limit its communicability. Since even a word of the disease could spread untold panic, the *Semi-vax* was hidden from the public's eye, although it eventually found its way into the black market. She was also responsible for re-discovering a cure for thirty-two different types of cancer, specifically lung and skin cancers; however the costs involved were such that only the richest people could afford the cure. Dr. Lee never married. She tended to her work, and to her son and then to his son. Dr. Lee died of heart failure on the day she became a great-grandmother.

Jaimee Lynn Burke: The child zombie drank a quart of human blood every day until the day Dr. Lee died. On that day she drank four quarts, all that Dr. Lee had in her. She did not kill Dr. Lee; it was a gift. Three days later Jaimee Lynn attended her funeral and, as she always did when she went outside, she wore dark glasses and gloves. Her hair was just as yellow as it had always been and her skin was an unblemished, unwrinkled alabaster. She was seventy-years-old and those around her thought she was seven or eight. After the funeral, Jaimee Lynn slipped out of her cell using a key that had been willed to her and disappeared into the world. It would be nice to say that she disappeared forever, but that would not be true.

The End

Author's Note:

Thank you so much for reading the Apocalypse Crusade series. I certainly hoped that you enjoyed it. I liked the story so much that I decided to write a sequel to the series, the first book of which is tentatively called: *Dead Eye Runner*. It's about half-zombies(much like Jaimee Lynn, Eng and Von Braun, hiding in the midst of the over-crowded slum-states of New York and Boston. Their existence is denied by the corrupt governments, who are afraid of what will happen if the word gets out. Dead Eye Runners, gritty men with few moral qualms about anything at all, hunt them down for the bounties paid. I expect it will be a lot of fun!

But before I write that book, I have to finish the Generation Z series. I will begin book 6 immediately and it should be ready by mid-2019. Luckily, there is a way for you to read Book 6, chapter by chapter, before anyone else! All you have to do is go to my Patreon page (**Here**) and support my writing. The tier levels are exceedingly generous with freebies running from autographed books, video podcasts, free Audible books, signed T-shirts, and swag of all sorts. At a high enough tier, you will even get to meet me in person as I take you and three friends out to dinner.

Patreon is a great way to help support me so I don't have to go back into the coal mines...back into the dark.

Another way to help is to write a review of this book on Amazon and/or on your own Facebook page. The review is the most practical and inexpensive form of advertisement an independent author has available to get his work known. I would greatly appreciate it.

PS If you are interested in autographed copies of my books, souvenir posters of the covers, Apocalypse T-shirts and other awesome Swag, please visit my website at **https:// www.petemeredith1.com**

PPS: I need to thank a number of people for their help in bringing you this book. My beta readers Joanna Niederer, KariAnn Morgan, Kari-Lyn Rakestraw, Monica Turner, Michelle Heeder, Mindy Wilkinson, Amber Carrol, Marinda Grindstaff, Amber Powell, Shamus McGuigan—Thanks so much!

Fictional works by Peter Meredith:

A Perfect America
Infinite Reality: Daggerland Online Novel 1
Infinite Assassins: Daggerland Online Novel 2
Generation Z
Generation Z: The Queen of the Dead
Generation Z: The Queen of War
Generation Z: The Queen Unthroned
Generation Z: The Queen Enslaved
The Sacrificial Daughter
The Apocalypse Crusade War of the Undead: Day One
The Apocalypse Crusade War of the Undead: Day Two
The Apocalypse Crusade War of the Undead Day Three
The Apocalypse Crusade War of the Undead Day Four
The Apocalypse Crusade War of the Undead Day Five
The Horror of the Shade: Trilogy of the Void 1
An Illusion of Hell: Trilogy of the Void 2
Hell Blade: Trilogy of the Void 3
The Punished
Sprite
The Blood Lure The Hidden Land Novel 1
The King's Trap The Hidden Land Novel 2
To Ensnare a Queen The Hidden Land Novel 3
The Apocalypse: The Undead World Novel 1
The Apocalypse Survivors: The Undead World Novel 2
The Apocalypse Outcasts: The Undead World Novel 3
The Apocalypse Fugitives: The Undead World Novel 4
The Apocalypse Renegades: The Undead World Novel 5
The Apocalypse Exile: The Undead World Novel 6
The Apocalypse War: The Undead World Novel 7
The Apocalypse Executioner: The Undead World Novel 8
The Apocalypse Revenge: The Undead World Novel 9
The Apocalypse Sacrifice: The Undead World 10
The Edge of Hell: Gods of the Undead Book One
The Edge of Temptation: Gods of the Undead Book Two
The Witch: Jillybean in the Undead World
Jillybean's First Adventure: An Undead World Expansion
Tales from the Butcher's Block

Printed by Amazon Italia Logistica S.r.l.
Torrazza Piemonte (TO), Italy